SABINA

A NOVEL SET IN THE ITALIAN RENAISSANCE

C. DE MELO

NOTE FROM THE AUTHOR

It has taken years of careful research in Florence, Italy, to write this novel. Many of the dates, major events, and characters are historically accurate. One must not forget, however, that this is a work of fiction. This entitles the author to take certain artistic liberties—the greatest being the independence I have bestowed upon my female characters. In reality, women of good breeding had little or no freedom in the patriarchal society of Renaissance Florence. While female chastity had to be protected at all costs, men behaved as they pleased. I have also taken the liberty to create personalities for historical figures, which are based on my research of Florentine society during the quattrocento, documented facts, and even a few spicy rumors.

ACKNOWLEDGEMENT

Special thanks to Dr. Cinzia Giorgio, award-winning author, Vatican University professor, and literary critic, for her support and stellar review of SABINA (translated from Italian):

"A literary scope that will not fail to conquer even the most refined public. Historical reconstructions are punctilious, a meticulous fresco of Renaissance society serves as the backdrop for a breathtaking novel full of twists and great characters. A story of passion, betrayal, and magic that transports us to the Florence of the Pazzi Conspiracy and the terrible Savonarola, right up to the restoration of the Medici power by the Grand Duke Cosimo I. A novel that you will not be able to put down."

"Let all Italy know, and all Christendom too, of the power, the strength, and the glory that the Florentines have at present in Tuscany."

–Historian Benedetto Dei describing "Florentie bella" in the book: *La cronica dall'anno 1400 all'anno 1500.*

DEDICATION

Thank you, D.

CHAPTER 1
LUCCA, TUSCANY
AUGUST 1, 1477

It was the first day of August and mercilessly hot. Not a single drop of rain had fallen for nearly a month, causing the crops, livestock, and Tuscans to suffer. Sabina Rossi sat on a stone bench outside her father's villa quietly reading a book, its pages well-worn from frequent use. It was a special book, and she took great pains to keep it hidden from her father's prying eyes.

Placing her fingertip on the page, she looked up at the cloudless sky. The endless expanse above her head was lapis lazuli, the noble blue favored by artists when painting the Madonna's cloak. She gazed into the distance, visually tracing the uneven line of Monte Pisano, the mountain separating Lucca from its rival city, Pisa. According to legend, God had deliberately placed it there to prevent the *Lucchese* from looking at the *Pisani*.

The distant bells of San Michele broke her reverie, and she recalled to mind its colonnaded façade. At the church's pinnacle, flanked by two angels, stood a large statue of St. Michael spearing the great dragon. Each metal feather of his sculpted wings quivered in the wind, making it seem as if the archangel could take flight at any given moment.

The crow at Sabina's feet hopped around to capture her attention. Throwing another crumb from the chunk of stale bread in her lap, she inquired sweetly, "Still hungry, Mendi?"

The savvy bird visited her about the same time every day in order to receive a free meal, so she eventually nicknamed it Mendi—a shortened version of *mendicante*, or beggar.

"Sono disgraziato!"

Startled by the sound of her father's voice, Sabina tossed the book into a nearby rosemary bush as Mendi flew away with an agitated cry.

Don Antonio strode into the courtyard. "Where are you?"

"Here, Papa," Sabina replied.

The old man stomped toward his daughter with a scowl on his face. "Why do you disgrace us? Have you no shame?"

"What's wrong?" she asked, her face as innocent as an angel's.

"You continue to swim naked after I strictly forbade you to do so! People will think you're a common slut!"

"No one was around, so I decided to take a quick swim."

"No one was around, eh? Donna Francesca saw you on her way home from the market. She was so shocked that she dropped her basket. What were you thinking?"

"It's so hot, Papa. Who wouldn't relish the feel of cool water on their skin on a day like this? I didn't mean to offend anyone."

"Sabina!" Cecilia exited the villa carrying a potted plant with her three year old son, Paolo, in tow. "Did you pluck the leaves from my basil plant?"

Sabina regarded her older sister with disdain. Since the death of her husband, Cecilia had ceased to care for her appearance and had gained weight. The twenty-three-year-old widow looked tired and matronly.

"Well? Did you?" Cecilia pressed, frowning at the bare stems.

Don Antonio peered at Sabina suspiciously. "You're not still concocting silly love potions for those stupid village girls, are you?"

Although she remained silent, he saw the familiar look of guilt on her face and proceeded to administer a sound beating. Sabina cringed from the assault as Cecilia attempted to placate their father.

The old man eventually regained his composure and balled his hands into fists. "What am I going to do with you, Sabina?"

Paolo spotted the book in the rosemary bush and picked it up.

Cecilia moved toward her son. "What do you have there?"

Sabina snatched the book from her nephew's hands and

placed it behind her back. "It's only a silly book of poetry."

"Let me see it," Don Antonio demanded.

Sabina shook her head and his face darkened in anger. Knowing her father's temper, she relented.

He leafed through the pages. "A book of poetry, eh?"

"Papa—"

"Not only do you sit here reading books of witchcraft, but you lie to *me*—your own father!"

"It's not witchcraft, it's botany."

"Botany, my elbow! You should be reading the Bible or reciting prayers or anything that may save that soul of yours, which I'm certain is bound for Hell!" Turning to Cecilia, he added, "Why didn't you stop her from committing such mischief today?"

"I was gone for most of the afternoon," Cecilia explained. "Donna Filomena is sick, so I helped her look after the baby."

Don Antonio sighed tiredly, then narrowed his eyes at Sabina. "When you're not writing silly poems, you're reading silly books."

"You simply lack appreciation for literature, Papa."

"I *do* appreciate literature," the old man corrected. "What I don't appreciate is a rebellious daughter. Why can't you be like Cecilia? She goes to church willingly, while you have to be forced. She engages in Christian works, while you mix potions. Cecilia has never given me reason to worry, but you give me nothing but grief!" He paused, his face a mask of anger. "As God is my witness, I will see you married before the month's end. I've already begun discussing the arrangements."

"Arrangements?"

"I'm planning your future," he said, calmly adjusting his sleeve.

Sabina smiled, unfazed. "Very well."

"You're going to marry Signore Tommaso Caravelli."

The exceptionally wealthy widower lived in Florence. Twice married and still without an heir to inherit his sizeable fortune, he was one of the most sought-after men in Tuscany.

Sabina stood, the smile vanishing from her face. "That's

9

quite funny, Papa…I almost believe you."

"You *should* believe me."

"I would rather you marry me off to a Pisano than to that old Florentine! He's almost old enough to be your father!"

"Bite your tongue, girl! Signore Tommaso is several years younger than I am, and strong enough to keep you in line."

Despite the harm done to her precious basil plant, Cecilia interceded on her sister's behalf. "Father, you cannot be serious. Signore Tommaso is in his fifties—he's far too old for Sabina."

"He's exactly forty-nine."

Cecilia winced. "That's a thirty-year age difference."

The old man snorted. "I'm getting too old for your sister's constant mischief. She needs a husband—not a foolish young man with his head in the clouds—but a strong man with worldly experience who won't tolerate her impudence." When Sabina shook her head defiantly, he added, "If you refuse to marry him, I will personally escort you to the convent of your choice."

"I'll be good, I promise," Sabina said. "I'll never swim naked or do anything that upsets you."

He crossed his arms. "You'll be obedient and do as I say."

Sabina crossed her arms, too. "I will not marry him."

"Do you realize how wealthy he is? Or the kind of life he can provide for you? There are countless women who would jump at the chance of marrying such a man."

"Then let him choose one of those women for his bride."

"You stupid, foolish girl! I should beat you until some good sense enters that hard head of yours."

Sabina's chin began to quiver. "Please, Papa…"

Don Antonio almost felt pity, then he remembered how she had recently cost him a considerable sum by letting out the neighbor's goat as a prank. The animal never returned, forcing him to offer monetary compensation. "You will either marry Tommaso or dedicate your life to God. The choice is yours to make."

"That's what I should have done at your age," Cecilia mused aloud.

Sabina frowned at her sister. "What?"

10

"I should have become a nun instead of getting married. They must enjoy a peaceful existence."

"Well, that kind of dull life may be appealing to you, but not to me."

"There's nothing wrong with dedicating your life to God," Don Antonio snapped. "It's a selfless and noble endeavor. Perhaps a convent would be a better choice for you, after all."

"Forgive me, Papa," Sabina said contritely. "I meant no disrespect."

His expression softened. "I can't continue to support you forever. Tommaso is willing to wed you without a dowry because he's desperate for an heir, and needs a strong young bride to provide him with one."

Sabina pursed her lips. "You expect me to be grateful?"

"You have no dowry."

"No, but I'm a Rossi. Does our noble name not account for anything? I'm sure our blood is purer than the common sludge coursing through Tommaso's veins."

"Our noble name is *all* we have now—a chance like this will not present itself again." Don Antonio was aware of his daughter's stunning beauty and how it drew the attention of the local men. Her chastity was in constant danger, so the sooner the girl was married, the better. "Tommaso is dining with us tomorrow evening."

"*Tomorrow*? When were you planning to tell me?"

The old man's patience was exceeding its limit. "I was on my way to tell you now, only Donna Francesca intercepted me at the gate. Tommaso wants to meet you before the official betrothal."

"Of course. All men wish to inspect a broodmare before making a purchase. I'm assuming it won't matter if I like him or not, will it?"

"*Sabina is going to marry Signore Tommaso! Sabina is going to marry Signore Tommaso!*"

Hearing her nephew's childish taunt, Sabina ran into the house and went straight to her small bedchamber, bolting the door. Going to the window, she gazed at the neat rows of olive

11

trees growing beyond the stone walls of the courtyard. Her late grandfather, Bernardo, had planted those trees before her father was born. They were tall and thriving now, but barely producing enough crop to make a profit.

Sabina was in this miserable predicament because of her grandfather and his bad gambling habit. She couldn't be angry with him, however. In life, Bernardo had been a charming man whom she had loved dearly.

"Open up," Cecilia cried from the other side of the door.

Ignoring her sister, she looked past the olive trees to the distant hills of the sun-scorched landscape. The grass was the color of straw thanks to the unusually dry summer. Oh, how she desperately longed for rain.

The Republic of Venice was never scorched or dry. In fact, there was plenty of water in La Serenissima; the very streets there made of it! She could run away to Venice and...

And what, you silly girl?

Shortly after her mother's death, her father became ill. He eventually recovered, but his health was never the same. Money was tight and the lack of decent suitors put a strain on the Rossi finances. To make matters worse, Cecilia was forced to return home with an extra mouth to feed after her husband died. Her father was right; he could not support the four of them forever. She would have to marry Tommaso.

"Sabina, please open the door," Cecilia implored.

"Go away. Leave me alone."

"Papa is right. You won't get another opportunity like this one. Stop behaving like a spoiled brat and be grateful."

"If you feel so strongly about it, sister, then you should marry him!"

She expected an angry reply, but instead she heard Cecilia's frustrated sigh and retreating footsteps.

CHAPTER 2

Sabina's contrary mood the following day prompted Don Antonio to threaten his daughter once again with a cloistered life in a remote convent. She was ordered to bathe and prepare for the evening's festivities while Cecilia and two kindly neighbors cooked an elaborate meal to impress their guest of honor.

Sabina spent a considerable amount of time fuming and pacing the floor of her bedchamber. Rather than wear something pretty for the special occasion, she chose a somber black frock with high neckline and long sleeves. Unmarried girls usually wore their hair loose—and Sabina was no exception, often allowing her thick, dark locks to cascade down her back. Despite this, she fashioned her hair into a severe style by coiling her tresses into a knot at the nape of her neck. When she was done, she smiled smugly at her reflection in the looking glass.

Cecilia pounded on the bedchamber door. "Make haste, Sabina! Signore Tommaso will be here at any moment."

"I'm almost done," Sabina replied in a cheerful voice.

Don Antonio and Cecilia exchanged a look of hopeful surprise, but when Sabina finally emerged from the room, their faces fell.

"You look like Mother," Cecilia commented.

Don Antonio was about to tell his stubborn daughter to change into something more suitable when he heard a carriage outside the door. "Santo Cristo, he's here." He gave Sabina a stern look and warned, "Behave." She rolled her eyes and crossed her arms. *That wretched girl*, he thought while opening the door for his guest.

"Buona sera! Your presence honors my humble home, Signore Tommaso. Please, come in."

Tommaso mumbled a polite reply, practically pushing past

13

the old man in order to get a better view of Cecilia and Sabina. The young women gaped in admiration of the Florentine's clothing, correctly assuming that his lavish outfit was worth more than both of their entire wardrobes put together.

Tommaso cut a fine figure in his knee-length black velvet robe trimmed with fox fur. Beneath the robe he wore a tunic fashioned from green silk with silver embroidery around the collar. He offered the sisters a gallant bow while studying each of them in turn. One was plump and rather plain, but she wore a decent gown of good quality linen. The other, although dressed like an austere matron in black, had an exquisite face with eyes the color of emeralds.

Tommaso turned to Don Antonio. "Which one is to be my bride?"

Before her father had a chance to answer, Sabina replied, "I am."

Ah, the beauty is to be mine. Tommaso masked his relief with a grimace. "She doesn't look hearty enough to bear children."

Sabina was about to take a step forward and give a sassy retort, but her sister restrained her with a painful pinch to her upper arm.

"I assure you, she's as healthy as an ox, Signore," Don Antonio gently contradicted. "Sabina will bear you many sons."

Feigning interest in Cecilia, Tommaso asked, "What about her?"

"Oh, my daughter Cecilia is a widow and has a small son."

The Florentine waved his hand dismissively and heaved a theatrical sigh of resignation. "I suppose Sabina will have to do."

"How dare you come in here and—"

Cecilia's hand clamped down over Sabina's mouth.

Tommaso raised an eyebrow. "I see she possesses a fiery spirit, Don Antonio. No wonder you wish to be rid of her."

The old man's face resembled the color of ripe pomegranates as he glared at Sabina, who stared back at him with fearless defiance.

14

Tommaso continued to study the untamed beauty with amusement. "Please remove your hand from your sister's mouth," he said calmly to Cecilia. "I would hear what she has to say."

Cecilia looked to her father, who nodded with obvious reluctance. Her hand had been so tightly cupped around her sister's mouth that rosy imprints of fingers were splayed across Sabina's cheek.

"Well?" Tommaso prompted. "Go on and speak your mind."

"How dare you come in here and inspect us as though we were farm animals that you wish to breed. How dare you comment on my appearance when you're practically old enough to be my father and—" Sabina was about to make a rude comment about his lack of good looks, but it would be untrue. Tommaso's face was lined, yes, but also strong and distinguished—almost handsome.

Tommaso eyed her expectantly. "And?"

Don Antonio stood aside, silently wishing for the earth to swallow him whole while Cecilia nervously bit her lip.

"You should know that I'm not the type who merely sits at home praying over rosary beads and doing needlework," Sabina warned. "I don't plan on changing my ways, either."

"Sabina!" Don Antonio cried.

Tommaso never broke eye contact with Sabina as he placed a hand on the old man's shoulder to restrain him. "I'm devout but not overly zealous, so I don't expect you to pray any more than you already do. Also, I don't need any more tapestries on the walls of my palazzo."

Sabina crossed her arms. "I dislike being told what to do."

Mortified, Don Antonio covered his face with his hands.

"That makes two of us," Tommaso admitted quietly as he patted the old man's back in a gesture of comfort. "Anything else, Signorina?"

"That's all I have to say…*for now*."

The relief in the air was almost palpable.

"It seems as though you and I have much in common, Sabina," Tommaso said. Turning to Don Antonio, he inquired cheerfully, "Well, when do we eat? I'm absolutely famished."

The three of them stared at him in surprise.

"What can we do about Sabina?" Tommaso asked in response to the curious stares. "Shall we thrash her within inches of her life? It won't change how she thinks or feels, will it? Besides, I like her spirit. I think she'll make a fine wife."

The old man's eyes widened in disbelief. "You still wish to marry my daughter?"

"Of course I do." Taking a step closer to Sabina, Tommaso whispered, "Hopefully, you'll grow to like me someday."

Don Antonio and Cecilia looked immensely relieved as they sat down at the table. Sabina was silent throughout the meal as Tommaso regaled them with tales of his travels. At one point he noticed a book on a stool, carefully bound in red velvet.

Reaching for it, he inquired, "What's this?"

Sabina stood. "Please, Signore, I insist that you give me the book."

Realization dawned on him when he noticed the pages were written by a neat, female hand. "This is your writing."

She was tempted to snatch the book out of his hands, but her father shot her a warning look. "Yes, it is."

"I would love to know what sort of things my future bride writes about." Sabina remained stoically silent. Not wanting to torment the girl further, he relinquished the book. "You have pretty penmanship."

"Thank you," she replied, clasping the book to her chest.

The evening soon came to an end and Don Antonio insisted that his guest spend the night. "After all," he reasoned, "you'll be my son-in-law soon, and I hope you will think of this as your home in Lucca."

"I appreciate the offer, Don Antonio, but I have urgent business early in the morning." Tommaso bent over Sabina's hand, and said in a low voice meant only for her ears, *"Goodnight, Tempesta."*

Sabina received a thorough tongue-lashing from her father, then helped her sister clean up. Cecilia swept the floor while Sabina scrubbed the plates, lost in thought. She was relieved that Tommaso was not the ogre she had imagined—after all, she could do worse.

Three days later, a messenger from Florence arrived at the villa with a posy and a small wooden box.

Cecilia went to the kitchen door and called out to her younger sister who was picking rosemary in the garden. "Something has arrived for you! Come inside!"

Sabina took the box from her sister's hands once she entered the kitchen. "What's this?"

"Open it and find out."

Sabina opened the box and pulled out a string of pearls. Perfectly round orbs gleamed in the sunlight pouring in from the window.

"Oh, my!" Cecilia exclaimed. "There's a note and flowers, too." She shuffled inside and picked up a piece of vellum from the scarred wooden table. "Here, let me read it to you."

"I can read just fine," Sabina said, taking the note from her sister's hand.

" 'My dearest Sabina…Your beauty and spirit have enchanted me, and I look forward to our next encounter. Until then, enjoy the humble token I have sent you. Your servant, Tommaso.' "

"He's incredibly generous and kind," Cecilia pointed out. "You're a fortunate girl."

Sabina put the necklace on with her sister's help, then placed the flowers in a ceramic pitcher filled with water.

"Sabina? Are you home?"

Cecilia frowned as she peered out the window. "It's that good-for-nothing Marco! You should send him away. Signore Tommaso won't appreciate men visiting you now that you're officially betrothed."

Marco's tall, stocky frame filled the doorway. "I heard you're getting married to Tommaso Caravelli," he said sourly. "Is it true?"

Cecilia took it upon herself to reply. "Yes, it's true. My father has arranged for Sabina to marry—and about time, too!"

Sabina intercepted. "Come with me, Marco."

17

Cecilia moved to block her path. "Papa and Signore Tommaso wouldn't approve of you wandering off alone with Marco now that you're spoken for."

"I will handle things the way I see fit," Sabina retorted as she exited the house with Marco in tow. When they were out of earshot, she added, "My father is forcing me to marry him."

"What about us?" Marco asked, his brown eyes lacking their usual twinkle. "How will we continue to see each other if you're married and living in Florence?"

Sabina looked over her shoulder to make sure Cecilia was not following them. "Let's walk far from the house."

They followed the stream that snaked behind the olive grove and led into a wooded glen. Hidden beneath a thick canopy of trees, Marco gripped Sabina's shoulders and pulled her against him.

"You're hurting me, Marco."

Easing his grip, he noticed the expensive pearls around her neck for the first time. "Are those from him?"

"Yes."

"My God, what is your father thinking? He's too old for you."

She felt a strange urge to defend Tommaso, but refrained. "There's nothing I can do."

"Marry me, instead."

"What?"

"Marry me."

In all the time they had known each other, and throughout the many embraces they had shared, Marco had never mentioned the word 'marriage.'

When they were children, Marco ran with a pack of older boys who enjoyed making mischief and wreaking havoc on younger, weaker children. He was the imp, the bully who had teased her incessantly—sometimes even cruelly. The moment she blossomed into a young woman, his demeanor toward her changed from aggressive to possessive. At first, she resisted his amorous advances, but he was persistent. To make matters worse, her mother died unexpectedly. With her father overcome

18

by illness and grief, and Cecilia caring for a husband and child, she had no one to turn to for comfort. Marco came to the rescue, filling the sudden, agonizing void in her life with his constant company and piquant humor. In exchange for this emotional salve, she had finally given in to his physical demands.

Although Marco was attractive, their relationship was far from the romantic ones described by troubadours.

"I can't marry you," Sabina stated firmly.

Taking hold of her chin, he bent his head and plundered her mouth. Unable to resist the familiar comfort of his body, she wound her arms around his neck and played with the dark curls at the nape.

"Are you ready to give this up," he asked against her lips, his big hands trailing down the length of her spine.

"I'll learn to live without it, and so shall you."

The house was far enough away to allow Marco to ease Sabina onto the soft grass and lift her skirts. His lovemaking was urgent, and he took his lustful pleasure as selfishly as a common stallion. She bore his considerable weight and hard thrusts placidly, knowing it was the last time they would ever be together in a carnal sense.

Satiated, Marco placed his head on her bosom afterward. Trailing a blade of grass along her collar bone, he said, "Don't marry him."

She stifled a yawn. "I can't disobey my father."

He raised himself on his elbow and stared at her in disbelief. "Since when are you the good, obedient daughter? The role of martyr doesn't suit you at all."

"Hush or I'll find a potion that will turn you into a toad."

"Be careful, Sabina," he warned, his face serious. "You'll end up burned at the stake someday if you continue to make such jests."

Despite Marco's blatant disregard for the divine admonition against the sin of fornication, he came from an extremely devout and superstitious family.

"Who said I was jesting?" she challenged with a twinkle in her eye.

19

Marco frowned at her in disapproval. He knew the love potions Sabina created for the village girls weren't real—or at least he hoped they weren't. "You try my patience at times."

"Then I've succeeded in my task."

To break the tension, he tickled her roughly. "Vixen!"

"Stop that, Marco Alfani!"

Lowering his head, he kissed her heartily on the mouth. "Marry me."

"I cannot," she replied, wriggling out of his grasp and smoothing the creases from her skirt.

"Let me speak to your father and ask for your hand in marriage."

"No!"

Marco's expression was one of puzzlement verging on anger. "Do you *want* to marry him?"

"Do you realize that you've never told me you loved me? What difference does it make if I marry you or Tommaso? Neither of you love me. I'm only a pawn to be used in a game played by men."

"Please, let me ask your father for your hand."

"Why? Is my marriage to another man an assault on your pride?"

Marco appeared wounded. "I do love you, Sabina."

***

Marco arrived at Don Antonio's villa later that day. Cecilia and Sabina were both in the kitchen preparing supper while Paolo played at their feet.

"Don Antonio, may I have a word with you, please?" he said from the doorway as he fidgeted nervously with his hands. Despite the August heat, he had worn his best wool tunic in an attempt to look presentable and there was a sheen of perspiration on his brow.

Don Antonio eyed the uninvited guest suspiciously. He never cared much for the young man who eyed his daughter like a stud seeking to rut, but said, "Come in, Marco. What can I do for you?"

Marco cleared his throat. "As you know, sir, I'm a simple

man but I come from a decent family."

"Yes, your father is a good man and I've known him for many years."

Encouraged by this, Marco continued, "I don't have much now because I'm still young, but I'm a hard worker. I would like to ask—"

"—for my daughter's hand in marriage."

"Yes, I want to marry Sabina."

"She is already spoken for."

"But, Don Antonio—"

"I'm sorry, Marco. The answer is no."

Although his pride was deeply wounded, Marco inclined his head respectfully and gave Sabina a wistful glance before taking his leave.

Don Antonio sat down at the table and allowed his daughters to set a plate of steaming stewed tripe before him. "Have you been allowing Marco to court you?" he asked, staring pointedly at Sabina.

Sabina poured wine into his cup and re-corked the bottle. "You know how Marco has always been fond of me."

"That's not what I asked you."

"We are not courting."

Cecilia snorted. Don Antonio glanced at his eldest daughter before fixing his gaze on Sabina. "Well, whatever is going on between you two must end. *Now*. You're going to be married soon, and I will not have you sullying yourself or our family name, do you understand?"

"Yes."

"I'm serious, Sabina."

Placing a loaf of bread on the table, she said, "I know, Papa."

"Don't worry, Father," Cecilia said. "Sabina is not so foolish as to throw away her entire future."

"I hope you're correct," he said. "I'm entrusting her into your care."

Cecilia's eyebrows shot upward. "Into my care?"

"Yes. From now until the wedding day, don't let your sister out of your sight."

Was there ever a city more glorious than Florence? It was no wonder the royal courts of Europe recognized it as the epicenter of art, culture, and classical expression. Tommaso had sent a carriage to fetch his bride and her family a few days before the wedding. When the vehicle passed through the massive city gates, Don Antonio pointed out the Medici crest— a gold shield with several red balls. Since the Medici commissioned many public artworks and paid for structural repairs, the family's coat of arms was ostentatiously displayed throughout the city. This cunning strategy served as a visual testament to any foreigner entering Florence that Medici authority was both unchallenged and absolute.

The horses were forced to slow their pace within the crowded streets, thus allowing the occupants inside the carriage to marvel at the grand palazzos and public statues carved from dazzling white Carrara marble. The elegant piazzas teemed with Florentines, many flaunting expensive jewels and sumptuous clothing. The majority of people wore red, but not just any red; *Florentine Red* was currently the most fashionable color in Europe. Sabina mentally likened it to the color of blood— vibrant, yet deep, and extremely flattering to the complexion. Some wore Florentine Red in the form of plush velvet with a luxuriously thick pile while others sported brocade with decorative flowers and leaves fashioned from gold or silver thread.

"Red everywhere," Paolo chirped.

"What a clever boy you are," Cecilia cooed as she kissed the top of her son's head.

"Florence is overflowing with wealth and it shows," Don Antonio mused aloud, his gaze fixed on a well-heeled pair of gentlemen.

The city consisted of successful bankers, artists, sculptors, wool and silk merchants, carpenters—too many talented people to mention. The staggering net worth of some bourgeoisie families rivaled that of royal princes.

The carriage turned down an impossibly narrow street and finally came to a stop in front of a long stone wall with an iron-studded wooden door at its center. Above the door was Tommaso's family crest, marking the residence as the Palazzo Caravelli. The carved stone shield portrayed a cylindrical tower with an eagle poised atop Guelph crenellations. Two servants appeared, helping them alight from the carriage. Sabina and her family followed them into a courtyard surrounded by low stone buildings and a tower that appeared to be at least five hundred years old. There was a cistern in the center of the courtyard and a bronze fountain fashioned like a mermaid.

"Welcome," Tommaso said as he emerged from within the shadowy interior of the tower.

Greetings were exchanged, then Sabina eyes were drawn to the ceramic bas-relief sculpture of the Madonna and Christ child adorning the wall behind his head. The exquisitely carved figures, along with the boughs of decorative leaves and fruits framing the charming scene, were painted in brilliant white, yellow ochre, and blue.

Following her gaze, Tommaso smiled. "Do you like it?"

"It's lovely."

"You have good taste. Luca della Robbia's work is in high demand." Taking her hands into his own, he said, "I trust that you'll find your chamber comfortable. If there's anything you or your family requires, please don't hesitate to ask the servants."

She was charmed by his courteous hospitality. "Thank you."

Motioning to the servants, he instructed, "See that our guests are given some refreshment and show the ladies to their bedchambers."

Turning to Don Antonio, he inquired, "Would you care to take some wine with me under the shade of my fruit trees before going to your room, or would you prefer to rest first?"

"I would be delighted to have some wine with you."

"Very well," Tommaso said as he put his arm around the old man in a friendly gesture. "Ladies, we shall see you at supper."

The cool interior of the palazzo was a relief from the heat outside. Sabina, Cecilia, and Paolo ascended a long flight of stairs separating the servant's ground floor from the *piano nobile*. Sabina took in the attractive surroundings, liking her new home instantly. She smiled in delight when she entered her new private quarters, which were spacious and well-lit. The wide bed boasted a canopy fashioned from the softest yellow silk. The servants had carefully strewn lavender and tansy onto the comfortable straw and down-filled mattress in order to give the bed a pleasant scent while simultaneously repelling bedbugs. There was an antechamber for bathing and a sitting room with a small writing desk.

The Rossi family enjoyed the best of what Florence had to offer, including the hospitality of their gracious host. Sabina, who had always taken an interest in the arts, immediately noticed that the paintings and sculptures of Florence possessed a different style than those of Lucca. Many of the themes were the same—Annunciation of Christ, Madonna Enthroned or the martyrdom of various saints, but in Florence the figures seemed to be alive. The Virgin Mary was often depicted as a pretty young woman flaunting current fashion rather than a stiff matronly figure in traditional dark blue cloak. Instead of static religious effigies, Florentine sculptors adopted the style of ancient Greece and Rome to create idealized gods. One could easily imagine these impressive figures stepping down from their marble pedestals at any moment to walk among the people.

Interestingly, it was common for wealthy Florentine families to commission religious paintings for their private chapels with their own likenesses included in the holy scenes. Family members stood alongside Jesus or their patron saints dressed like royals and dripping in jewels. Sabina wondered if these people were trying to be seen as godly, or if they were attempting to drag God down to their level. Although unsure of the answer, she was certain that Florentine art was magnificent.

Artists, architects, sculptors, writers, philosophers, and musicians thrived under the patronage of guilds and generous commissions from wealthy families. Tommaso mentioned the names of the city's most prominent families and Sabina committed a few of them to memory: Strozzi, Pazzi, Rucellai, and Tornabuoni. Of these great families, none was more generous in their patronage than the powerful House of Medici.

The day before their wedding, Tommaso and Sabina attended Holy Mass in the church where they would be married.

"This is the Basilica of San Lorenzo, a revered church in the city," Tommaso stated proudly. "Brunelleschi, who is considered the most talented architect in the city, designed the basilica's interior."

"Did the Medici pay for this church?" she inquired, her eyes darting to the Medici coat of arms displayed throughout the church.

"Yes."

Sabina was again impressed by the wealth and power of Florence's leading family. "Will I have the honor of meeting them soon?"

"Most certainly."

After the service, Tommaso led Sabina to the front of the church. On the floor before the high altar was a big circle of porphyry, a rare and expensive Egyptian marble the color of mulberries—a stone normally reserved for emperors. "Lorenzo's grandfather, Cosimo, was buried beneath the circle upon which we are standing. So beloved is he by the Florentines that they've bestowed upon him the Latin title of *Pater Patriae*, or—"

"Father of the Fatherland," Sabina supplied.

"Correct," he beamed. "Cosimo adopted the turtle as his personal emblem during his lifetime, thus alluding to his infinite patience. He was a man who waited for the right moment to strike. The great grandfather of Lorenzo, Giovanni di Bicci, was buried in the sacristy beneath that communion table." Sabina followed his pointed finger. "His location is also marked by a circular slab of costly porphyry."

"What about that beautiful porphyry sarcophagus over there?" she asked, indicating the iron grate in the sacristy's wall.

"That's the final resting place of Lorenzo's father, Piero, commonly known as Piero il Gottoso. The Medici are plagued by gout, thus the nickname. Do you see how the sarcophagus rests on four turtles? It's an homage to Cosimo."

The precious materials and prestigious locations of the tombs hinted at the Medici family's enormous pride, but Sabina wisely refrained from voicing such an unkind speculation.

***

The last day of August dawned clear and predictably hot. Tuscany was still in the midst of a drought with no relief in sight. True to her father's words, Sabina would be married before the month was over. Tomorrow was the first of September and, by then, she would be the legal wife of Tommaso Caravelli. She was pleased that her future husband treated her and her family like royalty. She had even been allowed to bring Mendi, who was now calling out loudly from his wired brass cage near the windowsill. The bird took flight at whim throughout the day, yet always returned in the evening to roost.

Every fine lady in Florence possessed a talented lady's maid, so Tommaso had procured one for his bride as a wedding gift. A girl by the name of Teresa plaited Sabina's hair, expertly coiling the braids into two rolls at the top of each ear then tucking the rolls into templers adorned with pearls. She then pinned a length of silk as sheer as mist to the headdress, allowing a measure of the fabric to fall in front of her mistress's face.

Sabina admired her reflection in the highly polished looking glass. The long-sleeved gown she wore was cut from gold brocade with an intricate pearl design sewn into the front panel of a snug-fitting bodice.

A page eventually knocked on the door, signaling that it was time to go. Tommaso had arranged for a litter to carry his bride the short distance to the church.

Don Antonio began his familiar speech the moment he saw his daughter descend the stairs. "We have long since lost the family fortune—thanks to your grandfather's gambling—but our name is still one of great fame, going as far back as—"

"—the first fathers of Tuscany," Sabina interjected with a huff. "I know, Papa. The Rossi family were once the great Guelphs who possessed considerable wealth...*I know*...but we are not rich and we no longer hold any power, political or otherwise."

"Show some respect, Sabina," Cecilia snapped.

Sabina shot Cecilia a withering look before taking her father's hands into her own. "Don't worry, Papa. I won't disrespect our good family name," she assured in a gentler tone.

Hurt by Sabina's initial harshness, Don Antonio nodded sadly.

"Forgive me," Sabina offered before entering the litter.

Cecilia placed her arm around her father's slumped shoulders. "Come, our carriage awaits."

As a rule, Tommaso Caravelli avoided ostentatious behavior whenever possible. Unlike some noblemen who flaunted their wealth by strutting around like peacocks in the latest fashions, he preferred understated elegance. While he adhered to this personal code of conduct, he had no qualms bending the rules where Sabina was concerned. It was a popular custom in Florence for veiled brides to ride to the church on a white horse on their wedding day, but that was not good enough for Tommaso. He insisted that his future wife be transported to the basilica in a gilded litter with the Caravelli crest painted on the door.

Family, friends, and curious onlookers gathered to see Tommaso Caravelli get married—again. They stared at the golden litter as it was carried up the stairs of San Lorenzo by two liveried pages, then gaped as Sabina emerged from the velvet-lined interior with all the pomp of a queen arriving at her own coronation. She walked into the church, drawing the eyes of many lustful men and envious maidens. Tommaso stood by the altar looking handsome in a brocade tunic of deep amber, the golden beads sewn into the fabric gleaming in the candlelight.

The moment Sabina stood beside the groom, the priest began the long, monotonous marriage ceremony. Everyone appeared relieved when Tommaso lifted the sheer veil from the bride's face and kissed her cheek. Invited guests made their way to the Palazzo Caravelli in the blazing heat of the midday sun to partake of the marriage feast.

The lavish meal was served in the spacious main hall, which was airy and cool. The cooks prepared roasted fowl, stag, hare, and swan, each served with various sauces. Fresh breads, aged cheeses, and stewed vegetables accompanied the meats. Honeyed treats of every size and shape mixed with nuts, fruits, or rare spices were available in abundance for those with a sweet tooth. Acrobats and troubadours performed to entertain the many guests as minstrels sang songs of love to honor the newlywed couple.

Sabina sat beside her husband at the high table with a look of sheer amazement on her face. Never in her life had she attended such an extravagant affair!

Tommaso leaned over and whispered, "Are you enjoying yourself, my Tempesta?" She nodded and he smiled in satisfaction. "I did this all for you. I hope you are pleased, Sabina."

For a brief instant, Tommaso resembled a lovesick young man. Did this mean he could be easily swayed? She smiled at the possibility and said, "I'm very pleased. Thank you."

Later, after eating and drinking more than she should have, Sabina wandered away from her husband's side to a staircase located at the far corner of the main hall. Feeling excessively warm, she decided to get away from the revelry and cool off for a bit. Several of the florid-faced guests were already drunk and dancing merrily as she ascended the stairs. At the top was a spacious room with cream-painted walls and a red-tiled floor. There was a big window in the room, its green shutters thrown back to reveal the tiny orange grove in the courtyard below. The wide wooden bench beneath the window was piled high with

28

soft cushions, and it beckoned invitingly.

Sabina sat down and pulled the heavy brocade skirt up past her knees, revealing a set of shapely bare legs. Teresa had tried to convince her to wear stockings for propriety's sake, but flaunting rules for the sake of comfort was nothing new for Sabina. She kicked off her shoes, relishing the deliciously cold tile beneath her toes. Resting her head against the windowsill, she closed her eyes and allowed the breeze to caress her clammy skin. The lazy hum of bumblebees in the courtyard almost lulled her to sleep. After several minutes, she felt a presence in the room and her eyes snapped open.

It was Marco, dressed in a black tunic and hose as if attending a funeral. "*Signora*, should you not be with your husband and your guests?" he inquired drily from the doorway.

She sat up straight, quickly slipping her feet into her shoes. "What are you doing here?"

"An old friend can't offer his congratulations on your wedding day?"

"I know you too well to believe this is your true intention."

His gaze swept over her bare legs, her cleavage, and finally rested on her full mouth. She let her skirt fall to the floor and adjusted her bodice as he sauntered into the room. "So, how does it feel to be the wife of such a wealthy man, *Signora*?"

"Stop calling me that!"

"You are now married, are you not?"

"Yes, but—"

"I'm merely giving a married woman the respect she is due."

He sat beside her on the bench and boldly traced the curve of her breast with his fingertip, compelling her to slap his hand away.

"Marco, I don't know how you got here—or even why you came—but you must leave right now." Ignoring her words, he leaned forward in an attempt to kiss her lips and she shoved him. "I'm serious. Go!"

"You know you'll always be mine," he whispered.

She stood and walked to the center of the room. "Leave now or I shall be forced to summon my husband's guards."

"You wouldn't dare," he said menacingly.

Tommaso walked into the room and looked from Marco to Sabina. "Some of the guests have been wondering where you went off to, my dear."

Her face paled. "Forgive me, Signore Tommaso. It was sweltering downstairs…I came up here to cool off."

"First of all, you must stop calling me *Signore* Tommaso. I'm your husband now. Secondly, who is this man?"

"Signore—I mean, Tommaso, this is an old family friend," she replied. "He is Marco, son of Signore Niccolò Alfani."

The men nodded to each other without saying a word.

Tommaso offered his arm to Sabina. "If you will excuse us, Signore Marco, my wife and I must return to our guests."

Marco did not move as he silently watched them leave.

"I never want you to be alone with that man again," Tommaso whispered as they descended the stairs. To drive his point home, he gave her arm a painful squeeze. "Do you understand me?"

She winced. "Yes."

He released his vice-like grip. "Good. We shall get along fine if you do as I say."

Obviously, her husband was no lovesick fool, nor would he be easily influenced by feminine wiles.

"Sabina! Come and dance with me," Cecilia called out when she caught sight of her sister.

Sabina allowed herself to be pulled away from Tommaso and into the throng of dancing guests. The smell of sweet perfume, wine, and perspiration permeated the air, making her feel nauseous.

"What in God's name are you doing?" Cecilia demanded.

"What are you talking about?"

"I saw Marco follow you upstairs. Please tell me you haven't done anything dishonorable on your wedding day."

"I'm insulted that you would insinuate such a thing. I didn't even know Marco was here."

"Well, no one invited him. Two of Signore Tommaso's guards just escorted him outside. What an embarrassment to our family."

"An embarrassment not caused by me, I assure you."

"Don't be stupid and ruin the wonderful opportunity you've been given. You could have married someone poor, like I did." Cecilia sighed. "If only I'd been blessed with your beauty, I would have fared better in life."

Sabina was tired of her sister's constant disparaging comments. "Enough, Cecilia!"

Some of the nearby guests tossed curious glances in their direction, causing Cecilia's cheeks to redden with shame. "How dare you speak to me in such a manner?"

"How dare you insult me on my wedding day! I've endured enough of your reproaches. Papa's too, for that matter."

Cecilia raised an eyebrow. "Now that you've married a man with prestige and wealth, you think you're better than me."

"That's not what I think at all—Cecilia, wait," Sabina protested, but her sister was already walking away.

First her father, then Tommaso, and now her sister. How many more people would she offend today?

Tommaso came to stand beside his wife. "Is anything amiss?"

"Not at all."

He knew harsh words were exchanged between the two sisters, and he was willing to bet they had to do with Marco Alfani. "May I have the pleasure of this dance?"

"Since when does a husband ask permission of his wife?"

"You have much to learn, my dear," he said as he slipped a hand around her slim waist.

Sabina was pleasantly surprised to learn that Tommaso was not only surefooted, but also physically fit for a man of his age.

"Are you feeling unwell?" Tommaso inquired.

"Why do you ask?"

"Your face is flushed."

"Perhaps it was the wine," she lied.

"Perhaps," he repeated. "Tell me, is Marco your lover?"

"Marco?"

"Yes, *Marco*, the man whom you were alone with upstairs

31

during our wedding celebration. Do not bother lying to me, Sabina, I'll know when you do."

"How will you know if I lie?"

"Your lips lie, but your eyes do not. I have dealt with enough people in my life to know when someone is being dishonest, especially women."

She looked away before admitting, "Yes, he was my lover."

"And now?" he demanded, taking hold of her chin and forcing her to meet his gaze.

"Now I'm married and have no lovers."

"Did you invite him here today?"

"No. I didn't know he was here, I swear."

"Are you still in love with him?"

Sabina hesitated. It would be improper either way she responded. If she said "yes," it would threaten her marriage, but if she said "no," she would seem like a whore. She decided to be honest. "I was never in love with him."

"You're telling me the truth."

She nodded. "I was a stupid girl."

He found her honesty refreshing. Of all the women he had known, and he had known many, Sabina Rossi was the most peculiar. She was strong and rebellious but possessed a childlike quality that was almost endearing.

"Good," he said, pulling her against him. "I prefer a stupid girl over a woman who is in love with another man."

Don Antonio tapped Tommaso on his shoulder. "May I have a dance with my daughter on her wedding day?"

Tommaso handed his wife to his father-in-law. Don Antonio beamed with pride. "Signore Tommaso is a fine man, Sabina. I'm certain he will make your life very comfortable and offer you many niceties that I cannot."

"You've given me everything I need, Papa."

"Yes, but you deserve more and I know you want more. You are nothing like your sister, Cecilia, who was content to marry a simple man and now basks in motherhood. Such a dull existence would kill your spirit. Life would have been easier had you been born male, but Fate can be cruel." He paused. "I wouldn't have married you to Tommaso if I didn't think he could provide you with what you need in life."

"What is it that I need?"

"Excitement."

She could not deny it. "Thank you, Papa," she said, kissing his cheek.

Don Antonio narrowed his eyes. "You may think me a simple old man but pay heed to the counsel I'm about to give you. Do not let your heart or your headstrong ways lead you astray."

Sabina rolled her eyes in anticipation of another onslaught of admonitions when her father took both of her hands firmly in his own and pulled her forward. His face was serious, his eyes fearful.

She frowned. "Papa?"

"Listen carefully to what I'm about to say, my child. Be wary now that you are a member of Florentine society. You should know who your friends are but, more importantly, know your enemies. Watch that tongue of yours; be mindful of what you say and to whom you say it. Control your temper. Never reveal anything you do not want repeated—speak little and listen twofold." Don Antonio cast a furtive glance over his shoulder and whispered, "And for God's sake, do not concoct any of your silly potions! Being accused of witchcraft is no trivial matter here in Florence. Signore Tommaso deals with important and influential people, and you would not want to jeopardize your husband's position in society."

Don Antonio's wise words hit Sabina with great impact. As she scanned the room, she noticed several sets of eyes watching her carefully. For the first time since her arrival in Florence, she felt insecure of her new role. She had been afforded a good education and learned basic court manners but never had the opportunity to actually mingle in high society until now.

"Papa, take me home. I don't want to stay here in Florence," she said, gripping her father's hands tightly.

Don Antonio saw the panic in his daughter's eyes and found her vulnerability disconcerting, especially since it was

33

something she rarely, if ever, displayed. "Now, now, Sabina," he said soothingly. "There's no need for you to fear. You are a lovely young woman and you know how to behave properly. You'll be fine as long as you heed my counsel."

She immediately straightened her shoulders. "You're right, Papa," she said, glancing around the room and coolly meeting the eyes of those who stared in her direction. "I know what to do. I'll be fine."

Don Antonio embraced Sabina and walked away, leaving her alone in the center of the room. With her head held high and several eyes following her, she walked to where Tommaso stood and placed a hand upon his arm.

He gazed down at her and smiled. "Come, dearest, there is someone I want you to meet," he said, leading her through the throng of guests. "Giuliano de' Medici has arrived from Milan only a moment ago and is here to offer his congratulations."

Sabina was led to a group of well-dressed men. The most exquisitely dressed was an attractive young man in his mid-twenties with brown, shoulder-length hair and a serene face. He smiled at Tommaso before embracing him with great affection.

"Giuliano, I'm so happy you could come," Tommaso said.

"I wanted to arrive earlier, but we were delayed," Giuliano explained. Noticing the stunning woman at his friend's side, he added, "Is this bella donna your new bride?"

"Giuliano, may I present to you my wife, Sabina, daughter of Don Antonio Rossi."

The dark eyes that studied Sabina were alert and intelligent. Giuliano stepped forward and gallantly kissed her hand. "It's an honor to meet you, Signora. You are living proof of Tommaso's impeccable taste."

She smiled. "You are too kind, Signore Giuliano."

Giuliano turned to Tommaso. "I congratulate you on finding such a lovely treasure."

"Thank you, my friend. Where is Lorenzo?"

"Unfortunately, my brother was forced to remain in Milan and instructed me to convey his best wishes to you both. He regrets not being able to attend your wedding today."

"I know the business he tends to is urgent; there is no need for him to feel any regrets. I shall see him soon enough."

"You must present your wife at the palazzo when Lorenzo returns," Giuliano said, winking at Sabina. "He will be charmed."

"It will be an honor. Now, please, I want you and your men to eat, drink, and enjoy the festivities," Tommaso said before quickly summoning his servants and instructing them to pay special attention to the Medici entourage.

Giuliano mingled easily with the guests since he knew everyone.

Sabina was duly impressed that her husband was on such friendly terms with the wealthiest and most politically influential family in Tuscany. "How long have you known the Medici brothers?"

"I was a good friend of their father, so I've known them since birth. Before that, my father and their grandfather did business together."

"Oh? What kind of business?"

"Why, banking, of course."

"I see. Do you regularly attend court at their palazzo?"

Tommaso stepped closer to Sabina and lowered his voice. "You must never refer to the Palazzo Medici as a royal court, my dear. It's offensive."

"Forgive me."

He waved away her apology. "You must always keep in mind that Florence is a republic, not a monarchy."

Her brow creased in confusion. "Oh."

"You will be presented to Lorenzo, who, although not being a prince, assumes the role of one." He paused. "Do you understand?"

"So I should treat him like a prince but never call him that to his face."

Tommaso nodded in approval. "Correct."

"And the Palazzo Medici is not an official royal court but it operates as such, although everyone pretends it doesn't because Florence is a republic."

"I think you'll learn how this city operates very quickly."

The wedding festivities lasted until nightfall. Don Antonio wished many blessings upon the marital union and kissed his daughter's cheek before retiring to his guest chamber. Cecilia also approached her sister and brother-in-law before retiring. She hugged her sister coolly, muttering a blessing on their marriage before heading off to bed.

Later that night, after the guests had gone home, Sabina sat at the dressing table in her bedchamber. Teresa had already helped her mistress out of the wedding gown and was now brushing her hair in the light of three flickering candles.

"You are very lucky, Signora Sabina."

"Why do you say that?"

"Signore Tommaso is a good man who gives with an open hand to those whom he loves. He is always helping people and never asks the cost, which is why God has blessed him with so much wealth."

"How do you know this?"

"My father was cousin to his first wife."

"Tell me about her."

"We're not allowed to speak of her because... Well, she fled with another man."

Sabina hid her surprise. "I see..."

"Signore Tommaso helped us very much after my mother died."

"I'm sorry for your loss, Teresa. My mother is dead, too."

"May her soul be blessed in Heaven," Teresa said before crossing herself and kissing the tiny gold crucifix that hung from a chain around her neck.

"How well do you know my husband?"

"Well enough to assure you that he loathes impropriety and does not tolerate disrespect," she replied candidly.

"I'll keep that in mind."

"He seems very fond of you, Signora Sabina. One of my cousins served as the lady's maid to his second wife, Signora Mariella." Teresa lowered her voice and added, "She and Signore Tommaso were never in accord. She died in childbirth.

The baby died, too."

"What happened to your cousin after her mistress died?"

"She was sent to another Florentine lady across the city."

How clever of her husband to get rid of the girl. It certainly prevented any gossip about the late Signora Mariella. "Anything else I should know?"

Teresa froze, her cheeks bright red in the reflection of the looking glass.

Tommaso stood in the doorway. "Leave us."

Teresa bowed her head. "Yes, Signore Tommaso." She laid down the brush, curtsied to her master and mistress, and started to walk out of the room when Mendi began to caw loudly from within his cage.

Tommaso frowned. "Take that damned bird with you. I know you love that wretched crow, Sabina, but there is room for only one male in your bedchamber tonight."

Teresa retraced her steps and picked up the cage. Mendi, unhappy at being moved, threatened to peck at the girl's hand, but Sabina's sharp reprimand kept him from doing so. Holding the cage as far away from her as she could, the maid hastily vacated the room.

"What do you think of Teresa?" Tommaso asked with feigned nonchalance.

"I like her," Sabina replied cautiously, wondering how much of the conversation he had heard before entering her room.

"Good. I want you to be happy." He stood behind her and placed his hands on her shoulders. "I don't expect you to love me." She stiffened at the unexpected statement and tried to turn around in order to face him, but his grip on her shoulders tightened. "I'm well aware your beauty and youth, Sabina. After seeing what your former lover looks like, I know you'll probably never love me."

"Tommaso, I—"

"Don't interrupt me again," he warned. "Unlike other men, I do not care that my bride is not a virgin. I'm no longer a young man prone to frivolous jealousies, nor do I wish to engage in any hot-tempered duels for the sake of your virtue. Time is precious to me."

He moved her hair aside to expose her nape and bent to kiss the soft skin. "Now that you're my wife, I expect your loyalty and respect. I want you to provide me with a son and not make a cuckold of me. In return, you will be afforded freedoms that are usually denied most women. You can read as many books as you wish, learn any subject you desire—with my approval, of course. I may even share political views with you, but only if you adhere to my conditions. If you refuse to abide by my rules and decide to take on a lover, or dishonor me in any way through improper conduct, you will be cast out of this house in shame. Your reputation will be ruined forever." His hands fell to his sides. "Do we have an agreement, Sabina?"

"Yes, Tommaso."

Without further words, he led her to the bed. Sabina was surprised by the unexpected finesse of his lovemaking. Marco had been lustful and clumsy in comparison with Tommaso's expertise. When they finished, she stared at the exposed timbers on the ceiling. The act itself had been pleasant enough, which was somewhat of a relief.

"You must be tired," he said, kissing her cheek before getting out of bed. "I will retire to my chamber now. Goodnight, Sabina."

"Goodnight, Tommaso, and thank you."

"For what?"

"For everything."

He cast a wry smile over his shoulder and left the room.

CHAPTER 4

By the middle of September, two important things occurred: first, rain—blessed, glorious rain! The second, Sabina learned that being the wife of an important Florentine was a serious responsibility. The merchant republican society of Florence was committed to communal, Christian, and classical values. This meant that the honor of men should reside in their public image and service, and in the personal virtue of their wives. It was one of the reasons why Tommaso had warned her never to dishonor him in any way.

The constant male preoccupation to ensure their wives' purity—and that of the bloodline through which their property descended—was so great that the majority of Florentine women were excluded from public life. Several of these women were sequestered to their homes, much to their frustration. The educated and genteel wives of affluent men were forced to deal with a certain measure of patriarchal demands. The only women who were free from any of these societal burdens were peasants, prostitutes and the mistresses of powerful men. For them, purity of bloodline and familial reputation were of little or no concern.

A mature man and a liberal thinker, Tommaso allowed Sabina the freedom that many other women were denied. Like other respectable husbands, he forbade his wife to wander the streets unescorted but saw no problem in allowing her to go out in the company of her lady's maid and armed guards. Sabina attended church regularly with her husband, gave alms to the poor, and behaved modestly at all times.

Of the many rules she was expected to follow, behaving modestly was perhaps the most difficult. She desired to run barefoot through the fields while holding her skirts high in order to feel the tall grass on her legs. On hot days, she wanted to swim naked in the cool ponds and rivers located in the Florentine hills. In Lucca, she could easily escape into the woods and enjoy these simple pleasures in secret. In Florence, this proved to be impossible. As the wife of a prominent citizen, she could never indulge in any of her wild childhood activities. Her husband's personal library was a wonderful consolation, however, and he granted her access to many books.

As the weeks passed, Tommaso noticed an array of books on his wife's bedside table when he entered her bedchamber, but her red velvet journal was always absent; hidden.

One night, after making love to his wife, he noticed a sheet of parchment on the floor. He made sure she was asleep before holding the sheet toward the light of a sputtering candle. As he read the dark, elegant verse, he was genuinely impressed with Sabina's talent. When he finished, he placed the sheet back on the floor.

***

On the last day of October, a page arrived early in the morning as Tommaso and Sabina were breaking their fast. He handed Tommaso a scroll sealed with red wax and imprinted with the Medici crest.

Tommaso broke the seal and read the message. "Lorenzo de' Medici is back from Milan, and a banquet will be held to celebrate his return."

"I will finally see the Palazzo Medici and meet Lorenzo?"

"Yes, my dear. I shall summon the seamstress today."

"Why? You've already given me several fine gowns. I can wear any one of them."

"This is no common banquet. You are being officially presented to the Ruler of Florence."

Donna Maria arrived the following day with several swatches of fabric. After many years of creating gowns for Florentine ladies, she was one of the most sought-after seamstresses in the city. She was a tiny older woman with hands made rough from years of sewing. The only color she ever wore was black, and the only jewelry she flaunted was a gold crucifix.

After obtaining her husband's opinion, Sabina settled on deep red silk with gold leaf pattern. Since the fabric was ornate,

Donna Maria designed a simple style with a low neckline, flowing train, and long, bell-shaped sleeves. For the next few days, the seamstress and her apprentices worked hard to create a splendid gown.

On the day of the Medici party, Teresa gave her mistress a series of beauty treatments consisting of a milk bath and a lengthy massage with scented oil. Sabina's hair was washed with rose water and brushed until it shone, then styled into a braided knot at the back of her neck.

"Lorenzo de' Medici is an extraordinary man," Teresa said as she pinned small gold beads into her mistress's coiffure.

Sabina sat in front of the looking glass and met her maid's gaze in the reflection. "Have you met him?"

"Only once. It was here, in fact, shortly before your arrival. I served him wine while he waited for Signore Tommaso. I will never forget that strong face or the fine clothes he wore." She paused. "He made me shiver."

"Fear?"

"Not fear, although he is feared by many. It was more like a presence."

"How interesting."

"You'll know what I mean when you meet him," Teresa said, smoothing an errant strand of hair.

"I was told that Lorenzo is politically shrewd and fond of the arts."

Teresa laughed slightly, holding the ivory comb in her hand mid-air. "Fond of the arts? No, Signora, he *loves* the arts. Signore Lorenzo is patron to many artists and intellectuals living in Florence. He is also a philosopher who embraces Plato." She tucked another gold bead into place before adding, "Rumor has it that he's good friends with Signore Marsilio Ficino."

Sabina had heard of the controversial philosopher. Most people avoided company with such types, afraid of the negative social repercussions. Only a man in a high position of power possessed the luxury of not caring what others thought. "Is that so? I assume he acts as Ficino's protector."

"Most definitely. There are those with closed minds who would destroy such great thinkers of our time," Teresa replied. "I admire Signore Lorenzo for not being one of them."

"You surprise me, Teresa."

"How so?"

"Well, you seem to know so much."

"I've always worked in important households and, since it's my duty to keep quiet and listen attentively, I learn many things."

"Well, I'm glad you share your knowledge with me."

"You surprise me, too, Signora."

Sabina's brows lifted slightly in surprise. "Oh?"

"Many ladies care only for the trivialities of life, such as fashion and gossip. Some walk about with great airs, believing themselves superior to everyone else. You're not like them— and I mean this as the greatest compliment. I hope my honesty doesn't offend you. My father has warned me many times to bite my tongue."

"As did mine. I'm not offended. On the contrary, I'm flattered."

Both women turned in surprise at the sound of fluttering feathers. Mendi, who had disappeared three days ago, flew into the room and perched on a chair.

"He must be hungry," Teresa said.

"Or perhaps he misses my company," Sabina countered hopefully.

The plate of cheese, bread, and fruit that a servant had brought up earlier for breakfast was still on the table.

Sabina reached for a crust of leftover bread and tossed it at the crow. Mendi gobbled it up immediately. "You were right. He's hungry," she said sourly. Turning back to her maid, she asked, "Have you ever met his wife?"

"Signore Lorenzo's wife?" Sabina nodded and Teresa replied, "No. I know he married a Roman noblewoman named Clarice Orsini eight years ago, but I have only caught glimpses of her. She rarely ventures out."

"What is she like? Is she witty? Pretty?"

Teresa set down the comb and took a step back to admire her handiwork. "She is considered to be quite plain, but well-mannered. Many Florentines find her exceedingly prudish and resent her for being foreign."

Teresa's gossip was priceless!

The maid continued in a conspiratorial tone, "From what I've heard, Signora Clarice is a dutiful wife and Signore Lorenzo is fond of her, but she is rumored to be as cold as a winter's day in Venice."

"How unfortunate for Signore Lorenzo."

"Do not pity him, Signora. It's common knowledge that he gives vent to his appetites by keeping numerous mistresses."

Sabina's eyes widened. "How many?"

"Too many to count…but there is one mistress that reigns supreme above all other women." She paused and whispered, "Even his wife."

I wonder what Tommaso would say if he caught me gossiping like a scullery maid. "Who?" Sabina demanded shamelessly, leaning closer.

"Her name is Lucrezia Donati. You must have seen her in passing by now." Sabina tried to place a face to the name and shook her head. Teresa continued, "You will probably meet her soon enough."

"So, in addition to a wife, he has a main mistress as well as several other mistresses on the side." Her maid nodded and Sabina smirked. "Lorenzo de' Medici must be a very busy man."

"He's reputed to be a good lover," Teresa said, giggling.

"Teresa!"

The maid had the decency to blush, if only slightly. "I'm only repeating what I've heard."

"We should end this conversation right now for the sake of propriety," Sabina announced with mock rigidness.

"I'm sure he'll be impressed with you," Teresa said slyly, ignoring her mistress's suggestion. "Lorenzo admires beautiful women, but what he truly appreciates is intelligence, and you possess both in abundance."

43

"How do you know so much about the Medici household?"

"I know one of Signora Clarice's lady's maids," Teresa replied as she helped Sabina into the new red gown. "You look exquisite, Signora. I know you'll enjoy yourself tonight."

"Thank you, Teresa. Don't wait up for me."

After casting a critical eye over her reflection one last time, Sabina fetched a fur-lined cloak and met her husband in the main hall. Tommaso complimented her lavishly as they made their way outside. The autumn chill had already set in and Sabina shivered, nuzzling her chin into the cloak's downy fur.

Two of Tommaso's guards accompanied them, each one armed with a deadly rapier. The Medici had many enemies and, since Tommaso was a friend and supporter of the family, he was considered a foe.

The impressive Palazzo Medici was a striking three-story structure located a stone's throw from the Basilica of San Lorenzo. The ground floor of the palazzo, which led to the inner courtyard, consisted of open arches. Constructed of heavy rustic stones, it reminded Sabina of a fortress. The second and third floors boasted smooth masonry and double lancet windows, creating an elegant façade. A stone bench wrapped around the exterior of the palazzo.

They passed the Medici guards and entered the main gate. Sabina was impressed by the series of tall arches surrounding the large square area within the tiled courtyard. Silky white plaster walls and ceilings were paired with smooth gray stone columns the locals referred to as pietra serena. The malleable stone was easy to carve and therefore served a popular building material for many architects.

"This courtyard design reminds me of the church where we were wed," Sabina commented.

"This entire palazzo was inspired by Brunelleschi's passion for classical lines, but it was designed by Michelozzo," Tommaso explained.

Sabina gasped and pointed. "Oh, look!"

Tommaso smiled at her childlike pleasure at seeing ornate wooden birdcages suspended from every other arch. Each one

44

contained a colorful songbird within.

Sabina moved toward the birdcages, then stopped when she noticed a bronze statue of David. Depicted as a lithe boy sporting a helmet, he stood coquettishly with the massive decapitated head of Goliath at his feet. An oversized sword was propped at his side. If the sculpture miraculously came to life, there was no way the delicate David would have the strength to wield such a heavy weapon.

Sabina continued to stare at the sensuous figure as she slowly walked around its base. The feather on Goliath's helmet was so long that its tip caressed the bottom of David's buttocks—*and beyond*. The shocking eroticism made her blush.

Tommaso moved to stand behind his wife. "It was created by the sculptor Donatello. Elegant, is it not?

"I've never seen David depicted so...so..."

"Come," he said, urging her forward. A smile played upon his lips as if he knew exactly what she was thinking.

Tommaso informed her that the statue had been privately commissioned almost forty years ago by one of the Medici rumored to have homosexual appetites. Sodomy, although illegal, was rampant in Florence. In fact, in some European cities, the words "sodomite" and "Florentine" were interchangeable.

They came upon yet another bronze statue set upon a fairly high base, gilded with pure gold. There was nothing erotic about this piece because the two figures depicted were Judith and Holofernes. Judith had just hacked into the neck of Holofernes with her sword. The defeated, dying man was at her feet, and the heroine's arm was raised to deliver another savage blow.

"This one is also by Donatello," Tommaso said. "It's a fountain—see here?" He indicated a small hole in the sculpted cushion where Holofernes sat, in which water poured out and quietly trickled into a small pool below. "Sometimes, Lorenzo runs red wine through this fountain instead of water, allowing his guests to fill their chalices with the 'blood' of the villain."

Sabina shuddered in disgust. "Why would anyone want to

have such a violent, gruesome statue in a courtyard?"

"Many foreign dignitaries come here to discuss business and politics with Lorenzo. This contrived statue makes a mighty statement and sends an equally powerful warning."

Sabina understood. By instilling fear into the hearts of others, the Medici secured the loyalty of the people. "It's hard to believe that the artist who carved the elegant David also carved this piece."

"Donatello was legend within his own lifetime. A genius, really."

Music flowed into the courtyard from inside the impressive palazzo. Tommaso gently took Sabina's arm and led her toward the sound. They climbed the great staircase and saw the musicians' horns draped with the coat of arms of the Florentine Republic: a red *giglio*, or lily, on a white background. As soon as Tommaso's political companions spotted him, they were drawn into a circle of chatting guests. Sabina had already met many of them at her wedding celebration, so she felt at ease. The men eventually began talking about politics and far-off wars, and the women edged closer together in order to be out of earshot.

One of the older ladies said, "Sabina is such a lovely young thing, is she not? *Una bella fanciulla.*"

"Yes," another lady agreed, almost begrudgingly.

"Are you enjoying married life, my dear?"

"I'm fortunate to have married such a good man," Sabina replied.

"I only hope that my daughter can make such an advantageous match."

The lady changed the subject by commenting on a new fashion trend, and Sabina listened quietly, contributing little to the conversation. She focused her attention on those around her, hoping to catch a glimpse of Lorenzo. It was Giuliano who eventually caught her eye as he approached her husband.

"Tommaso," he said, placing a hand on the older man's shoulder.

"Giuliano, my friend. I haven't seen you since the day of my wedding. Where have you been?"

"Where have I been? The question is where have you been?" Giuliano shot back playfully.

"I've been dutifully fulfilling my political obligations at the Signoria, like a good citizen should."

"I'm sure my brother has given you many assignments to keep you busy and away from your comely wife," he teased, tossing a glance at Sabina.

"Indeed he has," Tommaso confessed. "But that's no reason why we can't see more of each other."

"I'm usually running errands or doing some other business for Lorenzo. He's so busy these days," Giuliano confided. "But you're right, there's no reason for us not to see more of each other—and we will, starting tonight."

"I see that your brother has been teaching you the art of diplomacy. Soon, your skill will land you the role of Ambassador."

Giuliano blushed slightly at the compliment and turned to Sabina, kissing her hand. "I bid you welcome, Signora. Your presence graces our home."

"Thank you," she said. "The palazzo is truly grand."

"My grandfather, Cosimo, wanted to build a palazzo like no other in Florence and I think he succeeded in his goal. I'm glad you like it."

"The artwork is divine."

"Then we shall make sure that you are a frequent visitor here. My brother is always planning concertos, discourses, banquets—this is not only our home but also the cultural center of the city."

Thrilled by the prospect, Sabina said, "I would be honored to be in the presence of so many talented and enlightened people."

"Come, Tommaso. Lorenzo is eager to see you and to meet your new wife," Giuliano said, offering Sabina his arm.

They walked to the far corner of the large main hall where a chair was set upon a slightly raised platform. Seated like a king on a throne was Lorenzo de' Medici, elegantly dressed in a brown brocade tunic and black velvet surcoat trimmed with ermine. There was a marble bust of his father beside him. The sculpture was life-sized and Piero looked to be fairly young when it was created; one could see a slight resemblance between father and son.

Sabina discreetly studied Lorenzo from where she stood. His olive complexion stood out in contrast to his shoulder-length black hair and dark, piercing eyes. A strong jaw jutting slightly outward was contrasted by a generous mouth boasting full lips. His nose, which was long and crooked, afforded him a harsh profile. He wasn't nearly as handsome as Giuliano, but he possessed a certain sensuality that was attractive in its own right. She deemed his face to be interesting, yet easily capable of instilling fear upon his enemies.

Lorenzo unexpectedly turned his head and captured her gaze, causing her face to redden. His eyes bore into her own, giving Sabina the impression that he could read her mind if he chose to do so. The intensity and power he emitted was so great that she shivered. In that moment, she knew without a doubt that beneath the calm and cool exterior existed a lethal man. The image of a cat ready to pounce crept into her mind.

Sabina knew she should drop her gaze for propriety's sake, but found she could not. Instead, she stood there staring like an idiot at the most important man in Tuscany. A slow grin spread across his face before he looked away, leaving her mortified.

What was it about this man?

"It's good to see you again, my friend," Lorenzo said as he rose from his chair to embrace Tommaso. It was a gesture noticed by those who stood nearby. He added cryptically, "Forgive me for not attending your wedding. You knew the problem I had to deal with in the North."

"There's nothing to forgive. It's good to have you back in Florence."

"You've brought your wife," Lorenzo said, his eyes taking in Sabina's shapely form beneath the gown. "She is lovelier than Giuliano described."

"Thank you," Tommaso said, turning to Sabina and urging

her forward.

Lorenzo bent over her hand and lightly brushed his lips against her knuckles. "Welcome to Florence, Signora Sabina. Your beauty graces my home this evening." To Tommaso, he added, "You will have to be a watchdog tonight, my friend."

"It's an honor to be here and to finally meet you."

Lorenzo smiled. "I'm familiar with your family name. In fact, I remember my grandfather speaking highly of Signore Bernardo Rossi. It's a name you should be proud of."

"Thank you. I've heard many things about *you*, Signore Lorenzo," she said, ignoring her husband's raised brow.

"Good things, I hope," Lorenzo shot back, casting a curious glance in Tommaso's direction.

"Oh, yes. Very good things."

Tommaso was about to lead his wife away when Lorenzo stopped him with a subtle gesture. "Such as?"

"I was told that you're one of the greatest patrons of the arts," she replied. "You also embrace the new philosophies of our time."

"I encourage artists and writers to express themselves freely, yes. After all, man was created by God, therefore, man has much to offer. God creates good things, does He not?"

"God also created Hell," she countered.

"She is a clever one, Tommaso," Lorenzo commented, his eyes never leaving Sabina's face. "Yes, but even Hell can be good."

"How so?"

"There are good lessons to be learned. I'm sure you're familiar with *La Divina Commedia*?"

"Yes, of course."

He spread out his hands. "Well, there you have it." When Sabina's brow creased in confusion, he inquired rhetorically, "What do we learn from Dante's description of Hell? That we should strive to become godly people in life. Otherwise, we may end up with the same fate as those sorry souls doomed to eternal suffering."

They laughed and Lorenzo gave Sabina a playful wink. "If

you'll excuse me, Signora, I have to discuss a boring political matter with your husband."

"I do not find politics boring in the least. It's what shapes our society." Lorenzo raised an amused eyebrow, but Tommaso was not smiling. Fearing she had spoken out of turn, she added, "Forgive me."

"I'll see you at supper, Signora," Lorenzo said. "I hope you've brought your appetite—my cooks have prepared a grand feast. Afterward, I'll show you the chapel. Tommaso, I believe your wife would enjoy that."

"She would indeed," Tommaso agreed.

"I look forward to it." Sabina curtsied to both men and quickly walked toward a page carrying a tray of wine-filled goblets. She selected one, then took a long sip to calm her racing heart.

Later, during the delicious meal, Sabina noticed Lorenzo's wife for the first time. Clarice Orsini had descended from her private chambers to dine with her guests. Although she was only twenty-five years old, her plain, high-cut gown made her appear older. Long, delicate fingers graced her hands, and she flaunted an ivory complexion that many women undoubtedly envied. She kept her brown eyes downcast for the most part, and almost every strand of her reddish-brown hair was tucked inside a veiled headdress.

Lorenzo spoke to his wife occasionally, pointing out different guests or making amusing comments. Clarice returned his attempts at joviality with a wan smile as she picked at her food.

Tommaso glanced at his wife. "It's impolite to stare."

Sabina looked down at her plate. "I'm too curious for my own good."

"It's natural to be curious about the Medici, especially Lorenzo."

"Tell me about him."

He took a sip of wine and cleared his throat. "He was only twenty years old when his father died. The Signoria, as well as the heads of many leading families, doubted his ability to assume a position of leadership in the city."

"Did *you* doubt him?"

"I'm afraid so."

"Why?"

"I'd always known Lorenzo as a kind, sensitive boy. Intelligent, too. He was quiet, kept to himself, and he hated speaking in public. Even now, he's a man of little words. I grossly underestimated him—we all did. He's proven himself to be a political genius: strong, cunning, and shrewd. These qualities have gotten him far. Nothing escapes his notice— *nothing.*"

"You make him sound intimidating."

"There's no need for you to feel intimidated by him, but be aware with whom you are dealing. Never mistake his silence for weakness, and remember that he can be a formidable enemy if the need arises. Here," he said, offering her a choice piece of meat from his plate. "Lorenzo is a fair man, good natured, too— until you cross him. I wouldn't want him as my enemy; therefore, I'm careful not to offend him in any way. You would be wise to follow suit."

"I'll be sure to heed your advice."

Seeing the worry in his wife's eyes, Tommaso decided to lighten the mood. "Lorenzo has quite the sense of humor." A faraway look came into his eyes, as if recalling a memory, and he chuckled softly. "He used to write poetry when he was a boy. He even recited some for me, once."

Sabina's face lit up with interest. "He writes, too?"

"He's been writing poetry since childhood and can also compose music. No doubt he inherited these traits and talents from his mother, who was an accomplished musician."

"I see."

"Before you get excited, I should warn you that Lorenzo enjoyed writing and singing bawdy carnival tunes. The local Florentines loved them!" Lowering his voice, he added, "He also wrote some tawdry verses full of sexual references to various vegetables. Some would call his work vulgar, but it was all in good fun. He was a spirited lad with an awful voice,

51

causing many to cover their ears when he sang."

She stole a glimpse at Lorenzo then stared at her husband in disbelief. "I thought you said he was shy and hated speaking in public."

He shrugged. "Not when it came to mingling with the common people. I still have some of the poems Lorenzo wrote when he was a fiery adolescent, but I don't think them proper for a lady to read."

"The raucous youth has become a man to be reckoned with."

"Exactly," he agreed, turning his attention to his food.

When everyone had eaten to their satisfaction, the musicians struck up a tune and a boy began to sing. The high-pitched voice betrayed that he was *castrato*. The guests, feeling somnolent after the abundant meal, settled comfortably in their seats to listen and digest. After a few solos, the boy bowed to his audience and left. The musicians immediately began playing a livelier melody, encouraging the guests to dance.

At that point, Lorenzo escorted Sabina and Tommaso to the palazzo's chapel. As she walked into the space, she gasped aloud in delight. Every wall was frescoed with vibrant colors and heavily detailed with rich, shining gold.

"It's magnificent," Sabina said, turning around in circles before examining each painted scene. "Who is the artist?"

"My father commissioned Benozzo Gozzoli to paint the interior, but the architectural elements were designed by Michelozzo." Pointing upward, Lorenzo added, "The ceiling was done by Portigiano but according to Michelozzo's design."

The ceiling was of inlaid wood, painted, and gilded. Sabina was enchanted by the skill so lavishly displayed by Florentine artisans. Turning her attention back to the walls, she stood in silent awe as Lorenzo highlighted details within the scenes.

"These are the three magi who make their way to Bethlehem and, as you can see, each of them has his own entourage," he explained. "And there, on the north wall are the portraits of my grandfather, my father, and my uncles—Giovanni and Carlo."

"Let us not forget the two princes in the scene," Tommaso interjected.

Lorenzo chuckled. "Ah, yes. Those two boys are Giuliano and myself."

Sabina's eyes took in the elaborate costumes of the kings, the carefully rendered pastoral scenes in the background, the serene angels, and the Medici men who were so meticulously portrayed. She noticed that Cosimo was seated on a mule rather than a horse, but the trappings on the animal were of luxurious gold. She walked to the altar and surveyed the Adoration of Christ painted on the panel. She recognized the artist at once.

"This was painted by Filippo Lippi, was it not?"

"Brava," Tommaso said, impressed.

Lorenzo inquired, "What do you think of our chapel?"

Sabina clasped her hands together and whirled around. "It feels as if I'm inside a jewelry box filled with gold and precious gemstones."

"A fitting comparison. My grandfather was a man of excellent taste, and my father inherited that trait."

"And you, Signore Lorenzo, have obviously inherited your refined taste from them. Thank you for showing me your beautiful chapel."

Tommaso said, "Lorenzo, you are spoiling my wife."

As they retreated to rejoin the other guests, Sabina noticed fragile crystal vases with silver handles, a display of delicately carved cameos encased in copper, and bejeweled boxes crafted of silver. It seemed as if everywhere one looked, there was something to delight the eyes.

The festivities continued well into the night with dancing and singing. Even though Florence had a strict curfew and everyone was expected to be indoors after sunset, the Medici and their guests were immune to the law.

At one point during the evening, Sabina caught Clarice staring at her. Clarice averted her gaze quickly, almost nervously. Sabina thought it odd. The woman's matronly appearance was overshadowed by the primness she displayed during the festivities by refusing to dance or participate in rowdy conversations. She kept quietly to herself as though in disapproval of the entire affair, while Lorenzo laughed and mingled amiably with the guests.

When the time came for Sabina and Tommaso to take their leave and thank their hosts, Lorenzo held Sabina's hand—lingering for a few minutes—as he invited them to return soon. If Tommaso noticed Lorenzo's overt flirtation, he made no mention of it as they melted into the night and made their way home.

CHAPTER 5

Although the Signoria was the city's House of Lords where laws were created and implemented, the Palazzo Medici swarmed with politicians and other prominent members of Florentine society on a regular basis. Decisions regarding the city's policies were discussed at length with Lorenzo before any official action was taken by the Signoria. In fact, whenever a foreign dignitary visited Florence he was expected to announce his presence at the Palazzo Medici before stepping foot in the Signoria. This silent code of ethics was acceptable to the majority, especially since Lorenzo gave them little choice to do otherwise. Tommaso, who had always played an important role in Florentine politics, spent about as much time in the Medici household as he did his own.

In addition to being the city's political center, the Palazzo Medici was a platform to launch newly discovered talent. On the occasions that Lorenzo wished musicians, artists, philosophers, writers, or poets to entertain his intimate friends, Sabina was permitted to accompany Tommaso to the Palazzo Medici and socialize freely with the other ladies present. The ever-reserved Clarice and her ladies-in-waiting were usually nearby, quietly sewing or reading prayer books, but seldom did they mingle or contribute to conversations.

One sunny day in late November, Sabina accompanied her husband to the Palazzo Medici for a dinner followed by a concerto. Lorenzo needed to speak privately with Tommaso regarding a legal matter, so Sabina was asked to wait in the garden. Relishing the opportunity to explore more of the magnificent palazzo, she walked outside. Two ladies sat on a bench, deeply engrossed in conversation. Not wishing to disturb them, she went to sit on an empty bench by a fountain.

A moment later, a pretty young woman with blonde curly hair and blue eyes approached her. In a high-pitched voice, she inquired, "May I sit with you?"

"Certainly," Sabina replied, moving over to afford her more room.

"I've seen you from afar a few times, but haven't had the chance to speak with you. My name is Angelina Bardi."

"It's a pleasure to make your acquaintance, Signora Angelina."

"Signorina," Angelina corrected. "I know your husband is a loyal supporter of the Medici and the Signoria holds him in high esteem. He's a man respected by many." When Sabina expressed mild surprise, she added, "I make it my business to know everything about everyone."

"I see."

"Do you like the arts?" Angelina asked, changing the subject.

"Very much."

"Painting, sculpture, music, or literature?"

"All of them, I suppose."

"Which is your favorite?"

Although Sabina didn't appreciate the young woman's tone, she replied, "I would have to say literature."

"Humph." Sabina waited for her to say more, but she did not. Instead, she asked, "Have you met Clarice?"

"Yes, of course."

"Terribly dull, is she not? Lacks fashion sense as well," Angelina mused aloud as she smoothed the skirt of her pink velvet gown.

"She is rather quiet," Sabina said neutrally.

"I didn't say she's quiet, I said she's dull. There's a difference."

"To be honest, I haven't spent as much time with our hostess as you obviously have."

"One doesn't need to spend much time with Clarice to discover that she has the personality of a dead fish."

Sabina felt suddenly uncomfortable and tried to think of a reason to excuse herself from Angelina's company. She felt it was a terrible breach of etiquette to speak ill of their hostess.

Besides, who was this woman? If she wasn't at the palazzo accompanied by her husband, what was she doing here in the first place?

Noticing Sabina's slight frown, Angelina asked sweetly, "Who is your seamstress? Every time I see you, I'm simply enchanted by your fine garments."

"My seamstress is Donna Maria."

"I should have known. She has made many gowns for me, too. Perhaps we should pass her name along to Clarice so she can get out of those nun habits."

Clarice and her ladies-in-waiting entered the garden and sat on the benches located beneath a sprawling fig tree.

Sabina noticed how Angelina's eyes narrowed at the sight of Lorenzo's wife. Clarice pulled out what appeared to be a prayer book and began to read while some of her ladies did needlepoint. A woman of graceful stature with light brown hair and intelligent eyes entered the garden soon afterward, causing the ladies to look up from their task. Clarice glared at the woman, compelling her to turn around and reenter the palazzo.

Filled with burning curiosity, Sabina whispered, "Who was that?"

"No one of importance," Angelina replied sourly. Then, as an afterthought, she demanded, "Do you think her beautiful?"

"She is quite attractive."

"You do know who she is, don't you?"

"Angelina!"

Both women turned around to see a good-looking young man standing a few feet away from them. His blonde hair shone in the sunlight and his big hazel eyes were fixed on Angelina.

"Giovanni, where have you been hiding?" Angelina chided playfully.

"I was looking for you," he replied in a whiny voice.

"I've been here, speaking with my new friend. Now, go inside and wait for me. There's to be a concerto this afternoon with a musical prodigy recently discovered by Lorenzo." Then, turning to Sabina, she added, "He has such a gift for finding good talent, don't you agree?"

"Yes."

Angelina frowned at Giovanni, who was still standing in the same spot. As if commanding a dog, she pointed to the palazzo's entrance. "Go!"

Defeated, Giovanni shuffled away.

Sabina hid her shock as she inquired, "Is he your betrothed?"

Angelina laughed. "Him? Oh, no!" She eyed Sabina intently. "Signore Tommaso Caravelli is a good man. You're fortunate that your father made such a fine match. I only hope that my father does the same for me."

"I'm sure your father will choose someone appropriate for you."

Angelina took one of Sabina's hands. "I'm so happy to have finally met you. One should always be selective when choosing social companions, and I have a feeling that you and I shall become good friends."

The display of camaraderie was a bit premature, but Sabina smiled.

"I better not keep Giovanni waiting too long," Angelina said with a mischievous grin. "I do hope to see you again soon."

Later, while Sabina and her husband partook of the midday meal, she inquired, "What do you know about Angelina Bardi?"

"Why do you ask?"

"I met her in the garden and she seemed intent on becoming fast friends."

Tommaso rolled his eyes. "Angelina is the spoiled daughter of one of my colleagues—she's also a notorious gossip. You should be wary of that one."

"Because she likes to gossip?"

He broke off a piece of bread and put it in his mouth. "No, because she's rumored to be a whore."

"Is it true or is it just a rumor?"

"There is usually some truth in rumors."

"Perhaps," she mused as she picked at her roasted venison.

"Either way, it's unfitting for my wife to keep close company with such a woman." The corners of his lips lifted. "Besides, you may frighten her."

58

"Frighten her? How?"

"You are the Tempesta, are you not? It would only be a matter of time before she felt the sting of your sharp tongue."

"Is that what you really think of me?"

"No, my sweet, I'm only teasing you. I believe that marriage has tamed you, but only a little bit."

"Why is Angelina wandering alone throughout the palazzo?" Sabina pressed, returning to the former topic. "It's most inappropriate for an unmarried girl her age."

"It most certainly is," he assured her. "Her father is a distant cousin of Lorenzo's mother, so she's considered a family member."

"Such a far-off familial relation is dubious."

"True, but her father is a wealthy and valuable supporter of Lorenzo. Angelina insists on accompanying him when he comes to the Palazzo Medici, and he usually gives in to his daughter's whims."

"He indulges her too much."

"I agree with you. Angelina should be home practicing her embroidery, as should you."

"Tommaso!"

"I only jest. Is there anything else you wish to know, my insatiably curious wife?"

Sabina's cheeks reddened. "No."

"Good. Now please allow me to eat so that I may get back to business," he chided. "This morning's affairs are still unresolved, so we must meet again this afternoon."

"What about the concerto? Will you make it in time?"

He shook his head. "I had planned on attending, but I cannot. I will be occupied well into the evening."

Sabina's face fell in disappointment. "Does that mean I must go home?"

"You should stay and enjoy the concerto," he replied, much to her surprise. "I'll send word for Teresa and my men to meet you here. They will accompany you home when it's over."

"Thank you."

Afterward, Sabina chatted with some of the ladies as they

59

waited for the concerto to commence. It was to be held in the salon, which supposedly had excellent acoustics. Sabina took a seat and watched as the room filled with guests. She noticed that Angelina was missing.

Lorenzo, who stole away from his many responsibilities to see his protégé perform, came into the crowded room late and took his reserved seat in the front row. Angelina came in immediately afterward with flushed cheeks and slightly disheveled hair. Both appeared to be out of breath, as if they had run down the corridor. Sabina scanned the room and noticed that Clarice was not in attendance.

The musician played the lute with great skill and sang in a sublime voice. Lorenzo greeted his guests at the performance's end, yet appeared to go out of his way to ignore Angelina.

He kissed Sabina's hand. "My dear Sabina. Enchanting, as usual, I see. One might say you look almost dangerous."

"Dangerous?" she repeated, taken aback.

His eyes glittered with mischief. "Beauty is a weapon and, when coupled with intelligence, it makes a woman powerful. I consider anyone with that kind of influence to be dangerous."

Sabina flushed to the roots of her hair. "You exaggerate, sir."

Grinning, he inquired, "What did you think of the performance?"

"It was wonderful, thank you for inviting me. Your protégé is truly gifted."

"See? I told you God creates good things. In this case, it was a perfect tenor."

"You were correct, Signore Lorenzo."

"How I wish you would stop saying 'Signore' and call me by my Christian name when we speak privately. After all, I love your husband like my own father, and consider you both part of my family." When Sabina hesitated, he added softly, "It would please me."

"As you wish, Lorenzo."

"Good," he said. "I hear that you're a lover of literature."

"What else has my husband told you?"

"Many things." Cupping her elbow and leading her away from the other guests, he asked, "Has he shown you my library yet?"

"The one adjacent to the Basilica of San Lorenzo?"

"Yes."

"Tommaso pointed it out to me from the street, but we didn't go inside, of course. I admit that I was curious to see its interior."

It was socially forbidden for a respectable woman to wander into a place where only men gathered, even if it was only a library. Sabina had begged her husband to accompany her inside, but he had refused.

"Tommaso cannot risk your reputation. Or his, for that matter. He speaks highly of you and is impressed with your intellectual capacity. Life must not be easy for a woman who possesses a clever mind." He paused in quiet debate. "Come. I want to show you something."

Sabina caught Angelina's sharp look as Lorenzo led her out of the room. They ascended a flight of stairs, walked down a long hall, and stopped before a small door with ornate iron hinges.

He extracted a key from his pocket. "Do you know what this is?"

"It's a key."

"Yes, but not just any key. This one is special because it opens the door to my personal library. Only a select few have ever been inside these sacred walls. Tommaso told me you have a great passion for books, so I want to show you my treasured collection."

Sabina's heart leapt for joy as she entered the small room filled with ancient scrolls and antique books. Lorenzo picked up an old scroll made of a peculiar paper that Sabina had never seen before.

"This is a papyrus scroll from Egypt. It was written before Christ was born." Picking up another scroll, he added, "And this one was written by Socrates himself."

Sabina was speechless. She saw original works by Dante,

various philosophers, and well-known poets. Lorenzo watched with a smile as she gingerly picked up a book and gently leafed through the pages.

He looked at her expectantly. "Well, what do you think?"

"You are a fortunate man to possess such an astonishing collection," she replied without hesitation.

"What if I gave you access to this room? What if I allowed you to come here whenever you wished?" he asked, taking a step closer.

Her heart skipped several beats "I don't think my husband would approve," she reluctantly confessed.

"Well, there is no risk of your reputation being tarnished here."

"I appreciate your generosity, Lorenzo, but I would need to obtain Tommaso's permission."

"Spoken like a good wife. Tommaso is a fortunate man, indeed. For your information, he knows I'm making this offer to you and has given his approval."

So this was a test. Sabina said nothing.

He raised a finger and continued, "Very few people have this privilege, so don't tell anyone about it. Understood?"

"Yes." She paused. "I don't know what to say…"

"Thank you would suffice."

"Thank you."

"I'll give you a copy of this key, and you must be escorted by one of the pages whenever you come here. Instruct the servant to remain outside the door while you read."

"Yes, Lorenzo."

"Good. Let us return to the salon before wild rumors begin circulating."

Most of the guests had already dispersed, except Angelina.

"What a splendid concerto!" she cried the moment she saw Lorenzo.

"I'm glad you enjoyed it, Angelina." A page arrived and whispered in Lorenzo's ear. He turned to both women and said, "I must go, ladies."

The moment he was gone, Angelina pounced on Sabina.

"Where did Lorenzo take you?"

"He showed me one of his new paintings," Sabina lied.

Angelina's eyes narrowed slightly, yet the smile remained on her face. "How nice. Perhaps you will sit with me in the courtyard?"

"Alas, I cannot. My maid and my husband's men will be meeting me soon to accompany me home."

Angelina turned on her heel and practically stormed out of the salon. Sabina was left alone with an unpleasant feeling in the pit of her stomach.

CHAPTER 6

The crisp, bright days of autumn soon gave way to winter. The weather changed drastically; days passed without the merest glimpse of sun. The frequent rain and gloominess plaguing the first weeks of December made the Florentines miserable. Tommaso complained of the inclement weather, the damp causing his bones to ache.

Sabina, on the other hand, never complained. Winter was her favorite season; a time to curl up with a good book or sit before a cozy fire with quill in hand. She would write for hours, sipping hot mulled wine while her ink-stained fingers flew across the pages of her journal.

Tommaso's presence was usually required at either the Signoria or the Palazzo Medici on an almost daily basis. Concerned that his wife may be feeling lonely, he suggested, "Perhaps you should invite your family to spend Christmas with us in Florence."

Sabina's face brightened. "You wouldn't mind a houseful of guests?"

"Not at all."

She smiled mischievously. "Good."

"Why are you grinning so wickedly?"

"I sent them an invitation two days ago."

***

Don Antonio, Cecilia, and little Paolo arrived in Florence at the beginning of Advent. Tommaso wasted no time inviting his father-in-law to accompany him whenever he went out, introducing Don Antonio to several colleagues. Since the old man enjoyed meeting and talking with new people, he truly appreciated his son-in-law's gesture. It was a break from the quiet life he led in Lucca, and a chance for him to feel like a useful member of society once again.

Cecilia insisted on going to church daily. Sabina, who only

attended mass when required, found her sister's religious zeal tiresome. Despite this, she accompanied her sister. While Cecilia prayed fervently, Sabina allowed her imagination to wander, conjuring fantastic stories. Oftentimes, she would return from church and immediately scribble down ideas.

A messenger arrived a few days later with an invitation to a Christmas Feast at the Palazzo Medici. As a courtesy, the invitation was extended to the visiting Rossi family. A seamstress was summoned to create something suitable for Cecilia to wear, and a tailor was sent for Don Antonio.

On the way home from church one morning, an icy drizzle began to fall, forcing Sabina and Cecilia to hasten their steps. It was one week before Christmas, and it seemed as if the weather was worsening daily.

As they shuffled along the street, Cecilia announced, "Papa is planning on building an addition to the house in Lucca."

Sabina grimaced. "Are you sure that's a good idea?"

"We need the space."

"Perhaps you should wait."

Cecilia glanced at Sabina as she avoided a puddle. "Why? We're only building two more rooms."

"I thought that you, Papa, and Paolo would eventually move in with us. In fact, I've already discussed the possibility with Tommaso, and he thinks it would be a good idea."

Cecilia took hold of her sister's hand. "I appreciate the offer, but Florence is not for me. I enjoy the peace and quiet of our family villa. Papa feels the same way. Besides, we would only be in the way."

"Nonsense! How could anyone ever be in the way in that big palazzo? We could go days without seeing one another. Can you not imagine us calling out to each other in the hallways? Paolo would get lost all the time."

Cecilia laughed. "Your tendency to exaggerate has not changed."

"If you and Papa truly wish to remain in Lucca, I'm sure Tommaso will pay for the addition on the house," Sabina said, her tone serious. "Save your money for other things.

Remember, if you change your mind, the invitation to live with us is always open."

"Perhaps when Paolo is older we'll accept your gracious offer. I'm sure your husband can introduce my son to the right people so that he may have the opportunity to make something of himself in this world."

"You have nothing to worry about as far as Paolo's future is concerned," Sabina assured. "I can understand your reluctance to move here. I, too, miss the peacefulness of Lucca at times."

They turned down a wider street and walked quietly for a few minutes.

Cecilia offered contritely, "I never apologized to you for what happened at your wedding. I should not have insulted you in that manner."

The rain fell harder and Sabina pulled her sister into a deep doorway. "I've already forgiven you. I only hope that you can forgive me, too."

They embraced and Sabina noticed that the wetness on her sister's face was not solely from the rain. A small carriage stopped in front of them. Painted on its door was a gold crest with red balls.

Giuliano's handsome face appeared through the window. "Get in!"

The grateful women scrambled into the carriage.

"You two look like drowned kittens," he observed, amused. "Signora Sabina, how good to see you again. And this is?"

"My older sister, Cecilia." Turning to her sister, she added, "This is Signore Giuliano de' Medici."

Cecilia's eyes widened in surprise. "A pleasure, sir."

Giuliano settled back into the cushioned seat. "Good thing I came this way or you would surely catch your death of cold. Why did you not take Tommaso's carriage today?"

"One of the wheels is being fixed," Sabina replied.

"I see. I assume both of you will be attending our Christmas feast." Sabina nodded and his face broke into a grin. "I'm glad to hear it. My sister-in-law, Clarice, loves Christmas, whereas my brother and I prefer the celebration of Easter."

"I prefer Easter to Christmas as well," Sabina said. "There's something so pure about the springtime, as if the earth is experiencing rebirth."

Cecilia added, "It's the perfect season to celebrate our Lord's resurrection."

"Exactly," Giuliano agreed. "In the springtime, everything is being born anew; the buds on the trees, the first bloom of the flowers. It's a most joyous time." A shadow crossed his face. "If only our sins could be wiped clean so we could start anew. That would be a true rebirth, would it not?"

Neither woman knew how to respond.

Sensing that he had made them uncomfortable, he said to Sabina, "Let us talk of pleasant things. Lorenzo tells me you're a lover of books."

"I am."

"Who is your favorite author?"

"A difficult question, but I would have to say Dante Alighieri. He blends drama with comedy, and his moral lessons are subtle yet indelible."

"His cantos are brimming with imagination and filled with poetic justice. I still prefer Boccaccio, however." His eyes glittered mischievously. "The *Decameron* is brilliant, full of the bawdy humor we vulgar Tuscans cannot seem to get enough of."

Sabina laughed. "Boccaccio's work is truly remarkable."

"What about you?" he asked of Cecilia.

Unlike Sabina, Cecilia did not have an appreciation for literature. Between caring for a small son and an ailing father, she had little time to read anything except the Bible. "Aside from the required readings selected by my childhood tutor, I'm afraid I'm dull-witted when it comes to discussions of literature."

"Nonsense," Sabina chided. "You are quite clever."

Cecilia offered Giuliano a deprecating smile. "My sister is being kind."

Giuliano smoothly rerouted the topic. "Tommaso has quite a collection of books. After all, he is close friends with Messer

Bisticci."

Vespasiano da Bisticci owned the most prosperous cartolaio in the city. In addition to servicing the Florentine nobility, the famous book merchant enjoyed an international clientele that included Europe's royalty.

He continued, "Have you met him?"

Sabina preened. "We had the pleasure of his company for dinner last month. He came bearing a gift—*Le Livre de la Cité des Dames*. I already owned a copy, but I appreciated the gesture nonetheless."

"You admire Christine di Pisan, then?"

"Oh, yes."

He smiled. "Why am I not surprised?"

Cecilia was relieved when the carriage stopped in front of the Palazzo Caravelli.

"Thank you, Signore Giuliano," Sabina said. "Will you not come inside? You could enjoy some hot mulled wine with us."

"That's most kind, but I must decline. I'll see you soon. Good day."

Sabina and Cecilia rushed inside and went upstairs. Two servants helped them out of their wet garments and into clothes that were warm and dry.

As they sat before the fire sipping hot mulled wine, Sabina studied Cecilia. "You shouldn't sell yourself short, sister," she advised. "It's not fitting to call yourself 'dull-witted' to a member of the Medici family."

Cecilia snorted. "Why should I care what he thinks?"

"He's one of the most important men in Florence."

"My life is very different from yours, Sabina. I have no time for such idle activities as keeping up with the latest literary trends or trying to put on airs to impress others."

"You chose your life," Sabina pointed out gently. "We were both afforded the same education and noble name. Papa tried to persuade you to marry that well-to-do merchant from Arezzo, but you refused."

"I had no desire to live in Arezzo," Cecilia retorted, annoyed.

"Had you accepted his proposal, you would have had an easy life with servants, and plenty of time for all the idle activities in the world."

Cecilia looked at her sister for a long time. "I made my choice and you made yours, and now we each must live with the consequences."

"We all reap what we sow," Sabina agreed quietly.

"Amen to that."

They silently watched the flames in the hearth until Paolo came in crying because Mendi had bitten him.

"Why Tommaso lets you keep that malignant creature is a mystery to me," Cecilia mumbled under her breath as she examined the peck mark on her son's hand.

"Mendi is not prone to biting unless he's provoked," Sabina said. "Paolo, did you tease him?"

"I held the bread away from him," the little boy admitted.

"Don't tease him and he won't bite," Sabina admonished. "Go on and play with the wooden sword your uncle gave you."

Paolo scampered away, leaving them alone again. Sabina refilled her sister's cup.

After drinking deeply, Cecilia said, "Marco is getting married."

Sabina was surprised to hear her old lover's name. "To whom?"

"A girl named Lisa from a nearby village. I hear she comes from a good family." Cecilia stole a sidelong glance to gauge her sister's reaction.

"Good as in virtuous or good as in wealthy?"

Cecilia cocked an eyebrow. "Is that jealousy or bitterness in your voice?"

"Neither. I'm merely curious."

"I believe her father is involved in trade and owns a small shop."

"I wish them much happiness," Sabina said coolly, betraying nothing.

Feeling daring, Cecilia inquired, "Don't you miss him?"

"I've found contentment in my marriage."

"What if Marco had followed you here to Florence?"

"And?"

"Would you have entertained the thought of making him your lover?"

Sabina almost choked on her wine. "No!"

"Are you being truthful?"

"I made a promise to God to be faithful to my husband, and I intend to keep it. Tommaso is a good man. Marriage has changed me, Cecilia. I'm no longer the wild child that father used to scold."

"No more swimming naked on hot days?"

"Definitely not."

"No more potions?"

"I haven't concocted a single love potion here, nor would I dare to do so."

"I knew about you and Marco all along, you know."

Stunned, Sabina tried to feign ignorance. "What do you mean?"

"Those long walks alone, or when Papa and I were out of the house…"

Cecilia rarely drank wine because it went straight to her head and loosened her lips. Now was one of those times.

"You speak nonsense when you drink wine," Sabina teased, pretending to take the cup away from her sister.

Cecilia gave her sister a tight, humorless smile. "I saw the pair of you together with my own eyes on two different occasions."

"It must have been your imagination."

"I have a son, remember? I know what happens between a man and a woman. I know for a fact that you weren't a virgin on your wedding day."

Cecilia moved to take another sip of wine, but Sabina grabbed the cup away. "Does Papa know?"

"I would never break his heart like that."

Sabina heaved a sigh of relief. "I ended it with Marco the day I received the pearls from Tommaso, but he insisted on asking for my hand in marriage anyway. He never touched me again after that day, I swear. Thank you for not telling Papa. Oh, Cecilia, I feel such shame right now."

"You *have* changed," Cecilia observed while reaching for her sister's hand. "The old Sabina would not have been ashamed. Let's put the past where it belongs—in the past."

Later that day, Don Antonio took Sabina aside privately. "You've only been married for a short period and already I see a big transformation in you."

Cecilia said the same thing earlier. Had she actually changed so much?

He continued, "I'm impressed by the smooth running of your household, and how highly Tommaso speaks of you. Apparently, you take your role as wife very seriously."

"Thank you for the compliment, Papa."

"It's no mere compliment, Sabina. The manner in which the Florentines have received me indicates how well you have played your part in society."

"They behave graciously toward you because you are in the company of an important man," she pointed out.

"True," he conceded. "But it's also because of your chaste behavior, your charitable works, and your husband's favorable opinion of you. You have elevated the Rossi name to its former greatness."

Up until now, her father had either mocked or criticized her unruly behavior. For the first time in her life, he offered sincere praise.

And it felt good.

The heavy rain continued, the sound of it echoing throughout the large rooms. Fires burned in the hearths, but it was still cold and uncomfortably damp. Sabina touched her father's hand and noticed it was icy.

"Come upstairs, Papa." She urged. "It's cold here."

Don Antonio allowed his daughter to lead him to her private quarters. She stoked the fire and, because the room was small, the heat of the flames spread quickly. He sat down, extending his hands toward the warmth.

"Ah, that's better," the old man said.

"Cecilia tells me that you wish to build an addition to the house."

"We need the space. Paolo is growing up fast."

"I will pay for it."

He shook his head. "It's enough that your husband is a generous host and has provided us with new clothing for Christmas."

"Tommaso is a wealthy man. An addition to a small house is of little cost for him. Do not argue with me, please. Do it for Paolo's sake."

Don Antonio said nothing and Sabina took it as silent acquiescence.

The rain persisted for the next few days. On the morning of the Medici Christmas party, the weather was cold, but at least it was dry.

Don Antonio had attended such grand social events before his father gambled away his inheritance; therefore, he felt somewhat comfortable among the nobility. Cecilia, on the other hand, felt apprehensive. Once inside the Palazzo Medici, Tommaso and Don Antonio spotted a group of familiar male faces and excused themselves from the women.

"Do you think Paolo is all right?" Cecilia asked for the second time since they left the Palazzo Caravelli half hour ago.

"He's fine," Sabina assured. "Our servants are more than capable of feeding him and putting him to bed. I also instructed Teresa to read him a bedtime story. Now stop worrying and enjoy yourself. It's not every day you get to attend such a splendid party."

"I suppose you're right."

They joined a group of ladies who rambled about pointless topics. Cecilia contributed little to the conversation. She was visibly relieved when they were finally seated and the meal was served.

Leaning over to whisper into Sabina's ear, she asked, "How can you stand it here?"

Sabina swallowed a bite of braised rabbit. "In what sense?"

"These people with their ridiculous airs, speaking such

nonsense," Cecilia continued in a low tone. "How can you stomach them?"

"It's a very different world from the one in which we were raised, but there is much beauty and culture here. I've learned to appreciate the good and ignore the bad. For example, I've met writers, artists, and musicians with incredible talent. Do you see that young man over there?" Sabina asked, discreetly pointing to a good-looking man seated not far from them.

Cecilia glanced at him. "Yes."

"He's one of Lorenzo's favorite artists. His paintings are highly refined—unlike anything I've ever seen. I honestly believe the artwork being created in this city must be divinely inspired because it has the power to touch your soul."

"What is the artist's name?"

"Alessandro Botticelli."

"Never heard of him."

"I'm sure you will eventually."

Cecilia shrugged. "These artists are all the same to me."

Sabina let the matter drop.

After the delicious meal, they enjoyed the melodies of minstrels and musicians. The guests, feeling full and sated, were either milling around to induce digestion or dancing.

Angelina Bardi approached the Rossi sisters with a smile on her face. "Signora Sabina! I've been wanting to speak with you all night," she said, eyeing Cecilia curiously from head to toe.

"Greetings Signorina Angelina," Sabina said. "Please allow me to introduce you to my sister, Signora Cecilia."

The two women exchanged polite greetings.

Angelina inquired, "Where are you from, originally?"

"Lucca."

"Are you enjoying Florence? It's vastly different from Lucca, which can be so very provincial."

"Yes."

"Do you live inside the city center of Lucca?"

"No, we live in the countryside," Cecilia replied, growing weary of the interrogation.

"How terribly dull." Taking hold of Sabina's wrist, Angelina said, "Come and see the latest painting Lorenzo has acquired."

She led both women up a flight of stairs to an empty corridor where several paintings hung on the walls. They came to a stop before a large depiction of Heaven and Hell with Jesus in the center of the composition. The colors were luminous, and the figures were rendered in various active poses.

"Impressive, is it not?" When Sabina nodded, Angelina added, "He asked *my* opinion before making the purchase."

Sabina wondered what sort of relationship she and Lorenzo shared.

Turning to Cecilia, Angelina inquired, "Do you like it?"

Staring at the scene, Cecilia replied, "I find it rather frightening."

"Nonsense! Why, look here," Angelina exclaimed, pointing to one of the damned members of humanity struggling to reach the Righteous gathered at the right hand of Jesus. "This poor creature is trying to sneak his way into the Kingdom of God, but do you see what the angel is doing?"

Cecilia saw that the angel was leading the man away from the Righteous and back toward the Damned congregated at Christ's left.

Angelina continued, "He represents the majority of us on Judgement Day. Once we realize that we're doomed, we'll attempt to sneak over to the other side." At that point, she laughed. "I know I will!"

Cecilia was horrified that Angelina found such a notion humorous, but she was even more disturbed when Sabina muffled a giggle.

"I'm going to sit in the courtyard for a moment," Cecilia said coolly. "I think I may have had too much wine, and I need to clear my head."

Sensing her sister's unease, Sabina offered, "I'll accompany you."

Angelina shivered. "Are you daft? It's cold outside."

Cecilia glared at Angelina with unmasked contempt before walking away. Sabina followed closely behind.

"That girl is intolerable," Cecilia whispered as they

descended the stairs. "Who is she, anyway?"

"One of the biggest gossipmongers in Florence."

"Please tell me she is no friend of yours. Her lack of respect for Christ's divine judgment is deplorable." Sabina merely shook her head, prompting Cecilia to add, "Is Angelina a courtier at the palazzo?"

"This isn't a royal court," Sabina corrected. "Florence is a—"

"Republic. Yes, I know. What exactly is Angelina's relationship to Lorenzo?"

"A distant cousin."

Cecilia smirked. "*Cousin?* I may not be as sophisticated as you are, Sabina, but it's clear that she's on intimate terms with him."

"There's no proof of that."

"She speaks of him as though she owns him—Lorenzo this and Lorenzo that. What more proof do you need of a woman's obsession with a man?"

"You're right, sister," Sabina agreed. "She did make a good point about the cold weather, however. Let's stay inside where it's warm."

"Fine, but I would appreciate it if we could avoid Signora Angelina."

"Signorina," Sabina reminded her.

"What that impertinent girl needs is a stern, religious husband to set her straight."

"I do not doubt it. Come, let's socialize a bit, shall we?"

While they chatted with a group of older ladies, Sabina noticed Tommaso's grim expression as he stood beside Giuliano and several of Lorenzo's men. When the men dispersed, Sabina excused herself and sought out her husband. Cecilia remained behind, engrossed in a deep conversation about the expansion of a local church.

Taking her husband's arm, she inquired, "You seem upset, Tommaso. Is everything all right?"

"Jacopo de' Pazzi had the nerve to show his face here tonight."

75

"Was he not invited?"

"Of course not! You know the Pazzi are enemies of the Medici."

"I saw two members of the Strozzi family here tonight," she countered. "I thought they were enemies, too."

Tommaso waved his hand dismissively. "The Strozzi are mere rivals. It's different with the Pazzi."

"How did he get in? Medici guards are posted around the entire palazzo."

He indicated a pretty woman across the room with flowing hair the color of honey and skin as pale as alabaster. "That is Fiona, younger sister of the famed beauty, Simonetta Vespucci. Fiona saw Jacopo slip past the guards, nestled within a group of guests."

Famed beauty? "Is Jacopo still here?"

"No, he was escorted out."

Sabina cleared her throat and inquired, "Who is Simonetta Vespucci?"

"She was Botticelli's favorite model and is considered to be the ideal of feminine beauty—at least here in Florence."

"Oh."

"Unfortunately, La Bella Simonetta died in April of last year."

"Such a shame. If Simonetta was as lovely as Fiona, I can understand why women strive to look like her."

"Me, too," he agreed a bit too readily for Sabina's taste.

"My complexion is golden and my hair is almost black. I suppose I'm the opposite of the Florentine ideal."

Tommaso's serious mood was lifted by his wife's jealousy. "Perhaps, but you are no less beautiful, my dear. As for Simonetta, she was not a chaste wife to her husband."

"Oh no?"

He shook his head. "She was Giuliano de' Medici's mistress."

Gossip lurked in every corner of this city! Sabina looked around. "By the way, where is my father? I thought he was with you?"

"He was, until he ran into an old friend of his. I'm sure Don Antonio is sitting in some quiet corner talking of old times."

A gentleman approached Tommaso and began to speak with him in a hushed tone. Not wanting to intrude on their conversation, Sabina wandered aimlessly until she reached a corner of the main hall where she could observe the festivities unnoticed. She soon felt a presence behind her.

"Why are you alone, Sabina?"

She spun around and was face to face with Lorenzo de' Medici. He was arrayed in black velvet with an under tunic the color of fresh blood. Florentine Red. A heavy gold chain in the shape of a rope hung around his neck and at the end was a medallion sporting a miniature head of the Marzocco lion. She recalled that the original Marzocco, symbol of the Florentine Republic, was carved by Donatello and stood in the Piazza della Signoria.

He continued, "Are you enjoying yourself?"

She nodded. "It's a lovely party." Whenever she found herself in close proximity to Lorenzo it seemed as if her cheeks automatically burned and her heart raced.

"Angelina informed me that she showed you my new painting depicting the Last Judgement. Do you approve?"

"It's marvelous, like all of your artwork. I'm sure the artist will obtain many commissions now that you own one of his pieces."

"Yes," he agreed, never taking his eyes off her. "You have not visited my library lately." Her face must have registered surprise because he added, "My servants tell me everything."

"Your servants are correct."

"You cannot be bored of my collection so soon."

"I could spend years in your library."

He took a step closer to her. "What has you so occupied these days?"

She detected the subtle scent of fragrant oil on his skin. The appealing, masculine scent distracted her thoughts. "The inclement weather has kept me indoors, so I've been busy writing."

Lorenzo's eyes widened. "What do you write?"

"Foolish verses," she replied dismissively.

"Something tells me that nothing you set your mind to is foolish."

"Why would you think that?"

"You are not that kind of woman."

There was an awkward silence and she changed the subject. "The musicians are playing such merry melodies tonight."

He would not be swayed, however. "I would like to see your work."

She gave a nervous little laugh. "Ah, no."

"Are you denying my request?"

"That's not what I meant."

"What *do* you mean?"

"I write for my own pleasure, Lorenzo. My work would pale in comparison to the fine literature to which you are accustomed."

Putting his face close to hers, he said, "Let me be the judge of that."

For an instant, she thought he was going to kiss her. As if reading her thoughts, his eyes dropped to her mouth and a slow smile spread across his face before he backed away. Out of the corner of her eye, she saw Angelina Bardi walking toward them.

"I was wondering where you'd wandered off to, Lorenzo," she said, taking his arm. "Your wife has retired for the evening."

"Perhaps the wine has made her sleepy," he commented while keeping his eyes on Sabina.

"Perhaps," she agreed, casting a steely glance in Sabina's direction.

"Angelina, did you know that Sabina possesses a talent for writing?"

"I did not," she replied with sticky sweetness.

"I would love to see her work, but she's too shy to show it to me."

"There's no need for shyness, Signora Sabina," Angelina chided. "Lorenzo is the best critic in Florence."

"I have no doubt of that," Sabina said.

78

"Then we shall read your work and give it a proper critique, won't we, Lorenzo?"

Sabina, who was unsure about showing her work to Lorenzo, relished the prospect of doing so even less after Angelina's comment. She hoped that her annoyance at the other woman's meddling did not show too plainly on her face.

Noticing Sabina's discomfort, Lorenzo immediately reverted to being the perfect host. "We have taunted our lovely writer enough for one night. I look forward to our next meeting," he said to Sabina as he bowed over her hand.

Sabina shivered as his warm lips touched her knuckles. "As do I."

She watched the two of them walk away arm in arm, and was relieved a moment later when Tommaso expressed his desire to go home. She was tired from the festivities and longed for the comfort of her bed.

CHAPTER 7

Don Antonio, Cecilia, and Paolo remained in Florence until the end of Epiphany.

Prior to their departure, Don Antonio said to Sabina, "You must come to Lucca soon."

"I will, Papa," she assured. "Promise me that you will spend Easter with us in Florence."

"If God wills it."

Sabina turned to Paolo and held out her arms to him. "Did you have fun?"

"Yes!" he replied, waving the wooden sword Tommaso had given him before embracing his aunt.

Sabina kissed his cheek. "Do you want to come visit me at Easter?"

Paolo nodded. "Will I get a shield next time?"

Sabina felt a pang of envy. She suddenly wanted a child, too. "I will make sure that you do. Go inside the carriage now, Paolo. I love you."

Don Antonio and Cecilia said their farewells, then Sabina watched the carriage roll down the narrow street.

***

January proved to be a dreary month with very few days of sunshine. The rain began the day after Epiphany and continued intermittently for almost a week. When it finally stopped, several clouds convened over the city like a giant wet blanket. Sabina remembered the arid, sultry days of August and longed for one such day to break up the gray monotony.

The weather improved slightly in February, but it was still too cold to sit outside and enjoy the courtyard garden. She took advantage of the inclement weather and completely gave herself over to writing in her journal. When no more blank pages were left, she decided to present it to Lorenzo. She was still uncomfortable with the idea of allowing him to see her work, but she was in no position to deny his request.

Another musical protégé was scheduled to perform at the Palazzo Medici during the first week of March. Tommaso had mentioned to her in passing that Messer Bardi was taking his family to Verona to visit relatives, so Angelina would not be present. Sabina would seize the opportunity to see Lorenzo privately.

The day of the concerto dawned clear and, despite the chilliness, the sun's fragile rays broke through the clouds. Sabina held her red journal close to her chest as she walked beside her husband and two armed guards. A well-dressed man passed them on the street and inclined his head toward Tommaso, who politely returned the gesture. Sabina was quick to notice there was no friendliness in her husband's eyes, only anger and distrust. The guards immediately placed their hands upon the hilts of their swords, closely watching the man until he was completely out of sight.

"Damned Pazzi," Tommaso muttered under his breath.

"There's that name again," Sabina said. "You told me they were our enemies, but you never explained why."

"They're devious and power-hungry—a dangerous combination."

"So are many other families in the city."

"Other families have not openly defied Medici rule."

"What have the Pazzi done that is so wrong?"

"These are matters meant to be discussed among men."

Sabina gave him a disbelieving look. "You have said yourself on more than one occasion that I'm smarter than many of your peers in the Signoria, and what a pity for Florence that I wasn't born male. Now you imply that my ears are not meant to hear the matters of men?"

"Still the Tempesta, I see. Very well. The pope demanded an exorbitant bank loan. Lorenzo felt inclined to deny the request."

"Why on earth would Lorenzo do something like that? It's the pope."

"It's not that simple. Pope Sixtus is an extremely ambitious

81

man. If he were to secure such a large sum of money, he would become powerful enough to threaten Lorenzo's authority in Florence."

"What does this have to do with the Pazzi?"

Tommaso glanced over his shoulder at the guards. "The Pazzi went behind Lorenzo's back and secured the loan for the pope."

"Thus making the Medici an enemy," she concluded.

"Correct."

"I would be angry if I was Lorenzo."

Tommaso laughed without humor. "You can rest assured that he is."

They arrived at the Palazzo Medici as Giotto's bell tower chimed. Giuliano quickly found Tommaso and led him down a hall while Sabina made her way to the salon. The musician was an attractive, large breasted woman with a commanding voice. She sang in perfect harmony with a harp player. Sabina closed her eyes and simply allowed the music to fill her soul.

Lorenzo eventually emerged from one of the rooms to mingle with the people present, and Sabina wondered why he wasn't with the rest of the men today. Perhaps it had to do with the lustful manner in which the singer's eyes followed him throughout the room. Was she one of his many lovers? He caught Sabina's eye and walked toward her.

He kissed her hand, then asked, "What did you think of her voice?"

"Once again, you've exhibited your talent for finding gifted people."

His eyes were drawn to the journal in her hand. "I see you have something for me. I haven't forgotten, you know."

"Nor I," she said, handing over the journal.

"Come," he said, lightly placing his hand on the small of her back.

Sabina was led into a large room where two maps dominated an entire wall, and a wooden globe rested upon a desk. He indicated a window seat overlooking the courtyard. Despite the cold weather outside, the area in which they sat was pleasantly warm due to the sunshine pouring in from the round glass panes. He examined the journal's red velvet cover before turning the pages, pausing whenever something caught his eye.

"You don't mind me reading your work?" he asked. "Be truthful."

"I was initially frightened because my work is, well, odd," she confessed. "But I know you're an intelligent man and possess an open mind, so I don't mind—as long as you promise not to judge my writing too harshly."

He placed his finger on a written line and read aloud, " 'Ascending to purity with demons lapping at my heels…' Such provocative words."

Sabina stared out the window as he continued to read silently. After a long moment, Lorenzo looked up and studied her face for what seemed like an eternity. Finally, he gently touched her cheek. Her written words were dark and melancholic, yet full of beauty and grace.

What was it about this woman?

Lorenzo cleared his throat. "Would you mind if I kept this journal for a few days?" Her apprehension was apparent, so he quickly added, "I'll be very careful with it, I promise."

She nodded reluctantly. "Please show it to no one else."

"I will honor your privacy."

For some unknown reason, she trusted him implicitly. The sound of several approaching footsteps made them both look up. Clarice and her retinue of ladies passed by the doorway. None of them bothered to glance into the room.

"They are headed to my wife's private chapel," he explained. "They pray every day at this hour. Clarice is very devout."

"A most commendable trait."

"She's a good woman," he said distractedly before turning his attention back to the journal in his hands. He flipped through the pages until he reached the end. "You have no more blank pages left."

"I used up the last page several days ago. I suppose you can blame it on the bad weather. I prefer writing to boring needlework." Realizing that Lorenzo's wife most likely did needlework, Sabina said, "Forgive me, I didn't mean—I know many women who love needlework and are quite good at it. I'm not one of them."

Lorenzo chuckled softly. "Thank God for that," he said with a twinkle in his eye. "In all seriousness, you must continue to write, Sabina. It would please me greatly if you do. I'll get you a new journal."

"There's no need for you to do that."

"It's my way of thanking you for sharing your thoughts with me," he insisted, casually taking hold of her hand. He began caressing her knuckles with his thumb as he read a few more poems.

Sabina found the absentminded gesture distracting. His touch was warm and strong, making her feel safe, apprehensive, excited—all at the same time. In an attempt to mask her giddiness, she blurted the first thought that popped into her head. "Tommaso told me about the Pazzi."

Lorenzo was well aware of the effect he had on people, especially women. He squeezed her hand before letting it go. "What exactly did he tell you?"

"They gave money to the pope behind your back."

"Obviously, Tommaso deems you trustworthy." She remained silent and he asked, "Tell me, how would you react to such an insolent act if you were in my shoes?"

She was not expecting such a question. "I…I don't know."

"Surely a writer with such a vivid imagination can think of something," he prompted. "Pretend the whole thing is merely a story. How would it end? Go on, indulge me."

Sabina thought for a moment. "I suppose you could send the entire Pazzi family into exile."

"Pity you were born a woman. You would have been an asset to the Republic." She blushed and he continued, "Tommaso is a fortunate man."

"Thank you."

"And I'm fortunate that he trusts you in my company."

"He has no reason not to trust me."

Lorenzo stood and she followed him out of the room. "Speaking of Tommaso, I have some matters to discuss with him. I promise I won't keep him long today. I'm sure you can entertain yourself in the meanwhile."

Sabina went directly to the library while she waited for her husband to finish his business. It was not long before Tommaso was ready to escort her home.

"Where's your journal?" he asked as they navigated the streets toward home. "You had it with you this morning."

"I left it with Lorenzo."

Tommaso's mouth became a hard line, but he said nothing more.

Tommaso announced their imminent departure for Pisa the next day.

Sabina, who was reading in her study, looked up from her book. "Why are we going to Pisa?"

"My aunt lives there. She's my only living relative, and I received news that she's very ill."

"I'm sorry to hear it. I didn't know you had an aunt."

"My father's only sibling. I haven't seen her in years."

"Why is she living in Pisa?"

The Florentines hated the Pisans almost as much as the people of Lucca did.

"She married a wealthy Pisan in the shipping business. After he died, she remained because her life was already established there."

"Why did she not attend our wedding?"

"She's too old to travel."

She closed her book. "Do you stay in contact with her?"

"You're full of questions this morning, aren't you? My aunt stopped corresponding with me almost two years ago when her fingers stiffened from old age. She refuses to dictate to a servant because she doesn't want anyone to know her business."

"She sounds like an interesting woman. What's her name?"

"Donna Maddalena Moroni."

Sabina smiled. "I look forward to meeting her."

They departed for Pisa a few days later, accompanied by

their personal servants and a pair of guards. During the short journey, Sabina marveled at the snowcapped mountains in the distance.

"That's not snow," Tommaso corrected. "Those are the quarries of Carrara. Many Florentine sculptors go there to select their marble."

The late afternoon sun was casting long shadows by the time they arrived in Pisa. They were informed that Donna Maddalena was not feeling well and would see them in the morning. After being shown to their bedchambers, a servant brought them a cold meal and red wine.

Sabina woke up the next day and found Teresa in her room staring out the window with an expression of pure wonder on her face.

"Signora, you must see the view. Here, let's get you washed up first," Teresa said, carrying a basin of water and a linen towel toward the bed.

Sabina ran the damp cloth along her face and chest. "What is it?"

"I want it to be a surprise."

Sabina finished her toilette, then went to the window. "Oh!"

Outside stood three of the most spectacular buildings she had ever seen. There was an enormous baptistery, a huge cathedral with a Moorish-inspired dome shaped like an onion, and a circular bell tower that leaned ever so slightly. All three were constructed of gleaming white marble that shimmered in the morning sunshine.

Sabina turned away from the view. "Quick, help me dress and take special care with my hair because I want to impress my husband's aunt."

Ah hour later, a servant led Sabina and Tommaso into a stuffy room hung with many tapestries. Donna Maddalena's tiny form was propped up by several cushions heaped upon a great bed boasting a red velvet canopy. Seated beside the enormous bed was her nurse.

"Let's see this new bride of yours, Tommaso," Donna Maddalena said in a surprisingly loud voice after kissing her nephew. "Is this your fourth or fifth wife? I've lost count."

"Third," Tommaso replied. "Aunt, this is Sabina Rossi."

"Come closer, child, so I can get a proper look at you." She took hold of Sabina's wrist with surprising strength and pulled her toward the bed. "My eyesight is not what is used to be, dear. Ah, there you are." After a careful inspection, she turned to her nephew. "She is positively lovely."

Tommaso smiled proudly. "Yes, I know."

"Young enough to be your daughter, too," the old woman murmured.

"What was that?" he asked.

She waved her papery hand dismissively. "Are you expecting, girl?"

"Expecting what?" Sabina asked.

Donna Maddalena raised an eyebrow. "Pretty, but not too bright."

Tommaso glanced uncomfortably at his wife, hoping she would not take offense. He had warned Sabina beforehand of his aunt's propensity for speaking her mind regardless of consequence.

Sabina felt foolish when she realized what the old woman meant. "Forgive me, I misunderstood. No, I'm not carrying a child—*yet*."

"Why not? You've been married for several months. You should be pregnant by now. Do you realize how desperate my nephew is for an heir? Get to it, girl, and do your duty."

"Unfortunately, God has not seen fit to bless my womb."

"God has nothing to do with it," the old woman snapped. Addressing Tommaso, she asked, "How long will you be staying in Pisa?"

"For as long as you will have us."

"Then you would never leave," she said coyly. "I expect you will show your wife our city's pride and joy?"

"I have every intention of doing so."

Donna Maddalena looked to Sabina. "Your name is familiar to me. I once knew a Bernardo Rossi, but that was long ago."

"That was my grandfather's name."

Donna Maddalena shot Tommaso an accusatory look. "You failed to tell me that your new bride is from Lucca. All that stupid rivalry. I'm an old woman and life is too short to care about such ridiculous matters."

"You do well to ignore it, aunt," he said.

The old woman shifted her gaze to Sabina. "As for your grandfather, he and my late husband would spend hours at the gaming tables." She paused and added slyly, "Bernardo liked placing big bets."

Sabina shifted uncomfortably, hoping she would change the subject. Donna Maddalena looked at her knowingly and began to inquire about several Florentines. The old woman was hungry for gossip and Sabina dutifully provided a few snippets for her amusement.

Once Donna Maddalena had heard her fill of scandals, marriages, and deaths, she placed a birdlike hand to her brow. "I'm tired."

"We'll leave you to rest now," Tommaso said before kissing his aunt's forehead. Motioning for the nurse to follow him outside the room, he then asked the woman, "How bad is it?"

"Quite bad," the nurse whispered. "According to the physician, she will not last another fortnight."

Later that day, Tommaso accompanied his wife to Holy Mass in order to pray for his aunt's soul. The striped Romanesque arches and enormous monolithic columns of Santa Maria Assunta took Sabina's breath away. After the service, they climbed the bell tower.

"When was this tower built?" Sabina asked, gazing at the spectacular mountains in the distance.

"At the end of the twelfth century."

"Why does it lean so?"

"According to some architects, it wasn't properly constructed. Others say the soil underneath is not solid enough to withstand the weight."

"Which theory do you support?"

"I think it may be a combination of both," he replied. "It began leaning after the first three tiers were completed. The architect, Bonanno Pisano, was so ashamed that he simply abandoned the project and fled Pisa. It took two more centuries to complete the project."

"These are the most incredible buildings I have ever seen," Sabina commented as they headed for the baptistery.

"Never say that in the presence of a Florentine," he warned.

The baptistery, rumored to be the biggest in Europe, was as round as a drum. They hovered in the doorway and listened as several monks chanted inside the spacious interior. The acoustics were so impressive that Sabina got chills listening to the unified voices. She looked up at the ceiling to see the big hole that allowed the rain to fall and fill the large baptismal pool.

That evening, Donna Maddalena announced that she felt well enough to dine with them. Throughout the meal, the old woman regaled Sabina with home remedies to cure infertility and encourage conception.

The old woman slept throughout the following morning, allowing Tommaso to show his wife the University of Pisa and other noteworthy buildings. They stopped at a bakery so he could purchase some local pastries and Sabina's mouth watered at the sight of them.

"I'd like one of each, please," she said.

"How you manage to keep that stunning figure of yours is a mystery," Tommaso said as he paid the baker.

They bit the flaky pastries and laughed when crumbs stuck to their mouths. Sabina was thoroughly enjoying her husband's company and gave his cheek a spontaneous kiss.

He grinned. "What was that for?"

"I felt like it."

She tore off another piece and stuffed it in her husband's mouth, laughing as she did so.

Tommaso had not visited his wife's bed since their arrival in Pisa out of respect for his aunt. That night, he did.

Two days later, Donna Maddalena's nurse announced that her mistress had taken a turn for the worse. Tommaso was summoned and remained with his aunt for most of the morning as the physicians bled her by slashing her skin and securing leeches to the tiny cuts. The glossy black creatures greedily sucked her blood until they became engorged.

"How is she?" Sabina asked of Tommaso when he joined her for supper in the evening.

"The physicians have done all they can."

"Your aunt is in God's hands now."

"She's had a good life and will die at a ripe old age—may we all be so blessed. She told her nurse was that she 'was ready to go to God.' "

Donna Maddalena Moroni went to God the next day, and everything she owned was bequeathed to her nephew. They were forced to remain in Pisa while Tommaso met with his aunt's solicitors to sort things out.

It was almost April by the time they returned to Florence, and Tommaso was summoned to the Palazzo Medici shortly afterward. A new political matter had arisen during his absence that needed the Signoria's immediate attention. Sabina accompanied him, hoping to see Lorenzo in order to retrieve her journal. Unfortunately, he was closed up in his study with meetings for the entire morning.

Sabina waited in the ladies' quarters, a large area where women could await their escorts or simply enjoy one another's company. The spacious, well-appointed rooms were located off the Medici chapel, affording both safety and privacy. Clarice and her ladies were present, as were many other women. Some were reading while others were engaged in needlepoint. Sabina sat alone by the fire fingering a tiny prayer book. When nobody was looking, she stood and discreetly exited the nearest doorway. She wandered toward the chapel, then beyond. To her good fortune, Lorenzo rounded the corner of the corridor and stopped at the sight of her.

"Sabina," he said, surprised. "Tommaso failed to mention you were here. How good to see your pretty face again."

"I was in the ladies' quarters awaiting my husband."

"What have you got there?" he asked, eyeing the prayer book.

She shrugged. "I would prefer Boccaccio, but…"

Smiling at her piquant humor, he said, "Well, I'll leave you to the ladies, then."

"Actually, I was hoping to see you."

"I'm flattered. Come, I have something for you."

Lorenzo led her to his study where he removed the red journal from his desk drawer. He also removed a book bound in blue leather.

"This is your new journal," he said, handing her both books. "I had the leather dyed to my favorite shade of blue."

"How thoughtful of you, Lorenzo. Thank you, it's beautiful," she said, admiring the craftsmanship.

"Gifting you a new journal perfectly sums up my opinion of your work." He winked, adding, "I must go now. Don't stay away so long next time."

Clutching both journals to her chest, Sabina strolled down the picture gallery before rejoining the ladies. A heavy-set, middle-aged woman with a friendly face smiled as she entered the room.

"Signora Sabina Rossi?"

"Yes. Have we met?"

"No, but our husbands work closely together," she explained. "My name is Camelia Cantini."

"You are Signore Adolfo's wife, are you not?"

Her face lit up. "I am."

"I've heard my husband mention your name a few times. He speaks highly of you both. It's a pleasure to finally meet you, Signora Camelia."

"The pleasure is all mine, dear." She sighed, casting a glance at the ladies. "I don't come here often, you see. I'm getting old and prefer the comfort of my own home."

Camelia possessed an open face and exuded warmth and sincerity. Sabina liked her instantly.

"I hear you enjoy literature—writing, in particular," Camelia continued, changing the subject. Sabina's face showed surprise, so she quickly added, "I saw Lorenzo with his nose in a red journal recently. When I inquired if he was reading the work of a new literary protégé, he replied that the journal belonged to you." She paused. "Oh dear, I've made you uncomfortable."

"No, I...I didn't expect him to tell anyone he was reading my work."

"There was no one within earshot, I assure you. I'm certain he wouldn't share such information with others." Camelia reached out to touch the younger woman's hand. "I've known Lorenzo since he was a lad, so he treats me like a trusted aunt. No harm done, dear."

"I'm not exactly a literary protégé," Sabina confessed.

"You are being modest, Signora."

"Please, call me Sabina."

Camelia smiled broadly. "Very well, Sabina. Lorenzo said your work is very good; I know it must be true."

Sabina's heart skipped a beat at the thought of her writing being described as "very good" by the most important man in Florence. "Lorenzo de' Medici is kind to his friends."

"Nonsense," Camelia countered. "He is not one to flatter falsely."

A man walked past the doorway and paused to peek inside the room. Tall, broad shouldered, and exceptionally handsome, he grinned at Camelia and approached them.

"Pardon me for interrupting, ladies," he said with a gallant bow.

"Massimo!" Camelia cried. "How good to see you again."

Sabina took in the man's dashing attire and the thick gold chain which held his cloak in place. Dark, shoulder-length hair framed a face that could only be described as perfect. In fact, she was certain she had seen the classical profile sculpted on many of the city's masterpieces.

"It's wonderful to see you, too, Signora Camelia. I was on my way to meet with Lorenzo when I spotted you." His eyes slid toward Sabina. "May I be introduced to your lovely companion?"

"This is Signora Sabina Rossi, wife of Tommaso Caravelli," Camelia said, stressing the word "wife."

He bent over Sabina's hand, staring up at her through thick lashes.

Eyes as blue as the sea…

"It's a pleasure to meet you, Signora," he said in a husky voice. "I am Massimo Reni, at your service."

Sabina retracted her hand and they stared at each other in silence.

Camelia's head turned from right to left. *Oh dear.* "How long will you be staying in Florence, Massimo?"

"I plan to stay through Easter if my cousin will have me that long," he replied, still gazing at Sabina.

Sabina averted her eyes for the sake of modesty and finally found her voice. "Who is your cousin?"

"Clarice Orsini," he replied.

"Our dear Massimo is a Roman," Camelia explained.

He looked at Camelia. "So are you, my dear lady."

"True, but I married a Florentine. I've been away from my birth city for quite some time now, and almost consider myself more Florentine than Roman."

"I've never been to Rome," Sabina confessed.

"You should go," Massimo said, eyeing her intently. "It's one of the most amazing cities in the world."

"Ah, the Eternal City," Camelia said wistfully. "I'm long overdue for a visit."

"Do you still have family in Rome?"

"Yes, a sister," Camelia replied. "You are from Lucca, are you not?"

Sabina nodded.

"Do you still have family in Lucca?" Massimo inquired.

"Yes, my father, my sister, and my nephew."

"I have only been to Lucca once," Camelia said. "Charming city."

"I have yet to see its charm. Perhaps someday I'll be fortunate enough to have someone show me around," Massimo said, smiling at Sabina in such a way that seemed to imply she would be perfect for the task.

Camelia gave him a reproving look, which he responded to

with an impish grin. "If you will excuse us, Massimo. Signora Sabina and I were on our way to the garden to take in some fresh air. It was a pleasure to see you and I'm sure we'll meet again."

Taking the hint, Massimo inclined his head at them. "I can assure you the pleasure was entirely mine, ladies."

Sabina allowed herself to be led away by Camelia. Against her better judgment, she peeked over her shoulder and met Massimo's azure gaze before slipping through the doorway.

"He's harmless, I assure you," Camelia whispered. "Quite the charmer—clever and handsome, too! A young woman like you has to be careful around that one."

Camelia sat on a bench beneath the shade of a fig tree and urged her new friend to sit beside her. The older woman enjoyed talking and soon dominated the conversation, contributing various tidbits of interesting gossip. Suddenly, she squeezed Sabina's arm. "Look there," she whispered. "I have not seen her in months."

Sabina turned her head and saw an attractive woman dressed in a costly gown of plum velvet. It was the same mysterious woman she had seen the first time she met Angelina Bardi. "Who is she?"

Camelia looked at her in surprise. "Lucrezia Donati."

She recalled to mind Teresa's gossip. "Lorenzo's mistress?"

"His favorite, long before he married Clarice."

Sabina stared at the woman who held first place in Lorenzo de' Medici's heart. "The two women tolerate each other?"

"You could say that. Clarice is well aware of Lucrezia's existence but resents her presence in the palazzo. She considers it an affront."

"Does Lorenzo normally allow his mistresses to roam freely under his wife's nose?"

"Certainly not! An exception is made for Lucrezia because her father has always been an ally of the Medici. She and Lorenzo used to play together as children. She knows every nook and cranny of this palazzo."

"Yet, he has other mistresses."

"Yes, like Angelina Bardi," Camelia said with a comical eye roll, confirming Sabina's suspicion. "You've met her?"

"Yes."

Camelia shook her head dismissively. "Anyway, the reason Clarice and Lucrezia both have good, long-lasting relationships with Lorenzo is because they understand him as a man. Neither woman attempts to rein him in with jealous demands or petty ultimatums, so he returns to them of his own accord. It's a brilliant strategy on their part, and keeps everyone happy."

While Sabina pondered over Camelia's words, Lucrezia caught her eye and gave her a friendly smile.

CHAPTER 8

Lorenzo and Giuliano de' Medici held an outdoor tournament before Lent to celebrate the end of winter and the onset of spring. They generously provided the good citizens of Florence with plenty of sport and entertainment. No expense was spared to maintain the Medici popularity and ensure the public's loyalty. Vendors came from far and wide to set up stalls around the huge piazza of Santa Croce, where the joust would be held.

Sabina, Tommaso, and a few other friends decided to attend the event together. Seats had been thoughtfully reserved for their group.

As the crowd waited for the joust to begin, three men pulled a bear into the center of the piazza. They shouted commands to the great beast, which wore a red vest and a little green cap upon its massive head. The bear was obviously well-trained, for it obeyed the men rather than eating them. The crowd applauded and cheered as the bear did a somersault and other tricks. Coins were thrown in appreciation, and one of the men quickly began to gather the money as the bear waved to the crowd.

"I think I shall buy you that bear," Tommaso said to his wife.

She turned to him, surprised. "Whatever for?"

"You seem to be as enthralled with it as those children standing there," he said, indicating a group of wide-eyed children with mouths agape. He gave her hand an affectionate squeeze. "Your innocence is absolutely charming. It's moments like these that make me love you even more."

A trumpet sounded and Sabina gasped in delight as Lorenzo and Giuliano rode out on two powerful steeds. The brothers were dressed in matching armor fashioned from copper and gold. Their retinue followed closely behind, arrayed in colorful costumes and carrying jousting lances. Silk banners flaunting noble family crests billowed in the breeze.

Massimo was among them, dressed in black armor.

"Impressive, are they not?" Tommaso asked.

"Very," she replied, trying hard not to stare at Massimo.

"You should have seen the joust that was held here in 1475."

"Simonetta Vespucci was declared the most beautiful woman in Florence at that tournament, was she not?"

"Yes," he replied. "You would have loved it. Everyone of importance was in attendance. Giuliano de' Medici wore an armor made of pure silver. He looked like an ancient pagan god. The remarkable feast that followed was talked about for a long time afterward."

The crowd cheered loudly for the Medici brothers as they paraded around the piazza, waving at the people.

"They are like gods," she mused aloud.

"That's one way to look at them." Another group of riders entered the piazza and Tommaso added, "Those are the opponents."

The crowd began to boo the men who would challenge the Medici. Lorenzo rode to where his wife sat and bowed his head. Clarice held up a lace handkerchief for the crowd to see before tying it around her husband's arm and blowing him a kiss. The crowd roared in favor of their hero.

Massimo's horse paused relatively close to where Sabina sat. She was shocked when he looked directly at her. Tommaso clenched his fists and frowned in response to the young man's insolence. Undeterred, Massimo held Sabina's gaze for a long moment before urging his horse forward. He waved to his cousin, Clarice, who blew him a kiss.

"Do you know that man?" Tommaso demanded.

"Signora Camelia introduced him to me at the Palazzo Medici."

His jaw clenched and his eyes narrowed. "Did she, now?"

"I have only spoken to him that one time—and it was very brief," she assured hastily. "Did you know he is Clarice's cousin?"

"Of course I do," he retorted in a clipped tone.

Tommaso said nothing more. Sabina knew her husband was

upset. Thankfully, he was soon distracted by the men as they took their places for the joust. Sabina winced each time the wooden lances crashed together. It made an awful sound and sent countless splinters up in the air. Throughout the harrowing affair, six men fell off their horses, four suffered mild injuries, and one had to be dragged away. In the end, it was no surprise when the Medici brothers won the tournament. The crowd cheered for a long time.

It was a miracle that no one perished that day.

Lorenzo and Giuliano had generously arranged for bread, meat, and wine to be doled out to the people when the tournament was over. Since the majority of Florentines gave up eating meat entirely during the period between Lent and Easter, they seized the opportunity to gorge themselves. Florid-faced and sweaty, they feasted in the streets and made merry until sunset.

Sabina and Tommaso joined the private celebration held at the Palazzo Medici. They congratulated the victors and heaped lavish praise upon their sportsmanship. Sabina noticed Massimo chatting to a few of Clarice's ladies and looked away immediately. She took her seat beside her husband and feasted along with the other guests. Although she took great pains to ignore him, Massimo watched her discreetly throughout the entire evening. When Tommaso finally announced that it was time to go home, Massimo noticed the disappointment on Sabina's face. In that flickering moment, their eyes met and conveyed what their lips could not.

Later that night, she tossed and turned, unable to sleep.

***

Springtime came to Tuscany with so much verdant beauty and grace, it was as if Flora herself had descended upon the city. Delicate buds sprouted on trees and bushes while wildflowers sprang up in lush, green fields. Even the birds sang in praise of the season. Flowers bloomed in the countryside as well as in private courtyards, including that of the Palazzo Caravelli. Capable servants tended to the flower beds while Sabina nurtured her precious herbs. The rosemary, basil, and lavender gave off the sweetest of perfumes. She would sometimes spend hours in the garden writing in her new blue journal. On occasion, Tommaso would join her in the sunshine and catch up on his reading.

It was during one of these pleasant afternoons that Sabina handed Tommaso her red journal. "I have allowed Lorenzo de' Medici to read it. I suppose it's time I let you do the same."

To her chagrin, he returned the journal. "If that's the only reason, then I'm not interested."

"No, it's not. I've wanted to for quite some time, but I was unsure of what you would think," she countered, placing the journal in his hands.

"Are you being truthful with me?"

"Of course I am. I'd be honored if you would read my work and gave me an honest opinion of it."

"Very well."

"Thank you for being patient with me."

During the next few days, Sabina noticed Tommaso frequently reading out of the red journal. Try as she might, she could not discern the expressions on his face while he read her words.

Sabina was picking irises in the garden with Mendi at her side when Tommaso approached her with journal in hand. "I'm done."

She paused in her task and shaded her eyes against the sun. "Well?"

"I'm impressed."

"Are you being kind or honest?"

"Honest. I enjoyed the short stories, and the poetry intrigued me."

"That means so much to me, Tommaso."

Mendi cawed loudly and he shooed the crow away before setting the red journal on a nearby bench. "I have to go to Milan with Lorenzo."

"When?"

"Tomorrow. We leave at dawn."

She dropped the irises and stood. "How long will you be

away?"

"Not long, only a few days."

"You'll be missed."

Tommaso kissed Sabina's cheek and she watched him walk away. Sometimes, she pondered over the events of her life with wonder. A year ago, she would never have imagined being married to such a favorable husband. She was young, rich, and from what Lorenzo and Tommaso told her, a writer with a bit of actual talent. She would have offered a prayer of thanks to God, but since she was not as religious as Cecilia, she was content to thank Fate.

***

Don Antonio, Cecilia, and Paolo arrived in Florence a few days before Easter Sunday. Sabina, who had not seen her family since Epiphany, was quick to notice that her father looked frail.

"Papa is not well," Sabina said to Cecilia when they were alone.

"He's been sick again. We almost couldn't come for Easter."

"Why was I not informed of this in any of your letters?"

"He didn't want to worry you."

"I had every intention of going to Lucca in late February once the weather improved, but Tommaso's aunt was on her deathbed. We were stuck in Pisa for several weeks—"

"I know." Cecilia reached out for her sister's hand. "He knows. We understand. Life is full of unexpected circumstances."

"Still, I should have been informed of his condition…"

Cecilia sighed. "Papa wanted to keep his promise and spend Easter with you here in Florence. He was afraid you would tell him not to come if you knew he was sick."

"He's right. I would have gone to Lucca. How bad is it?"

"The pain he used to complain of occasionally is returning ever more frequently, and he has become quite weak."

"Perhaps he should remain here in Florence with us. We can hire the best physicians to care for him."

"I doubt he'll agree to that."

Sabina was annoyed. "How do you know?"

100

"I've made that same suggestion to him more than once."

"Did you summon the physician in Lucca?"

Cecilia's eyes were sad as she looked away and nodded.

"And?" Sabina prompted.

"He doesn't have much longer to live."

Sabina looked outside the window and saw her father sitting in the garden watching Paolo play with his wooden sword. He seemed so small and fragile, and her heart ached at the thought of losing him forever.

Cecilia continued, "He begged me not to tell you any of this, but I didn't wish to keep you in ignorance."

Sabina nodded and continued to stare at her father. Cecilia placed her hand on her sister's shoulder and gave it a reassuring squeeze before walking away.

***

The pope's sixteen-year-old grandnephew, Raffaello Riario, would be traveling to Pisa to attend university. A recently elected cardinal, this was a required duty for him. The archbishop of Pisa, Francesco Salviati, would accompany the boy. On his way to Pisa, Riario was expected to visit the Medici out of social and political courtesy. A lavish banquet was scheduled at the house of another noble Florentine family for the twenty-fifth of April, which was Holy Saturday, the day before Easter.

"Are you going to attend?" Sabina asked of Tommaso after he had apprised her of the event.

The spring evening was unusually warm and they had dined under the stars in the courtyard. Don Antonio, Cecilia, and Paolo had already retired for the evening.

"The heads of Florence are expected to attend, myself included. As my wife, you will accompany me." He drank the remainder of his wine, then added, "Actually, I wish we weren't invited."

"Why not? The Medici will be there, too, won't they?"

"Yes, but so will the other rival families, including the Pazzi."

"I'm sure the host will seat the Medici far from the Pazzi.

101

Besides, isn't Lorenzo's sister, Bianca, married to a Pazzi?"

"Yes, but that marriage did little to bring the families together."

***

The temperature dropped and the evening of Holy Saturday was gray and chilly. Don Antonio and Cecilia were settled comfortably before the fire in Sabina's sitting room. Between the two of them were a pile of books and a basket of needlepoint. Paolo played at their feet.

Sabina entered the room and took in the scene with a smile. "I've instructed the servants to serve the evening meal in here."

"Thank you," Don Antonio said.

Cecilia added, "You should get ready or you'll be late."

Teresa stood waiting in her mistress's bedchamber with a basin of fragrant water and a linen cloth. Sabina washed up and changed into a formal gown before allowing her maid to dress her hair.

"Teresa, please keep an eye on my father," Sabina said while admiring her reflection in the looking glass. "See to his comfort and be sure to offer him a hot draught before he retires."

"Yes, Signora."

Tommaso and Sabina made their way to the palazzo where the young cardinal and the archbishop were staying. Private guards surrounded the building granting entry to those with an invitation.

Once inside, Sabina saw a few familiar faces. She was properly introduced to Archbishop Salviati and Cardinal Riario before taking her assigned place beside her husband. It was not long before Lorenzo arrived and, after dutifully greeting his hosts, he took his seat near Tommaso at the cardinal's right hand.

"Where is Giuliano?" Tommaso asked.

"He injured his leg during this morning's hunt."

Sabina craned her neck to ask, "Is he hurt badly?"

"A bit bruised and sore, but he should be fine by tomorrow," Lorenzo replied. "I'll let him know of your kind concern."

Lorenzo, Tommaso, and Sabina ate sparingly of the

delicious food, their anxious eyes darting around the room. The Pazzi, on the other hand, ate with gusto and appeared to be having a good time. Clearly, they were on friendly terms with the foreign guests.

Hired minstrels sang and the wine flowed freely until the wee hours. Archbishop Salviati's florid face was covered in a sheen of perspiration. Someone spoke in his ear and he burst into peals of laughter. A moment later, two robust women sporting indecently low-cut gowns emerged from a side door. They wore gaudy jewelry and their cosmetics had been applied with a heavy hand. The young cardinal's face paled with apprehension at the sight of the whores.

"He's still a virgin!" one of the men shouted, smacking the boy on the shoulder.

The archbishop made a crude joke before pulling one of the women onto his lap. The other whore circled the adolescent cardinal like a cat about to pounce upon a mouse.

Sabina put her lips to Tommaso's ear. "These men make me uneasy."

"Me too," he admitted.

Tommaso and Lorenzo thanked their hosts and prepared to depart. Once outside, the Caravelli and Medici armed guards surrounded them. Their eyes were wary, hands resting on the hilts of their weapons.

"That was almost painful," Lorenzo admitted quietly.

Tommaso nodded. "My sentiments exactly."

"I don't trust Salviati."

"Neither do I."

It was a strange night and Sabina felt relief the moment they arrived home. To her surprise, Tommaso entered her bedchamber a moment later, his eyes reflecting lust. Their lovemaking was surprisingly intense, and they lingered in each other's arms afterward.

"Tommaso?"

"Yes, my love?"

"Are you disappointed with me for not providing you with a son?"

"*Yet*," he amended, tracing the curve of her hip with his fingertip. "I greatly desire a son and often wonder why you haven't conceived, but I'm not disappointed with you. It's as God wishes it to be."

"Do you think I'm barren?"

"No, Sabina. I think you're a strong, healthy girl who will produce fine children when the time is right."

"I hope it's soon."

"Are you eager to become a mother?"

"Isn't every woman?"

"Most are, yes, but you're not 'every woman.' You may reply honestly."

"How can I be eager for something I don't know? I'm enjoying my life with you, but I'm aware of how much you want a son. As your wife, it's my duty to provide you with your heart's desire—an heir."

"Don't worry about these things, my love. We shall have our son one day, and all will be well," he said reassuringly. "Now get some sleep."

CHAPTER 9
EASTER SUNDAY
APRIL 26, 1478

Sabina awoke from a strange dream she could not recall, and it made her oddly anxious. She broke her fast and washed up before selecting a gown for Easter Mass.

"You look pale, Signora," Teresa said. "Are you feeling unwell?"

Sabina rubbed her temples. "I'm a bit tired from last night."

"Shall I prepare an invigorating tonic for you?"

"No, thank you, I'll be fine. Would you please accompany us this morning and help mind Paolo?"

"With pleasure."

It was a short distance to Santa Maria del Fiore cathedral. Sabina and Tommaso were relieved to see Giuliano limping across the piazza. Apparently, the injuries he'd sustained from the hunting accident were minor. Handsome as ever, he flashed his charming smile at a pair of young girls who almost swooned at the gesture.

"He must be feeling better," Tommaso commented drily before leading them through the cathedral's porta santa.

They padded down the nave toward the high altar, the area reserved for the Medici family and their allies. Clarice was already present with her ladies, her head bent over a prayer book. It was not long before Lorenzo and Giuliano took their places among the armed guards and loyal supporters.

Sabina yawned several times during the tediously long mass. Inevitably, her mind and eyes wandered throughout the massive space.

Cecilia gave her sister a reproving look, but it did no good. "Paolo seems to be paying more attention than you are," she whispered.

It was true. The little boy quietly offered the priest his rapt attention.

"I'm sure God will reward him for it," Sabina shot back.

Don Antonio put his finger to his lips, admonishing his daughters to be silent. Seeing this, Tommaso hid his amusement.

At the high point of the Easter Mass, several people bowed their heads in respectful anticipation of the holy act of transubstantiation. Sabina's stomach churned as the anxiety she felt earlier intensified. There was a chill in the air and the tiny hairs on the back of her neck prickled. She discreetly looked around while the congregation bent their heads in solemn reverence. As the priest lifted the wine-filled chalice toward Heaven, Giuliano de' Medici was viciously attacked by two assassins. Using razor-sharp daggers, they repeatedly stabbed him with such ferocity that poor Giuliano was dead even before he collapsed onto the floor in a pool of his own blood.

Sabina witnessed the sacrilegious slaughter and looked to Lorenzo. A man stood behind him with eyes revealing murderous intention. Without a moment's hesitation, she cried, "Lorenzo! Behind you!"

Lorenzo turned around, his body tense and coiled for action. The cold steel of a dagger nicked his neck, missing the arterial vein by a fraction of an inch. Had he not moved, the assassin's blade would have accurately hit its mark, causing fatal consequences. Lorenzo quickly undid the clasp of his cloak, threw the garment at the man's face, and unsheathed his sword. Undeterred, the assassin also drew his sword. Onlookers cried out in fear. Two guards helped Lorenzo flee the scene by jumping over the high altar and slipping into the sacristy. Before the door closed, Sabina saw one of the guards sucking the blood out of the wound in Lorenzo's neck—a precautionary measure against a blade laced with venom.

The conspirators were soon surrounded by Medici allies, and a vicious fight ensued. Don Antonio clutched at his chest when he saw Giuliano sprawled on the cathedral floor. Following her father's gaze, Cecilia gasped in horror. Sabina was relieved that Lorenzo was alive, but now Tommaso was lost in the melee.

"Where is Paolo?" Cecilia demanded, her voice shrill.

Teresa looked around frantically. "He was right here a moment ago."

People ran toward the doors in a state of sheer panic.

"Oh my God, where is my Paolo?"

While Cecilia, Teresa, and Don Antonio went off to find Paolo, Sabina searched for Tommaso. She finally spotted her husband on the south transept, defending himself against one of the assassins. Tommaso was a decent swordsman, but he faced a younger, stronger opponent who was highly trained in the art of murder. Tommaso continued to wield his sword bravely until a second man arrived on the scene.

Sabina cried out in horror as the newcomer lunged forward and ran his sword right through Tommaso's belly. The cold-blooded killer then pulled out the sword, wiped the blade on Tommaso's cloak, and ran off.

With no concern for her own safety, Sabina ran toward Tommaso. She knelt beside him and put her hand over the wound. Hot blood oozed between her fingers. "Oh, God, no! Tommaso!"

His eyes fluttered. "Sabina…"

"I'll fetch the physician!"

He clasped her hand with surprising strength. "Don't leave me."

"I need to get help—the wound is deep."

"So deep that it's fatal." He winced. "I'll be dead before you return."

"No! You will live, but I need to go now."

"I'm already feeling dizzy and cold…I would rather spend my last few moments with you, gazing at your lovely face."

Teresa ran up to them and began to cry hysterically when she saw her master sprawled out on the floor in a pool of blood.

Sabina turned to her maid and shouted, "Get help!"

Teresa nodded and obediently ran off.

Tommaso's face was ashen. Shivering, he whispered, "I'm so cold."

She removed her cloak and covered her husband's body as best she could. "I promise I'll bear you a son if you live. Stay with me."

"Kiss me, Sabina," he said through chattering teeth.

With tears streaming down her face, she leaned over and tenderly kissed her husband's lips for the last time. He attempted a smile, then froze.

"Tommaso," she cried, shaking him. "No!"

It was too late. She had lost her dear husband and good friend.

"You meddlesome bitch!"

Sabina looked up to see the man who had tried to kill Lorenzo standing over her and wielding a dagger. She scrambled to her feet in an attempt to run away, but he grabbed her arm and yanked her backward, causing her to fall to the floor.

I'll be joining you shortly, Tommaso.

Suddenly, the assassin let out a loud groan. His eyes bulged and he fell to his knees, revealing another man standing behind him with a bloody sword in his hand. It was Massimo.

"Come," he said, taking her hand and pulling her toward the exit.

"Wait, my husband! I can't leave him here like this!"

"There's nothing we can do for him now." When Sabina resisted, he cried, "It's unsafe for us to remain here!"

Massimo continued to pull Sabina through the throng of people. They were separated at one point and she tripped over a dead body, banging her arm against the stone floor of the cathedral. Massimo picked her up effortlessly in his arms and carried her across the piazza to safety.

Pale and trembling from shock, she whispered, "Tommaso."

"I'm taking you to the Palazzo Medici." She began to cry and he added gently, "I'm sorry. Your husband was a good man."

"My family is still inside...Paolo, my nephew, is lost."

"I'll find them. Stay here."

Sabina huddled in the deep doorway of a building and

108

watched the madness unfold in the piazza. A few of the conspirators attempted to mount horses in order to escape, but Medici supporters dragged them down and stabbed them to death. One nervous horse reared its front legs and galloped across the piazza, evoking screams in its wake. She remained perfectly still in the shadows, cringing at the smell of blood in the air. Massimo returned several minutes later carrying a child who Sabina immediately recognized as Paolo. Her father and sister staggered at Massimo's side, both white with shock.

"My son! My son!" Cecilia wailed, falling to her knees.

Don Antonio and Teresa helped Cecilia to her feet.

Massimo said quietly, "Your sister was leading her son across the piazza when a horse came at them."

Sabina felt sick. "Oh, God."

A nearby woman screamed, prompting Massimo to urge them toward the Palazzo Medici. "We need to get inside *now*."

Sabina put her arm around Cecilia and led her out of the piazza. There was chaos in the streets of Florence as they blindly followed Massimo. Once inside the palazzo, he gently set Paolo down on a long table. Cecilia embraced her son and made a sound akin to that of a wounded animal. Don Antonio sat in a chair, covered his eyes with his hand, and wept for his daughter and grandson.

Clarice entered the room and her face paled as she took in the scene. "Is my husband dead?" she demanded. "Has anyone seen Lorenzo?"

"He vanished after Giuliano was stabbed," someone replied.

"He escaped into the sacristy," Sabina said. "I saw him."

"Santo Cristo," Clarice exclaimed with gratitude, crossing herself and kissing the crucifix that hung around her neck.

A moment later, Lorenzo arrived at the palazzo accompanied by the same two men who helped him escape. Clarice immediately ran to her husband and embraced him.

"Your neck," she said, trying to pull aside the bloody cloth that Lorenzo held against the wound.

"A cut, nothing more," he assured, untangling himself from her arms. "The people think me dead. They must know that I'm alive."

Leaning out the window as far as he could, he showed himself to the Florentines who had gathered around the palazzo.

Someone in the crowd shouted, "There he is!"

Florence's most beloved son was alive! As if on cue, the people began to chant loudly, 'Palle! Palle! Palle!' in reference to the familiar balls on the Medici coat of arms.

Sabina heard their cries and, despite the gruesome carnage she'd just witnessed, something in her heart stirred. Oh, how the people loved him.

And so do you, Sabina.

Lorenzo turned away from the window and called out the names of his closest friends and associates. When he called for Tommaso and received no reply, he frowned. "Where is Tommaso?"

Massimo cast a glance at Sabina and said softly, "He's dead."

Lorenzo's face registered shock before a sinister shadow settled across his features. Sabina immediately recalled Tommaso's words: 'he can be a formidable enemy if the need arises.' He walked toward Sabina, his gaze locked on the dead little boy and his inconsolable mother.

Taking her hands into his own, he stared into her eyes and vowed, "You may rest assured that I will do everything within my power to avenge Tommaso's death and the death of your nephew."

"I know," she whispered.

"Had you not cried out in warning, I would be dead." Cupping her face with his hands, he leaned forward and kissed her forehead. "I promise you, Sabina, from this day forth, you will be cared for as one of my own. You and your family are now under my personal protection. It's the least I can do to honor Tommaso in death."

Lorenzo turned to Don Antonio and put a hand on the old man's shoulder. He gave him a look that required no words. Cecilia was lost in an ocean of tears and Teresa did her best to console her.

"Tommaso and the boy will have the best funerals Florence can provide," Lorenzo promised. To his assembled men, he said, "Tell me what you saw and what you know."

Someone confirmed the identity of the treacherous men who led the attack, then added, "They are crying 'death to the tyrants' as they ride through the streets of Florence. They plan to take the Signoria."

Lorenzo's hands curled into fists as he listened to the man. He recalled the image of Giuliano's lifeless body on the floor as he had made his way down the nave toward the sacristy. There had been no time for him to stop, no time for last words or a simple farewell. The grisly image of his younger brother would haunt him forever.

"We are going to take back the Signoria," Lorenzo declared. "First, we must bury the dead."

Giuliano's funeral was attended by almost every Florentine in the city. Tommaso and Paolo were buried the day afterward. Sabina had never been in love with Tommaso, but she did foster genuine affection and respect for him during their brief time together. She would miss him, but the death of her husband paled in comparison to losing Paolo. Her beloved nephew, the precious little boy she had come to love as her own, was gone forever.

Don Antonio and Cecilia were inconsolable. Sabina desperately tried to convince them to stay in Florence with her, but they refused. Cecilia claimed that she could not bear to look at the cathedral. The enormous dome of Santa Maria del Fiore was visible throughout the city, forcing her to relive the horrific memory every day. Teary-eyed and brokenhearted, Sabina said farewell to her father and sister, and she remained at the window long after their carriage had disappeared.

Hell broke loose in Florence when it was discovered that Archbishop Salviati and the Pazzi family were deeply involved in the Medici assassination plot. Lorenzo and his men stormed the Signoria, and the enemies lurking within were put to death immediately. This in itself did not surprise the Florentines. What did surprise and disturb them was the gruesome manner

111

in which they were killed—defenestration. Lorenzo threw the conspirators out of the highest windows of the Signoria, their bodies smashing into bloody bits on the stones below. The people in the crowded piazza cringed at the gory spectacle. It was later said that the Piazza della Signoria was drenched in blood.

The manhunt continued and the people of Florence aided the Medici in this vengeful endeavor. What the scheming conspirators never anticipated was the love the Florentines held for their leader. It did not take long before another twenty traitors were found and killed. Salviati's men were surrounded in the courtyard and stabbed to death by Medici supporters. Salviati himself was brought before Lorenzo, who saw fit to hang and disembowel the archbishop. Jacopo de' Pazzi, the patriarch of the Pazzi family, had tried to escape by hiding in a nearby village. The villagers, being loyal supporters of the Medici, seized him and dragged him back to Florence where he was executed. Francesco de' Pazzi, one of the two murderers who had stabbed Giuliano to death, was also executed. The only member spared was Guglielmo de' Pazzi, husband of Bianca de' Medici. Lorenzo, ever merciful, condemned his brother-in-law and his sister to exile.

Lorenzo insisted that the corpses of the traitors be strung up and publicly displayed outside the Signoria for several days. The bloated, rotting bodies served as a warning to anyone who dared raise a hand against the Medici.

The bile rose in Sabina's throat one morning as she and her maid passed by the Signoria and saw crows picking at the flesh of the decaying corpses. She fervently hoped that Mendi was not among them.

In the end, eighty people died in what was later to be called the Pazzi Conspiracy. The incident had a profound and noticeable effect on Lorenzo. The Ruler of Florence became withdrawn, serious, and overly suspicious. The days of carefree living, jousts, carnivals, and other public forms of entertainment were over.

An ominous cloud had settled over Florence.

Lorenzo had placed some of his armed guards around the Palazzo Caravelli during those dark days, and Sabina was grateful for the extra protection. Several weeks later, he sent her an invitation to come and dine at the Palazzo Medici. It was to be an intimate gathering of family and close friends, the first social event since her widowhood.

Wearing a black gown and no jewelry except for an onyx brooch to hold her cloak in place, she went to the Palazzo Medici accompanied by two guards. She was greeted with newfound respect for having aided in saving Lorenzo's life.

Clarice, who had never sought Sabina's company in private, did so that evening. She approached wearing a high-collared black gown and a severe hairstyle that made her look much older.

"I wanted to personally thank you for what you did, Signora Sabina."

"There's no need to thank me, Signora Clarice."

Clarice held out a tiny box. "A token of our gratitude."

Nestled inside was an exquisite diamond brooch. "It's lovely, but I cannot accept such a gift."

"Please accept it. For my sake."

Sabina inclined her head. "Thank you."

Clarice attempted a smile, then walked back to her ladies.

There were only a handful of guests seated at the dinner table, and Lorenzo had insisted that his brother's chair be kept vacant out of respect for his memory. Sabina found herself positioned between Massimo and Lorenzo, who naturally sat at the head of the table.

Lorenzo turned to Sabina and asked, "Have you started writing again?"

The other guests were deeply engrossed in conversation, so only she and Massimo heard his question.

"I find it difficult to concentrate these days," she replied. "I'm sure that in time…"

Lorenzo nodded in understanding. "It would be a shame if you stopped. You know Tommaso would not have wanted that."

"I know."

Someone asked Lorenzo a question and he turned his attention from Sabina to answer it.

Massimo seized the opportunity. "You're a writer?"

"No." She sipped her wine, nervously aware of his closeness.

"I'm a great fan of female writers." She threw him a disbelieving look, yet he continued, undaunted. "Take Christine di Pisan, for example, or Hildegard of Bingen."

"You're serious."

"Of course, I am. Those women possessed a sensitivity and inner strength that shone through their writing."

"Are you a lover of literature, then?"

"Very much so."

"Dante?"

"Genius."

"Boccaccio?"

"Brilliant." Massimo reached for his goblet and took a sip of wine. She was impressed and he knew it. "What do you write?"

"Poems, short stories. I have a passion for penning my thoughts."

Massimo imagined many other ways the intriguing woman seated beside him expressed her passion, then quickly reminded himself that she was recently widowed. "Perhaps you would honor me by allowing me to read some of your work?"

She lowered her eyes. "Perhaps."

Lorenzo turned his attention back to Sabina in time to hear the end of their conversation, prompting him to give Massimo a warning look.

Someone at the table said, "Bianca has sent word to me, Lorenzo. She is begging for you to reconsider her exile."

A hush fell over the room. The person who spoke was an older man who appeared to be sympathetic to Bianca's situation. Lorenzo slammed his fist on the table, causing everyone to jump in their seats.

Flustered, the man inquired, "How shall I reply to her

letter?"

Lorenzo replied in an eerily calm voice that unsettled everyone, "Tell my sister this: as long as her Pazzi husband lives, neither of them are welcome in Florence. She is fortunate that I didn't hang him with the others. Remind her that her husband's family killed our brother before attempting to kill me."

After a brief silence, the man said, "I will tell Bianca exactly what you have told me. Forgive me, if I spoke out of turn."

Lorenzo waved away the apology with his bejeweled hand and gulped down the rest of his wine. Sabina could see that he was in pain, and she wanted to ease his suffering, but she couldn't slay the demons that tortured his soul. No one but God could accomplish that feat.

As though reading her mind, Massimo leaned over and whispered, "I wish there was some way to comfort him."

"As do I."

"My cousin is sick over Giuliano's death. She truly mourns his loss. I regret that I must leave her side when she needs me the most."

"Must you go?" she asked, barely masking her disappointment.

Pleased by her displeasure, he replied, "I've been summoned to Rome in order to deal with an unpleasant legal matter."

"I'm sure your presence will be missed in Florence."

"I promised Clarice I'd return the moment the matter is resolved. Hopefully, it won't take too long."

"Hopefully."

To Sabina's chagrin, Lorenzo was eyeing her steadily.

CHAPTER 10

In the wake of the Pazzi Conspiracy, Pope Sixtus IV excommunicated Lorenzo de' Medici for his bloody vendetta against the Pazzi family, their supporters, and Archbishop Salviati. The Signoria was ordered by papal decree to surrender Lorenzo. Of course, they refused. The Tuscan Church supported the Signoria's decision, which eventually led to its excommunication.

Such open rebellion against the Vatican created more enemies for Florence, and Lorenzo was soon faced with political threats from Milan, Urbino, and Siena. The most serious threat came from Ferdinand, King of Naples. In order to solidify Florence's position and keep peace in Italy, Lorenzo set off on several campaigns to secure political alliances.

With Tommaso gone and Lorenzo away from Florence for long periods at a time, Sabina no longer visited the Palazzo Medici. In fact, despite being a widow of wealth and prestige, she rarely left her home.

The blood-drenched spring of 1478 eventually gave birth to the glorious verdure of summer. The days were long and hot; the evenings, sultry. The constant sunshine lifted the spirits and inspired hope for good things to come.

Massimo and Lorenzo were back in Florence by early September, and the Palazzo Medici came alive once again. Sabina was happy when the invitations began arriving at her door. Mindful of her recent state of widowhood, Massimo was respectful when speaking with Sabina, and always discreet in his attempts at flirtation. In time, she grew to appreciate his quick wit and his propensity for making her laugh.

On a mild November evening, after enjoying a concerto of stringed instruments, Massimo informed Sabina of his imminent departure.

"You're always running off to Rome," she said wistfully.

"I *am* Roman," he reminded her, snatching two goblets of diluted red wine from a servant's tray.

She accepted one of the goblets from his hand. "Yes, I know."

"Will you miss me?"

She shrugged. "Perhaps."

"Are you teasing me, Signora Sabina?"

Smiling mischievously, she took a sip of wine. "Perhaps."

"Rest assured that I'll miss you," he confessed, his tone and expression sincere. "In fact, I'll be counting the days until I see your lovely face again."

Sabina stared into the ruby contents of her goblet and said nothing.

He said tentatively, "If I spoke out of turn, I beg your—"

"Stop," she interjected. Meeting his eyes, she said quietly, "You will be missed, Massimo."

***

Lorenzo went off on another campaign and his absence, combined with lack of sunshine, made for a bleak winter. There would be no Christmas banquet at the Palazzo Medici to foster good cheer. People went about their business with sullen expressions, wincing against the gusts of cold wind.

Sabina decided to spend a quiet Christmas in Lucca with her family rather than be alone in Florence. Despite the painful loss of Paolo, they managed to enjoy and comfort each other during the holiday season. In mid-February she received a letter from Cecilia stating that their father was on his deathbed. She departed for Lucca at once.

"Thank God you're here," Cecilia said upon her sister's arrival.

"Where is he?"

Cecilia led her into their father's room where he lay sleeping.

To Sabina's horror, his face was ashen. "What happened?"

"He woke up a few days ago complaining of terrible pain, more than the usual. The fever started yesterday."

"He wasn't like this last month. I left sufficient funds—did you summon the physician?"

"Of course I did," Cecilia replied defensively.

"Why is he not here now?"

"He's on his way."

Sabina sighed. "Forgive me. I'm only thinking of Papa's health."

Cecilia placed an arm around her sister. "I'm worried, too. He sleeps several hours a day due to the pain medication the physician prescribed."

"The thought of losing him so soon after losing Paolo and Tommaso is too much to bear," Sabina said, looking down at her sleeping father.

"I know," Cecilia agreed sadly.

The physician arrived a while later. He was a tall, thin man with a bland face and thinning hair. Sabina took note of his long fingers as he removed powders and leaves from a leather satchel.

"Is he any better today?" he asked.

"The same as yesterday," Cecilia replied.

"I'll make another batch of medicine, which you will mix with his food," he instructed before blending together various herbs.

The physician left with the promise to return the same time tomorrow. Don Antonio woke up while Cecilia was preparing some porridge.

"What a nice surprise," Don Antonio said weakly when he spotted Sabina sitting by the bed. It was a great effort for him to speak.

She took his hand and smiled. "Hello Papa."

"Look at me. Absolutely useless—an old bag of bones."

"Do not say such things," she reprimanded gently. "The best physician in Lucca is taking care of you."

He placed his frail, veined hand over hers. "Sabina, my dear. My only regret is dying so soon after Tommaso and Paolo. You girls have suffered so much already…forgive me."

Cecilia entered the room with a bowl of porridge in her hands. She sat in the vacant chair beside the bed and began spoon-feeding their father. After one mouthful, Don Antonio made a face.

"What's that bitter taste?"

"The medicine the physician instructed me to mix with your food."

Like a child, he pushed the bowl aside. "Good God, woman. You'll kill me before my time. I would prefer some bread."

"I baked some this morning," Cecilia said, rising to her feet.

"And some of that good cheese we purchased at the market. Oh, and do we have any of that fine wine from Sabina's last visit?"

"Papa, I don't think you should be eating such rich foods or drinking undiluted wine," Cecilia pointed out. "The porridge is better for you."

Sabina went into the kitchen and began preparing a tray with the foods her father had requested.

Seeing this, Cecilia asked, "What are you doing?"

She continued scavenging for the best food in the house. "What does it look like I'm doing? Do you have any sausage?"

"He should not be eating these things."

"Papa is *dying*, Cecilia. Let him enjoy a bit of pleasure while he still can. What good will come from eating that foul porridge, anyway? Buy him a few more hours? A day or two? Let him go to his grave satisfied."

Cecilia looked down at the bowl of lumpy, unappealing porridge and placed it on the table. "You're right. Let him eat what he wants to eat. I purchased some sausage with fennel the other day. He loves that. Oh, we still have olives, too."

Sabina smiled. "Thank you."

Don Antonio eyed the tray his daughters had prepared for him and grinned like a little boy. He savored the simple meal so much that he momentarily forgot his pain. Cecilia administered the potent medicine, which he consumed without complaint. Later in the evening, as their father slept, the two sisters ate their supper.

Cecilia announced, "I plan to join the convent. It's something I've always wanted to do, and now there's nothing to hold me back."

"I think it would be good for you."

"You should join with me," Cecilia suggested with a straight face.

Sabina almost choked on her wine and her sister laughed. It was the first time she had cracked a smile since the death of her son.

Cecilia grew serious. "I think of Paolo every moment of every day."

"I miss him, too."

"If I dedicate my life to God, it will bring me closer to my son. I know he's in Heaven right now. I'll most likely sell the villa, too."

"I love this house. It's been in the family for years. We've already lost the palazzo in the city, thanks to grandfather's gambling. Let's not lose the country villa as well."

"Who will tend to it? What about the olive groves?"

"I will hire servants. We can sell the produce if you wish. I have more than enough money for us to live quite comfortably—more than I know what to do with! Perhaps we should donate the crops to the poor."

"Or to the convent I plan to join," Cecilia suggested.

"That's a very good idea."

Suddenly, Don Antonio screamed. Sabina and Cecilia ran to their father's side to see him clutching his abdomen and groaning in pain.

"I felt something burst!" he managed to say between moans.

"I'll fetch the physician," Cecilia said, darting out of the room.

Sabina procured a damp cloth and placed it on her father's forehead.

"The pain medicine," he muttered between clenched teeth.

She found the small pot containing the ground-up herbs and sprinkled some into a cup of watered wine.

"Drink, Papa," she urged, holding the vessel to his lips.

Some of the liquid dribbled down his chin, but he managed to drink most of it. The pain subsided enough for him to breathe easier.

"Tonight, I die," he whispered.

Taking hold of his hand, Sabina said, "Be strong, Papa. Cecilia went to fetch the physician."

He struggled to keep his eyes open, the potent herbs making him drowsy.

"Papa? Papa!" Sabina gently shook him. "Wake up!"

Cecilia arrived a half hour later with the physician, who removed implements and herbs from his satchel.

"He said he felt something burst from within," Sabina informed him. "I gave him some of the pain medicine."

He nodded and gently pushed her aside in order to tend to his patient. "It's best if you and your sister remain in the kitchen."

Alarmed, Cecilia asked, "Why?"

"I need to cut him open," he replied. "Fetch me some water, clean cloths, and a bucket."

"Cut him open?" Sabina demanded as Cecilia procured the requested items. "He's already in immense pain—"

"I'll administer another potent dose."

Sabina reluctantly left the room and closed the door. The two women paced back and forth in the small kitchen for what seemed like eternity. When the physician emerged, his face was grim.

"How is he?" Sabina asked.

"I have done all I could."

Impatient, Sabina pushed past him and froze. The bed was soaked with blood and a bloody bandage was wrapped around Don Antonio's lower abdomen. Her poor father was unconscious. Several engorged leeches squirmed around in a jar. The water in the bowl that held the physician's instruments was dark pink.

"Papa, can you hear me?" Cecilia asked.

Sabina glared at the physician. "What have you done?"

"Your father is in God's hands now," he replied.

"God be damned, you butcher!"

Cecilia gasped. "Sabina! My sister is upset. She didn't mean

121

that."

Sabina clenched her teeth. "I most certainly meant it. Get out!"

The physician shook his head and left.

"What's wrong with you?" Cecilia demanded. "He did his best."

Sabina ignored her. "Papa? Can you hear me?"

Don Antonio did not respond. Long after the physician went home, the two sisters remained by their father's side. He opened his eyes once and smiled faintly at each one of them. By early dawn, he was dead. He was buried beside his beloved wife. Sabina returned to Florence one week following the funeral and Cecilia joined the Convento di Santa Lucia.

***

In the spring of 1479, one of Tommaso's solicitors came to Sabina with a proposal. The head of a noble Florentine family wanted to purchase the Palazzo Caravelli as a wedding gift for his son.

Sabina's brow creased. "Sell Tommaso's home?"

"It's your home now, Signora Sabina, to do with as you please." The solicitor spread his arms wide. "Besides, this palazzo is too big for only one woman—unless, of course, you plan to remarry soon."

"I have neither suitors nor intention at present."

"He's offered a high price. If you choose to sell, you could purchase a home more suitable for a young widow. A bit smaller and closer to the city center, perhaps. You would have a considerable amount of money left over, and I would be happy to advise you on investments."

"I will think on it."

Sabina thought it over for a few days and decided to take the solicitor's advice. He was right, she didn't need all that space. She sought the help of her friend, Camelia, to find a suitable new home.

One morning, as she and Camelia walked along the Arno River, the older woman said, "The intense heat of summer will be upon us soon. We are only in May and it's already too warm.

You would do well to buy a villa in the hills, where it's cooler. What about Fiesole?"

"I spent most of my life living on the outskirts of Lucca. While the countryside is pleasant, I find it dull at times."

"Ah, you're young and need excitement. What about living by the river? There's always a breeze near water."

Sabina's eyes traveled to the oldest bridge in the city, the Ponte Vecchio. Several butcher shops spanned the length of the bridge, and animal entrails were unceremoniously dumped into the river on a daily basis. In the stifling heat of summer, the stench of rotting offal would be unbearable.

"I would prefer to live closer to the Piazza del Duomo. Isn't that where you live, too?"

"Yes, Adolfo and I enjoy the area." Her eyes lit up and she exclaimed, "I know someone who is selling a wonderful home only a stone's throw from the cathedral. Why didn't I think of it sooner?"

"Is it a good house?"

"Oh, it would be perfect for you, Sabina. It has a charming little courtyard with a fountain and a spacious main floor for entertaining. It's not too big—a splendid palazzina. Would you care to see it?"

"Very much so."

"Come. No sense in wasting time, is there?"

"Perhaps I should send a servant to make an appointment."

"Nonsense. I know Signora Berta well. There's no need for formalities."

"But she will not be expecting us."

"Signora Berta is recently widowed and rarely receives visitors. She'll be thrilled to have someone to talk with." Camelia nodded in greeting to a passing lady before adding, "Poor old dear has taken ill, so she's going to live with her daughter."

They walked along the river then turned down a narrow alley leading to the Piazza della Signoria. As they crossed the large square, Sabina shuddered at the memory of the hanging corpses swaying in the breeze last spring. The eyes of the two armed guards accompanying them darted left and right. They reached the Piazza del Duomo and skirted the cathedral until Camelia stopped in front of a small palazzo.

"Here it is," she announced.

Sabina took in the arched oak door with black iron hinges. The pediment over the door sported three playful gargoyles.

Camelia took hold of the iron knocker in the form of a lion's head with a ring in its mouth and banged it against the door with considerable force. "Signora Berta!" She paused. "She's a bit hard of hearing."

Nothing.

Camelia knocked and called out again. Finally, a young girl opened the small viewing door located above the knocker. "Yes?"

"Tell Signora Berta that Signora Camelia is here with a friend."

The oak door swung open. The young girl's hands were red and wet.

"I've brought a prospective buyer to see the house," Camelia explained.

The girl curtsied respectfully and invited them inside. They walked into a spacious courtyard featuring a whimsical fountain at its center; a nymph coyly turning her face away from an amorous satyr. Two stone benches had been placed under the shade of carefully pruned fruit trees. A shriveled old woman sat on one of the benches eating an orange.

Camelia said loudly, "Buongiorno, Signora Berta!"

The old woman peered upward while putting an orange wedge in her mouth, and some of the fruit's juice ran down her wrinkled chin. She did not seem to recognize Camelia.

"Do you remember me? I made you that lovely torta with apples and pine nuts," Camelia said, trying to jostle the old woman's memory.

A flicker of recognition registered in Signora Berta's eyes and she smiled. "You tried to fatten me up with that rich cake!"

Camelia turned and motioned for Sabina to come closer. "I want you to meet my friend, Signora Sabina Rossi."

The old woman looked at Sabina, pointed to Camelia, and said, "She wants me to be fat like her."

Sabina stifled a giggle. Camelia frowned slightly and said, "She is interested in taking a look at your house."

"Look!" Signora Berta exclaimed as she held out the partially eaten orange. "Oranges in May! Can you believe it? My daughter's gardener grows them indoors. Would you like some?"

"No, thank you," Sabina said.

The old woman looked extremely disappointed that her oranges were being rejected.

"We will try them next time, dear. I promise," Camelia assured. "Signora Sabina wishes to buy a house."

Cupping her hand around her ear, Signora Berta cried, "What?"

"SHE WISHES TO BUY A HOUSE!"

"Ah…I see. She should find a husband and make him buy her a house," Signora Berta said then cackled hoarsely.

"I'm recently widowed," Sabina explained.

The old woman crossed herself. "Forgive me, Signora. I'll have Gloria show you around. Gloria! Where are you? That good-for-nothing girl. Where is she? Always has her head in the clouds, that one."

The girl with the red, wet hands crept into the courtyard.

"There you are!" Signora Berta exclaimed. "Show these ladies inside—and take off that dirty apron!"

Gloria led them up a flight of stairs to the main floor. It was spacious with many windows to allow in natural sunlight, and there was a big library that could house the books she had inherited from Tommaso.

Massimo would like this house. Sabina froze mid-step at the thought.

"Would you like to see upstairs?" Gloria asked.

"Of course we would, you daft child," Camelia replied. "Would you buy a house without seeing it top to bottom?"

Gloria showed them the upstairs bedchambers and a private sitting area that looked down into the courtyard.

"What do you think?" Camelia asked of Sabina.

"It's perfect. I'll make Signora Berta an offer. Thank you, Camelia."

Camelia grinned and they hurried outside to speak with Signora Berta, who agreed to a fair price. Sabina realized this was the first major purchase she had ever made in her life. She was pleasantly overcome by the power of her wealth, but more importantly, her newfound independence.

"A new house for a new life," Camelia commented as they left the palazzo "And perhaps a new love...?"

"What do you mean?"

"A beautiful rich widow like yourself will not be left alone for long." Sabina said nothing and Camelia added, "Have you not noticed the eligible men of Florence circling you like ravenous vultures?"

"I've noticed no such thing."

"Open your eyes, my dear girl. The men are being cautious because of who your husband was and who your protector is. When the time is right, they'll swoop in on you."

"Stop," Sabina said, smiling.

"I know you were fond of Tommaso—we all were—but what are you going to do now that he's gone? Sit in your room and knit for the rest of your life? Trust me, if the roles were reversed, Tommaso would not hesitate to remarry or, at the very least, take on a lover. Men are like that. Their needs must be met."

"But it's been such a short time."

"It's been over a year."

Sabina sighed. "Maybe you're right."

"I'm rarely wrong," Camelia boasted. "How old are you, anyway?""

"I turned twenty last October."

"An old maid," Camelia teased.

"Really?"

"I merely jest! Sabina, your life has not even begun. You're fortunate to have inherited such a great sum of money, but please take my advice: Do not be in a hurry to give it away."

"Give it away? What do you mean?"

"By getting married."

"Oh. I thought you were encouraging me to do just that."

Camelia rolled her eyes. "I'm encouraging you to find love, but I'm also advising you to take your time. You have a great advantage over other women. Your wealth allows you to be selective. There's no need for you to rush into a marriage to give away your money and freedom. With Lorenzo de' Medici as your protector, you may do as you please—as long as you employ caution, of course. Being discreet is imperative in Florentine society. One must appear chaste and avoid scandal."

Sabina pondered the older woman's words.

Camelia sighed. "If only I was as young, beautiful, and rich as you are…"

"Go on," Sabina prompted. "What would you do if you were me?"

Camelia smiled slyly as she peeked over her shoulder at the two guards. "Knowing what I know today, I would discreetly take on a lover, keep my independence, and enjoy my wealth!"

Sabina's mouth gaped open in surprise. "Camelia, I would never have expected such scandalous advice from you!"

Both women burst into laughter as they walked toward the cathedral.

***

Sabina assembled her servants and announced her intention to sell the Palazzo Caravelli. Only a handful of the best servants would follow their mistress to her new home. Although the buyer insisted on purchasing most of the furniture, there was still much work to be done before the move. Tommaso's clothing was sorted and either sold or given to charities. The same was done with his books since there was no room for all of them in her new home. Messer da Bisticci was given first choice and expressed his gratitude with a gift copy of *Le Livre des Trois Vertus*.

The day prior to the move, the solicitor came by with official paperwork requiring her signature. Before handing over the keys, she wandered through the rooms, her memories bittersweet.

Goodbye, my dear Tommaso.

Sabina descended the stairs to where her few servants were ready and waiting to depart. A sturdy horse-drawn cart was piled high with her belongings. She took one last look at the Palazzo Caravelli before locking the gate and handing the keys to the solicitor.

One chapter of her life was over and another was about to begin.

CHAPTER 11

Sabina was enchanted with her new home. One of the first things she did was plant a garden full of her favorite herbs. She decorated the walls with tapestries, and even commissioned a painting from one of Lorenzo's protégées. She made it a regular habit to buy fresh flowers in the market and display them in vases throughout the house. Bit by bit, she filled her home with items she loved, and soon it became a special place; her refuge.

When the flowers were in full bloom, her desire to write outdoors compelled her to procure a small wooden desk and a chair. She placed them in the courtyard under the portico, which afforded her a view of the fountain. Her days were long and quiet, but fulfilling. She read and wrote, and even tried her hand at tatting. Camelia came over frequently when her husband was away, which provided some merriment in her otherwise solitary life.

Sabina sat outside scribbling a short story on a sunny June day when someone knocked on the door. Teresa, who was seated in the garden reading, went to open the tiny viewing door to see who it was.

A moment later she came back and said, "Signore Massimo is here."

Sabina set down her quill. The last time she saw Massimo was seven months ago at the Palazzo Medici. It was unconventional for a man to visit a woman's home, but inviting him inside could incur rumors. "Show him in and have one of the servants fetch some refreshment." Looking down in dismay at her ink-stained fingers, she said, "I need to clean my hands."

She ran inside, scrubbed her hands clean, then stared at her reflection in the looking glass. Pinching her cheeks to give them some color, she slowed her breathing, then calmly walked outside. Massimo sat on one of the stone benches accepting a goblet of wine from a servant girl.

"Massimo, what a pleasant surprise."

He set down the wine and stood. "Sabina."

"When did you arrive in Florence?"

He reached for her hand and kissed it. "Last night. Forgive my intrusion. It's been too long…I simply had to come."

She withdrew her hand and dismissed the servant with a look.

"I've thought of you often," he confessed, his eyes sweeping over the parchment-strewn desk and quills. "I've disturbed your writing."

"It's only some notes."

"So, this is your new home."

"Yes. How did you know where I lived?"

"*Everyone* knows where Sabina Rossi lives." He paused, smiling. "It's charming. Do you like it?"

"I love it."

"Do you not miss the grandeur of the Palazzo Caravelli?"

"Sometimes, but this is more fitting for me. Would you like to see the rest of it?" she asked, indicating the open door that led inside.

Massimo nodded and she felt self-conscious as he followed her upstairs to the main floor. She showed him around, pointing out various works of art, and he seemed genuinely interested in everything she had to say. He picked up the blue journal on the desk in her study.

"What a finely bound book," he commented.

"It was a gift from Lorenzo. I filled the pages of my other journal, so he had this one made for me."

He frowned slightly. "How generous of him. Have you filled these pages, too?"

"Almost."

"Do you mind if I take a peek?"

Normally, Sabina would have been reluctant to honor such a request. For some reason, she trusted Massimo. *Implicitly*. "If it pleases you."

He turned the first few pages and read aloud, " 'and there began her uncertain journey to the edge of night, where she found sweet solace in the shadows, in the absence of light.' " He stopped, his fingers hovering above the page. "Do you often taste the salt of your own tears, Sabina?"

No one had ever asked her such a direct, personal question. His gaze pierced her soul. Without a word, she gently took the book from him and placed it upon her desk.

He looked stricken. "Forgive me, I did not mean—"

"Stop. There's nothing to forgive."

"I know you've suffered great losses since your arrival to Florence."

"All I have left in this world is my sister," she whispered, willing herself not to cry. "Everyone else is dead."

"You have so many friends who admire and care about you," he pointed out. "I care about you."

She took a deep breath and put on her best smile. "I appreciate your words more than you know."

"Let's talk of happy things," he prompted. "There's been too much sadness in Florence lately, and we need to put it behind us."

She looked out the window and noticed that her well-trained staff had set two chairs and a table by the fountain. "It's past midday. Are you hungry?"

"I had no intention of dining with you."

"Nor I with you, but you're here and the day is lovely, so why not enjoy a meal in each other's company?"

"You have not shown me your bedchamber," he countered softly.

In an attempt to maintain a sliver of propriety, she avoided showing him the most intimate room in her home. "It's the last door on the right."

Massimo walked into the largest of the bedchambers. There were two big windows with shutters thrown open to reveal a sea of terracotta rooftops and the shimmering Arno River beyond. The scents of roses and lilacs wafted up from the courtyard below. Sabina's bed was big and comfortable, hung with green velvet and gold-patterned silk. An enormous tapestry depicted a traditional scene of a maiden with a lion at her feet and a

131

unicorn in the background.

"I feel like the lion," he said, pointing to the tapestry.

"Why?"

"Because I'm at your mercy, my lady."

Sabina's heart raced but she said nothing.

Massimo walked to the window and jumped back when a black crow landed on the sill and snapped at him.

"No, Mendi!" Sabina admonished. The bird flew into the room and landed on her shoulder. "Sorry. He tends to be possessive about his territory. I'm afraid it's my fault for spoiling him."

He stared at the crow in astonishment. "You have a crow as a pet?"

"Oh, for quite some time now."

"Does he ever bite you?"

"Never. It's my hand that feeds him. Is that not so, Mendi?" she cooed to the ominous bird.

Massimo was oddly intrigued. "Do you own an owl as well?"

"An owl? No, why?"

"It just seems fitting...if you have a crow, why not an owl?"

"Next you'll ask if I own a black cat."

"I assume you do."

She shook her head. "Mendi actually chose me."

The crow gave a loud caw at the sound of its name.

He eyed her intently. "You're an interesting woman, Sabina."

"Interesting is a polite way to describe unusual," she accused playfully.

"Perhaps mysterious would please you?"

"Perhaps." There was an awkward silence and she felt the intensity of his presence in her bedchamber. "Let's take some refreshment downstairs."

Rather than accept Sabina's suggestion, Massimo stepped closer and casually waved Mendi off her shoulder.

"How I missed your face," he whispered while caressing her cheek.

She held her breath, standing very still as he bent his head and softly kissed her lips. The kiss did not remain soft for long as they finally gave in to their pent-up passion. A dozen thoughts ran through her head in that blissful moment; Camelia's advice among them.

Kissing her urgently, Massimo carried Sabina to the bed. She made no attempt to stop him. Why should she? Tommaso was dead. She had mourned a respectful period and was free to love again if she chose. Yet, there was a pang of uncertainty in her heart. His hands caressed her back and neck and she moaned softly, giving in to the pleasure of his touch. She decided to cast aside her doubts and enjoy the moment. Did Camelia not advise her to take on a lover as long as she was discreet? Did she not deserve to be loved and to love in return? Had she not secretly desired Massimo since the day they first met?

Yes, yes, and yes.

With firm resolve, she allowed him to untie the laces of her bodice. His tongue sought the sweetness of her mouth as she unfastened the clasp of his cloak. They undressed eagerly.

"I've wanted you since the moment I met you," he confessed as he nuzzled her neck and inhaled the fragrance of her skin.

"As have I," she admitted into his ear as he held her close.

Sabina surrendered to the lovemaking, meeting his passion with her own. They looked into each other's eyes with intense wonderment when it was over. After a few more languid kisses and caresses, she sat up and noticed that the sun was casting long shadows on the floor. They had lost track of time during their passionate tryst, and neither of them was sorry for it.

Massimo's eyes were pleading. "Please let me come see you tomorrow."

Sabina nodded in consent and snuggled into his warm embrace.

Massimo visited Sabina on a daily basis. Their hunger and need for each other was overwhelming. When not wrapped in each other's arms, they talked for hours about anything and everything. To their mutual delight, they shared many interests.

Sabina studied Massimo's handsome features in the

133

candlelight one night after he had fallen asleep. He was perfect—*perhaps too perfect*—and for the first time she felt something sinister lurking beneath the surface of her newfound joy. A premonition? She ignored the nagging doubt. Throwing caution to the wind, she fell headfirst into the blissful arms of love.

***

Lorenzo returned to Florence after a successful campaign in the South. There were other enemies to convert and his work was far from over, but he decided to celebrate the small victory with a summer fête. Massimo was forced to leave Sabina's bed early on the day of the Medici party.

"Stay a bit longer," she pleaded.

"I promised Clarice that I would help her with the music selection. The minstrels will arrive this morning to practice," he replied, kissing the tip of her nose. "Besides, she nags me enough as it is."

"Does she? About what?"

"Clarice is no fool. She begs to know the identity of the lady claiming my attention."

"What do you tell her?"

He sat up in bed. "I tell her I'm out with friends."

She pulled him back down. "Drinking, gambling, and whoring?"

"Something like that. Don't pout, dolcezza, I would scream your name from the rooftops if I could, but your reputation is at stake." He kissed her deeply then added, "We must be discreet tonight."

He was right. Their relationship had to remain secret to prevent gossip and scandal. Lorenzo was Sabina's protector and Massimo was Clarice's cousin; neither wanted to risk Medici displeasure.

She wrapped her arms around him. "Make love to me before you go."

"How can I refuse such a sweet request?"

Their lovemaking was brief and intense. Sabina stretched languidly and remained in bed after he departed.

"Love is a natural cosmetic," Teresa observed, entering the room with a pile of laundered linens. "Your skin glows and your eyes are bright, Signora Sabina. Which gown shall you wear tonight?"

"The light blue silk."

Later, Sabina set out into the sultry evening looking fresh and cool in the azure gown. Accompanied by her guard, they walked the short distance to the Palazzo Medici. The outside torches burned brightly against the violet twilight sky. Inside the courtyard, a riot of colorful potted flowers delighted the guests. Lorenzo decided to pay homage to Bacchus by filtering wine into the statue of Judith and Holofernes. Some of the guests were already filling their goblets with the "blood" and becoming inebriated by the ruby elixir.

Lorenzo materialized before her and inquired, "Sabina. How are you enjoying your new home?"

She offered him a heartfelt smile. "I'm enjoying it very much, thank you. You'll have to make time to visit me someday."

"I may accept your invitation."

"I hope you do. You've been missed, Lorenzo," she confessed. "Congratulations on your recent victory, and welcome home."

"The victory is insignificant compared to the losses we've suffered."

"Yes, but things will soon change for the better."

"Will they? Look around you. Everything is different now." His eyes swept over the many guests making merry around them. "I'm not the same man, Sabina. Florence is not the same city."

"I know."

"Times are changing. The people, their ideals—*everything* is changing right before our very eyes." He sighed tiredly. "I wish my brother was here with me now."

"We all miss Giuliano."

"I've thought about that dreadful day many times over," he whispered fiercely. "I wonder what I could have done differently to prevent his death."

Lorenzo was under tremendous stress and his guilty conscience only wore him down further. Sabina leaned forward and tenderly kissed his cheek, making him look at her in surprise.

"I see you torture yourself over Giuliano's death and it breaks my heart. There's nothing you could have done to prevent it." She boldly reached for his hand. "You granted me access to your library, now let me return the favor. My new home is humble, but there's a delightful little courtyard with a fountain. It's blissfully quiet and peaceful but, more importantly, it's private. I can hide from the world and forget my troubles there—so can you. Whenever you want to. I'll make a copy of the key to the gate for you."

Lorenzo was intrigued, and her invitation was tempting. Sabina was maturing into the type of woman who could cast a spell upon a man and have him eating out of the palm of her hand before he even realized it. He grasped her hand suddenly. "Come."

She almost stumbled over one of the peacocks roaming throughout the courtyard as he tugged her forward. Several eyes followed them, including Angelina Bardi's.

Sabina whispered, "Where are we going?"

Lorenzo did not reply. He led her through a maze of hallways until they stood by the door of his library. "What do you think of me?"

She was taken aback. "What do you mean?"

Lorenzo gripped her shoulders and his dark eyes searched her face with such intensity that she instinctively pulled away. "As a man, Sabina. Am I a heathen for what I've done?"

She saw the pain in his eyes, heard the desperation in his voice. "For incurring the Vatican's disapproval?"

He nodded curtly and fumbled for the key to unlock the door. "Ah, yes, the excommunication from the pope," he muttered, shaking his head in disgust as they entered the small space. "He's scheming against me as we speak."

"The church leaders of Tuscany are still on your side," she

pointed out as he closed the door behind them. "They said you had every right to avenge Giuliano and bring his murderers to justice. The pope's decision was wrong. He's no man of God as far as I'm concerned."

For a woman to say such a thing was not only improper, it was dangerous. The fact that Sabina spoke her mind only deepened Lorenzo's trust. "I'm not concerned with Holy Mother Church or the pope," he said. "I'm concerned about *me*, about being a good man…I'm concerned for my immortal soul."

With so much blood on his hands, it was no surprise his conscience felt heavy. *He should be speaking with a priest, not me.* "Why would you ask me such a question, Lorenzo? I'm only a woman."

"A woman who thinks like a man. A woman who was married to one of my oldest and dearest friends; he was like a father to me. Tommaso trusted you and so do I."

"But still only a woman," she reasoned. "I'm in no position to—"

"You're perceptive, intelligent, and honest…I've grown fond of you, Sabina, and I value your opinion."

"Perhaps a priest would be—"

He cut her off again, and this time his eyes blazed. "Am I a monster?"

Dressed in somber black with his dark hair neatly combed back from his forehead, he looked formidable yet elegant. The dark shadows under his eyes betrayed restless nights; a tortured soul. As intimidating as he could be, as feared as he was by many, in that instant, Lorenzo de' Medici was as fragile as a little boy.

Gently placing her palm against his cheek, she said, "You are no monster, Lorenzo. Banish the thought from your head immediately."

Hearing her words, he clasped her wrist and held her hand in place. "You speak as my friend."

"I speak the truth. Do you not remember how the people shouted your name in the streets on that dark day? Is it not

137

obvious they love you? We all love you. Surely, that brings you some measure of comfort?"

"The people would love you, too, if you entertained them and fed them the way I have all these years."

"It's more than that, and you know it. Look at everything you've done for Florence—the art, the schools, the orphanages, the public feasts. You're a generous patron who has brought honor and glory to this city. The people love you because you're a remarkable man and a wise ruler. What you did to the Pazzi and the other traitors was unpleasant—bestial even—but necessary."

"Some say that I went too far."

"They murdered your innocent brother in cold blood during Easter Mass. They committed sacrilege on top of mortal sin." She added icily, "They *deserved* to die."

Lorenzo was stunned by her vehemence and loyalty to him. "They would have killed me were it not for you."

"I thank God every day for sparing your life."

He studied her intently with an expression she could not discern. Suddenly, he pushed her against a bookcase and kissed her, forcing his tongue into her mouth. Overwhelmed by his ferocity and the spicy scent of his skin, Sabina was momentarily swept up in the madness. His hand slid down her back, pulling her tightly against him.

She felt him harden against her thigh and whispered, "Lorenzo…"

He stepped back abruptly, his breathing ragged, his eyes unusually bright. They stared at one another in shocked surprise.

Placing both hands against his chest, she stammered, "I…I think it's best—I should get back."

"Yes, you should," he agreed huskily. When she hesitated, he added, "You should go *now*."

Sabina fled the library and almost ran into Angelina in the hallway. Her curls bobbed up and down as she stopped short to avoid collision. She looked from Sabina to Lorenzo, then to Sabina's mouth.

"Angelina, my dear," Lorenzo said from inside the library. "Come and see my new book."

"You bitch," Angelina said to Sabina before walking into the library and closing the door.

Stunned, Sabina stood in the hallway. A moment later, the unmistakable sounds of kissing and moaning came through the door. Leaning against the wall, she pressed her fingers to her throbbing lips. She could still feel Lorenzo's kiss, taste his mouth…

She walked away quickly, her mind reeling.

Massimo spotted Sabina as she entered the main hall, and pretended to greet her formally. "Where were you?"

She smiled. "I was with Lorenzo."

He brought her knuckles to his lips. "He's in love with you."

"Don't be ridiculous."

"I'm serious. He mentions your name far too many times for my taste—and my cousin's, for that matter."

"Does he really mention me often?"

"Yes." His eyebrow shot upward. "Does that please you?"

"Your jealousy is rather charming."

He discreetly placed his lips to her ear. "Oh, the things I would do to you right now…I can't blame Lorenzo if he's in love with you. After all, what chance does a mortal man have against a goddess?"

She laughed at his outrageous flattery.

He continued, "Accompany me to the garden. The sky is filled with shining stars and the full moon is rising."

"Do you think it wise? People will talk if we wander off alone."

"On a night as magical as this, who can resist temptation?"

A peacock strutted past them. "Oh, look!"

"I gave Clarice the idea for the peacocks, you know."

"They're splendid."

"Yet they pale in comparison to your beauty and charm."

"Please, Massimo, we must be discreet."

"Come to the garden. I'll take you into a dark corner and—
"

"Sabina!" Camelia exclaimed. They both turned their heads. "Hello, Massimo, what a surprise to see you here."

Sabina happily embraced her friend. Massimo tried to hide his disappointment as he bowed over the older woman's hand.

Camelia looked from Sabina to Massimo with a knowing grin. "Was I interrupting anything?"

"Not at all," Sabina replied smoothly. "How are you?"

"Fine, aside from the normal aches and pains of old age. I wanted to tell you about Signora Berta's daughter. Apparently, she caught her husband—"

Signore Adolfo appeared at his wife's side and, after inclining his head at Sabina and Massimo, said, "The podestà's wife wishes to have a word with you, my dear."

Camelia placed her hand on Sabina's arm. "I'll speak to you in a bit."

"Camelia loves to gossip, doesn't she?" Massimo said when they were alone again. "Let's go outside."

"Men gossip, too." Sabina said, following him into the garden.

They strolled the pebbled path and he led her into a shadowy corner where they were hidden by fruit trees and flower bushes. There, he plundered her mouth and fondled her breast.

"I'm coming home with you tonight," he said between kisses.

"Someone is going to see us," she whispered, pulling away.

"Stop worrying. No one is around."

She stiffened in his embrace and he sighed in frustration. They walked nonchalantly toward the courtyard where three old women had gathered to gossip. They looked at Massimo and Sabina suspiciously before delving back into their conversation. The minstrels played gaily as some of the guests participated in a lively dance. Servants carried out trays filled with sweetmeats and a variety of delicacies, then set them on long tables.

"Wait here, dearest, while I get us some wine," Massimo said.

Sabina watched his broad shoulders cut through the throng of guests. She heard the tinkling sound of Angelina's laughter and spotted her by the tables. Apparently, her tryst with Lorenzo had been brief. Massimo picked up two goblets of wine and Angelina beckoned him to lean closer so that she could whisper in his ear.

Accepting a glass goblet from him a moment later, Sabina demanded, "What was that all about?"

"What?"

"Angelina Bardi whispered in your ear."

He feigned shock. "Sabina Rossi, are you jealous?"

"The correct word is curious."

"She made a few banal comments about the evening's entertainment. Nothing to worry your pretty head over."

One of Massimo's acquaintances stopped to greet him. As the two men chatted, Sabina took a sip of the wine. It tasted bitter, but she was thirsty and took another swallow. This time, the bitterness was enough to make her recoil in disgust. She handed the half-empty goblet to a passing servant and put a hand to her forehead.

Noticing this, Massimo inquired, "Are you all right?"

"I think I drank the wine too quickly. It tasted bitter."

"Lorenzo de' Medici serve bad wine? Never!"

"You have a good…point," she said breathlessly.

"It could be a combination of the excitement and the heat."

"Yes," she agreed, her voice sounding far-off to her own ears.

"You look terribly pale."

A buzzing sound filled her ears and she swayed from dizziness. Her limbs became heavy as lead and she felt suddenly queasy. She caught Lorenzo's eye from across the room. His face registered worry and fear as he excused himself from a group of men.

Massimo took a step closer. "Sabina?"

She staggered against him, causing the goblet in his hand to fall and shatter against the tiled floor. "I think I'm going to be ill."

The last thing Sabina saw before everything went black was Lorenzo running toward her. As her knees buckled and gave way, he scooped her up effortlessly in his arms.

Ascending the stairs, Lorenzo shouted, "Summon my physician!"

Sabina awoke in a strange bedroom where two female servants fretted over her. She tried to lean on her elbow, retched, and vomited violently in the wooden bucket one of the girls placed below her chin. The taste in her mouth was vile. Her stomach was in pain and she was drenched with perspiration. Black spittle pooled on her lower lip.

"Where…am…"

"Do not speak, Signora. Save your strength. Signore Lorenzo's physician has arrived," said the girl holding the bucket.

Sabina heard the voices of Massimo and Lorenzo outside the closed door. The room spun out of control and she closed her eyes tightly to stop the nausea. The door creaked open. A distinguished older man peered down at her and frowned when he noticed that her tongue and teeth were black.

"Who told you to administer charcoal?"

"Signore Lorenzo did," replied one of the girls. "We mixed it with water and forced it down her throat."

"Has she been vomiting since then?"

"Yes."

"Let me see that bucket."

The girl handed him the bucket, and he covered his nose with a linen handkerchief as he looked inside. "Hmmm," he said. "Did you drink wine before fainting, Signora?"

Sabina replied in a weak voice, "Yes."

"Did you eat anything?"

She shook her head.

"Lay back."

She obeyed and he proceeded to gently press various points of her abdomen with his fingers. When she flinched in pain, he asked, "Did the wine taste bitter?"

She nodded feebly.

He leaned closer. "I regret to tell you this, but you've been poisoned. Thankfully, Signore Lorenzo acted wisely and in a timely manner. The charcoal has expelled most of the toxin from your body."

Poisoned? Sabina could only stare at him in disbelief.

"Signore Lorenzo insists that you spend the night where you'll be under constant supervision. I'm going to administer a remedy to soothe your stomach and help you sleep."

The physician made her swallow a strange tasting serum that made her want to retch again, then thanked him.

"Do not let anyone else come in," Sabina whispered to the girl after the physician had departed.

***

Massimo, Camelia, and Lorenzo were waiting in the hallway to bombard the physician with questions.

"She is young and strong." Looking at Lorenzo, the physician added, "The charcoal was administered in time to rid her body of the poison."

Camelia's eyes were wide. "Poison?" she repeated. "Surely, you're mistaken. Who would want to poison our Sabina? That sweet girl!"

Lorenzo grimaced. At first he thought it was a second assassination plot; that the wine had been meant for him. He quickly ruled out that possibility since everyone knew he rarely ate anything that had not first passed the lips of his food-taster. Someone had deliberately attempted to kill Sabina—and he had a good idea of who it was and why.

"Does anyone know how this happened?" the physician asked.

"I'm not sure," Massimo said. "I fetched two goblets of wine from the table and Sabina complained of the taste."

"Did your wine taste bitter?" Camelia asked him.

"Not at all."

"Sabina needs rest. I'll send word when she's fully recovered," Lorenzo said dismissively. "For her safety's sake, it's best to keep this matter between us. If anyone inquires, simply tell them she fainted from heat exhaustion and is now resting."

"Yes, of course." Camelia said, turning to go.

143

Massimo nodded in agreement but remained rooted to the spot. His obvious reluctance to leave struck Lorenzo as odd.

Camelia tugged on his arm. "Would you accompany me, Massimo?"

"With pleasure," he replied, nodding to Lorenzo before leading the older woman downstairs.

Sabina felt groggy the following morning. "What time is it?"

"Almost midday," replied the girl who held the bucket last night.

"I would like some water, please."

She poured water into a cup. "Here. Shall I fetch some broth?"

Sabina sipped the water before nodding. Her stomach felt so empty that it hurt. The girl sent her companion to the kitchen.

She then proceeded to help Sabina wash. "Signore Lorenzo wishes to speak with you as soon as you're ready to receive him."

The other girl eventually returned carrying a tray laden with bread, beef broth, and fruit. Sabina ate ravenously. When she was finished, she looked down at her dress. In addition to being completely wrinkled from having been slept in, there was dried vomit on the bodice.

The girl smiled reassuringly. "One of Signora Clarice's ladies is about your size."

"Thank you," Sabina said in relief.

After the servants had combed Sabina's hair and helped her into a fresh gown, she was ready to see Lorenzo.

"How are you feeling?" he asked as soon as he entered the room.

"Was I really poisoned?"

His expression was grim as he nodded slowly in response.

She frowned. "My God, who would do such a thing? I've no enemies—at least none that I'm aware of."

"You should leave Florence," he said quietly.

"You can't be serious, Lorenzo. I recently purchased a home."

"Not permanently, of course. Only for a few weeks."

144

"Why would I do that?"

"For your own safety."

"There's no safer place for me to be than here in Florence under your protection," she pointed out, baffled.

He smiled wryly and caressed her cheek. "I can protect you from many things, my dear, but I'm powerless against the envy of other women."

"That's ridiculous!"

"Not to a woman who is obsessed."

"Obsessed with whom? You?"

"It's no secret that I have mistresses. Unfortunately, some of them are extremely jealous of anyone who claims my affection or attention."

Sabina eyed him knowingly. "Angelina."

Lorenzo sighed and spread out his hands. "She denies it completely, claiming that you're one of her friends," he said, but his tone betrayed a lack of conviction.

"That spoiled, stupid girl!"

"Don't underestimate her capabilities. She failed in her attempt but could easily hire someone to kill you. It's best if you go."

Her head throbbed. "Can't you restrain her?"

"Sabina…"

"I should go to the Signoria and accuse her of attempted murder!"

"Angelina would deny the accusation. Besides, you have no proof. Her father is a wealthy man with important political ties. Allowing you to accuse his daughter of such a crime would be a great dishonor to his family. I cannot risk losing any allies right now."

"But, Lorenzo—"

"You must do as I say. It's only for a brief period, I promise," he said, wiping away her tears with his finger. "I would never forgive myself if a second attempt on your life achieved the desired results."

Oh, how she hated her new enemy, Angelina Bardi!

"Why not visit your sister?" he suggested.

Although she dreaded the thought of spending time in a dreary convent, she nodded for the sake of argument.

"Good girl," he said, giving her hand a squeeze. "My men will escort you home and you can prepare for your departure."

"You want me to leave now?"

"The sooner, the better."

Lorenzo embraced Sabina and gave her lips a quick kiss before leaving the room. As promised, four of his armed guards were waiting in the courtyard. Looking over her shoulder, she thought she saw Angelina in the window.

Massimo was already waiting for her when she arrived home. "Dearest," he said, taking her in his arms. "I've been up all night, sick with worry!"

"There's something I must tell you."

"You're weak and need rest. Let me help you to your room," he said, leading her toward the stairs.

"Lorenzo believes I was poisoned by one of his jealous mistresses."

Massimo paused, mid-step. "Which one?"

Sabina shook her head tiredly. "It doesn't matter. He told me to leave Florence for the sake of my safety."

"Where can you be safer than here, under his protection?"

"That's exactly what I said, too. He can fight off an army, but I suppose he cannot protect me against a scheming girl."

"Where will you go?"

"Lorenzo suggested that I visit Cecilia in Lucca."

"I can't imagine you praying beside the pious nuns in a convent."

"I don't have many options. I suppose I could go to Fiesole."

"That's not far enough from Florence for you to be truly safe."

Defeated, she said, "I'll go to Lucca."

They entered the room and she stretched out on the bed fully clothed. Massimo sat beside her. "Why not come to Rome with me?"

She hesitated. "I don't' think that's a good idea."

"Would you rather be in a dull convent?"

She knew he was right, yet running off to Rome with her lover could lead to disastrous consequences.

As if reading her thoughts, he said, "I live in a villa outside the city. No one would even know you were there."

She stared at him dubiously. It was a tempting offer.

He caressed her cheek. "Come with me. I want to care for you."

Sabina gazed into his pleading blue eyes. It would be nice to have a man care for her again the way Tommaso did. "I'll go to Rome."

Pleased, he leaned over and kissed her lips. "I'll leave in the morning and you'll follow a few days later. I'll send my manservant here to fetch you. Don't worry, my love, all will be well."

Massimo left for Rome at dawn, and Sabina informed Teresa of their imminent trip.

"How long do you plan to stay in Rome, Signora?"

"Pack enough gowns for a month—or two."

"Who will accompany you?"

"Only you."

"I have always wanted to see Rome."

"Now you have your chance," Sabina said as she picked up a jewelry box, opened the lid, and inventoried the contents. "Discretion is of the utmost importance."

"No one in this household has ever talked of Signore Massimo's visits. They wouldn't dare betray you."

"Good," Sabina said, handing the jewelry box to Teresa. "Pack this as well. Massimo's manservant will be arriving soon to accompany us."

Sabina was in deep thought throughout the day, still unsure if it was wise to disregard Lorenzo's suggestion of staying with Cecilia. Before going to bed that night, she walked to the open window and gazed up at the sky. Only a thin sliver of a moon was visible, making the night inky black.

I wish I had a sign to let me know I'm doing the right thing.

A loud cry broke the silence. Mendi flew inside to perch on her shoulder.

"Are you my sign?" she asked as she stroked the smooth, black feathers on the crow's head. Mendi replied with a caw. "I bet you want to come to Rome, too. God knows none of the servants want to look after you."

Mendi snapped at her hair, pulling a few strands in his beak. She lovingly reproved her odd pet and placed him in his cage along with some bread.

"Goodnight, Mendi."

Later that night, she tossed and turned in her bed, unable to sleep. When she finally drifted off, she dreamt of her father and Paolo. She awoke with a start and realized that her face was cold and wet from tears.

CHAPTER 12

Leo, Massimo's servant, arrived a few days later. His youthful skin was so smooth and unblemished that it incurred Sabina's envy. Light eyes and wavy blonde hair contributed to his angelic appearance.

Sabina could barely contain her excitement on the morning of her departure. Aside from the one time she accompanied Tommaso to Pisa, the only journeys she had ever made in her life were between Lucca and Florence. The thought of visiting a new destination was thrilling, especially under such romantic circumstances.

As their hired carriage passed under the archway of Porta Romana, she bade Florence a temporary farewell, then sat back as the driver urged the horses down the old Roman road leading south. She took in the beauty of the Tuscan countryside and breathed in deeply. The air was fresh and sweet, and free of the vile odors her nose had grown accustomed to within the city walls. Across from her sat Teresa and Leo, her two companions on this secret rendezvous. The rhythmic motion of the carriage soon lulled the three of them to sleep.

They spent the night at an inn, and arrived in Rome before sunset on the following day. Sabina and Teresa marveled at the Imperial Roman Forum, the Coliseum, and the Pantheon. The piazzas were full of people sporting different hair and clothing styles than the Florentines. The carriage continued through the crowded city center and across the Tiber River, where they saw the magnificent Castello Sant'Angelo. They were soon out of the urban bustle and on a quiet road lined with lush pine trees. The carriage eventually stopped before a gracious villa painted the color of apricots.

Massimo greeted them warmly, then took Sabina aside to kiss her lips. "Come, I have something to show you."

They walked down a side path that sloped into a delightful

lemon grove. In its center was a trellised canopy heavy with fragrant grapes. A small table for two was set underneath the shade of the vineyard.

"I know how much you like to dine outside," he said.

"This is wonderful, Massimo. Thank you."

"I want you to feel at home here." He traced the curve of her neck with his fingertip, making her shiver. "I want to make you happy."

"I've never been happier."

"Yet I sense that you're anxious."

"I've never done anything so….so bold before."

"You'll feel better after a few days. Trust me, my love." He paused. "Would you like to rest or would you prefer to dine first?"

"I'm ravenous," she confessed. "As long as my disheveled appearance doesn't offend you."

"You look as fresh as a rose. Besides, you could wear a beggar's rags and still look elegant. Here, sit down," he said as he pulled out a chair.

They dined on stewed hare with freshly baked bread, crisp greens, and fine wine. Afterward, they toured the grounds and the private walled courtyard adjacent to the villa. A large marble fountain boasting a life-size statue of a mythological pan playing a flute made an impressive centerpiece to the space. Well-tended flowers grew along the walls and the soft buzz of insects blended with the bubbling sound of the fountain's water.

"This is such a splendid villa," Sabina commented. "Did you have it designed to your specifications or did you procure it as is?"

A shadow crossed his face. "I inherited it. Let me show you inside."

She followed him from room to room, commenting on the finely painted frescoes on the walls and ceilings. "Do you live here year-round, or do you have another home in the city center?"

"This is my only residence. So many questions, Sabina."

"I'm only curious. Forgive me."

"There's nothing to forgive," he said, taking her hands in his and bringing them up to his lips so that he could kiss each one. "While you're here, I want to live each day as though it was our last, full of love and laughter—without a care in the world. What do you think of that?"

She lightly kissed his lips. "I think it's a good plan."

Massimo pulled her in for a deeper kiss before sweeping her into his bedchamber. Once inside, he locked the door and walked toward Sabina with a sly smile. She allowed her lover to ravish her with his mouth and hands. They made love throughout the afternoon and into the evening, not bothering to dress for dinner or care about anything else.

"This is how I wish it to be between us all the time," he said, teasing her earlobe with his teeth.

Nestled in his embrace, she sighed. "Me, too."

"Your skin is like silk," he said sleepily. "Sabina…mia donna."

Her eyes grew heavy and, just before she drifted off to sleep, she thanked God and Fate for her good fortune.

Life was blissful for the next few weeks. They ate, drank, made love, rode horses, took long walks, and talked for hours on end.

By mid-July, Massimo made it clear that he wanted Sabina to stay with him indefinitely. They sat under the shade of a linden tree when he proposed the idea. She refused at first, claiming that she should return to Florence. After several kisses, he managed to change her mind.

One day, a thought struck her: *Why hasn't he proposed marriage?*

While taking a walk with Massimo in the countryside that afternoon, Sabina noticed two children playing in the nearby hills. It was the perfect opportunity to broach the topic of marriage.

"Look at those children playing over there," she said, pointing. "Aren't they darling? Who are they?"

"They belong to a peasant farmer who works the land bordering this property."

151

"I miss my little nephew," she admitted quietly.

"I'm sorry, my love. Someday, God-willing, you'll have children of your own to bring you comfort," he said in an attempt to soothe her.

She snatched the opportunity. "Of course we will."

"We?"

He had repeated the word with such surprise that she stopped walking and faced him. "Who else would I be referring to?"

"Naturally…"

"We would have to get married first."

His face visibly flushed from discomfort. "Sabina, my dearest—"

"You *do* have intentions of marrying me, don't you?"

"I adore you!" he exclaimed passionately. "I love you!"

"But not enough to wed me."

"I never said that. You're upset and jumping to conclusions."

"A moment ago you seemed shocked at the thought of having children with me," she pressed. "Do you not like children?"

"Of course I do. I was surprised, nothing more. Who wouldn't want to marry someone as perfect as you?" he countered. His lips brushed against her cheek, then her lips. "I would be proud to be your husband and the father of your children."

"What if you spoke with Lorenzo? Tell him you wish to officially court me. I've mourned Tommaso's death long enough, and no one would speak ill of a young widow who wishes to remarry."

"I know you hate sneaking around like this—so do I—but now wouldn't be a good time to bring up the topic of courtship. Lorenzo has too much to worry about these days. We should wait a bit longer."

Satisfied that his intention matched her own, she said, "Very well."

***

On a sunny September morning a messenger arrived at the

villa with a letter for Massimo. He and Sabina were in the middle of breaking their fast, so he wiped his fingers clean before reading the penned words.

Seeing his troubled expression, she asked, "Is something wrong?"

"It's nothing for you to worry about." He stood and kissed her lips lightly. "Would you please excuse me?"

"Where are you going?"

"An urgent matter needs my immediate attention."

She stood. "Can I help with anything?"

Pain crept into his eyes. "No, my love. I'm going into my study, but I want you to enjoy the fine morning. I'll see you a bit later."

Massimo walked out of the room and she stared after him, perplexed. Sabina tried to distract herself by playing cards with Teresa in the garden, but it was no use. At midday she went to check on him. The door of his study was locked, but she heard him pacing back and forth. Something was clearly troubling him. Was a family member sick? Was a debt called in early? Had someone threatened him? She lifted her hand to knock on the door and froze. Should she disturb his privacy? She backed away, opting to wait until he was ready to reveal the problem.

Massimo finally emerged several hours later and Sabina greeted him with a kiss. "Would you like to go out for a walk? It's a lovely afternoon and you've spent most of the day indoors."

"Forgive me, but I don't feel well," he replied tiredly. "Take Teresa or Leo with you if you want some company."

There was a film of perspiration on his brow. "Massimo, are you ill?" she asked, touching his forehead. "Tell me what's happened, my love."

He gently removed her hand. "Please, Sabina, give me some time alone for a little while. I need to sort something out."

Massimo walked away and she knew instinctively that something was terribly wrong. The uneasiness she had first felt in Florence resurfaced, and this time she couldn't ignore the ominous premonition. She went out for a long walk, but it did little to relieve her anxiety.

Another possibility entered Sabina's head and she stopped in her tracks. Had Massimo tired of her already? She chided herself for being insecure. Did he not make love to her every day? Was he not constantly declaring his love? Everything would be clarified this evening during supper. After all, they were not just lovers, they were good friends.

Massimo did not come out of his room for supper, and Sabina was forced to dine alone with her unpleasant thoughts. His behavior had been extremely uncharacteristic throughout the day, but now it bordered on rudeness. She pushed aside the plate containing her half-eaten meal and went to his study.

Placing her hand on the closed door, she called out, "Massimo?"

Nothing but silence greeted her from the other side.

She tried the doorknob and it turned. "Forgive my intrusion—"

The room was a complete mess and Massimo was nowhere to be found. The desk drawer was open and empty. She went into his bedchamber and found the large armoire empty, too. A few articles of clothing had been left behind on the floor.

Sabina felt instantly sick. "Teresa!" Her maid poked her head inside the doorway and she demanded, "Have you seen Massimo today?"

"I saw him getting into a carriage."

An icy chill settled over her. "When?"

"He left this afternoon while you were out taking a walk…"

"Why didn't you tell me?"

"I assumed you already knew."

"Where did he go?"

"Forgive me, Signora, but I didn't feel it was my place to question the master of the house. Leo was with him—they left together."

"Massimo has abandoned me."

Teresa placed a comforting hand on her mistress's shoulder. "He would never do such a thing," she reasoned quietly. "He's a good man and he loves you. There must be a reasonable

154

explanation."

Sabina shook her head in dismay. "A letter arrived this morning. I have no idea what it contained, but Massimo was terribly upset and remained locked inside his study all afternoon—and now this," she lamented, indicating the vacated room.

"Look! There's a note on the bedside table," Teresa said, pointing to the small piece of folded parchment. She picked it up and handed it to Sabina. "Your name is written on the outside."

Sabina unfolded the note and recognized Massimo's handwriting:

My dearest Sabina,

Our days together have been the happiest I've ever known. I don't know how to convey this troublesome news, but I can no longer live with my deceitfulness. I was afraid to tell you the truth because I wanted you so badly—even if only for a short time. Please forgive my selfishness. My dearest love, I'm a married man and cannot provide the future you deserve. My wife and I are estranged, but she discovered that I have been keeping a mistress. She demands that I come home immediately under threat of divorce. Her family is powerful and her father is a close associate to the pope. Divorce would cause a rift in their political alliances. Unfortunately, I'm also utterly destitute. My wife owns everything—even the villa where we have shared so many unforgettable moments. Thank you for the sweet memories. I shall cherish them forever. Please be comforted by the fact that I wish you nothing but happiness. I will love you forever.

Massimo

Sabina reread the note before allowing it to fall from her hand. "He's married and penniless..." Her knees felt weak and she leaned against the wall for support. "His wife knows he has a mistress and threatened to divorce him."

Teresa embraced her mistress as she wept.

Sabina wiped her eyes with the back of her hand. "We have no time for this," she said crisply as she squared her shoulders.

155

"I wish to leave here immediately. I'll help you pack our belongings."

"Are you certain, Signora?" Teresa asked, clearly seeing through the false bravado. "You've just suffered a terrible shock. Maybe we should leave in the morning after you've had some sleep."

"I'm not spending one more day in another woman's villa," Sabina replied, fighting back a fresh onslaught of tears. "We leave tonight."

"As you wish."

Sabina instructed a kitchen knave to ride into the city center to procure a carriage. By the time they left Rome, the sun was making its ascent. While Sabina watched the golden rays kiss the sky, she vowed not to shed another tear for Massimo Reni.

CHAPTER 13

"You cannot go alone! I won't allow it!" Clarice Orsini cried. It was the first time she had ever raised her voice to her husband.

Lorenzo shot his wife a look that silenced her instantly and made her cheeks burn with shame. "You forget your place, Clarice. I'm unaccustomed to taking orders from men, much less from women."

In a softer tone, she said, "What if something happens to you? What will become of us? Think of your family."

"You'll be well cared for in the event of my demise."

"Think of your sons."

"That's exactly why I'm going to negotiate with Ferdinand."

"Why go alone? Do you not see the danger?"

"Of course I do! Do you think me a fool, woman?"

Clarice shook her head. "Not a fool but foolishly brave."

"You think this has to do with bravery?" Lorenzo cursed under his breath. "If I show up in Naples with an army, Ferdinand will think it an act of aggression. If I show up alone, he'll realize that I'm not a threat and hopefully be more inclined to listen to what I have to say."

Clarice paced the room, unconvinced. "Lorenzo, please—"

"The pope has promoted an anti-Florentine league in an attempt to destroy me. If the Kingdom of Naples joins him, I won't stand a chance and neither will Florence. This is why I must speak to Ferdinand face to face, man to man," he explained as patiently as possible.

"When do you depart?" she asked, her tone one of resignation.

"I leave for Pisa tomorrow. From there, I shall set sail to Naples."

"Will you at least reconsider the timing of your departure and spend Christmas with us?"

"Go to your prayers now, Clarice," he retorted gruffly.

No sooner had Clarice left and closed the door, a small side door opened and Lucrezia Donati walked into the room. Lorenzo knew she had been waiting for his wife's departure. The regal way in which she carried herself was always a source of wonderment to him.

Lucrezia's head was tilted back and she looked down her nose at him in disapproval. "Clarice is right, you know. It's extremely dangerous for you to travel to Naples alone."

"Not you, too."

"I know better than to try and dissuade you."

Lorenzo pulled her into his arms. "I admit, I'm stubborn."

She cradled his head as one would a child. "Like a mule."

His hands began to roam her body. "I need you now."

Lucrezia kissed him as he pushed her against the wall and raised her skirts. She whispered soothingly as he entered her body. Throughout their intense lovemaking, she kept her lips to his ear, speaking in hushed tones until he filled her with his seed.

Gripping her around the waist, Lorenzo pulled her roughly toward him. "I wish I could take you with me," he confessed into the softness of her hair.

"I know you do, but I would only distract you from your goal."

He bit her earlobe. "A sweet distraction…"

"You will succeed in your endeavor, Lorenzo. I can sense it."

"I'm glad to hear it. Your predictions are never wrong."

"Never," she agreed with a confident smile.

"I hear the King of Naples is not a reasonable man."

"Every beast can be tamed, my love."

As Lorenzo began to pace, Lucrezia was reminded of the ferocious lions that were kept on display outside the Signoria. Her own Marzocco.

"I have every intention of taming this beast," he said. "Go now, dearest. I still have someone I need to see before I depart."

They stared at one another for a brief moment before

Lucrezia opened the side door. "Give my regards to Sabina Rossi."

His eyebrows shot up in surprise. "How do you know?"

"No one knows you better than I do, Lorenzo." She paused. "Besides, it's obvious that you're fond of her."

"Are you jealous?"

"Should I be?"

Silence.

She smiled knowingly. "Godspeed, my love. Come back to me victorious and unharmed."

***

It was cold and dreary outside, so Sabina decided to spend the afternoon reading a book inside her cozy sitting room.

Teresa came to the door. "Lorenzo de' Medici is here."

"Good God," Sabina said, surprised. "I'll be down at once. Serve our best wine and the finest refreshments we can muster from the kitchen."

Sabina waved her maid out of the room and heaved an anxious sigh as she crossed into her bedchamber. Peering into the looking glass, she bit her lips and pinched her cheeks for color. She retrieved the diamond brooch Clarice had given her from the jewelry box and pinned it to the center of the green velvet bodice of her gown.

She descended the stairs to the main hall and found him comfortably seated in her best chair. A servant was setting out small silver trays on the table beside him. They contained dried figs stuffed with blanched almonds, sugared apricots, and honeyed pastries topped with crunchy hazelnuts.

Sabina mustered a smile. "Lorenzo, what an honor. Had I known you were coming, I would have prepared something special."

He did not smile or speak, but studied her with a stony expression.

She continued, "I hope all is well with you and your family."

"Sit down," he instructed in soft voice laced with steel.

She obediently sat down in the chair opposite him.

He looked at the servant. "Leave us." When they were alone,

he demanded, "Why didn't you come to me when I summoned you?"

Three invitations had arrived since her return from Rome. The last had been written in Lorenzo's own hand.

"You sent invitations, not summons."

"I told you to leave Florence for a few weeks and you were gone the entire summer. You returned in mid-September and didn't bother to send word to me."

Unable to face anyone, Sabina had shut herself off from the world after Massimo had abandoned her. "I've been ill, Lorenzo."

His eyes narrowed. "Your cheeks glow with good health. You're not being honest with me."

"I've been here alone and…"

"And?" he urged. "Is there something you wish to tell me?"

Another servant came in with a bottle of her finest wine. Sabina took the bottle and waved the girl away. "You must try this vintage, Lorenzo. It's a fine Vernaccia di San Gimignano."

"Forgive the indelicacy of what I'm about to tell you."

"You can always speak freely with me," she assured, filling two silver chalices with wine.

"I'm aware of your relationship with Massimo and I know what happened in Rome."

Mortified, she almost spilled the wine. He leaned forward and steadied her hand, guiding the bottle toward the tabletop.

"How?" she managed to ask.

"Clarice had her suspicions, and so did I."

She lowered her head. "We tried to be discreet."

"My wife and I knew that Massimo had a secret lover in Florence, but we never imagined it was you. The day you were poisoned, he was reluctant to leave your side, which made me suspicious. Then he abruptly left for Rome and you departed a few days later."

"You told me to leave Florence."

"Yes, for a *brief* spell to visit your *sister*."

Sabina was too ashamed to speak. She possessed a genuine fear of displeasing Lorenzo—not even her own father had been capable of evoking such a sentiment.

"Sabina?" he prompted when she remained silent.

"I didn't want to go to a tedious convent."

"I can understand that."

"I've been hiding within these walls, dealing with my shame alone."

"And mending your broken heart."

She placed her head in her hands. "I feel so humiliated, Lorenzo. I can only imagine what you must think of me."

"I think no less of you. If Tommaso was alive today, and had you made him a cuckold, it would be a different story."

"I was loyal and devoted to my late husband."

"I know." He paused and took a hearty sip of his wine. "The problem is that you have no male relatives."

"What does that have to do with anything?"

"You're young, beautiful, rich—tempting prey to any predator. A male relative should have arranged a marriage for you by now, but you lack one. Had you satisfied your need for male companionship discreetly, it wouldn't be so objectionable. Unfortunately, you chose a married man who is related to my wife. That complicates matters."

"I didn't know Massimo was married. I swear."

"Rest assured that he'll answer directly to me for that deception when I see him. Your ignorance doesn't change what happened, however. Massimo's wife knows that his mistress is from Florence, and she's demanding to know the woman's identity. I strictly forbade Clarice from divulging that information. Massimo's father-in-law is quite influential and vindictive."

"How did she ever find out about us?"

"Servants, most likely. Maybe someone saw the two of you together while you were out in public. Who knows?"

"What do you want me to do?"

"You must avoid scandal at all cost. It may be prudent to visit your sister at this time. If anyone discovers your secret, you can claim that you're doing penance for your sins at the convent."

She nodded reluctantly before taking a deep swallow of wine. The liquid warmth spread throughout her body.

Lorenzo refilled his own chalice. "I'll summon you to Florence when the time is right."

"When do you want me to go?"

"Immediately."

"What will happen to Massimo?"

He gave her a dark look. "Don't waste your time thinking of him. It will be good for you to get out of this house and spend Christmas with your sister. Hopefully, this matter will be forgotten in a few months."

In a few months? She doubted that a drafty convent in winter would be good for anyone.

"Everything will turn out well if you do as I say." His tone was both affectionate and stern.

"How many people know?"

"There are rumors spreading throughout Rome, but I'm certain your name hasn't been mentioned since your identity hasn't been revealed. Here in Florence, only Clarice and I know the truth."

"Please know that I meant no disrespect to you or your wife."

"I know." He reached across to caress her face the way a father would his favorite child. His touch and the look in his eyes had nothing to do with paternal feelings, however. "Promise me that you'll leave for Lucca before the week's end."

"You have my word."

"I depart for Pisa tomorrow," he announced, changing the subject. "My ship will then set sail for Naples, where I will attempt to reason with the king and dissuade him from attacking Florence."

"How many men will accompany you?"

"None."

She touched his hand. "You intend to go alone?"

"I do."

"What does Clarice say about this?"

"She has no say in my decisions." Smirking, he added, "Do

you think all women are as brazen as you?"

"Traveling to Naples alone will be dangerous. God knows who could be waiting along the roads to ambush you."

"I know."

"Please reconsider, Lorenzo."

He was moved by Sabina's concern for his person, whereas his wife cared only for her own welfare and that of her children. Once again, the thought of bedding this remarkable woman crept into his mind, but he cast aside the urge. He could not disrespect Tommaso's memory.

"I must go alone to speak with the king. The future of Florence is in my hands. I cannot fail."

"What if something happens to you before you have a chance to speak with him? What will happen to Florence?"

"I'll be back to summon you home soon. I promise."

"You'd better keep your word," she said, her eyes filled with worry. "We've already suffered the loss of Giuliano. We can't lose you, too."

"If I keep my word and return, I expect you to present yourself at my home when I invite you. Understood?"

"Yes."

He stood. "You will come to the palazzo to feast with me after I succeed in Naples. For now, take care. Your reputation is at stake."

She stood, too. "What about Angelina?"

"By the time you return to Florence, everything will be resolved. I'm in the process of aiding her father arrange a marriage for her."

"Thank God."

"Let us not speak her name or of this matter again," he said, stepping forward to embrace her. "You should have been born a man."

Hugging him tightly, she said, "You've said this to me before."

"I'll probably say it to you again. You're too unconventional for womanhood. I could use a man with your innate perception to aid me in decision-making or to simply keep me in line. The fact that you're a woman leaves me with only two choices. I can either watch over you like a brother or make you my mistress." He kissed her cheek and walked toward the door. "I'll see you soon, Sabina."

She opened the door for him. "Be safe, Lorenzo. Godspeed."

The four Medici guards who had been waiting for their master outside the gate encompassed Lorenzo the moment he stepped into the street. Sabina locked the gate and immediately summoned Teresa.

"I'm going to Lucca to see my sister. Pack only the plainest gowns. There is no need for finery at the convent."

"Will I be accompanying you, Signora?"

"Do you wish to come with me?"

"It's my duty to follow you wherever you go."

"I appreciate your loyalty, but that's not what I asked."

Teresa blushed. "God forgive me, but I have no stomach for the severity of convents."

"Then my answer is no, you will not be accompanying me."

"You cannot go alone."

"I'll be surrounded by God and the angels," Sabina said drily. "Besides, I need someone to be my eyes and ears in Florence while I'm away. Oh, and to watch over that mischievous crow of mine."

"You won't be taking Mendi?" Teresa asked, disappointed.

"They wouldn't allow me through the gates of Hell with that little demon. I expect you to keep my home in order and the servants in line. I want to know what's happening in Florence, so write to me weekly."

"Yes, Signora."

"That's all for now. If I think of anything else, I'll let you know."

Teresa moved as if to go, then stopped. "Signora?"

"Yes?"

"Does Signora Cecilia know about your aversion to convents?"

Sabina laughed. "Oh, yes."

"If I may be so bold...what excuse will you use to explain

164

the purpose of your visit?"

"I'll tell Cecilia that I've come for a retreat in order to cleanse my soul of its many sins. She'll be ecstatic."

***

Cecilia was happy to see Sabina at Santa Lucia, and even happier when she discovered her sister's intention to stay indefinitely. "Everyone can benefit from a spiritual retreat," she said. "Come, let me give you a tour of our convent."

Sabina learned that the century-old structure had started out as a small convent with a handful of nuns before its expansion. Now, it housed over fifty nuns.

It began to drizzle as they crossed the courtyard, so they ducked beneath the arches of the cloisters and entered the church. Cecilia wore a rough linen habit the color of dirty water with nothing but a thin wool cape for warmth.

"Aren't you cold?" Sabina inquired.

"I am warmed by Holy Spirit," Cecilia replied cheerfully. "Tell me, what's the real reason for you coming here?"

"I wanted to see you."

Cecilia studied her sister through narrowed eyes. "You invite me to Florence when you want to see me. Come on. Out with it."

"I wanted to get away from the city."

"That's not like you, Sabina."

"Well, maybe I'm getting tired or bored—or both. I need a respite, and this seemed like a good place to get some peace."

Although Cecilia's expression remained skeptical, she seemed to accept Sabina's reason and said nothing more on the subject. They walked down the nave, then through a side door that led to the refectory.

Cecilia paused. "I have something to show you inside."

Sabina hoped it would be food because she was hungry. When they entered the spacious refectory, Cecilia pointed to the frescoed walls. "Are they not beautiful?"

The life-sized frescoes were indeed impressive. Painted in fresh colors that made the room come alive, three walls depicted scenes of Mary's life: The Birth of the Virgin, The Marriage of

165

the Virgin, and The Ascension of the Virgin. Of course, Santa Lucia was present in every scene as a silent witness to these blessed events.

Sabina liked the last one the best because it showed Mary's face in total rapture as she floated up toward Heaven in a beam of light. So many religious works of art dealt with serious or unpleasant themes; it was refreshing to see a holy figure looking pleased for a change.

"We take our meals here," Cecilia explained. "The Last Supper scene is usually depicted on refectory walls, but I suppose our late abbess wanted to be unique."

Sabina's stomach growled. She wasn't interested in frescoes at the moment. "Will I have to wear a nun's habit?"

"No." Cecilia smiled and stared at her sister.

"What?"

Her smile widened. "I knew God would answer my prayers."

"What do you mean?"

"Well, here you are!"

"Remember, it's only temporary."

Cecilia's smile remained glued in place. "I often pray that you'll take the vows someday and join me here in the convent. We could live out the rest of our years in peace, serving our dear Lord."

Sabina realized that Cecilia had grown more pious after Paolo's death—to the point of fanaticism. "My life is in Florence."

"You could sell the house and donate your money to the poor."

Sabina wondered if promising Lorenzo she would stay in Lucca had been such a good idea. Could she tolerate months of constant preaching and pressure from Cecilia? Was this the price she had to pay for her foolishness with Massimo?

She still loved him, although she hated to admit it. Did that not count for anything? Can love be deemed foolish if it goes terribly wrong? Massimo had not sent her any messages. The only thing she had from him was the note he had scribbled before abandoning her at the villa in Rome. There had been no further explanation, no words exchanged to offer any closure—just the note.

"Does that sound appealing to you?" Cecilia asked.

"What?"

"Are you listening to me?"

Sabina put her hand on her sister's shoulder. "Forgive me. I'm tired from the journey and this dreary weather is doing little to help."

"I asked you if you wanted to accompany me tomorrow."

"Where are you going?"

"The hospital."

"Is someone sick?"

"We give alms to the poor in the morning, then help at the orphanage and hospital in the afternoon."

"Yes, of course, charity."

"Wait and see how good you'll feel when God's Holy Spirit fills your soul. The Bible says that there's more pleasure in giving than in receiving. How true that is," Cecilia said, crossing herself.

Sabina's stomach growled again. "What time do we eat?"

"Let's get you something to ease your hunger until supper time."

The next morning, Sabina donned a plain gown and attended mass. Afterward, she was introduced to the abbess, Mother Marcella, a gaunt woman with inquisitive gray eyes.

"Welcome, Signora Sabina. Sister Cecilia has spoken of you many times," the abbess said as she regarded Sabina coolly. "We hope you benefit spiritually from the peacefulness of our humble convent."

"I'm sure I will. As a token of my gratitude, I would like to make a donation." Sabina handed over a heavy coin purse.

Mother Marcella's eyes widened with subtle glee. "Your gift is greatly appreciated and will be put to good use. God bless your generosity, Signora. If there's anything you need, simply ask."

Ah, the power of money. Had not Massimo abandoned her

167

and forsaken their love for his wife's money?

Sabina watched the fabric of Mother Marcella's wimple flap in the breeze as she walked briskly toward the chapel.

Sabina accompanied her sister to the Ospedale di Misericordia located across town. Sick people were scattered about on makeshift cots, and most of them were either extremely poor or very old. It was the first time she had ever been exposed to such raw human suffering, and it brought tears to her eyes.

She was impressed at Cecilia's compassion toward these people who had no one else to care for them. The lack of sanitary conditions, accompanied by the vile stench of human filth, would have frightened most people away. Not the sisters of Santa Lucia. The nuns sat alongside the sick and spoke consoling words as they bathed their patients, redressed their wounds, and fed them. Sabina watched in amazement as these unselfish women gave of themselves without taking, or even wanting, anything in return.

Sabina walked among the sick feeling nothing but gratitude for her good health. She joined the nuns and got busy cleaning wounds, feeding the sick, and trying to comfort the patients as best she could. Since she had never done such work before, she was surprised at the mental and physical exhaustion she felt at the end of the day.

Sabina hoped Lorenzo would summon her home soon.

***

Cecilia was excited at the prospect of Sabina spending Christmas at Santa Lucia and began to rally the nuns into putting together a night of wholesome festivities. Sabina knew there would be no fine gowns or dancing, but she would make sure there would be a bountiful feast.

"May I have a word with you, please?" Sabina said to Mother Marcella one day. When the abbess nodded, she continued, "I would like to provide the nuns with a special Christmas dinner."

"That's quite a generous offer, Signora Sabina. We usually have a small, humble feast. Some of the nuns with good voices sing a few hymns to honor the birth of our Lord."

"Allow me to provide the feast this year as my way of saying thank you for all the hospitality I have so graciously received from everyone."

"I'm sure your gift will be appreciated by all, including myself."

"What about music? Would you allow me to hire some musicians?"

"We do not normally indulge in such worldly entertainment—"

"They would be instructed to play only religious music. The scores can be approved by you beforehand."

The abbess thought about it. "As long as I pick out the music, I see no harm in allowing a few musicians as entertainment."

Sabina grinned at the prospect of having something fun to do during the long, cold days of December. She knew better than to push the matter of dancing, which would surely be rejected.

"Thank you, Mother Marcella. You will not be disappointed."

"No, Signora Sabina, thank you."

She proceeded to find Cecilia in order to tell her the news.

"Planning our Christmas feast should keep you busy," Cecilia said. "Remember, this is a convent and we have taken vows of poverty. We are unaccustomed to luxuries here."

"Well, I have taken no such vows and there's nothing wrong with accepting gifts from those who wish to bestow them."

"That's true," Cecilia conceded. "Promise me that you won't shame me by doing anything overly extravagant."

Sabina rolled her eyes. "A few dancers, some acrobats, and a couple of troubadours will do these nuns some good."

"Dancers? Acrobats? Troubadours?"

"I merely jest. Don't worry, sister. I won't do anything to shame you or compromise the Christian dignity of this convent."

Cecilia was visibly relieved. "Not to change the subject, but one of the sisters who I'm friendly with—"

"Sister Olivia?" Sabina interrupted.

"Yes, Sister Olivia. How did you know?"

"I see you two together often enough. Besides, it has come to my attention that she likes to gossip and I know how much you enjoy a spicy tale," Sabina replied with a smirk.

Cecilia frowned in mock outrage. "As I was saying, she informed me this morning that her cousin, Lisa, died recently. To make matters worse, she was expecting her first child."

"How tragic!"

"You'll never guess who the girl was married to." When Sabina shrugged, she said, "Marco."

"Marco?"

Cecilia raised an eyebrow. "Surely you remember him."

"Marco Alfani?"

Cecilia nodded. "It's a small world, indeed."

"Poor man."

"Oh, but there's more..."

"You nuns really do love to gossip."

"So do you, so do not judge."

"True. Tell me more."

"A few days after Lisa's funeral, Marco announced his desire to become a priest."

"No!" Sabina exclaimed in utter disbelief.

"Yes!"

Sabina rubbed her chin as she recalled the many passionate embraces she and Marco had shared prior to her marriage. From lustful beast to celibate priest? She was skeptical of his endeavor.

Cecilia continued, "A priest! Can you believe it?"

"Hardly. I hope it brings him peace and happiness."

Cecilia looked at Sabina slyly. "Would you not like to see him now that the two of you are widowed?"

"No."

"You don't miss him? Not even a little bit?"

"We had this conversation before, remember? Besides, I believe he harbors resentment against me for marrying

170

Tommaso."

"He doesn't know that you're widowed," Cecilia pointed out.

"So?"

"Maybe if he knew, he would be seeking you out rather than taking vows of celibacy."

"I suppose we'll never know, will we?" Sabina changed the subject. "What do you think of stuffed partridges? You told me not to be too extravagant, so I'll avoid roasted pheasants and peacocks."

"Partridges are fine. I'm sure the sisters will love whatever food you provide."

***

Christmas Day dawned wet and cold, and the weather worsened as the day progressed. Inside the convent, there was a flurry of activity as the cooks and servants that Sabina hired for the day prepared food for the nuns. Everyone appreciated the Christmas feast. Along with delicious stuffed partridges, there were meat pies, assorted breads, custard, sweet tarts, cheese, and generous quantities of good wine. A group of musicians played instrumental church melodies that everyone seemed to enjoy, especially the abbess.

At one point, Cecilia said to Sabina, "I've underestimated you."

"How so?"

"This feast is wonderful and not overly extravagant. It's just right."

"I'm glad you approve."

As the cold December rain pounded upon the roof, the nuns were warm and cozy, celebrating the birth of the Lord in high style.

CHAPTER 14

The passing of the New Year was quiet at Santa Lucia. Sabina had settled into her new life at the convent and, as Cecilia promised, she felt good about helping others. Sabina spent most of her time at the hospital, where her knowledge of herbs and roots—and how to use them in healing—was a valuable asset to the patients.

One afternoon in mid-January, an unconscious boy was brought into the hospital. He had developed a bad infection in his leg, and the barber surgeon had to amputate the limb in order to save the boy's life. The incision wound was not healing properly, causing the boy to suffer from fever. Since it was a hospital for the poor, medications were sparse and the treatments administered were sometimes less than ideal.

Sabina concocted every plaster and unguent that she could think of, but they failed to provide relief. Determined to help the boy, she left the hospital to purchase medicine from the best apothecary in the city. She returned late in the afternoon and administered the costly ointment to her young patient's wound.

One of the nuns approached the cot and Sabina inquired, "What do you know of this boy's family? Is he an orphan?"

The nun looked down at the sleeping boy. "His mother is forced to beg daily to feed her other children. I'm sure she'd be here with him if she could. Poor little angel."

"Where does she live?"

The nun proceeded to give her directions to a dubious neighborhood full of pickpockets and shabby dwellings.

Sabina sat down and studied the boy, who looked to be six or seven years old. When he opened his eyes, she leaned over and smiled at him.

"Who are you?" he asked weakly.

"My name is Sabina. What's your name?"

"Demetrio."

"Are you still in pain?" He nodded with tears in his eyes, prompting her to caress his cheek. "Would seeing your mother make you feel better?" He nodded and sniffed. "What's your mother's name?"

"Grazia."

"Rest now, Demetrio. I'll return in the morning."

Early the next day, Sabina donned her plainest gown and cloak, then hid a heavy coin pouch inside of her bodice.

"It's too dangerous for you to go alone," Cecilia said.

"God is pleased with me, remember? At least that's what you said. He wouldn't allow harm to come to me if I'm doing His will."

"Do not put God to the test, Sabina."

"I'm merely going to fetch a sick boy's mother."

"Apparently, all this time in the convent has done little to eradicate your stubbornness."

"Were you expecting miracles?"

Cecilia sighed tiredly. "Be careful and God be with you."

No one paid attention to Sabina as she walked toward the area where Demetrio's mother and siblings resided. She was sure to keep her head low and her pace quick. After finding the address, she knocked on the door of a dilapidated house. A woman with sad eyes came to the door.

Sabina inquired, "Are you Donna Grazia, Demetrio's mother?"

Stricken, Grazia's eyes filled with tears. "He died? Oh, please, no!"

Sabina reached for the woman's hand. "Demetrio is alive. I applied good medicine yesterday, and I expect he will be better today."

Grazia sagged with relief and crossed herself. "Thank God and all the saints. I miss him so much."

"He needs you."

Without a word, Grazia opened the door wider and stepped aside so that Sabina could see two twin girls playing with a doll made of straw. They appeared to be about three years of age. She looked at the children, then back at Sabina. "I'm alone in

173

this world and I have to beg in order for them to eat. If I could sit with Demetrio in the hospital, I would."

"May I come in?"

"Who are you?"

"My name is Sabina Rossi. I'm staying at Santa Lucia with my sister, Cecilia. We do charity work in the hospital."

Grazia ushered Sabina into the dingy, single-room dwelling. In the corner was a big straw mattress where Grazia and her children slept, and an empty cooking pot rested within the cold hearth.

Sabina extracted the coin-filled pouch from the inside of her bodice. "Here, this is for you to buy food and whatever else you may need."

Grazia opened the pouch and gasped at the sight of several gold florins. She gaped at Sabina in disbelief. "This is a fortune."

"Yes, so you don't need to beg anymore. You can properly care for your son while he heals and adapts to having only one leg."

Grazia burst into tears and knelt. "God has sent me an angel!"

"Please, get up," Sabina said feeling extremely uncomfortable. "God has given me so much. It's only fair that I share it with those in need."

Sabina learned that Grazia's husband died the year after she had given birth to the twins. With no husband to support her, she was soon drowning in debt and forced to sell almost everything they owned. After the money ran out, she chose begging over prostitution.

By the time Sabina left Grazia's house and the awful neighborhood, she was emotionally spent. Feeling incredibly grateful for all the good she had in her life, she went straight into the chapel as soon as she reached Santa Lucia. Dropping to her knees before the altar, she offered a heartfelt prayer to God.

Sabina was glad to see Grazia sitting by her son's cot the next time she was at the hospital. She and the twins were dressed in decent clothing instead of rags, and Demetrio was eating broth with bread.

"You're obviously feeling better, Demetrio," Sabina said.

He grinned. "Thank you for the medicine, Signora."

"You're welcome, my dear."

Sabina left them alone so that she could help the other nuns.

Cecilia approached and placed her arm around her sister's shoulders. "I'm very proud of you…Papa would be, too."

"Maybe now you'll stop pointing out my faults," Sabina teased.

"Never! After all, what are older sisters for?"

Both laughed as they helped prepare food for the hungry patients.

Demetrio healed quickly, as the young often do, and eventually learned to maneuver about with the use of two wooden crutches.

One morning, Sabina found Grazia at the hospital with a big smile on her face. "Signora Sabina, Demetrio is going home today!"

"That's good news. The nuns and I have taken quite a liking to your son. He'll be missed."

"I've managed to find work in a bakery. The baker's wife died and he has no one to help him. The pay is little, but I'll be allowed to take home some of the day-old bread that doesn't get sold."

"This is wonderful news, indeed! I wish you all the best."

Sabina bade farewell to Grazia and her son before walking around the hospital to see if any new patients had been admitted. She soon came upon a cot where a half-naked man lay with his eyes closed. He had a gentle face with sharp features that reminded her of a serene angel in one of the Botticelli paintings she'd seen at the Palazzo Medici. His wheat-colored hair was long, and his pale skin was as flawless as porcelain. His body, with the exception of the bandaged wound on his left side, was without blemish. Cecilia stood nearby when Sabina reached down and took one of the man's hands in her own. Turning it over, she examined the palm. It was devoid of calluses or blisters.

175

"What are you doing, Sabina?"

Lifting the palm toward Cecilia, she replied, "This man has never known a day of hard work in his life. Who is he?"

"I have no idea," Cecilia replied, turning her attention to an old woman who began to scream in pain.

Sabina studied the mysterious man. Could he be a member of nobility? If that was the case, he would be in his own fine bed attended by the best physicians, not lingering in a hospital that serviced the poor.

The man's breathing was shallow and he was covered in a film of perspiration. Touching his forehead, she realized he was burning with fever. She quickly procured a cool, wet cloth and applied it to his brow.

Sabina left the man's side and aided her sister with the care of the old woman, who was in the throes of death. With so many people needing medical attention, the dead were disposed of quickly in order to make room for the living. Sabina left her sister's side and walked toward one of the hospital workers in charge of admitting new patients.

Cecilia caught up with her. "What are you doing?"

"I want to know about that man. He shouldn't be here."

"Why? He's young and strong, and will heal quickly. It's the old and weak we should focus on first."

Sabina ignored her sister and interrogated the worker. She discovered that a passing merchant had found the man in a dark alley and had brought him to the hospital on his horse. Apparently, he had been stabbed on his left side, most likely robbed, and left for dead. Like the proverbial Good Samaritan, the merchant had provided the hospital caretakers with a few coins for the stranger's care.

"I'll take over his care," Sabina said.

Cecilia looked taken aback. "You don't even know him."

"I didn't know Demetrio either."

"That was different."

"How?"

"It was a child with a particularly cruel circumstance. This man was simply robbed and stabbed. He'll heal soon enough and be on his way."

Sabina removed several coins from the purse she kept hidden in the folds of her garment and instructed the worker to fetch a private physician. She took a seat by the man's cot, admiring his angelic face while administering wet cloths to his hot forehead. The fever was no doubt due to an infection brewing in the stab wound. Suddenly, his lashes fluttered, but his eyes remained closed.

She leaned closer. "Can you hear me? You're in the Ospedale di Misericordia in Lucca. A physician will be here soon."

His right hand flinched. She re-wet the cloth and applied it to his brow once more, then slightly lifted the bandages to see the extent of the wound. The cut was not long, but it was deep and must have bled quite a bit.

The man opened his amber eyes, making her shiver. She'd seen eyes like that only once before on a gypsy passing through town when she was a child.

"Can you hear me?" she asked again.

He stared into the distance for a brief moment, then slipped back into unconsciousness. She remained at his side until the physician arrived.

"How long has he been like this?" the physician inquired while touching his forehead.

"Someone brought him in this morning. He was left for dead."

The physician examined and cleaned the wound, then applied a poultice. Next, he removed a vial from his satchel and poured it down the man's throat. "The medicine will soon take effect. Someone should sit with him until he awakens and get him to drink some water."

The man began sweating profusely shortly after the physician departed. Sabina tried to keep him cool with wet strips of linen, but it did little good. He then twitched and moaned in feverish delirium, compelling Sabina to take hold of his hand. It was late and she was very tired by the time his body stopped fighting the fever. He was no longer flushed and perspiring, and his skin felt much cooler to the touch.

Sabina smiled wearily. "I knew you would win," she whispered, wiping his face and neck with a damp cloth.

The man's eyes suddenly flew open. His irises were like glittering topaz gemstones. Startled, she accidentally dropped the cloth.

They stared at each other before she reached for a cup of water. "You must be thirsty." He said nothing as she placed the cup to his lips. He looked as though he wanted to speak, but was too exhausted to do so.

"Don't talk," she said. "You need to save your strength."

The foxlike eyes remained locked on hers.

"My name is Sabina Rossi. You were brought here after someone found you in an alley." He nodded slightly and she continued, "You were stabbed, but you'll survive."

An expression of relief and gratitude crossed his face. He closed his eyes and was asleep almost immediately. She stood up, stretched, and looked around. The hospital was dark and only one candle burned by a bed where an old man was dying and a priest had been summoned by his family to perform the last rites.

Sabina had seen enough sickness and death to last a lifetime. She felt as though she had to get out of the hospital as soon as possible, but it was late at night. It would be unsafe to walk the streets alone at this hour. Sighing, she sat back down and fell asleep in the chair.

Sabina opened her eyes and the man was gone. She looked around, feeling disoriented and stiff from having slept on a hard surface in an upright position. She stood, smoothing the skirt of her gown.

Catching sight of a hospital worker, she demanded, "Where is the man who got stabbed?"

"He's gone, Signora. Two servants arrived at dawn inquiring about their master. Apparently, the man is of some importance and had been missing since last night. The servants were dressed as foreigners and could barely speak Tuscan."

She frowned. "And you did not bother to wake me? Did you

at least get his name?"

The worker began tapping the side of his head with his finger as if trying to remember. "For the love of Saint Peter, I can't recall it. The name was foreign. German? English? Forgive me, Signora."

Sabina left the hospital feeling extremely tired and slightly frustrated that she wouldn't be able to speak with her mysterious patient. She walked back to the convent in the cold morning air, thinking that perhaps it was God's wish. She stopped in her tracks. *God's wish?* She shook her head and smiled. Cecilia was beginning to rub off on her.

On the tenth day of February, a letter arrived from Teresa stating that Angelina Bardi was officially betrothed to a nobleman from Venice. Sabina breathed a sigh of relief. True to his word, Lorenzo had taken care of the problem. There was still no word of his return from Naples.

The following day, an unexpected visitor arrived at the Convento di Santa Lucia. Cecilia was in her cell reading the Bible by the window. Despite the cold wind outside, she kept one of the shutters open for light since burning candles during the day wasn't allowed. Sabina had gone out to buy various medicines for the hospital and was expected to return shortly. Cecilia heard a knock on the door and assumed it was her sister.

"Excuse the interruption," said Sister Olivia from the doorway.

"Nonsense, come in," Cecilia said, closing the Bible. "I was expecting Sabina. Tell me, what can I do for you?"

"Do you remember how I told you about my cousin Lisa— the one who died?" Cecilia nodded and she added, "You mentioned to me that you knew her husband, Marco."

"Yes, of course. How is he?"

"He's fine. He's here, in fact."

"Here?"

"Yes, in the courtyard below. He's waiting to see you."

Cecilia looked surprised. "How did he find out I was here?"

"When my sister came to visit, I told her that you knew him. He was horrified to hear about your dear little Paolo." Cecilia's

179

eyes watered at the mention of her son's name and Sister Olivia regretted her words immediately. "Forgive me if I have upset you."

Cecilia composed herself. "Let us not keep Marco waiting."

They both walked downstairs to the cloister garden.

As soon as Marco caught sight of Cecilia, he smiled. "Sister Cecilia."

Although she never cared for him when he was wooing her sister, her opinion changed the moment she learned of his "godly calling."

"It's good to see you, Marco," she said. "Sister Olivia told me about your wife and child. Please accept my condolences on your loss."

"Thank you." He looked to Sister Olivia. "Did she also tell you that I'm on my way to becoming a priest?"

"She did, and I'm happy for you. There is no higher calling than the service of our Lord."

Marco shrugged. "It was either join the priesthood or remarry and continue to work hard in the fields."

Cecilia was taken aback. "You make it sound so easy. Surely, you must have prayed on the matter before coming to such a big decision and entering the seminary."

"I love God, so why not work for Him?" He paused, his face serious. "I was deeply saddened when I heard about Paolo and your father. Take comfort that they are both in Heaven with God."

She nodded as she bit back tears. "I do."

Changing the subject, he asked, "How is your sister?"

"Sabina is staying here with me at the convent." Marco's eyes lit up in surprise, prompting her to add, "She needed a spiritual respite."

"I see," he said dubiously. The Sabina he remembered would never stay in a convent of her own volition. "Is she all right?"

Cecilia sighed sadly. "You know of the assassination attempt made on the Medici."

"Everyone knows. Giuliano was murdered during Easter

Mass."

"My father and I were in Florence visiting Sabina, and we were in the cathedral when that happened. The violence and chaos following the attack claimed the lives of Tommaso Caravelli and my son."

Stunned, he offered, "I'm so sorry to hear this. It seems as though we have all suffered tragic losses."

"True, but we still have much to be thankful for."

"Is Sabina here? May I speak with her?"

"She's out purchasing curatives for the hospital and I don't know when she'll be back. You're more than welcome to wait."

"Alas, I must leave this afternoon."

"Signora Sabina is very generous," Sister Olivia interjected. "She arranged a wonderful Christmas feast."

"May God bless her," Marco said. "Please convey my warm regards to your sister. Hopefully, our paths will cross in the future."

The nuns bade Marco farewell and he exited the convent with his mind still reeling. Turning a corner, his breath caught in his throat at the sight of Sabina lugging a large basket down the street.

She paused mid-step. "Marco?"

"Sabina—I spoke with your sister only a moment ago! How are you?" Taking the basket from her hand, he added, "Please, let me."

"What are you doing here?"

"I'm in Lucca for the day, so I paid Sister Olivia a visit."

"I see."

He hesitated. "Cecilia informed me about Tommaso...I'm sorry."

"Apparently, neither one of us has managed to escape the last few years unscathed. I was sad to learn about your wife."

He nodded. "Life is full of surprises, isn't it?"

"Like you wanting to become a priest."

"Why not? It's a profession like any other, only I answer to God rather than a man."

The Marco Alfani she knew was a carnal man, not a spiritual

one. They arrived at the convent gates and she moved to retrieve the basket. "Well, I wish you all the best."

"This basket is heavy, I'll take it inside for you," he said, going through the gate. "Cecilia told me you were buying curatives for the hospital. That's generous of you but very uncharacteristic."

She kept pace with him. "Are you implying that I'm uncharitable?"

"Not at all. The Sabina I knew would mix her own concoctions."

She chuckled and allowed him to carry the basket into the refectory. "Thank you, Marco. You can set it down there."

Marco set the basket down on a table and admired the frescoed walls.

Seeing this, she said, "You should see the frescoes in the chapel. They're exquisite." She regretted her thoughtless words instantly.

Predictably, he inquired, "May I see them?"

"I'm not sure if you're allowed to go in there. The nuns are strict about having visitors, especially men."

Unlike the refectory, which opened onto the cloisters and was in plain sight, the chapel was down a long transept at the back of the church. It would be empty this time of day. As innocent as the situation was, the last thing she wanted to do was upset Mother Marcella by taking a man to such a secluded place.

"Most of the nuns know me here. Besides, I'm currently enrolled at the seminary and soon to become a priest," he reminded her. "Priests are allowed to walk wherever they choose within God's houses."

He did have a valid point. What harm could come of showing him the lovely artwork? "Very well."

She led him to the chapel and hovered at the entrance as he looked at the vibrantly painted frescoes. He glanced at her on a few occasions, but she pretended not to notice.

Marco eventually walked to where she stood. "Now that we're alone, I'd like to ask you something. Did you ever think of me when you were married?"

Sabina took a step backward. "That's not a question for a future priest to be asking of a widow."

"Your tongue is as sharp as ever, I see."

"Sharp or not, it speaks the truth."

"I'm not a priest *yet*."

"No, but you will be soon."

"Does that upset you?"

She debated running toward the church's exit. "Why should it?"

"Because then I will be lost to you forever."

"You haven't changed a bit, Marco Alfani."

A shadow settled across his features. "Are you mocking me?"

She laughed derisively. "*Father* Marco."

"You *are* mocking me."

"People won't confess to you if they know about your bad temper."

His hands balled into fists and his face turned red. "My bad temper is nothing compared to your conniving character!"

Sabina was shocked by this unexpected outburst of rage. "Forgive me if my teasing offended you."

"You offended me long ago when you willingly ran off to marry that old Florentine," he said through clenched teeth.

He was serious. She knew he harbored some resentment against her, but she had no idea of its extent. "I know your pride was wounded, but it's not as if you and I were madly in love—"

"Of course I loved you!"

She looked at him incredulously. "Marco, I'm well aware that I was not the only girl you were satisfying yourself with. I know there were others. Did you love them, too?"

"Yes, I satisfied my needs wherever I could—that's what men do—but my heart was always yours."

Sabina shook her head dismissively. "None of this matters now."

Marco gripped her shoulders and forced her into a shadowy

corner within the chapel. "Say the word and I'll leave the seminary." She struggled and he pushed himself against her body. "Tell me that you want me, and we'll run away together."

"Stop speaking nonsense! You're about to become a priest!"

She felt him hardening. "Do you miss *this*?" he asked provocatively before nuzzling her throat. "I've thought of you so many times—of your body, your scent. No woman has ever compared to you."

"Please," she cried as she wriggled to free herself from his embrace.

Marco silenced Sabina's protests with a rough kiss, so she bit his lip. His head drew back in pain. "Stop it! You can't deny what we shared. You belong to me, do you understand? You'll always be mine."

She managed to free her arm and slapped him across his face as hard as she could. "I belong to no one!"

He shook her so violently that she thought her teeth would shatter. "You prissy little bitch! You lifted your skirts for me countless times, and now you want to play the high and mighty lady?"

"Marco, please," she reasoned, truly frightened now.

"Remember—if you hadn't married Tommaso, you'd still be in Lucca playing the whore with me."

"Let go of me! What madness has taken hold of you? The nuns are expecting me and will come looking for me at any moment."

"Let them come," he said, his lips curling into a sneer.

"I'll scream."

Extracting a handkerchief from his tunic, he gagged her with alarming speed. "I'm going to teach you the same lesson I taught the miller's daughter when she said she wouldn't have me."

Sabina's eyes reflected horror when she realized his intention. She desperately tried to get away, but Marco was too strong. He spun her around and pressed her face against the frescoed wall before pinning her arms behind her back. She screamed into the gag.

Placing his lips to her ear, he whispered, "Remember this?"

Tears of indignant rage filled her eyes as he entered her and took his sexual pleasure against her will. When he was finished, he removed the gag and let go of her arms. Too stunned to speak, she slumped against the wall for support. In all the time she had known Marco, she had never imagined him capable of such a vile deed.

He adjusted his clothing as if nothing happened. "You'd be wise to keep this to yourself," he advised. "Given that we were so close at one time, no one will believe that what took place was not of your free will."

She shot him a seething look. "Get out of here, Marco."

For an instant, she thought she saw guilt in his eyes, but it was soon replaced by anger. "Pride and arrogance are sins, Sabina. Consider this a much-needed lesson in humility."

Marco sauntered out of the chapel into the sunlight with his head held high, as if he'd committed no wrong.

Dazed, Sabina reached under her skirt and grimaced in disgust at the wetness between her legs. She needed to collect her wits and rid herself of his filth. Wincing with soreness, she stood and staggered out of the chapel toward the cloisters, then straight up to her cell.

Once inside, she hastily removed her clothing and kicked the pile of fabric into a corner. The gown would be donated to charity. Shivering with cold, she filled a basin with icy water, procured a linen cloth, and proceeded to wash her body. Tears blurred her vision as she scrubbed her skin vigorously, hoping to wipe away all traces of Marco.

***

Cecilia was quick to notice a change in her sister. Sabina normally chatted when they walked to the hospital or the orphanage, but she had grown sullen the last few days. "You haven't been yourself as of late. You're unusually quiet and your brow is furrowed. Is there something wrong?"

Sabina contemplated telling Cecilia what Marco had done, but what good would come of it? It would change nothing. "I miss Florence," she said with a forced smile. "I'm sorry if I haven't been good company."

Cecilia eyed her steadily. "There's nothing more?"

"No."

After that day, Sabina made an effort to put the entire episode with Marco behind her. It would be easier to pretend that it never happened than to relive the humiliation of being raped. Gradually, she became stronger, and the deep sorrow she felt was eventually replaced by indignation.

CHAPTER 15
FLORENCE, TUSCANY
MARCH 1480

Lorenzo de' Medici had departed from Pisa to Naples on December 14, 1479, and did not return to Florence until March the following year. He had risked his life for the peace and well-being of Florence, and the risk had paid off. Not only had he managed to successfully negotiate with the King of Naples but also with the pope, thus avoiding war. In short, he made his position in Florence stronger than ever before, and—although he never held political office within the Republic—the European rulers officially recognized him as the Head of Florence.

"Must you leave so soon?" Cecilia lamented after Sabina announced her imminent departure to Florence.

"I've been in Lucca for several months, dear sister. I miss my home."

"I know. I'm being selfish. I've enjoyed your company—we all have." She smiled indulgently. "More than that, I've enjoyed witnessing the positive changes in you."

"Was I such a bad person?"

"No, but you're leaving this convent a better person than when you arrived," Cecilia replied honestly before embracing her sister.

Sabina returned to Florence where she was affectionately greeted by Teresa, then bombarded with the latest gossip. For the next few days, she did little else but write and enjoy the comfort of her home. The time she spent in the convent had heightened her appreciation for warmth, soft cushions, and beautiful objects.

A few days later, she was at the Palazzo Medici. Lorenzo took her hands into his own when he saw her. "What a lovely sight for sore eyes," he said cheerfully. "Welcome home,

Sabina."

"Thank you, and congratulations on your great success."

"Have you heard? The Florentines have given me a new name—Il Magnifico."

"The Magnificent," she repeated. "It suits you perfectly."

He chuckled softly. "Do you think so?"

"I most certainly do. It's a relief to see you in such good spirits, too."

Peering at her closely, he commented, "There's something different about you. Tell me, how was your stay at the convent?"

"At first I hated it," she admitted. "But then I grew accustomed to the routine and actually enjoyed helping others."

"Did you miss Florence?"

"Every day."

He took a step closer. "Did you miss me?"

"Every day."

He smiled. "Come. Let's partake of some refreshment." They walked toward a servant bearing a tray of chalices and he took two of them. Handing one to Sabina, he asked, "Do you remember when you invited me to your home after Giuliano's death? You said I could find peace and privacy there."

"Of course I remember."

"I shall call upon you soon."

***

Sabina discovered that Signore Adolfo was away on business, so she invited Camelia to dine with her the following evening. The older woman was genuinely happy to see her friend and embraced her tightly.

"You simply disappeared without sending word to me," Camelia said, baffled. "Your maid, Teresa, would not divulge any details as to your whereabouts. Her loyalty to you is impressive."

"I'm sorry if I caused you any distress. I should have written to you. I was visiting my sister at the Convento di Santa Lucia."

Camelia frowned. "All those months with the nuns? Were you doing some kind of penance?" When Sabina did not smile,

188

her expression grew serious. "Oh, dear. I can sense there's something wrong."

"I'll tell you everything but, first, let's have some wine."

Sabina led her guest upstairs. She had instructed the servants to set a small table in her sitting room, where it was private and warm.

"How charming," Camelia commented as she took in the cozy surroundings. "Adolfo has been busy lately. With the Florentine economy expanding so rapidly, it won't be long before the major countries of Europe begin trading with us on a grander scale."

"Thanks to Lorenzo," Sabina added.

Camelia nodded in agreement and raised her goblet. "I'll drink to that." She took a hearty sip. "Now, tell me why you disappeared."

Sabina sighed. "I wanted to write to you many times, but I didn't know how to broach the matter with you."

Camelia reached out and patted Sabina's hand. "I think of you as the daughter I never had. What drove you into a convent?"

Sabina took a long sip of wine before confessing her love affair with Massimo and her temporary exile from Florence. Camelia remained silent with a look of compassion on her face as she listened intently. When Sabina had finished, she reached across the table and poured a second glass of wine for the both of them.

"My poor girl," Camelia observed.

"It's my fault for being so naïve."

"I sensed the attraction between the two of you—even a blind person could see it—but I didn't think Massimo would act upon it, given your status in Florence and his wife's vindictive nature."

"You knew he was married?" Sabina demanded incredulously.

"*Everyone* knows, so I assumed you did, too."

"I'm so ashamed."

"Well, Massimo should have been honest with you." She

shook her head. "What a terrible ordeal."

A terrible ordeal, yes, but it pales in comparison to being raped. Sabina forced the painful memory out of her head.

It never happened...it never happened...it never happened...

"Sabina?"

"Yes?"

"Has he?"

"Has who what?"

Camelia looked at her strangely. "Have you been listening?"

Sabina blushed. "Forgive me. Too much wine on an empty stomach."

"We've been busy talking while our food is getting cold. Let's eat something before we lose our wits."

They ate a few mouthfuls of stew before Camelia inquired, "Has Massimo sent word to you since the day he abandoned you in Rome?"

Sabina put down her knife and shook her head. "According to Teresa, he never came here while I was in Lucca. No letter, no messenger—it's as if he simply vanished into thin air. I sometimes wonder if I didn't dream the whole thing."

Camelia balled her hands into fists. "That scoundrel! The next time I see him, I'll—"

"You must do nothing. I beg you!" Sabina interjected. "I've told you this in the strictest of confidence."

"I'll honor your request, but he deserves a good tongue-lashing.' She paused in thought. "Now that you're back in Florence, I have a wonderful idea that will help to mend your broken heart."

Nothing will mend this heart of mine. "Oh?"

"Why not write a book?"

Sabina smiled ruefully. "And get it published, too?"

"With your money and connections, it shouldn't be that difficult."

"I wouldn't feel comfortable with my work being read by so many people."

"Write under a false name—a man's name."

Sabina stared at her friend. "Do you think I could get away

190

with it?"

"Why not? You could have a messenger deliver the manuscript to the appropriate sources and see what happens."

"What should I write about?"

"That's entirely up to you. I think it would be deliciously funny if your book became a success. Imagine the people asking one another 'Who is the author?' and only you and I knowing the truth!"

The appealing idea reeked of mischief and fun. Writing was a healthy distraction; it had saved her before and it would save her again.

Sabina chose to write about her own experiences as a foreigner in Florence, offering witty anecdotes on the Florentines and their customs. She wrote furiously throughout the spring season and, by early summer, she had completed a short manuscript. She invited Camelia to her home in order to celebrate her accomplishment.

"Would you like to read the manuscript before it reaches the hands of the public?" Sabina inquired, holding out a stack of parchment sheets.

Camelia shook her head. "As tempting as that may be, I prefer to be pleasantly surprised. I must say that I'm very impressed."

Sabina grinned as a servant filled their chalices with wine. "All I need now is a man's name. Help me select one."

"What about Luciano?"

Sabina wrinkled her nose. "I don't think it fits the tone of the book. What about Carlo?"

Camelia shook her head. "Giancarlo?"

"No. What about Salvatore?"

"Salvatore di Amato. That sounds romantic, don't you think?"

"Do you know anyone by that name?"

Camelia thought for a moment. "No."

Sabina ran to her desk, dipped her quill in ink, and wrote the name on the first page of the manuscript. "One of my servants will take this into town and act on behalf of 'Salvatore.' I suppose we'll have to wait and see what happens after that."

"What's the book's title?"

"A Foreign Perception."

***

A Foreign Perception not only managed to get published and make its way into the hands of several Florentines, it was also praised for being humorous and witty. It soon became the topic of many conversations and a popular novel among the upper class. It even won the approval of Vespasiano da Bisticci, who was overheard talking about the book with his clients in his famed cartolaio.

When the Florentines began to speculate on the origin and whereabouts of Salvatore di Amato, Camelia and Sabina laughed heartily at their little charade.

Lorenzo held a dinner party on the first of September and invited Sabina to attend the event. During the meal, she overheard one of the nobles speaking about her book.

"*A Foreign Perception* is worth reading," he declared to several people sitting nearby. "Salvatore di Amato should be commended."

Another man said, "He's a bit saucy, but definitely humorous. Has anyone here met the author?"

Sabina's heart pounded as she tried to appear nonchalant. Lorenzo, who was listening to the conversation with interest, said nothing.

A young woman preened in her seat. "I ran into the author the other day in the market and, I must say, he's quite handsome."

Sabina almost choked on her food. Several guests, including Lorenzo, looked to her in alarm. She drank some wine and smiled to let the guests know that she was fine.

"I was attending mass at Santa Croce and he stood a few feet away from me," said an elderly gentleman. "Perhaps our gracious host will invite Signore Salvatore to a meal so that we may get to know him."

Lorenzo sat back in his chair. "It's strange that I have not heard of this author before now."

The old man said, "He is a great admirer of yours, Signore Lorenzo. In fact, he mentions you several times in the book."

Lorenzo raised an eyebrow. "Odd, considering I know nothing of him." Looking at Sabina, who had not said a word, he asked, "Have you read Salvatore's work?"

"Me?" she asked, reaching for her chalice. "Ah, no, not yet."

"Then we should both read it soon."

All eyes turned to her and she swallowed hard. "Yes, we should."

A page walked in and whispered something into Lorenzo's ear, who nodded and said, "Show them in and set two more places at the table."

The page returned, followed by an older man and a young man, each lavishly dressed in a foreign style. Upon seeing the men, Lorenzo stood and welcomed them.

"Forgive the intrusion," said the older man in broken Tuscan.

"Your presence honors my home," Lorenzo said. He indicated the two seats that the servants had hastily set. "Please, sit and dine with me and my guests."

When the newcomers turned around to take their seats, the young man caught Sabina's incredulous gaze and a flicker of recognition mingled with uncertainty crossed his face.

Sabina waited for him to speak, but he didn't. With a racing heart, she lowered her head and finished her meal in silence.

Afterward, Lorenzo approached Sabina with the two foreign men in tow. "My new business associates have requested an introduction," he explained. "Gentlemen, I present to you Signora Sabina Rossi."

The young man bent over Sabina's hand and kissed it. "It's an honor, Signora. I am Sir James Wynne of Rochester and I never had the chance to thank you for your kindness."

Lorenzo looked from Sabina to James in confusion.

"You know each other," the older man asked.

James ignored the question. "This is my father, Thaddeus Wynne, Earl of Rochester."

Sabina curtsied and extended her hand. The earl bent over

193

it.

James never took his eyes off Sabina's face when he asked, "Father, do you remember when I was robbed and left for dead in Lucca?"

"How can I ever forget such a tragedy?"

"This is the young woman who nursed me back to health in that dreadful hospital."

Thaddeus's eyes widened with realization. "I see."

"My servants came for me during the night while I was unconscious," James explained. "I have never forgotten your eyes."

I haven't forgotten yours, either. Sabina smiled. "I'm happy to see you in good health, Sir James."

Thaddeus said, "Thank you for saving my son, Signora Sabina. If I may ask, what were you doing at the hospital in the first place?"

"My sister is a nun in the Convent di Santa Lucia. They do charity work at the hospital and orphanage. During my visit with her, I accompanied the nuns and worked alongside them."

"How commendable," Thaddeus said.

James placed his hand on the left side of his torso. "I would show you the scar right now if it was not considered inappropriate."

"I'll take your word for it. You speak our language well."

James blushed. "You are too kind."

"I'm sure it's better than my English."

"Do you speak English?" Thaddeus asked.

"No," she admitted, making the men laugh.

The musicians began to play a tune. Some of the guests gathered in the center of the main hall in order to dance.

"Perhaps Signora Sabina would like to dance," Thaddeus said to his son. "Go ahead and enjoy yourself for a bit while I speak with Signore Lorenzo."

James looked at Sabina. "Would you care to dance?"

Sabina glanced at Lorenzo, who gave her an imperceptible nod. She accepted James's hand and allowed him to lead her toward the other dancing guests. Lorenzo looked at Sabina thoughtfully before leading the earl to a more private location.

"What brings you so far from home?" Sabina asked while stepping in tune to the music.

"My father wishes to propose a trading deal with Signore Lorenzo," he replied, spinning her around once. "There are many fine goods produced in this region such as silk, wine, art, and gold. It seems as though the Tuscans have a talent for just about everything."

"I've never thought of it that way, but I suppose it's true."

"Well, we would like to bring some of that finery to England where it would be sold for a king's ransom."

"Aside from its economic potential, what do you think of Florence?"

"I enjoy the mild climate and find the art and literature sophisticated. The fashions are also impressive, and the women..." He flushed to the roots of his golden hair and did not finish the sentence.

"What about the women?" she prompted.

"They are exotic and colorful, like peacocks."

"What are English women like?"

"Bland in comparison," he said softly, his amber eyes twinkling.

She felt her cheeks burn and averted her gaze. After what Massimo had done to her heart, she wouldn't let anyone else in so easily. Not even a golden Englishman with the face of a Botticelli angel.

The music ended and James bowed. "Thank you for the dance."

"My pleasure. Now, if you'll excuse me—"

"May I join you?"

She was about to protest politely, but something in his eyes made her stop. They walked through the cluster of guests and out into the courtyard.

"Shall we sit for a while?" he suggested. "It's a lovely evening."

They sat down on a stone bench and gazed at the stars in the violet twilight sky. The air was velvety, heavy with the scent of rain and late blossoms. She remembered when Massimo had kissed her under those same stars in that same courtyard.

I wonder where you are now, Massimo...

"Have you ever been to England, Signora Sabina?"

She shook her head. "Tell me about it."

James proceeded to talk about his country with obvious pride. Sabina soon found herself engrossed in an intelligent and lively conversation. It seemed as though only a few moments had passed before Lorenzo and the earl found them outside.

"It's late and we should go," Thaddeus said to his son.

Reluctantly, James stood and Sabina followed suit. "It has truly been a pleasure speaking with you, Signora," he said before kissing her hand. "Hopefully, our paths will cross again soon."

Sabina smiled. "I'd like that."

Thaddeus inclined his head. "Thank you for entertaining my son. I bid you a good evening, Signora Sabina."

Lorenzo motioned to a page and said to the men, "My servant will show you out. Good evening, gentlemen."

James offered Sabina a wistful look before walking away.

"You're full of surprises," Lorenzo commented, eyeing her closely.

"James was left for dead at the hospital, so I arranged for a physician to examine the wound, then I sat with him until his fever broke."

"Several months later, you meet him in my home."

"An uncanny coincidence."

"The English, it seems, have developed a taste for fine things. They already foster a wonderful relationship with Portugal and wish to expand their trade territory. The earl is eager to engage with Florence and other cities within the Tuscan region. It's a wise move on his part, not only for business but also for political alliances."

"How long will they stay in Italy?"

He looked at her knowingly and, rather than answer her question, he said, "You and Sir James appear to have much in common."

Sabina's cheeks reddened. "He's polite and well-educated." She paused. "Is he married?"

Lorenzo chuckled. "No."

The Earl of Rochester made it clear to Lorenzo de' Medici that he was interested in learning more about "the lovely" Signora Sabina Rossi. Apparently, his son was a finicky man. Having recently lost his young wife after delivering their first, stillborn child, James had shown no interest in marrying again.

The death of Thaddeus's wife the previous year had only heightened the earl's own sense of mortality and intensified his need for a grandson. He was losing patience with James and wanted his son to marry again in order to procure an heir.

"She is of noble blood, is she not?" Thaddeus asked of Lorenzo.

"The Rossi name dates back to the forefathers of Tuscany. She is of the oldest and most noble blood," Lorenzo replied, closing the door of his study to assure privacy.

"What of her reputation?"

Lorenzo thought of Sabina's recent affair with Massimo. There had been no scandal and hardly anyone knew of it. "I can personally attest to Signora Sabina's reputation; it's immaculate. There is no blush upon her name. She was married briefly to one of my oldest and dearest friends, Tommaso Caravelli. An honorable man who lost his life only eight months into their marriage."

The earl rubbed his chin pensively. "No children?"

"No."

"Please excuse the indelicacy of this question, but…I assume her financial state is one that would enable her to marry someone of my son's rank?"

Ah, money. It was always a tool used at the bargaining table of marriages. "She is richer than many princesses."

The earl nodded, pleased. "My son has taken quite a fancy to her. Since I cannot convince him to take an English bride, I have no objection to a foreign one—given, of course, that she meets the proper criteria."

"I think she would be a fine choice for your son," Lorenzo

197

assured.

"She would have to learn English," Thaddeus said thoughtfully.

Lorenzo, wanting to secure a good alliance with the Earl of Rochester and see Sabina happily matched, invited her and James to his palazzo. It was an intimate gathering of friends and the perfect opportunity for two people to get to know each other better.

James showed great interest in everything Sabina said throughout dinner. At one point, Sabina saw Lorenzo looking at her in approval and she wondered what the meaning behind the look meant.

During the earl's stay in Florence, Lorenzo made it a point to invite Sabina to several dinners and performances and to make sure that she and James were seated together. On one such evening, after James had been called away by his father in order to meet some important Florentines, Sabina sought out Lorenzo.

"Are you trying to arrange a marriage between James and me?" she asked him bluntly when they were alone.

"There is no mincing words with you, is there, Sabina?"

"Not when my future is at stake," she replied levelly.

"The earl has made inquiries of you. It seems as though his son has taken a fancy to you and will most likely be proposing marriage soon."

"So you would have me marry a foreigner and move to England?" she asked, disappointed that he would not prefer to keep her close.

"I would not try to force you into anything. If you did accept his proposal, however, it would be most beneficial to me."

"I'm afraid, Lorenzo."

"I would not steer you toward anyone who would mistreat you. The earl is thrilled at the prospect of strengthening our relationship by his son taking a Tuscan bride."

"Who happens to be wealthy."

Sabina is no fool. "Your wealth does make you more attractive, yes."

198

"This match would be good for you and for Florence?"

"It would." Seeing the concern in her eyes, he said, "Do not be afraid of love. What happened between you and Massimo was unfortunate, but don't let that taint this opportunity. It's not good for you to remain alone. It's time you remarried, and what better way to forget Massimo than a new life in a new country? You should have children—many children, in fact. I cannot tell you the joy my sons bring me."

"You're right, Lorenzo." She hesitated. "I have a question to ask, but you must promise to answer it honestly and not be angry with me."

"Ask it."

"What has become of Massimo?"

A shadow settled across his features. "He's in Rome." When she continued to look at him expectantly for more news, he added, "Clarice was furious with me for taking your side in the matter."

"I'm sorry if I caused distress between you and your wife. I'm honored that you think highly enough of me to defend me."

"You should know by now that I care for you."

"Massimo has never attempted to contact you on my behalf?"

Again, his face grew dark. "No."

It's as though what transpired between us never existed. None of it mattered to him. I don't matter to him. "I will marry James of Rochester if it pleases you, Lorenzo."

He gently traced the curve of her cheek with his fingertip. "Dear Sabina, marry him only if it pleases you."

"What other option do I have? It's not as if Massimo—" She stopped once she saw the look on his face. "Forgive me."

"James is waiting to speak with you in my study."

Sabina found James standing by an open window with the sunlight washing over him like iridescent water, making his fair hair and amber eyes glimmer ethereally. As she walked toward him, his mouth curved into a smile, revealing his teeth. His canines were slightly sharp. It was intriguing how his pale features, which were almost pretty, mingled with the

199

savageness of his eyes and slightly animalistic teeth.

He took her hands into his own. "My father has informed me that he wishes to depart for England within a fortnight."

"I see."

He squeezed her hands slightly. "Come with us." She looked up at him and said nothing. "Marry me, Sabina."

"You hardly know me and I don't speak English. I'm not familiar with your country or its customs."

"None of that matters."

"What about your family in England? Will they not object to you bringing home a foreign bride? What of your mother?"

"She died several years ago."

"I'm sorry to hear it." She paused. "I have only one more question to ask before I give you an answer…Do you love me?"

"Does that matter to you?"

"Yes."

His eyes swept over her and he took a step closer. "I do."

Everything was happening so fast! Countless thoughts raced through Sabina's head: marriage, England, a new life, Lorenzo, Florence, Tommaso, Paolo, her father, Massimo…

Oh, Massimo…

"I will marry you, James."

He smiled. "Tell me that you care for me as I care for you."

She could not bring herself to say the words. Instead, she nodded. He bent his head and kissed her lips for the first time.

***

Sabina wrote to Cecilia about her upcoming marriage and voyage to England. She invited Cecilia to stay with her in Florence until her departure.

Cecilia arrived a few days later, surprised, sad, and happy all at the same time. "God works in mysterious ways," she said. "I would never have imagined that one of your patients from the hospital would find you in Florence and take you away."

"I know this is unexpected, but it feels like the right thing to do."

"I wish you the very best, Sabina. I hope he makes you happy."

"Me, too. I've invited James to sup with us so you can meet him."

Camelia and Signore Adolfo were also invited, and everyone seemed impressed with James. As sad as they were to see Sabina go, they rejoiced that she was marrying a man worthy enough to be her husband.

The day before Sabina's departure, Lorenzo called on her to say goodbye. "The earl could not be happier that his son has finally chosen a suitable bride," he said. "Fate is an unpredictable mistress."

"I only hope that I can live up to his expectations."

"I know you will. I've brought something for you—a parting gift."

"Lorenzo, how thoughtful."

He pulled out a book and she noticed the title on the cover: *A Foreign Perception*. "Have you read it?"

She smiled nervously, accepting the book from his hand. "No."

"There's something very familiar about the writing style of this mysterious author."

"Familiar?" she asked innocently, pretending to examine the pages.

Lorenzo narrowed his eyes at her. "Is there something you wish to tell me before you leave for England?"

"No…"

"Sabina," he said, his tone one of mild reproof.

"I wrote it," she finally confessed.

"Why the charade? People are going around town claiming they've met the elusive author. Does it humor you to make fools of others?"

"That wasn't my intention, I swear."

"Many would be angry at being tricked—and by a woman, no less."

"I wanted to have my words read, nothing more."

He crossed his arms and regarded her the way a father would an errant child. "I should make you confess the truth and offer a public apology."

201

"Please don't," she pleaded. "Let this remain a secret between us."

Lorenzo took his time pondering the matter while Sabina anxiously bit her lower lip. "I will let it pass—*this time*. No more pranks."

"I promise."

He let his stern guard down and finally chuckled. "Life in Florence will be dull without you," he admitted. "I shall miss you, and I'm grateful for the good memories we've shared in the past."

"You sound like my sister, Cecilia. She believes we'll never see each other again."

"England is far away and you'll be busy with your new life."

"As long as there are ships and horses, there's no reason why I cannot visit my loved ones."

He offered no reply. When a woman took a foreign husband, she often left her country never to return. "I regret that I cannot dally. I have a meeting with members of the Signoria today."

"You've only just arrived," she said, wanting to prolong the visit.

Lorenzo suddenly gathered her in his arms, and whispered in her ear, "Remember, I'll always be here if you need me."

Sabina's tears fell quietly as she embraced him. He pulled away to look down at her wet face and smiled softly. In an act of boldness, she pressed her lips against his in what was meant to be a swift kiss. Lorenzo, however, pulled her against him and kissed her hard. When he let her go, he smiled and winked at her.

"Godspeed, my beautiful Sabina," he said before walking out the door.

She was suddenly overwhelmed by sadness. She was leaving her beloved Florence.

She was leaving Massimo.

CHAPTER 16

On the morning of Sabina's departure Cecilia embraced her sister. Teresa, who would be accompanying Sabina to England, was enthralled with the idea of her mistress marrying into a noble family and moving to a foreign country.

Mendi, freed from his cage, was perched upon a low branch of a tree within the courtyard. Sabina feared the cold English weather would kill him after so many years in the mild Tuscan climate. She said goodbye to her feathered friend and wished him well. James was glad the eerie bird was staying behind in Tuscany.

Familiar with the unpredictability of life, Sabina thought it best to keep her charming palazzina. Even though the possibility of returning to Florence seemed slim, it was comforting to know that she owned a piece of property in her beloved Tuscany. She dismissed her servants and hired an old man named Iacopo to remain as caretaker.

"It's time to go," James said, placing his hand on the carriage door.

"I shall see you again, Cecilia," Sabina promised tearfully.

"I'll pray for you and ask God to keep you safe."

The sisters embraced again and Sabina entered the carriage. Cecilia waved and continued to stare down the street long after the carriage had disappeared from view.

Aside from Teresa, two servants accompanied Sabina on her journey. One of them was her cook, Maria, and the other, an Italian tutor named Umberto. She had insisted to James that their children would learn Tuscan culture and language. James had agreed to this condition.

Sabina gazed at the Tuscan hills as the carriage made its way to Pisa. The olive trees and vineyards were being harvested, and she saw many people working in the fields. The tall cypress trees used to mark property lines looked majestic against the horizon. It was delightfully picturesque, and she wondered if the English countryside was as pleasant. She was suddenly overwhelmed by nostalgia.

You haven't even left your native land and already you miss it.

The earl and his entourage were waiting for them in Pisa. Sabina stood to the side as her future father-in-law spoke to his son and the ship's captain in English. The language sounded guttural to her ears, and she hoped it would not be too difficult to learn.

"This is so exciting, Signora," Teresa said. "Will I be learning English, too?"

"Yes, of course."

"Sir James is most kind. I hope the English are as well-mannered as he is. I wonder what the English court is like. I've never been in the presence of a king before."

"Nor have I, but James and his father attend court regularly. I imagine that I'll be expected to accompany them."

"As your lady-in-waiting, I'll have to accompany you."

"Certainly," Sabina agreed, amused. Teresa was more excited than she was, and it made her wonder if she was doing the right thing.

James walked toward them and placed his hand on Sabina's arm. "The captain insists we leave now in order to avoid a storm that is headed for Pisa. Hopefully, we'll be far from here when it hits."

Sabina and her servants had never been on a ship before, and it was not long before they became seasick.

The ship sailed north to Genoa, then along the French coast until it reached Marseilles, the large seaport of southeast France. Rather than sail around Spain and Portugal and head north toward the British Isles, the earl thought it would be faster to travel across France to Le Havre and set sail across the English Channel from there. By now, she and her servants had earned their sea legs and the ship's movements no longer caused nausea.

Sabina was thrilled by the foreign sights and sounds. The

French had distinct fashion styles and their language sounded like an operatic staccato to her ears. As they walked along the pier into the city, James indulged his bride by purchasing some French sweetmeats, which she generously shared with her curious servants.

Later, while they were on the ship crossing the English Channel, James approached Sabina. "We're almost there."

"I'm glad to hear it."

"The journey is tedious, I know. You'll like England."

"Of that I am certain. Tell me about Edward IV."

James was happy to accommodate his future bride's request and recounted tales of his monarch. Sabina was surprised to learn that Edward had chosen a lowborn widow named Elizabeth Woodville for his wife. The queen had, at first, rejected the offer to be the king's mistress, so the king proposed marriage.

"How romantic."

"Some of the nobles believe it was foolish on the king's part," he explained. "They feel he could have made a better choice, one that would have provided a political alliance and strengthened his position."

"Your king married for love, and there's something noble in that."

"Perhaps you're right." He touched her cheek. "Thank you for agreeing to marry me. Leaving your home, your sister, and your friends is not easy. I promise you won't regret it."

"Land!"

The shout had come from one of the sailors. The ship sailed closer to the port of Dover, allowing Sabina to admire the impressive white cliffs that rose from the sea.

Everyone was exhausted by the time they reached Rochester. Torches burned outside the ancient stone walls of a mighty fortress. The impressive structure had been built for protection and lacked many of the decorative architectural elements so common in Florentine palazzos.

Sabina noticed numerous soldiers along the battlements. Following her gaze, James said, "Our army consists of nearly one hundred men. Fifty are garrisoned here, and the rest are stationed at various military posts throughout our territories."

The soldiers discreetly eyed the Tuscan beauty as she passed beneath them into the castle.

The interior was furnished with colorful tapestries and fur skins. The flagstones had been swept and the servants had taken the trouble to hang dried lavender in order to give off a pleasing aroma. The main hall was enormous, with the biggest hearth Sabina had ever seen—an entire tree could fit inside! They crossed its expanse and passed several spacious areas, some of which contained shelves of books and atlases.

Finally, they came to a stairwell. At this point, James and his father bid Sabina goodnight and instructed a page to take her and her servants to their respective quarters. Sabina found her room to be well appointed and pleasant. The bed canopy and drapes were of red velvet with gold trim. A fur rug was set to the side of the bed and on the far wall hung a large tapestry depicting a group of women primly seated in a garden reading what appeared to be prayer books. The tapestry's background was also red. Later, she would learn that the color red was as popular with the English as it was with the Florentines.

Teresa busily unpacked their belongings while Sabina noticed various small details throughout the room. There was a ceramic bowl thoughtfully filled with pears, a prayer book beside the bed, two empty storage chests, and a pretty little chair set before a small writing desk. Parchment, quills, and ink were neatly stacked on the desk's surface.

"It's a lovely room," Teresa said as she shook out a night shift.

"Yes, it is." Sabina paused. "I want to thank you for being here, Teresa. I can't imagine being alone right now."

"I would never abandon you, Signora Sabina."

Touched, Sabina took the night shift from her maid. "I'll finish unpacking. I know you're tired. Go and rest now."

Teresa smiled. "Thank you. Goodnight."

The next morning, James gave Sabina a tour of her new home, commonly known as Hart Castle. It derived its name from the Norman baron who built it in the late ninth century.

James pointed to a cluster of trees. "London is less than a day's ride in that direction."

"You and your father attend court quite often."

"My father is actually a distant cousin of the king and therefore favored by him. We must formally present you at court in order to obtain His Majesty's official blessing before the wedding ceremony can take place. Father has procured an English tutor for you."

"I shall start my lessons at once."

He chuckled. "I admire your enthusiasm. First, I would like to show you the land surrounding the castle."

Sabina knew how to ride a horse fairly well and did a decent job of keeping up with James as they rode along the river. The autumn trees were ablaze with color, making the landscape come alive. She expected James to lead her to a private spot where he could steal a few kisses, but he did not. In fact, aside from the brief kiss they shared on the ship, he hadn't touched her once since their departure from Tuscany.

Sabina's cheeks were red and slightly chapped from the cold wind. Teresa would need to concoct an emollient cream to protect her skin from the harsh English weather. Later in the afternoon, she was introduced to an old man by the name of John Bullock, who was to be her English tutor. John, who knew both French and Italian, insisted on being called Tutor John.

The first lesson proved to be difficult since Sabina's tongue was unaccustomed to the task of pronouncing English sounds. She would eventually speak her husband's language with a thick accent, and hoped it would not be too offensive to the ears of English courtiers.

Sabina was determined to memorize a few simple phrases before her introduction to the king. She took the time to learn which families were considered allies and which were enemies.

Shortly after Sabina's twenty-second birthday, the earl announced that it was time for her to meet the King of England. Unlike her first husband, who had summoned the seamstress for his bride's presentation at the Palazzo Medici, James did nothing.

Sabina was put out by this. "Will I not have a new gown, James?"

The earl, who stood nearby, took it upon himself to reply. "If you need a new one, of course we'll summon the seamstress, but if you have something suitable, why bother? No one has seen any of your dresses before. To the English courtiers, everything you own is new."

She looked to James, who shrugged in agreement.

"I suppose you're right, my lord," she replied in English.

"Very good, Sabina," Thaddeus said.

Sabina wanted James to act as Tommaso had, making her feel special—but the earl *did* make a valid point.

Sabina found London to be much dirtier than Florence. She chided herself for making comparisons and tried to look at the positive instead of the negative. It was dark when they arrived at the royal residence, and they were shown immediately to their rooms.

Teresa helped her mistress dress the next morning in the fine red gown she had worn for her presentation to Lorenzo de' Medici. A costly ruby and diamond necklace flaunted the creaminess of her skin.

Thaddeus and James arrived in order to accompany Sabina to the main hall. Eyeing her gown, the earl said, "The neckline is too low."

Stunned, she said, "This is the fashion in Tuscany, my lord."

"You're in England now. Our ways are not your ways."

Teresa did her best to tuck the edges of a flimsy scarf into the bodice of the gown so that it would appear as part of the garment's design.

They made their way to the main hall, which was full of people. Many of the courtiers greeted the Earl of Rochester and his son while staring at the dark-haired beauty beside them. Sabina's raven hair, emerald eyes, and dazzling attire stood out in stark contrast to the English female courtiers. The earl bowed before the king.

"You've finally come home," Edward said. "It's good to see

you."

"Likewise, sire. I have many things to tell you about my travels."

"We will speak later in private. Let us see this Tuscan treasure."

Sabina was officially presented to the king, whom she found to be rather plain in appearance but with a pleasant countenance. The queen, a striking woman, sat beside him with their son close at hand. The young prince appeared bored until he saw Sabina.

Edward gazed upon the beautiful foreigner as she bowed before him. "Welcome, my lady. I hope you find England to your liking."

"It is an honor to meet you, Your Majesty. I find England lovely and most agreeable," she said in the best English her stubborn tongue would allow.

Several people heard her foreign accent and narrowed their eyes to study her more closely.

Edward grinned. "Already speaking English! We shall make a proper English lady of you, yet."

Sabina didn't understand, so James quickly translated. She smiled at the king and said, "Nothing would please me more, my lord."

Edward turned to James. "You have chosen wisely, Sir James. Your betrothed is comely and well-mannered. God bless your union."

"Thank you, sire."

James and Sabina backed away from the king while Thaddeus remained close to the throne. Once it was appropriate to turn their backs, James ushered her toward a quiet corner. "The king likes you," he said.

She sagged with relief. "I'm glad."

"You doubted? Foolish girl." James placed his hand on her waist. So far, he had made no attempt to bed her during their brief courtship. There was desire in his eyes. "If we could wed now, I would do it."

Aroused, she whispered, "We could enjoy the pleasures of

man and wife tonight, if you wish."

"I won't do that," he countered, taking a step back.

"I merely jest," she lied in an attempt to conceal her wounded pride.

"What do you think of a quiet, private ceremony?"

She had hoped for a lively banquet with troubadours and dancers, yet said, "That would suit me." She was lucky to have been given a second chance at a respectable marriage and didn't want to go against her future husband's wishes.

Sabina and James were married one week later. A few of the earl's closest allies and relatives were invited and, to the bride's surprise, musicians and acrobats were hired to entertain the guests. The wedding feast consisted of roasted meats, breads cleverly woven into braids, cheeses, fruits, and Tuscan pastries prepared by Sabina's cook. The English cooks had prepared tasty, meat-filled tarts called chewets.

She danced with her husband and he spun her around until she became dizzy. English music and dancing was different than what she was accustomed to, but she liked it. The guests cheered the couple on and even followed them to the nuptial chamber that had been prepared in advance by the servants. Despite the door being bolted shut, the guests continued to bang on it, shouting vulgar warnings and scandalous advice on how to properly conceive.

Sabina laughed as she sat on the bed, which had been sprinkled with dried rose petals. Candles burned throughout the room and fresh tansy had been strewn into the mattress. James began to undress and she followed suit. They both got into the bed and James kissed her for several minutes. His lovemaking proved to be pleasant enough, but far from passionate.

It paled in comparison…

She cursed herself for thinking of *him*, especially during the first night with her new husband. Her kind, sweet, and decent husband who had not lied to her about having a wife! James would never abandon her or go through life without trying to at least contact her in some way or another. Unlike Massimo, James was a good man.

210

"I love you," James whispered before kissing her forehead.

"And I, you," she replied automatically.

Long after James had fallen asleep, she was still wide awake.

***

Massimo's horse came to a halt in front of Sabina's palazzina. He took a great risk coming to Florence.

This visit was long overdue.

He desperately hoped she would understand why he was unable to contact her sooner as he knocked on the gate.

A bleary-eyed old man eventually came to the door and peered at him. "What commotion is this at such a late hour?"

Massimo took a step back in surprise. "Who are you?"

"I'm Iacopo, the caretaker. Who are you?"

"I'm here to see your mistress. Please, it's of the utmost importance."

Iacopo bristled in irritation. "The house is closed, sir. My mistress is in England."

"England? What the hell is she doing there?"

The old man frowned. "She lives there with her husband."

Massimo felt as if he had been kicked in the stomach. His knees went weak and he placed his hand on the door for support. *"Husband?"*

"Didn't you know?" Iacopo paused in concern when the young man's face turned white in the moonlight. "Signore? Are you feeling all right?"

Massimo rubbed his temples. No one had told him. Not even Clarice. After a moment, he asked, "When did she go?"

"Almost two months ago."

Massimo left without saying another word. He had come to Florence in secret, wearing a disguise, and now he had to leave with the utmost caution. The moment he was safely outside the city gates, he rode at breakneck speed to the nearest inn. Once inside, he purchased tankard upon tankard of ale until his wits were thoroughly dulled. Placing several coins on the table, he demanded a bed for the night. Within the privacy of a simple room, Massimo Reni gave in to tears.

Oh, Sabina…

CHAPTER 17

Sabina became pregnant in the spring and, according to the midwife, the baby would be born around Christmastime. James and Thaddeus were ecstatic, and they looked at her with newfound admiration for having fulfilled her duty in such a timely manner.

Sabina was terribly disappointed when she came down with a fever in early June. She had passed through her first English winter unscathed, so it seemed odd that she would become ill when the weather finally warmed. After two harrowing weeks, she recovered from the ordeal with no harm to the child.

"She's as strong as an ox," Thaddeus told his son. "If she can withstand illness without incident, then she can easily deliver a child."

"I hope you're right."

The earl had been correct about Sabina's ability to deliver a child, but he had incorrectly predicted the part about it being easy. She gave birth to a healthy girl in December of the year 1481.

The earl's disappointment at having a female grandchild was only slightly overshadowed by James's joy at finally joining the ranks of fatherhood. "What shall we name her?" he asked of Sabina as he cradled the newborn in his arms.

"I've always been fond of the name Stefania."

James looked blankly at her. "Our daughter should have a respectable English name. What do you think of the Anne? It was my grandmother's name, and it would please my father."

She thought of Santa Anna, mother of the Madonna, a venerated icon. "I think it's a good name. Lady Anne Wynne."

Sabina wondered if the earl himself had not chosen the name and suggested it to James. Not wanting to cause problems, she dismissed the sly thought. Her father-in-law had a tremendous influence on his son, but she knew James would put his foot

212

down when it was needed—or at least she hoped he would, if and when the time came.

"We shall baptize her at the cathedral as soon as possible."

"We can't christen the baby in this weather. It's too cold."

"We must," he insisted. "Heaven forbid something happen to her. Our little Anne's soul would not make it to Heaven."

"Nonsense! God wouldn't do that to an innocent child."

James gaped at his wife. "You dare question the wisdom of God?" Handing the baby to Teresa, he instructed, "Bundle her up warmly and help your mistress get dressed."

"Teresa, give me my daughter." Looking pointedly at James she added, "She's going nowhere and neither am I."

"Sabina, I insist the child be baptized."

"I'm only asking that you wait until the weather is warm. The baby is newly born and will most likely die if you take her out in freezing temperatures," she said, using the tone one would reserve for a daft child. As an afterthought, she added, "If it's so important to you, why not have the priest come here?"

"It should be done in the house of God on holy consecrated ground."

"For God's sake! Jesus himself was baptized in a river!"

She is too clever and swift with her words. Flustered and lacking an appropriate counter argument, he said, "My father and I insist on taking her to the cathedral."

She let out a long breath in an attempt to regain her composure and patience. "What about the castle's private chapel?" He said nothing, so she added sweetly, "Will you at least not try to compromise?"

When she stared at him with those piercing green eyes, he felt helpless. "I'll speak to my father and find out what he thinks."

"Why?" she snapped, eyes flashing. "Are you not the child's father? Is it not your right to make such decisions on your own?"

"Apparently you don't think so."

She was silenced by his retort. "If it means that much to you, so be it, but please let us wait a few days. Let the baby thrive a

213

bit before she is forced out into this miserable weather. I'm very tired, James."

He stroked her cheek. "I didn't mean to worry you. All is well."

Her exhaustion was so great, that she fell asleep instantly.

Sabina woke up and asked for her baby. Teresa, who stood wringing her hands nervously, only stared at her.

"Where is my child?"

"I had no choice, Signora," Teresa said. "I bundled the baby up as warmly as I could. I even took one of the small fur-skin rugs from your bedchamber and wrapped her in that, too."

Sabina was livid. "Good thinking. The fur will keep her warm. I'm not angry with you, Teresa. I'm angry with my husband, who apparently lacks a spine and cannot stand up to his father."

Sabina was relieved when James returned later that afternoon with Anne, who was now baptized and no longer in spiritual danger. She accepted the child and smiled to her father-in-law, but the moment the earl left the room she gave her husband a good tongue-lashing.

***

Spring crept slowly over England. The warm weather melted what little remained of the snow and soon the fat buds became visible on the trees. Sabina went outside often, inhaling the sweet, fresh scent in the air and basking in the warmth of the sun. How she dreaded the following winter!

Anne was growing up healthy and strong. The baby's wet nurse was a burly woman with ruddy cheeks and fair hair, and she often had wet streaks down the front of her bodice due to leaking nipples. Sabina did not mind the girl's slovenly appearance, as long as her baby thrived.

She had written a letter to Cecilia and Camelia shortly after Christmas, and their responses had recently arrived. Both were doing well and assured Sabina that her company was much missed. Camelia's letter contained the latest gossip, while Cecilia's letter included stories about her charity work. Sabina read and reread them, then tucked them away in a small chest.

214

She wrote to Lorenzo as well, but he had not yet replied.

***

Sabina's English improved and her social life expanded. She partook in noble festivities and often attended court with James. Edward, who took a fancy to Sabina, would ask her many questions about Florence and the famed Palazzo Medici. She entertained the king with stories of various Florentine artists and philosophers. When he inquired about the great Il Magnifico, she offered him an honest assessment of Lorenzo's character and many talents, including his political shrewdness.

"You are quite impressed with him," Edward concluded.

"I am, Your Majesty. He is unlike any man I've ever met."

"That's a bold thing to say before your king, my lady."

"But, my lord, you are also unlike any man I have ever met."

He laughed aloud, drawing curious looks from several courtiers. Sabina caught a glimmer of envy in some of their eyes. "Your English has improved to the point that you've developed a silver tongue."

"You flatter me, sire. Thank you."

"I speak the truth, my lady." He cleared his throat. "Now, if you will excuse me."

It was a dismissal. Sabina curtsied low to the king as he walked away. James appeared before her and demanded to know what had made the king laugh so loudly. When she told him of their conversation, he was not amused.

"You risked the king's displeasure," he chided.

"I would never displease the king or disgrace you, for that matter."

"My father and I had an interesting conversation this morning."

"Did you?"

"He said he would like to see us attend mass more often." She wondered what had brought on such an unexpected comment. "It's unseemly how seldom we appear in church together."

"I've been at your side every Sunday for mass."

"True, but some noble ladies take communion daily, and one

215

must keep up appearances to prevent wagging tongues."

She was taken aback. "Has someone singled us out for gossip?"

"Why do you oppose going to church? Remember, if you had not been at the convent, you would never have met me and saved my life. God works in mysterious ways. I'm merely suggesting that we honor Him more often."

"Does your father not have anything better to do than run our lives?" Sabina regretted her words when she saw the pain in her husband's eyes. "Forgive me. I care deeply for your father and meant no disrespect."

He shook his head and walked toward a group of gentlemen. That day marked the first snag in the fabric of their marriage.

***

Edward IV died in April of the year 1483 and his twelve-year-old son, Edward V, succeeded to the throne. He was a good boy, well loved by the people, and a promising king for England. Fate, being cruel and cunning, had different plans for the young king. Edward V, along with his younger brother, died two months later—only four days before his coronation. The young monarch's reign lasted eighty-six days and was dominated by the influence of his uncle, Richard, Duke of Gloucester.

The nobles who resented Elizabeth Woodville, Edward IV's lowborn widow, deemed her children illegitimate and managed to convince the clergy of this. The scandalous turn of events worked in the duke's favor. He was crowned King Richard III at Westminster Abbey in July.

All nobles were expected to swear fealty to their new sovereign. Sabina knew that her father-in-law was among those who suspected foul play on the part of the duke, but that didn't deter the earl or his son. They dutifully went to London and pledged their allegiance to Richard.

Sabina studied England's new king. A thin man with shoulder-length brown hair, he possessed a somewhat pinched face and beady eyes. She noticed he had a habit of chewing his bottom lip, causing the skin to redden and chafe. In short, she wasn't impressed by his countenance.

Anne turned two the year Richard became king. She was a happy and healthy child with blonde curls and twinkling green eyes. James was completely smitten with his little girl. Thaddeus also doted on the child, but he barely hid his disappointment that Anne was not a boy.

Umberto instructed Anne on Tuscan culture and language, while Tutor John taught her English and Latin. The little girl proved to be a bright student and, by the time she turned four, she was fluent in three languages.

Whenever Anne spoke the Tuscan dialect in front of her grandfather, he corrected the child by saying, 'Italian in private, English in public.'

This annoyed Sabina, who didn't want Anne adopting the notion that her mother's native tongue was somehow shameful.

***

Time passed quickly for Sabina, who devoted her life to being a good wife and mother. In 1485, Richard died in battle on Bosworth Field. It would be the end of Plantagenet rule because Henry VII, a Tudor, seized the throne. Once again, the nobles were called upon to swear fealty to their new sovereign. Sabina found this new king to be much more agreeable than the last one. Henry was not exactly handsome, but he was far from ugly. He held himself proudly, as a true noble should, and seemed to take his royal responsibilities seriously. She later learned that in order to strengthen his position, Henry pursued a European bride—the Queen of Naples.

"Apparently, it's becoming fashionable for Englishmen to have Italian wives," Thaddeus said when he heard the news.

Fate did not want the marriage to take place, and the king ended up marrying an Englishwoman, Princess Elizabeth of York.

In 1487, Sabina received a letter from Camelia informing her that Clarice Orsini had died at only thirty-four years of age. Sabina knew Lorenzo must be suffering, and the thought of his pain made her own heart ache. Despite Lorenzo's many infidelities, Clarice had been a good wife and a devoted mother to their children.

Sabina wasted no time in writing a letter to him, offering condolences and comforting words. Throughout the many years, she had written to Lorenzo several times and had not received one letter in return. She was sure that he read her letters, so she continued to write them. She also knew through her correspondence with Camelia that gout, the family disease that plagued the Medici, was beginning to take its toll on Lorenzo's health. Apparently, he was spending more and more time away from Florence in order to take therapeutic thermal waters to ease his pain. Unfortunately, it did little good.

CHAPTER 18

The long shadows darkened as the sun set behind the Roman hills. Massimo's wife watched her husband reading a book in the courtyard below. She had once found him devastatingly handsome, but the stark differences in their personalities and his lack of funds earned him her scorn. Their marriage had been arranged due to the friendship between her father and her late father-in-law. It was a gesture that both men later regretted. Massimo was nothing like Luigi, the wealthy and cultured Sicilian nobleman she met a few months ago.

"Michela."

She turned toward her father's voice. "Yes?"

"Have you heard from Luigi?"

There were no secrets between them. She lifted the letter from her lap. "His letter arrived today."

"I spoke to the bishop." He hesitated, his expression grim. "The Church will not grant you a divorce, so I'm going to appeal to the pope himself."

"I know you'll succeed in your endeavor, Father. If only Luigi's wife would hurry up and die, then there would be one less impediment."

Luigi's bedridden wife had fluctuated between life and death for months. The woman's demise would certainly make things easier.

"A strong alliance could be made between the two families," her father mused aloud. He stroked his daughter's hair. Her brown eyes were two slits when she smiled up at him. Michela was no great beauty, but she was strong and determined, which was far more valuable. "In due time, my sweet girl. Everything will work out."

"What if we…" she trailed off and looked out the window.

He followed her gaze to where his son-in-law sat. "Lorenzo would strike back. Besides, it's a mortal sin to commit such a heinous act. I never want to hear such words from your lips again."

"Forgive me, but I can no longer stomach the sight of him."

"I can expel him from the city. It's the best I can do."

"Then do it. It's obvious he is still pining for his long-lost whore."

"Consider it done, sweetheart. I'll send him back to the villa, far away from you. Think of him as being in exile."

Michela held her lover's letter to her chest and continued to gaze down at Massimo with unmasked contempt.

***

Desperate for a grandson, the Earl of Rochester became increasingly impatient with Sabina. She was forced to endure unkind comments and even hostility. James, who was also disappointed, still loved his wife and found himself stuck in the middle.

Shortly after Anne's ninth birthday, Sabina suggested that her daughter be presented at court. "She's an accomplished and well-behaved young lady," she said to her husband and father-in-law one day. "It's time to present her to the king and start thinking of her future."

"We'll take Anne to court when she has a brother to accompany her," Thaddeus said coldly.

Appalled, Sabina glanced at her husband for support and, when none came, she said, "My lord forgets that I'm as anxious for a son as you are." In addition to having taken several potions and expensive tonics assured to promote fertility, she instructed Teresa to keep her eyes and ears open for the latest cures. A male child would ease the tension in her marriage and get her father-in-law to stop his constant nagging.

"Is that so, my lady?" the earl asked in an accusing tone. "It seems to me that you were content to have inherited your last husband's fortune without an heir."

James glared at his father. "Father!"

Finally, Sabina thought, satisfied to see James take a stand against his overbearing father.

"Sit down, James, I only speak the truth," Thaddeus

snapped. "You have been married for several years and she has given you only one child—a useless girl. You need a son."

"I won't have you treat my wife in such a disrespectful manner, nor will I tolerate you speaking ill of my daughter."

The earl turned toward Sabina and said without a trace of remorse, "Forgive me."

Fuming, Sabina nodded in acknowledgment to his feigned apology and excused herself in order to check on Anne, who, gratefully, was not present to hear her grandfather's unkind words.

No sooner had she left the room, than the earl said, "It's obvious that you love your wife. Sabina's beauty and charm are beguiling, and she has won the admiration of many with her quick wit, but you must think seriously of your future. Without a son, the Wynne name will die out and the family's money and lands will go to whomever your daughter marries. In other words, a total stranger. Is that what you want?"

"Sabina feels terrible as it is without you adding to her troubles. She has tried everything possible and wants a son as much as I do."

The earl paced the room quietly, his mind racing. It was time to try a different tactic. "This is God's punishment for your wife's aversion to the Church. If she prayed more and aligned her life according to the Holy Scriptures, God's divine spirit would pour over her and give you a son." He paused in thought. "Sabina has never summoned the physician to discover what ailment prevents her from conceiving."

"She has tried many cures."

"Useless potions!" Then, a sinister thought crossed his mind. "If one didn't know better, one may think her a witch."

"Father!"

Thaddeus sniffed. "I beg your pardon, I misspoke. Others may interpret her lack of religious zeal and affinity for flower lore as being…*ungodly*."

James paled. "Sabina is a God-fearing woman."

"Of course," Thaddeus agreed in a placating tone. "Don't you find it odd how the castle's cats are drawn to her whenever

221

she's outside? According to the kitchen staff, she's constantly dabbling with roots and herbs, crushing them down with her mortar and pestle while muttering to herself like Morgana in the Arthurian tale."

"You should not pay heed to gossip."

"What about that odious crow she once kept as a pet?"

"My wife is a good Christian," James insisted. "She reads from the Bible she keeps by her bed and partakes of Holy Communion regularly. There are many godly women who share her inability to bear a male child and no one accuses them of witchcraft."

Thaddeus nodded in order to end the argument. The seed of doubt was already sown. "Let's hope you're right, my son."

James pondered on his father's words for days afterward, and they gradually began to seem like truth. God was punishing his wife for her lack of faith. He felt personally responsible for Sabina's spiritual health, and began pressuring her to attend mass daily. He insisted that she dress more conservatively, even going as far as forbidding cosmetics or ostentatious jewelry. When she resisted this onslaught of fanatical religious zeal, James turned to his father for help.

The cunning earl seized the opportunity to rid himself of what he now called his "fruitless daughter-in-law." James needed a son and the earl would do everything in his power to make that happen, even if it meant putting the matter before the judicial courts.

Sabina was quick to notice the change in her husband and father-in-law. Whenever they were together, they would cease speaking the moment she entered the room. James became increasingly emotionally distant but continued to visit her bedchamber on a frequent basis.

"Something is afoot," Sabina said to Teresa one day after the men had departed for court without so much as inviting her to go along with them. "James is…*different*."

"I wish I could disagree, but the staff at the castle have been treating us differently, too."

"This is ridiculous," Sabina fumed. "I know they're both

aggrieved by the fact that I've not yet produced a male heir but to treat me—us—like this is unacceptable."

"Do you want me to procure more herbs? I can go into town. Maybe the apothecary has heard of a new cure."

Sabina shook her head. "I've done everything short of selling my soul to Satan for a son. I will do no more. It's in God's hands now."

James and Thaddeus returned from court a week later. Sabina watched from the window of her bedchamber as they dismounted in the courtyard below. The late afternoon sun made James's hair shimmer like rose gold. He glanced up and caught her eye. She turned her face away and wandered back to her desk.

He stormed into her bedchamber a moment later. "You don't come downstairs to greet your husband?"

"I thought you were angry with me."

He closed the door. "On the contrary, I've missed you."

Sabina was surprised when he lunged forward to embrace and kiss her lips. She tasted the salty perspiration on his skin. His traveling cloak and boots were dusty and caked with mud.

"Shouldn't you change into fresh clothes and wash your face?" she suggested when his mouth moved to kiss her throat.

James only grunted in response, pushing her against the wall. His greedy hands clutched at her skirt, pulling it upward.

"James, please…"

"I would have you now, wife."

He freed himself and entered her with desperate need, then stood perfectly still when it was over. She could feel his thundering heart.

"I'll see you at supper," he said, kissing her brow.

Sabina watched him leave the room. James had never been so lustful and it left her feeling bewildered.

Teresa poked her head into the room. "Your husband and father-in-law have arrived."

"Yes, I know. I'll dine in one of my finest gowns this evening." As an afterthought, she added, "I'll also don my best jewels."

223

"But his lordship forbids—"

"They are my jewels to wear whenever I choose. I wish to redden my cheeks and lips, too. I hope my rouge pot has not been misplaced."

Teresa helped Sabina dress, then said, "I haven't seen you look like this since the last time we were at court."

"A long time ago, indeed." Sabina peered into the looking glass. "I'm fit to visit the Palazzo Medici."

Teresa's eyes filled with tears and Sabina did her best to keep her own at bay. She left the room and went downstairs to greet her husband and father-in-law. The men's eyes swept over her in astonishment, but she held her head high.

James approached and took hold of her elbow. "I thought I made it clear that I prefer your adornment to be modest."

"Are you implying that a finely dressed woman is immodest? If so, then you and your father were surrounded by immodest women for a week. I wonder what the queen would think of such a notion."

Thaddeus cleared his throat and looked pointedly at his son.

James nodded to his father. "I need to speak with you, Sabina. Shall we walk in the garden? It's a lovely evening outside."

They walked outside under the twilight sky. The sun had already set and there were streaks of red in the sky.

"I wish to divorce you," he said quietly.

Stunned, she said, "Divorce me? We made love only a moment ago!"

"You *are* my wife and it's my husbandly right to seek carnal pleasure from you." When she continued to stare at him incredulously, he said, "You know I'm very fond of you, Sabina, but I can't remain married to a woman who will not produce an heir."

"*Will not*? You speak as though it's something I can control." She paused, indignant. "Are these your words or your father's?"

"It's no secret that my father feels the same way. We both care for you and had such high hopes that this marriage would

224

be a success."

"I suppose in England marital success is based on how many sons a woman can produce. You Englishmen don't want wives, you want cows capable of breeding only bulls."

"Sabina, please be reasonable."

She clenched her fists. "What is to become of me, James?"

"You can remain here in England, of course. You and Anne will be provided for and continue to live in comfort." He smiled. "We can even continue with our relationship. After all, I still desire you."

Sabina narrowed her eyes at him as realization dawned on her. "You want me to be your mistress?"

"Well, yes."

"You would have me remain in England as your whore while you take on another wife? Are you mad? Did you truly believe that I would agree to such an arrangement?"

"I would think you would want to remain in England for Anne's sake, if not for mine."

"If you divorce me, I'll take my daughter back to Tuscany with me. I would never leave her behind to become a disinherited bastard."

He appeared offended. "I would never do that to her."

"Oh, no? When your new wife starts bearing the sons you so desperately desire, my child will be cast aside—unloved and unwanted."

"I love Anne as much as you do!"

"You're a weak, spineless man! You wouldn't dare risk the disapproval of your new wife or your father. Anne goes where I go."

"The laws of England favor the fathers, not the mothers."

Sabina crossed her arms, suddenly remembering the contents of Camelia's last letter. The new pope, Innocent VII, was a good friend of the Medici. In addition, the pope's son married Lorenzo's daughter and Lorenzo's nephew was now a cardinal.

"I will contest this divorce."

James shrugged. "It will do no good. It would be better for

225

everyone if you submit to my wishes."

"You mean the earl's wishes," she spat. "I plan to inform Lorenzo of this wicked plot that you and the earl are conspiring against me."

James was well aware that the Medici controlled the papacy, but he didn't expect such vehement opposition from his wife. "I'll have to discuss this matter with my father."

"Coward," she seethed, turning her back on her husband.

Sabina ran upstairs to find Teresa. "James is speaking with the earl at this very moment," she whispered to her faithful maid. "I want you to go downstairs and listen to their conversation." She ripped a pearl from her bodice. "Here, take this and pretend to be searching for my lost jewel. Be as silent as possible. Go now!"

Teresa set off quietly, stopping only when she heard the earl's voice. He was in his private study with his son, so she crept to the door…

Thaddeus was furious when James repeated his conversation with Sabina. "Damn her. Your union with that woman was profitable, I admit, but fruitless. The king agrees with me. In fact, he's already selected a wife for you."

"Who is she?"

"Lady Catherine of Chartwell. She's rumored to be pretty. More importantly, she comes from a fertile family. She has many brothers and sisters, and her siblings have many children. *Male children.*"

"I doubt she's prettier than my Sabina," James said churlishly.

Thaddeus bit back an angry retort. "You can still have Sabina."

"She found the idea of being my mistress repugnant."

"Do you want a son or not?" Thaddeus demanded, annoyed with his lovesick son. "Has that witch cast a spell on you? An evil love potion preventing you from thinking clearly?"

"No, Father, but I still love her."

Thaddeus delivered a hard blow to his son's head. James recoiled and winced as he rubbed the sore spot near his ear.

"Forgive me," the earl said gruffly. "I had to knock sense into you."

"Can't we wait a little longer?"

"You've been married for ten years! That Tuscan bitch isn't getting any younger. Her childbearing years are over." He put his arm around his son's shoulders. "Lady Catherine is only seventeen—ripe fruit on the vine. Take my advice and let Sabina go back to Tuscany."

"What about Anne?" James demanded. "I love my daughter."

"You'll love the sons and daughters you sire with Catherine. You'll be giving up one child in exchange for several more."

"What if we insist that Anne remain here?"

Thaddeus resisted the urge to hit his son again. "We risk the pope getting involved and voting in favor of Sabina. We don't want the pope meddling in our affairs." Seeing the misery in his son's eyes compelled him to add, "*Unless…*"

There was an uncomfortable pause as he stared past James with a strange look in his eyes, as though a revelation had just come to him.

"Unless what, Father?"

"Unless there was an unfortunate accident. You would get to keep your daughter and remarry without any problem."

James stared at his father in disbelief. "Are you suggesting murder?"

Teresa crept away to deliver this disturbing news to her mistress.

Shocked, Sabina paced back and forth in her bedchamber. "I want you to summon Umberto and Maria at once. Bring them here. Be quiet and discreet."

Teresa left the room and Sabina scribbled a letter to Lorenzo informing him of her dire circumstances. When her maid returned with the two servants in tow, she supplied Umberto with enough money to buy ship passages, and warned them not to breathe a word to anyone.

Sabina interrupted Anne's lessons the following morning and had a serious conversation with her daughter while

227

Umberto stood by the door like a dutiful sentry.

Anne's brow creased with worry. "Why must we leave, Mother?"

"You're old enough to know the truth, so I'll be honest. Your father wishes to divorce me, take another wife, and keep you in England."

Anne shook her head. "Father would never do such a thing. He loves us." Sabina remained straight-faced and said nothing. The girl's brows knitted together in puzzlement. "Why would father want to rid himself of you? What have you done?"

"Your father needs a male child to carry the Wynne name. I have failed in my duty to provide a male heir and he wishes to be rid of me."

Anne began to cry and Sabina held her. "I do not wish to leave!"

"I will not force you to come with me."

"I want you to stay in England, too," Anne whined.

"Today is the day you become an adult, little one," Sabina said, tucking an errant strand of hair behind her daughter's ear. "Life is full of difficult choices. On one hand, you have your father and England and everything that's familiar to you. On the other hand, you have your mother and Tuscany—it would be an adventure. Only you can decide, but this must remain a secret between us. Tell no one. Do you understand?" She waited for Anne's solemn nod before continuing, "Tonight, while everyone is asleep, I will depart with my servants. If you wish to accompany me, I'll be the happiest woman on earth. If you decide to stay, my heart will remain here with you forever. I'll be waiting for you in my bedchamber at midnight. Remember: I love you no matter what you decide."

Anne's face was wet with tears. Sabina hugged her tightly and kissed her forehead before leaving the room and giving the girl time to think.

The day passed slowly. When it was Anne's bedtime, Sabina kissed her daughter goodnight, just as she had done countless times before.

"I'm going with you, Mother. I don't want to stay here with

a stepmother. She'll never love me the way you do."

Sabina's heart tightened at her daughter's perceptiveness.

Anne continued, "I didn't have time to pack."

"I'll purchase new dresses for you, and they will be far prettier than anything these English seamstresses can create," Sabina promised before embracing her daughter. "Come, we must make haste."

All three servants were packed, dressed, and ready to go. Umberto had secured five passages aboard a ship that would take them across the channel into France. From there, Sabina would figure out what to do. She led the way down the steps to the main floor.

"How will we get past the armed guards?" Teresa whispered.

"I drugged their ale," Maria replied. "They should be sleeping soundly by now. I took the liberty of adding a little bit to the wine, too."

"Good thinking," Sabina said.

They made their way outside without a problem. Umberto fetched the horses from the stable and the five of them rode south beneath a crescent moon. They arrived in Dover before dawn and watched the sun rise from the ship as it headed south toward France.

***

James and his father were surprised to have slept much later than usual. The sun was high in the sky before they managed to drag themselves from their beds. The earl quickly ascertained that he had been drugged and sent a servant to check the rest of the castle.

The servant came back with puzzling news. "Lady Sabina is missing. Her bedchamber has been vacated and her clothing is gone. Lady Anne's room is untouched, but the girl is nowhere to be found."

"James!" Thaddeus bellowed as he scrambled out of bed.

The earl strode through the castle in his night shift, not caring about the cold stone floor beneath his bare feet. He found his son sitting on his bed rubbing his head.

James looked up groggily. "Father?"

"Your wife and daughter are gone."

James stood up and swayed. "Gone? How?"

"We were drugged, as I'm sure the soldiers were."

"Then we shall go after them."

"No, we won't, you fool!"

James's brow creased in confusion, forcing Thaddeus to point out the obvious. "Your wife has deserted you, James, which leaves you free to remarry." His spirited daughter-in-law was now guilty of abandonment and kidnapping. The pope couldn't possibly deny his son a divorce on such serious charges.

James stared straight ahead and said quietly, "I need to be alone, Father. Please go."

The earl closed the door. A moment later, he heard the pitiful sobbing of his brokenhearted son.

Sabina arrived in Florence and found it a very different city than the one she had left behind. While Anne admired the city's unique architecture from within the carriage, her perceptive mother studied the Florentines—more specifically, the expressions on their faces. There was a shadow over the city, even darker than the one cast by the Pazzi Conspiracy over a decade ago. The people seemed to have lost their joy and, in its place, there was something else, something that weighed heavily on their minds and hearts.

In her sudden haste to leave England, Sabina lacked the opportunity to write to Iacopo and inform him of their imminent arrival. Hearing the noise, the old man came out into the courtyard.

"Signora, you did not warn me!"

"Do not worry yourself, Iacopo," Sabina assured him. Iacopo's eyes swept over Anne, compelling her to add, "This is my daughter, Anne."

Iacopo greeted the girl with courtesy before shuffling off to help Umberto, Teresa, and Maria with the few travel trunks. Before long, rooms were aired, linens changed, and inventories made to replenish supplies. Sabina hired two young girls to help with the cooking and cleaning, and in a matter of days, her household ran smoothly.

Anne explored every nook and cranny of her new home, delighted by her foreign surroundings. Sabina sent a message to Camelia announcing their arrival, and her friend came over that same day.

After a tearful embrace, the older woman pulled away and looked Sabina up and down. "Why did you not write to let me know you were coming?"

"I didn't have the chance to do so."

"Is James with you?"

Sabina pursed her lips and shook her head. "I came with my daughter. Anne, where are you?"

Anne exited one of the rooms. "Yes, Mother?"

"Camelia, this is my daughter, Lady Anne Wynne of Rochester."

"It's a pleasure to meet you, Signora Camelia," the girl said with a respectful curtsy.

Camelia smiled warmly at the girl. "What a lovely girl you are, Anna! You have your mother's eyes." She turned to Sabina. "How long will you be staying in Florence?"

"Forever," Anne blurted out.

Camelia's brows came together as she looked askance at Sabina. "Oh, dear. Is everything all right?"

"It is now. Let's take some refreshment, then you and I shall talk."

The three of them ate some freshly baked apple cake and Sabina allowed Anne a bit of sweet wine before sending the girl to her room.

"Have you left your husband?" Camelia asked once they were alone.

"He was going to divorce me."

"On what grounds?"

"Failure to provide an heir. I tried every fertility cure in England but, for some reason, I couldn't conceive after having Anne. James is going to remarry as soon as we're officially divorced."

Camelia made a face. "Men!"

"I don't seem to have much luck with them," Sabina said sadly. "Maybe I'm meant to be alone in life."

"Don't think such a thing, my dear. Coming back to Florence was a wise decision. I'm surprised he allowed you to bring your daughter."

"I threatened to take the case before the pope and my father-in-law was against that idea. My maid overheard them conspiring against me. I was an obstacle in the way of their ambition. I think they meant to harm me in some way, although I can't prove it. We escaped in the middle of the night."

"You poor girl! At least you're safe now."

"Camelia, I feel as if my life is nothing more than a tawdry novel."

"There are enough lies, intrigues, and affairs in Florence to write thousands of tawdry novels. The cunning know-how to keep dirty secrets, and others pretend not to notice. Never feel as if you're the only person who has gone through scandal or heartache."

Sabina felt somewhat better after hearing this.

Camelia continued, "Speaking of scandals, have you heard what has been taking place in Florence?"

"No, but I noticed the Florentines seem grim."

"It's no wonder! Sermon upon sermon in the churches proclaiming God's punishments on the immoral city of Florence. Somber-faced monks walk through the streets shouting warnings of our imminent doom if we do not repent. People crying hysterically and beating themselves bloody in the piazzas to wash away their sins. Things have become intolerable."

The city Sabina remembered and esteemed supported new ideas, new thinking, and embraced ancient secular philosophies. The bile rose to her throat at the thought of facing more religious fanaticism.

"Who is responsible for this surge of zealotry?"

"A Dominican friar by the name of Girolamo Savonarola. His fiery sermons against social corruption are drawing in many followers—most of them poor, of course. The Florentines are in an uproar. He preaches against the lavish lifestyle of the nobility and the members of the Signoria. Even Lorenzo has not escaped his criticism."

"He speaks out against the Medici?"

"Repeatedly. He accuses Lorenzo of supporting the artists and writers who produce unholy, pagan works."

"How does this man get away with such impertinence?"

"The people love him."

"What of Lorenzo?"

"The last I heard he was taking in the thermal waters to soothe his gout. He spends more time in his villa in Careggi than in Florence. His son, Piero, is already preparing to take over when he dies."

"Lorenzo isn't old; he has many years yet to live."

"He's very ill, Sabina," Camelia pointed out gently. "The people are worried. Piero is not as clever or as politically shrewd as his father."

Sabina and Anne departed for the Palazzo Medici the following morning in the company of two newly hired guards. A page led them to a room where Lorenzo sat behind a desk. Dressed in black, he studied the document in his hand with a grave face. The lines between his brows and around his taut mouth were deep, evidence of stress and chronic pain. At the sight of Sabina in the doorway, he stood and opened his arms. She ran into them without a moment's hesitation.

Lorenzo gazed deeply into Sabina's eyes before kissing her forehead. "Ten years, is it? One would think ten hours by looking at you."

"It's wonderful to see you again."

"I read your last letter and was much aggrieved by it. I've written to the Earl of Rochester on your behalf. You're safe now, Sabina."

Moved, she inclined her head and kissed his hand in gratitude.

Suddenly, he winced in pain. "This wretched gout is killing me," he whispered through clenched teeth. He turned to Anne, who stood quietly near the door. "Who is this charming young lady?"

Sabina motioned for Anne to come forward. "My daughter, Anne."

Anne curtsied with surprising elegance. "It's an honor to make your acquaintance, my lord."

Lorenzo smiled and chucked the girl under the chin. "Pale and golden like her father, but the mischief I glimpse in her eyes is yours, Sabina."

Sabina stroked her daughter's hair. "She is my pride and joy."

"At least something good came from your union with James," he whispered. "Please, sit with me a moment. How do you find Florence after being away so long?"

She noticed that he moved with difficulty. "I find it quite changed."

He sighed tiredly. "I fear for the future of this city."

"Camelia told me the monk, Savonarola, speaks out against you. Why do you allow it?"

"My grandfather always taught me to keep my friends close and my enemies closer. Whenever he delivers a sermon, I try to attend. If I can't go, someone from my household attends on my behalf. He challenges me, among others, but I never dignify his words with a response. To do so would make me appear defensive, weak. The Florentines know who I am and they remember everything I've done for them."

"People can be fickle, Lorenzo. The masses have short memories. It's disrespectful for this monk to speak of you in such a manner."

"I don't worry about the poor people who support him, but my rich and powerful enemies see this fanatic as a means to get rid of me."

"You're going through so much right now. What can I do?"

"Nothing."

"There must be something, some way to help you."

He forced a smile. "Keep your eyes and ears open. Stay loyal to me. That's all I ask."

"My eyes and ears are always open. I'm forever your loyal servant."

"Are you happy to be back in your palazzina?"

"Yes." She glanced at her daughter. "Anne likes it, too."

His gaze shifted to Anne. "Do you, now?"

"Yes," Anne replied. "My room has a lovely view of the city."

There was a knock at the door. A young man walked in and handed Lorenzo a pile of documents. "You remember my eldest son, Piero?"

Sabina suddenly felt the weight of the last ten years.

Lorenzo's face paled abruptly, as if seized by a painful spasm.

"Father!" Piero cried. "Are you all right?"

"Forgive me, Sabina, but I must rest," Lorenzo allowed his son to help him stand. "I'm overjoyed that you're back in Florence, where you belong."

"I hope to see you again very soon." She looked to Piero and added, "If there's anything you need, please send word."

"Thank you, Signora Sabina."

Sabina led Anne out of the room and closed the door.

"He is very sick," Anne commented.

"Yes, he is."

"What's wrong with him?"

Sabina led her daughter to the palazzo's exit. "Gout. The Medici have always suffered from it."

"Is Lorenzo de' Medici the most important man in Florence?"

Although she was not sure anymore, she replied, "Yes."

Anne's eyes took in the fine furnishings and rare artwork on their way out. "Did you come here often before going to England?"

"I did. It was a magical place back in those days," Sabina replied, her eyes glazing as she remembered the banquets, the concertos, the talented artists...

Massimo.

"You seem to be a good friend of Signore Lorenzo."

The question broke her reverie. "I would like to think so."

"When will I meet my Aunt Cecilia?"

"Soon."

"Mother, I think I'm going to like living in Florence."

"I can't tell you how happy that makes me."

Cecilia arrived in Florence a few days later. She and Anne took to each other quickly, like two kindred souls coming together. Anne was fascinated by the fact that her aunt was a nun.

"May I visit the convent someday?" Anne asked of Sabina.

"If your Aunt Cecilia doesn't mind."

Cecilia smiled indulgently at her niece. "You're more than welcome to visit me and stay for as long as you like." To Sabina, she whispered, "She certainly didn't take after you."

Anne excused herself in order to prepare for her studies with Umberto, giving the sisters an opportunity to speak privately.

"He threatened to kill you?" Cecilia asked, aghast, after Sabina explained the circumstances which led to her hasty departure from England. "I had no idea you were suffering so much."

"James was a good husband at first, and I enjoyed my life in England—until recently."

Cecilia was pensive. "Did James spend all of your money?"

"No, and whatever remains of it will be returned once he marries whichever English bride his father chooses."

"Dear sister, God must have something special in store for you."

Sabina snickered and replied, "Hopefully, it does not involve a man."

***

James procured his divorce from Sabina and immediately married Lady Catherine of Chartwell. Tutor John, who had always admired Sabina, occasionally sent her letters from England.

In John's most recent letter, he stated that Lady Catherine was already pregnant. The earl rejoiced at the prospect of finally having a grandson, but happiness came with a price. Several people at court inquired about Sabina's sudden disappearance, forcing the earl to invent excuses until the truth of the divorce became public knowledge. Scandal was inevitable. John went on to describe Catherine as "rather plain and prone to corpulence." Sabina placed the letter in her lap when she had finished reading it and laughed aloud.

"What's so funny, Mother?" Anne asked, entering the room.

"Nothing, my love."

"What are you reading?"

237

She folded the letter and tucked it into her bodice. "A letter."

"About father?"

"Yes, he has remarried."

A shadow settled upon Anne's small features. "Who is it?"

"An English noblewoman. Lady Catherine of Chartwell. She'll soon be the mother of your half-brothers and half-sisters. When you're old enough to travel to England—"

Anne frowned. "Travel to England? What for?"

Sabina was taken aback by her daughter's tone. "To visit them."

"Why would I do that?"

"Whatever transpired between your father and me has nothing to do with you," she said gently.

"Yes, it does," Anne countered with tears in her eyes. "If I'd been born a boy, Father and Grandfather would not have been so cruel to you. I prayed to God every day when we lived in England. I wanted Him to forgive me for not being a boy."

"Anne, dearest, you being a girl does not make your father and grandfather love you any less."

"I once overheard Grandfather refer to me as a 'worthless girl' and father did not disagree with him."

Sabina suddenly hated James and Thaddeus for making their obsession for a male heir so apparent to her innocent child.

"Listen to me, Anne, and listen well, because this is the only time I will say this to you. I don't care what stupid thoughts filled the heads of your father and grandfather. In England, they may be important, but here they are nothing. Do you understand me? *Nothing*." Anne nodded, her expression solemn. Sabina continued, "I'm the widow of Signore Tommaso Caravelli, who was an important man in the city. I was born in Lucca, and my noble name goes back to the forefathers of Tuscany. I am respected here in Florence and enjoy not only the friendship of the most powerful man in the city, Lorenzo de' Medici, but also his protection. Furthermore, I'm happy you were born a girl, for women possess special gifts that men do not. From today onward, you will hold your head high and be proud of who you are. You will not shed another tear. Have I made myself clear?"

"Yes, Mother."

"Do not forget that half the blood running through your veins is my blood. *Rossi blood*."

Anne embraced her mother tightly. "You were a widow when you married father?"

"I was married for a brief period before my first husband was killed."

"Killed?" Anne asked, interested in hearing more.

Sabina patted the seat beside her. "Sit down. It's time you learned a few things about me."

***

After her serious talk with Anne, Sabina noticed a change in her daughter's demeanor. She wanted to know more about Tuscan culture and the history of the Rossi family. She even informed Umberto that she wanted to read Dante and Boccaccio.

Sabina had promised to take Anne to Santa Lucia, and her daughter reminded her periodically of that oath. According to Cecilia, a few changes had taken place at the convent while she was away in England. The most tragic was the sudden death of Mother Marcella. The new abbess, Mother Alfonsina, was a great admirer of Savonarola and adopted his strict rules. This made Sabina uneasy, but it didn't stop her from going to Lucca with Anne.

The day they visited the convent, Sabina fell ill. What had started out as mild apprehension in the cloisters became actual nausea when Cecilia led them toward the church that housed the frescoed chapel in the back—the same chapel where Marco had raped her so many years ago. She froze, unable to follow them.

"Mother are you feeling unwell?" Anne asked.

"You're as white as a sheet," Cecilia observed.

"Please, continue with the tour. I'll stay here."

Cecilia frowned. "Are you certain?"

Sabina nodded and sat on the low wall. She rested her head against one of the cloister's columns and gazed at the fruit trees in the garden. They were much taller than she remembered.

"Signora Sabina, is that you?"

Sabina turned her head. "Hello, Sister Olivia."

"How good to see you. Sister Cecilia told me that you married and moved to England. How long will you be staying in Tuscany?"

"I won't be returning to England."

Sister Olivia's face crumbled. "Oh no. Did your husband die?"

"He is alive and well."

The gossipy nun waited for some kind of explanation, but Sabina offered none. "I see," she finally said. "Well, the others are waiting for me. We're going to the orphanage today."

"A most commendable endeavor."

Sister Olivia turned to go, then stopped. "Your friend, Marco Alfani, is now a priest. I thought you'd like to know."

Sabina's stomach lurched, but she managed a polite nod.

The nun continued, "He's an avid supporter of Savonarola— a true man of God. Thanks to his many loyal parishioners, Father Marco is growing more powerful by the day."

Sister Olivia walked away, leaving Sabina alone to ponder over the information. Power given to a man like Marco could be dangerous.

Anne eventually emerged from the church with a grin on her face. "What a beautiful chapel! Zia Cecilia said that I could spend the summer here at Santa Lucia. May I, please?"

Cecilia gave Sabina a victorious look.

CHAPTER 20

Anne spent the summer of 1491 with her aunt at the Convento di Santa Lucia. She returned to Florence at the end of August a different person. Sabina later confided to Camelia that her daughter was "filled with the fire of the Holy Spirit." Even Umberto noticed a great change in his pupil's tastes once her studies commenced. Anne no longer wished to learn about pagan myths or literature with questionable moral themes, and—much to Sabina's disappointment—Dante and Boccaccio were of no interest to her.

Sabina displayed great patience toward her daughter, dismissing this newfound zeal as a mere phase of youth. Anne's strange behavior persisted, however, and she begged to be allowed to spend the following summer with Cecilia. Sabina decided it was time for a serious talk.

"Anne, I would like to speak with you about something," she said as they walked along the Arno River on a Saturday afternoon.

Florence had become dangerous for people who were not Savonarola's followers, so two armed guards followed them at a discreet distance.

Sabina continued, "Umberto tells me that you refuse to read certain books because of their immoral content. Is this true?"

Anne squinted against the sunshine to look at her mother. "Yes."

"I personally approved the books used in your lessons. Do you think I would allow any material that would morally corrupt you?"

"No…not intentionally."

Not intentionally? "Mythology and philosophy are part of history. Umberto also mentioned that you believe music is wicked. Where are you getting these radical ideas?"

"Fra Girolamo."

241

"How do you know so much about that fanatic?" When Anne didn't respond, Sabina prompted, "Answer me."

"I've heard his sermons."

It took Sabina a moment to understand the implication of her reply. "Have you been sneaking out of the house?" Anne nodded, her expression one of guilt. "Are you mad? Do you realize how dangerous it is to be walking the streets of the city alone?"

"I'll be ten years old this winter."

"You're still very much a child and know nothing of the world. Promise me that you will never sneak out of the house alone."

"I promise."

"You will allow Umberto to do what I pay him to do—educate you. Most girls your age are being groomed for marriage and receive barely enough instruction to run a household. Their lot in life is to wait upon a man and bear his children. I want much more for you."

"I am grateful, Mother. It's just…"

Sabina waited, but nothing came. "It's just—*what*? I've always been honest with you and I want you to be honest with me."

"I don't want to learn about things that may displease God."

"Let me ask you a question. Did God create man?"

"Yes."

"Man, in turn, creates wonderful things like music, poetry, and art. This is a tribute to God, not something wicked. Does that make sense?" Anne nodded reluctantly and Sabina continued, "There will be no more talk of moral corruption and wickedness. You will not make Umberto's task more difficult than it already is."

"Signore Lorenzo is getting worse," Anne said, changing the subject.

Sabina froze in her tracks. "Who told you this?"

"Fra Girolamo said the Medici have provoked God with their wickedness and He will soon put an end to their rule."

Sabina was furious. "Fra Girolamo should not be saying

242

such terrible things about the family who has done so much for the city of Florence."

"If what the friar said is not true, then why is Signore Lorenzo sick?"

"Many good people get sick and die. Even newborn babies die, and what wrongdoings are they guilty of?"

Anne pondered her mother's words before asking, "Will you allow me to spend this coming summer with Zia Cecilia?"

"We shall see."

***

By the end of March 1492, two things happened. First, a letter arrived from Tutor John stating that Lady Catherine was pregnant again. The woman had recently birthed a baby girl in January. James finally had what he wanted: a fertile wife. Despite this, there was still no male heir.

The second piece of news Sabina received was far more distressing. Lorenzo's gout had finally gotten the best of him. Feeling the end was close at hand, he insisted on being taken to his favorite villa in Careggi. His body was so wracked with pain that he couldn't ride a horse and had to be transported on a stretcher.

Upon hearing the news, Sabina left Florence at once and went to the villa to see her dear friend for the last time. There was already a crowd of people gathered at the villa, each waiting to bid farewell to Lorenzo. When it was finally Sabina's turn, she was not prepared for what she saw. Lorenzo, the strong, virile man she had always known—the Great Il Magnifico—looked frail upon his deathbed.

She knelt beside the bed and took his hand in her own. Gazing into his glassy eyes, she could tell he'd been drugged. "Lorenzo…"

He smiled slightly, his lips cracked and dry.

She whispered, "How I hate seeing you like this."

"I cannot complain," he said softly. "Life has been good to me. Tell me, how is your daughter?"

"She's fine."

"Anne is beautiful, like her mother."

243

Sabina's eyes watered and she brought Lorenzo's hand to her lips.

He swallowed hard. "I've instructed my son to keep you under our family's protection. I don't know if he'll rule as I have. Pray for him. Piero is weak and young. Ask God to give him strength and wisdom."

"I will." She noticed the physicians quietly working in the corner of the room, grinding pearls and other precious gems into fine dust.

Following her gaze, he whispered, "They keep insisting the jewels will cure me. I drank pulverized rubies this morning, but I feel worse."

"Oh, Lorenzo. If I could take your pain away, I would."

"I know you would. You've always been so good to me...so loyal."

A spasm of pain washed over him and he clenched his teeth. One of the physicians came over and made him drink a foul-smelling potion. Some of it ran dribbled down his chin and she could see iridescent flecks from the crushed pearls. Within minutes, he became groggy.

Lorenzo gave her a lopsided grin. "I should have bedded you long ago," he slurred. "Go now. There are others I must speak to before this useless body fails me once and for all."

Sabina's tears flowed freely as she put her face close to his and kissed his cheek. "I love you, Lorenzo," she whispered softly in his ear.

They shared a meaningful look before he closed his eyes and nodded. Sabina was led away from the bed by one of the Medici guards. Several people watched as she made her way downstairs to where others awaited Lorenzo's inevitable death. She knew many of those present and spoke to some. She was in the middle of a conversation with an older woman when two men dressed in black priestly robes appeared in the doorway.

The woman whispered, "Savonarola."

Sabina turned to gaze upon the individual who had caused such a radical change in Florence. She saw an unattractive man with an oversized hooked nose and thick lips. His companion was broader and taller, but the black hood of his cloak fell so low over his eyes that his face remained hidden.

"This way, Fra Girolamo," one of the guards said as he ushered in the monks. "Signore Lorenzo has been expecting you."

Surprised, Sabina whispered, "Lorenzo sent for him?"

The woman shrugged, perplexed.

"Sabina."

Her name was uttered by Savonarola's hooded companion. Slowly, he pushed back the hood to reveal his identity. She gasped in horror when she realized it was Marco Alfani. He had changed little except for the few strands of gray hair mingled with the black curls.

The memory of that terrible day in the chapel loomed in her mind, prompting her to recoil from him.

Marco put a hand on her arm. "Please—"

"Don't touch me!" Sabina cried, drawing several looks.

"Let me speak with you," he insisted.

She turned her back on him and rushed out of the villa.

He followed. "Sabina, wait!"

"Leave me alone!"

"I'm not that man anymore."

Sabina called out to her guards. Two burly men came running toward their mistress with weapons drawn. Marco stopped his pursuit at the sight of them. The men stared at the priest with steely eyes.

Standing behind the guards, she warned, "Lay a hand on me and you'll know the sharpness of their daggers."

Marco held up his hands and took a step forward. The men advanced and he froze. "I'm a follower of Savonarola—a man of peace."

"You can follow whomever you choose and go to Hell."

"I'm no longer the wicked man you once knew, Sabina."

She shook her head. "It doesn't change what you did to me. I'll never forgive you, nor will I ever forget."

Defeated, Marco walked back toward the villa. As Sabina watched him go, she began to tremble and cry.

One of the guards whispered, "Do you want us to follow him?"

The other added, "We can take care of him discreetly."

She would not stoop to murder, no matter how tempting. "That won't be necessary. Please take me home now."

Sabina walked away, her eyes drawn to the villa. She thought of the man dying within it. Lorenzo her friend, Lorenzo her protector, Lorenzo the man. She would never forget him for as long as she lived.

***

Lorenzo de' Medici died on the ninth of April 1492, at the age of forty-three. Sabina later learned that Savonarola had been summoned by Lorenzo to hear his final confession. This sudden change of heart on his part came as a surprise to many.

Florence was left in the hands of twenty-one-year-old Piero de' Medici, who had already acquired the nickname of Piero Sfortunato for his "unfortunate" lack of ability to successfully complete any project. Piero's Roman wife, also member of the Orsini family, was a coarse woman who didn't fit in with Florentine society.

In December of that same year, Camelia's husband died. Sabina made it a point to visit her widowed friend often in order to lift her spirits. A few weeks after Signore Adolfo's death, she received a letter from Tutor John informing her that Thaddeus had died only a few weeks before James's wife delivered a healthy son. The irony was almost comical, and Sabina didn't know whether to laugh or cry.

Later that night, in the privacy of her study, she reread the letter then tossed it into the flames within the hearth. "I hope you're happy now, James," she whispered as she watched the parchment blacken and burn.

"Mother?"

She turned around to see her daughter standing in the doorway. "What are you doing up at this late hour? You should be in bed."

"I can't sleep." Anne noticed the letter burning and asked, "Is that the letter from England? I heard the servants talking about it this afternoon."

"I have some unpleasant news. Your grandfather is dead." Anne stared at her mother blankly, unsure of what to do or say. Sabina continued, "Also, you now have a half-brother."

"That whore finally bore my father a son?"

"Anne!"

Shocked by her own outburst, Anne covered her mouth with her hand. "Forgive me, Mother." She then burst into tears. "He'll never want to see me again now that he has his precious son."

Stunned, Sabina asked, "You wish to see your father? I thought you were happy here."

"I am, but I sometimes miss him. Surely, you can't fault me for that!"

Anne's words pierced Sabina's heart like an arrow. Despite the contempt she harbored for James, he had always been a good father. "I don't fault you, Anne. Calm yourself. I'll write to him and arrange for your swift and safe return, if that's what you want."

Anne ran out of the room and locked herself in her bedchamber. Sabina knocked on the door, but she refused to open it. Having heard the commotion, Teresa poked her head into the hallway.

"Is everything all right, Signora?"

Sabina sighed tiredly and moved away from the door. "I've received news of the earl's death. Also, James's wife bore a son. Anne admitted that she misses her father, but believes he'll forsake her in favor of his son. I hate to see her suffering. I don't know what to do at this point."

"It's difficult for a child to comprehend the follies of adults," Teresa observed. "Don't worry. When she's older, she'll understand better."

"She's so stubborn and rebellious."

"Passionate and caring, too. The traits of her mother. Why don't you get ready for bed? I'll fix Anne a soothing draught in the meantime. I'll make one for you, too."

Throughout the years, Teresa had become more of a friend

than a servant. "Thank you. I don't know what I'd do without you."

Sabina undressed and studied her naked body in the looking glass. Despite having had a child and being thirty-four years of age, her figure had changed little during the last fifteen years. She was still slim and shapely with firm breasts and smooth legs. Shivering, she put on her shift and got under the warm covers.

She stretched out on the bed and, to her surprise, she thought of Tommaso. Life was carefree and pleasant when he and Lorenzo were alive. She treasured the memories of them almost as much as she treasured the memories of Massimo.

Cursing softly, she tried to think of something else, but it was no use. No matter how hard she tried to prevent them, thoughts of Massimo always managed to sneak their way into her head. She had never stopped loving him, even after all these years. Admitting this fact, after what he did, was not only difficult but also humiliating. The brief time they spent together was amazing and unlike anything she had ever known.

What if I tried to find him?

It was a tempting notion. Over a decade had passed since she had seen or heard from Massimo. For all she knew, he could be dead.

I could send a spy...

After all, her servants were discreet and loyal.

What if your spy returns with news that Massimo is alive and well?

Teresa came into the room and handed Sabina a steaming cup.

"How is Anne?" Sabina inquired before taking a cautious sip.

"I sat with her until she fell asleep."

"Good. She is resilient."

"Like her mother."

"There is something I want to do." Sabina hesitated. "I want to know what became of Massimo Reni."

Surprised, Teresa said, "I don't think that's wise."

"I'll send a spy."

"Have you forgotten how badly he hurt you?"

"I must know if Massimo is dead or alive."

"He doesn't seem to care if you're dead or alive."

The words hit Sabina hard. "That's true."

"Forgive me for speaking out of turn, but I don't wish to see you in pain again. He was a scoundrel for lying and abandoning you."

"Yes, he was."

"I wouldn't waste my time on him."

"Nor should I, yet this is something I must do."

"You still love him," Teresa accused. "Even after what he did?"

"The heart is a treacherous thing."

Teresa shook her head in dismay.

Sabina continued, "I need to find a trustworthy spy. Of all the servants, who do you think would be the best for the job?"

"Simone or Iacopo."

Iacopo was too old. Simone was one of her guards. He was quiet and intelligent with a military background.

The next day, Sabina summoned Simone to her study.

"Please sit," she said to the burly young man, indicating a chair.

Simone sat down and clasped his hands together, his hazel eyes taking in every detail of the room.

"I have an important task that needs to be carried out with the utmost of caution and secrecy. Not even the other servants must know."

He frowned and leaned forward in his seat. "Do you want me to kill that impertinent monk?"

"Ah, no. I want you to gather information about a man, a Roman. I need to know if he's still alive, if he's still married, where he is, what he's doing…I want to know everything about him." As an afterthought, she added, "And his wife."

"As you wish, Signora."

Sabina handed him a piece of parchment with Massimo's full name and the address of his Roman villa. "He was cousin

249

to Clarice Orsini, so it should not be too difficult a task."

"I'll do my best."

"I know you will. You must depart as soon as possible," she said, handing him a heavy purse. "Take this money for your expenses. Keep the rest as payment."

Simone returned to Florence two weeks later and was admitted directly into his mistress's private quarters.

"You found him?" Sabina demanded.

"He's alive and living in the villa."

Too nervous to sit, she paced the room. "Is he still married?"

"Yes, but they live separate lives."

"Does he have a lover?" Simone shook his head and she asked, "What about his wife? Does she have a lover?"

"Michela lives with her parents in Rome, but it's rumored that she's in love with a Sicilian. Her father tried annulling the marriage because he despises his son-in-law, but the Church refused to grant them a divorce."

"Did you speak with Massimo?"

Simone's eye followed his mistress from one side of the room to the other. "I thought you wanted me to be discreet and not be seen or heard."

Sabina nodded. "You did the right thing."

"May I give you a personal observation?"

"Yes, please."

"Signore Massimo appears to be a very sad and lonely man."

After her meeting with Simone, Sabina went to her bedchamber and locked the door. Anne was busy with her lessons and Teresa had gone to the market. She stared out the window at the pearl gray sky. Thunder clouds in the distance threatened rain. Two crows landed on a nearby branch and cawed loudly.

"Mendi," Sabina whispered, suddenly nostalgic for her odd pet that was long dead.

What am I to do?

Massimo was obviously in an unhappy situation and she felt sorry for him, but she was also in an unhappy situation, and where were his spies? Why did he not seek her out? Or, at the very least, send a letter? Did he not love her at all? Surely, no one could act that convincingly.

Sabina instructed Teresa to watch over Anne for the next few days, then left Florence in the company of her two guards. By the time she arrived at Massimo's villa in Rome, she had second thoughts about her hasty decision. Memories of that blissful summer rushed through her mind like a tidal wave and she trembled with nervous anticipation.

"Are you all right?" Simone asked when Sabina hesitated to descend from the carriage.

She nodded and gave him her hand. When he moved to follow her to the front door, she said, "No, I wish to go alone. Wait here."

It was cold and a light drizzle began to fall. Her fur-lined cloak was warm and she tightened it around her shoulders. Determined, she took hold of the brass ring and knocked. It was too early for bedtime but too late for receiving uninvited guests. The door opened and it took Sabina a moment to recognize an older looking Leo.

"Signora Sabina!"

"Greetings, Leo. I have come to see your master. Is he here? I know it's late…" she said, trailing off. "My men are outside."

"I'll see that they receive a hot meal and some wine at once." Leo's lips stretched into toothy grin. "My master will be very happy to see you. I'll let him know you're here."

"No—I mean, I would prefer to surprise him. It's important for me to see his reaction. Surely, you understand."

"He's reading in his study."

Sabina's hands shook and her heart raced as she walked toward the study. She stopped outside the open doorway and peered into the room. A sliver of Massimo's profile was visible as he sat reading by the light of a single candle. Like herself, he had aged little. Suddenly, he glanced up from his book and caught sight of her in the doorway.

"My God, Sabina!" His eyes narrowed. "Is it really you? Or has my loneliness driven me to madness?"

"It is I, Massimo."

251

He stood, wearing an expression of pure shock mingled with joy. It was the latter expression that made her run into his open arms. They embraced for what seemed like a small eternity. He inhaled the scent of her hair and pressed her against his body.

"I thought I'd never see you again," he said, his voice laden with relief. "I've missed you more than you'll ever know. Forgive me, my love. Please forgive me, even if I have not yet forgiven myself."

She had rehearsed what to say but after hearing the heartfelt remorse in his voice, her wounded pride no longer mattered. "Why didn't you contact me?" she asked when he pulled away to look down at her face.

"Lorenzo was furious. He warned me never to step foot in Florence again on penalty of death."

"You could have sent a letter."

"Lorenzo strictly forbade me to have any contact with you. I think it was because he loved you and felt jealous that you shared my bed and not his."

"You know he died this past spring."

"All of Europe knows."

"You could have come to Florence after his death."

"Why? As far as I knew, you were married and living in England."

"Did Lorenzo or Clarice tell you of my marriage?"

"No, I spoke to your man, Iacopo."

"What? When?"

"A few months after your departure. I had managed to sneak into Florence to see you and offer you the explanation you so greatly deserved. Needless to say, I was devastated when he told me the news."

"All these years so needlessly wasted," she lamented.

"My conscience has been weighing on me ever since."

"You could have told me you had a wife when I came to stay with you in Rome," she pointed out. "You should have been honest with me. After all, I thought we were not only lovers but also good friends."

"I didn't want you to think poorly of me. That was selfish

252

on my part and I'm sorry. I never meant to hurt you. I have never loved my wife and she outright despises me. We stopped sharing a bed long before I met you."

"Then why should she care if you keep a mistress?"

"Pride. Michela is a most arrogant and spoiled creature. She cannot stomach the idea of sharing her husband with another woman. Since her family has wealth and prestige, I must be her loyal dog. My father and her father were friends at one time, and my marriage was arranged to secure my family's financial future. We had lost our fortune, you see. My wife threatened to cut off all money to my family if I continued to see you, and I couldn't let my loved ones fall into ruin."

"Dear God, Massimo, I have more money than I can spend in a lifetime! Why did you not come to me with your predicament?"

"I'm practically owned by one woman and her money. I didn't want to be in the same predicament with you. I do have some pride."

Having grown up as an impoverished noble herself, she understood completely. "What now?"

"Well, now I live here in exile. My father-in-law wishes me dead so his precious daughter can remarry her wealthy Sicilian lover. He's an older man who will increase their fortunes and political ties. I think he has kept me alive because of Lorenzo."

"Now that Lorenzo is dead, your life may be in serious danger."

"I often think it's only a matter of time before he hires an assassin to get rid of me. He's already banished me from society. I want to leave, but my family will suffer if I cause my wife any embarrassment. The only way he would continue to help my family is if I die, and, believe me, the thought of ending my miserable existence has crossed my mind a hundred times."

"I thought your father and your father-in-law were friends."

"They were, but my father is long dead and circumstances have changed drastically."

"And your mother?"

"It's because of her and my sister that I remain here."

253

"Your ties with the Orsini family can help you, no?"

"We are distantly related; Clarice's uncle married my cousin. We grew up near each other and socialized within the same circles. There was more friendship between us than blood ties. Besides, she's dead."

"I see."

"Do you? Do you truly understand why I deceived you?"

She looked into his eyes and replied, "You can put your conscience to rest now. I forgive you, Massimo."

"Thank you," he said softly, then paused. "What of your marriage? Are you happy? Is your husband here visiting Tuscany with you?"

"My husband divorced me when I could not provide him with a son."

"He is a fool."

"Yes, he is. I have a beautiful daughter named Anne. She and I are living in Florence now."

"I would love to meet her someday."

There was an awkward silence as he stared at her intently. She felt foolishly aware of her disheveled appearance in that moment. She had been traveling in a coach for two days before barging in on Massimo.

Closing the gap between them, he inquired, "May I kiss you?"

Sabina nodded. It was not long before the fiery passion they shared all those years ago reignited. When she felt his hands undoing the ties of her bodice, she pulled away and shook her head.

He stopped. "Forgive me—"

She placed her fingertips against his lips to silence him. "I want to be sure you're never going to abandon me again."

"I will hurt myself before I hurt you again."

Without further words, Massimo lifted Sabina in his arms and carried her to his bedchamber. Like two hungry young lovers, they made love for most of the night.

Before they fell asleep at dawn, he whispered, "Do you think we have made up for the lost time?"

254

Despite being totally spent, she replied, "No."

The sun was high in the sky when they finally awoke. Both were ravenously hungry for food and for each other. A servant came in with bread, cheese, fruit, and wine. They ate and lounged in bed afterward.

Sabina sighed contentedly. "You must pack your things and return with me to Florence."

Massimo's face fell. "I can't do that…"

"To hell with your father-in-law and your spoiled wife!"

"What about my mother and my sister?"

"They can come to Florence, too." He shook his head and she said, "What's the problem? My money is as good as your wife's money."

"It's more than a matter of money, Sabina. It's our family's good name and reputation that's at stake. My mother would be devastated, and my sister is still young and unmarried."

"Hmmm," she mused, rubbing her chin as her mind raced. "So your death really would solve everything quite neatly."

"It would but…what's going through that lovely head of yours?"

She looked up at him and smiled mischievously. "I'm going to kill you, my love—or at least pretend to."

"How?" he asked, refilling her goblet with wine, then his own.

"I know a thing or two about herbs and roots that can mimic death."

"You're joking."

"I can mix a potion that will cause you to sleep so heavily that everyone will believe you're dead."

"What about the funeral?"

"You'll sleep for at least a day—maybe two."

"And the burial?"

"There's nothing money cannot fix. I'll pay the gravediggers and the priest a hefty sum if they bury someone else's body in your place."

He shook his head. "It's too dangerous. Think of the ramifications if we get caught."

"Do you want to miss out on the next decade of our lives?"

"No."

"Then trust me."

"I do."

"Good. How much do you trust your servant, Leo?"

"I trust him implicitly. He's my only companion here and he knows of everything that goes on in my life." He paused in thought. "What about my family? They'll be devastated."

"We'll contact them secretly a few weeks after the funeral and invite them to Florence. Nothing is impossible."

He looked at her in awe. "How do you do it?"

"Do what?"

"Stay so strong and determined and resourceful."

"I have no choice."

Later that day, Sabina summoned Leo and told him of her plan.

Leo listened quietly, then said, "There's only one thing that worries me, Signora. How will you keep Signore Massimo's wife and father from ever discovering the truth?"

"Massimo must never step foot in Rome again. So, you know exactly what to do?" He nodded and she continued, "Good. I'll mix the potion tonight and leave it with you. Tomorrow morning, after I've departed, you'll send a message to Michela informing her of Massimo's death. You must also tell her that Massimo's mother and sister will handle *all* the funeral arrangements."

"Yes, but my master's mother and sister will want to view the body."

"I've taken that into account. Have Massimo bathe in cold water and take the potion a few minutes prior to being displayed in the casket. He will fall into a deep sleep. You will give this letter to the priest along with this," she said, holding up a small purse filled with gold florins. Leo took the letter and coins. "Tell the priest that if he does not follow the specific directions of the letter, he will have to answer to the Medici." She wasn't really sure if Piero would help her cause or not, but she used the threat nonetheless. "Are we clear on everything?"

He nodded and turned to go.

"Oh, and Leo?" He stopped and turned. "You'll receive a handsome reward for your service and a good position within my home."

"Thank you, Signora."

Sabina went in search of Massimo and found him in the study, writing. "I sent Leo off with clear instructions.'

He placed the stylus he was using back into the inkwell. "Good. I want to leave this villa and never step foot in it again. I want to make new memories with you in Florence." He paused and smiled. "I also want to know everything you did and every place you saw during the time we've been apart. I feel like I missed out on so much."

"I'll tell you everything," she assured. *Except for being raped by Marco Alfani...that nightmare will accompany me to the grave.* "We should take advantage of the mild weather and go for a walk."

"I would prefer to ride."

Massimo owned only one stallion now. Sabina climbed up into the saddle behind him, snaking her arms tightly around his body. The cold wind felt exhilarating as they rode through farmland and past cottages. When he led his horse to a stream to drink, she dismounted.

"We shouldn't stay too long, the sun is about to duck behind the clouds," Massimo said, gazing up at the sky.

Sitting on a fallen tree, she said, "Stop fretting and sit beside me."

He took a seat and reached for her hand. "I still can't believe you're here. It's like a dream." After a moment, he blurted out, "You must have hated me after reading that letter."

"I never hated you. I cursed you a thousand times, however."

He chuckled without mirth. "I deserved it."

"Even when I was with James, I thought of you." It was the first time she had mentioned her former husband's name.

"Your English husband?"

She nodded. "He's now the Earl of Rochester."

"Do you speak English?"

257

"Yes."

"Say something in English."

She gazed deeply into his eyes, and said, "*The English winters were cold but not as cold as my heart without your love.*"

He clapped his hands together. "Splendid! Now translate."

"I said, 'Your horse will burst if it continues to drink so greedily.' "

"That's not what you said," he accused playfully.

Massimo sprang forward to grab her, but Sabina eluded him and ran off giggling. He proceeded to chase her around the clearing. She had not felt so young and free since she was a girl living in her father's house in Lucca.

When he finally caught her, he kissed her deeply and held her close. "God, I love you so much it frightens me."

They were breathing hard, their cheeks and lips red from the cold. "Make love to me, Massimo."

"Let's go back to the house where it's warm."

"No, I want to make love to you right here, in this place, right now."

Massimo accommodated his lady's request without further delay. The sun played hide and seek with the clouds while they touched and teased each other with their hands and lips.

Sabina was apprehensive the next morning as she said farewell to Massimo. "Remember to drink the entire vial. Leo will handle the rest."

"I'll see you in Florence after I'm reborn," he teased.

"You may feel dizzy at first, but sleep will quickly overtake you."

He raised an eyebrow. "How many people have you done this to?" She shrugged. "Sabina…"

"I made this potion only one other time for a woman who lived in Lucca. She paid me very dearly for it, too."

"So, you were the town witch?"

She shook her head. "Just a girl with an interest in botany."

"Why did this woman want such a potion in the first place?"

"I didn't ask her," she lied. The woman's husband beat her

mercilessly. Since the she lacked the strength for self-defense and couldn't bring herself to commit murder, the potion offered the woman a way out. Sabina never learned if the man had been buried alive or not, nor did she care to know.

"I trust you," he said.

"You will awaken and feel fine. I promise."

"I have no doubt of that. Now go back to Florence and let me carry out this farce."

She kissed him before joining her guards within the carriage.

***

The moment Sabina arrived in Florence, she informed Teresa of everything that had transpired in Rome.

As Teresa listened, her opinion of Massimo changed for the better. "He must love you very much if he's willing to swallow a potion to feign his own death."

"He does love me. I'm sure of it," Looking around, Sabina asked, "Where's my daughter?"

"With Umberto. Would you like me to fetch her for you?"

"No, I'll wait until her lessons are over."

Later, she found her daughter reading quietly by the hearth. "Hello Anne, I'm back. How I've missed you!"

"I've missed you, too," Anne said, accepting her mother's embrace.

"I'm glad to hear it. What are you reading, sweetheart?"

Anne held up the Bible. "God's word."

Sabina smiled slightly and tried to hide her disappointment. "I need to talk to you about a man named Signore Massimo."

"Who is that?"

Sabina replied to the question with a tactful version of the truth. Her daughter was old enough to know certain things but not everything.

Anne's brow creased. "So, you loved Signore Massimo before you met my father." Sabina nodded. "Do you still love him?"

"Yes."

"Why didn't you marry him when you had the chance?"

"It's a long and complicated story…"

259

"Did you love him while you were married to my father?"

There was no correct way to answer the question. "I still loved Signore Massimo, but I was a loyal and devoted wife to your father."

Anne was silent for a moment. "Will you marry Signore Massimo now that you're free?"

"Only if you approve of him. Signore Massimo will need a place to stay when he comes to Florence, and I've offered our spacious home. I want you and him to get to know each other." When Anne said nothing, she added, "Surely you're old enough to understand."

"Yes, Mother." She smiled and picked up the Bible. "I was reading the Song of Solomon. Have you ever read anything so beautiful?"

Sabina, who had read the verses years ago during catechism, recalled their poetic value. "No, I have not," she agreed, before leaving her daughter alone to read in peace.

CHAPTER 21

Sabina's scheme to feign Massimo's death was carried out smoothly. Nestled within his coffin, he slept deeply during the funeral mass. According to Leo, Massimo's wife and father-in-law were expressionless throughout the entire affair. Massimo's mother and sister, on the other hand, cried copiously. Once his coffin was closed, everyone filed out of the church to accompany the deceased to the cemetery. It was then that Massimo's coffin was hastily switched with another containing the body of a poor beggar.

It was after midnight when Massimo finally awoke in the church's sacristy. Leo was already waiting for him. "Signore, can you hear me?"

Massimo forced himself up onto his elbows and immediately placed a hand to his pounding head, a nasty side-effect Sabina had forgotten to mention.

Leo grinned. "We did it, Signore! You are now officially dead."

"Wonderful...the words any man long to hear," Massimo retorted sarcastically. "No one suspected?"

Leo helped his master get out of the coffin. "No one."

Massimo glanced at the wooden box and shuddered. "Did many people attend my funeral mass?"

"Not many."

"Evidence of my popularity."

"Your mother and sister were heartbroken."

"God bless them."

"We should leave Rome as soon as possible. No one must see you. There's only a sliver of a moon tonight, so it will be very dark."

"Let us go now."

"Wait, Signore! You'll need a new name for your new identity."

261

Massimo thought for a moment, then said, "Let it be Ferrara, which was my great-grandmother's name and birthplace. From today forth, I'm a Reni no longer."

***

Sabina and Anne were enjoying their supper when Teresa announced Massimo's arrival. Anne noticed how her mother's face glowed upon hearing the news.

"You love this man very much, Mother."

"Why do you say that?"

"I've never seen you look so joyful around my father."

Sabina blushed and felt a pang of guilt. Stifling the desire to run into Massimo's arms as soon as he entered the room, she stood up and placed a hand on Anne's shoulder. "How good to see you, Massimo. How was your journey?"

Understanding the situation at once, he resisted the temptation to kiss Sabina's lips and respectfully kissed her hand instead. "Good, thank you. It's a joy to see you again." He smiled at Anne. "And who is this?"

She smiled in gratitude. "This is my daughter, Anne."

"It's an honor to finally meet you, my lady," he said, bending over her small hand like a courtier. "I'm Signore Massimo Ferrara."

Sabina caught his eye when he uttered his new surname.

"Mother has told me about you, Signore. Welcome to our home."

"Such charming manners from one so young. Thank you, Anne."

Flattered by the attention of the handsome, blue-eyed man, Anne blushed.

Leo hovered quietly in the doorway and he beckoned the young man forward. "Allow me to introduce you to my faithful servant, Leo."

Leo bowed and made a coin disappear before Anne's eyes.

Anne's face lit up. "Mother, did you see that?"

Leo showed Anne his empty hands, then reached for her ear and pulled out the coin.

Anne snatched it and laughed with glee. "Please show me

262

how the trick is done."

"A magician must never reveal his secrets," Leo teased.

Anne turned to Sabina and whined, "Mother?"

Sabina shrugged. "I think Leo is right."

"Leo is full of tricks," Massimo said. "He can keep you entertained for hours."

"Mother, may I be excused?" Anne inquired.

"Yes, you may."

Anne took Leo by the hand. "Come and meet my tutor, Umberto. He is usually reading in the library at this hour. He knows a few tricks, too."

"Anne, Leo must be tired and hungry," Sabina pointed out. "He's been traveling a long time."

"I'm fine, Signora," Leo assured. "It will be a pleasure to meet your daughter's tutor."

Anne pulled Leo along and he followed her upstairs.

Sabina turned to Teresa. "Be sure Leo gets a hot meal and show him to his quarters. Oh, and have one of the servants set a plate at the table for Signore Massimo."

Teresa nodded and left the room.

Massimo pulled Sabina into his arms and kissed her mouth hungrily, then said, "I can't believe I'm back in this house with you."

"It's your house now."

He kissed her forehead. "Thank you, my love. Anne is like you in so many ways, so bold and charming."

"She is a blessing to me."

Sabina took her seat at the dining table and motioned for Massimo to sit down, too. A moment later, two servants entered the room. One carried a plate, a silver chalice, and cutlery, while the other carried a bowl of fragrant water so Massimo could wash his hands. They patiently waited for the servants to leave before resuming their conversation.

"At least something good came from your marriage to the Englishman," Massimo said, helping himself to the roasted meat heaped upon a silver platter.

Lorenzo had said the same thing. "Very true," Sabina said, filling his chalice with red wine.

He stifled a yawn. "Forgive me, my love. Pretending to be dead is not an easy task."

"You slept through most of it," she reminded him playfully. She watched as he placed a tender morsel in his mouth. "I hope the veal isn't too cold."

"It's delicious," he assured. "What have you told Anne about us?"

"That you and I were once in love, and you needed a place to stay."

"I assume we'll be sleeping in separate bedchambers?"

"You assumed correctly," she said, refilling her own chalice. "Anne believes our intention is to marry and that I have brought you here to meet her."

"I see."

"Do you?" she asked, reaching across the table to touch his arm.

He covered her hand with his own. "Certainly. As a good mother, you must think of your daughter. You've done the right thing."

"Thank you." She smiled and added mischievously, "I expect you in my bedchamber once everyone has retired for the night."

***

Massimo kept a low profile for the first few weeks. He went out only when necessary and decided to grow a goatee, which Sabina thought looked quite attractive on him.

When they received confirmation of Michela's marriage to the Sicilian, Leo was sent to inform Massimo's mother and sister of his fictitious death. Massimo's mother, Signora Giovanna, was so shocked that she took to her bed for a day. She arrived in Florence a week later accompanied by his sister, Caterina, who had the same stunning blue eyes and black hair as her brother.

Caterina embraced Sabina the moment they met. "Thank you so much, Signora Sabina," she said with great emotion. "My poor brother is finally free from that viper."

"Che bella," Signora Giovanna said as she stroked Sabina's cheek. "Una santa! Una vera santa!"

"I can assure you, Signora Giovanna, I'm no saint," Sabina said. "I love your son with all of my heart."

"They would have killed him, you know," the old woman said in a conspiratorial tone.

Caterina cut her off. "Mamma, please—"

"Without Clarice or Lorenzo in their way it was only a matter of time before an assassin slit my son's throat," Signora Giovanna insisted. "Now he is finally safe."

"And free," Massimo chimed in as he stepped forward and greeted his mother and sister with warm embraces.

Signora Giovanna's face crumbled and she began to cry. "Mio figlio! Seeing you dead…"

"I couldn't risk telling you beforehand, Mamma. It had to appear real in order for the plan to work," he said gently. "Forgive me for putting you through that pain."

"We understand, Massimo," Caterina said. "Mamma, stop crying."

Sabina waited until the old woman dried her eyes and calmed down before ushering them into the house. "You must be tired and hungry from your journey."

"We're starving," Caterina confessed. "It was a long ride and Mamma did not wish to stop."

"Any mother would have done the same in my shoes," Signora Giovanna retorted.

Caterina linked her arm through Sabina's and whispered, "You're the best thing that ever happened to my brother. He told me the whole story, you know—it made me cry. He was so heartbroken when he discovered you had married and moved to England."

"If only he had told me the truth about his situation. We would not have wasted so much precious time," Sabina said, glancing over her shoulder at Massimo.

Caterina followed her gaze. "He didn't have the courage to tell you. Men are strange creatures."

"They are, indeed."

"Massimo has suffered a decade of tremendous guilt and regret."

"I suppose everything happens in life for a reason. Our experiences make us grow and become more appreciative. Sometimes good things come from bad situations. Had I not married the Englishman, I would not have my daughter—and I would not trade Anne for the world. Ah, there she is now… Anne, come and meet our guests."

Anne, who was descending the stairs, walked toward her mother and curtsied politely to the guests. Sabina put her arm around her and said, "Ladies, this is my daughter, Anne."

"Welcome to Florence," Anne said.

Sabina stroked her daughter's hair. "Anne, this is Signora Giovanna, Massimo's mother, and Signorina Caterina, Massimo's sister. They will be staying with us for a while."

Caterina said, "What a pretty girl you are! It won't be long before suitors come knocking on your mother's door."

Anne became stone-faced. "I already know who I'm going to marry."

Caterina clapped her hands in expectation of hearing about some local boy and teased, "Who may that be?"

Anne replied, "Jesus Christ."

Caterina's face fell and Signora Giovanna tilted her head to the side. They both looked to Sabina for an explanation when Anne offered none.

"My daughter wishes to become a nun like her Aunt Cecilia," Sabina explained.

"Ahhh…" both women said in unison.

"A most commendable endeavor for a young woman," Signora Giovanna said. "You'll have a guaranteed place in Heaven, my dear."

Anne smiled at the old woman.

***

Signora Giovanna and Caterina stayed for a month, taking in the wondrous sights of Florence and enjoying the hospitality Sabina generously provided. Prior to their teary-eyed departure, she made them promise to return soon.

Massimo put his arm around Sabina when they were alone and said, "My mother told me I would be a fool not to marry you as soon as possible. She loves you like a daughter, you know."

Sabina smiled. "Your mother possesses infinite wisdom."

Sabina invited Anne to accompany her to the market the next day. Massimo and Leo had already left for the Piazza della Signoria, where the local men often congregated to obtain information on current events.

"Why not send Teresa?" Anne inquired.

Sabina motioned to the open window and added, "It's a lovely day."

Anne rubbed her temples. "I have a slight headache."

"Are you feeling all right?" Sabina asked, placing her hand on the girl's forehead to check for fever.

"I think I strained my eyes…too much reading. Please don't worry about me, Mother. I'm old enough to stay home with the servants."

Sabina nodded reluctantly and left the house alone. She walked halfway down the street before the weather turned unexpectedly. Dark clouds gathered and threatened rain, so she decided to return home. As she ascended the stairs she heard strange noises coming from Anne's room. Slowly, she tiptoed to the door and pushed it open.

Sabina recoiled in shock. "Anne!"

Anne stood in the center of the room stripped to the waist. In her fist was a wicked-looking leather strap. Angry red welts swelled across her back and some of them were bleeding slightly.

"Spiritual purification, Mother," Anne explained simply. "I don't expect you to understand."

Sabina's eyes filled with tears. "How long has this been going on?"

"Self-flagellation is good for the soul."

Sabina knew the practice. It was a sick, perverted form of religious fanaticism. She approached her daughter with her hand outstretched to touch the wounds splayed across the delicate white skin, but Anne moved to avoid her mother's touch. "Why do this to yourself?" she demanded, anger quickly replacing the shock.

"Because I'm a wicked sinner."

Sabina grabbed her daughter's shoulders and shook her with force. "Are you mad? What sins have you committed? You're a mere child!"

"My thoughts are wicked."

Sabina stared at her daughter with mouth agape.

Anne continued, "This makes me feel pure… cleansed."

"You are so innocent in the ways of this world, child. You have no idea what sin is and—believe me—you are not guilty of it. You're so good, Anne, such a good girl..."

Tears ran down Anne's face as she shook her head. "I'm not good."

"Why would you say such a thing?"

"I have evil thoughts—so evil that I can't even confess them in church. This is the only way to cleanse myself!"

"Tell me what you've done. Give me an explanation."

"Father and his new wife…I wish they were both dead."

Sabina covered her mouth with her hand to keep from sobbing aloud. She reached for her daughter with her free arm and pulled the girl close. Anne threw her arms around her mother's neck and wept. "Why did you not come to me sooner? Why suffer in silence? You can tell me *anything*, Anne."

"How can you confess such wicked thoughts to another person?"

"It's normal for you to be angry with your father," Sabina reasoned gently. "I'm angry with him, too."

"Do you wish death upon him?"

"I bear him no ill will. You should do the same for the sake of your own sanity. Promise me that you'll never do this to yourself again." When Anne remained silent, Sabina urged, "Promise me, Anne."

"I promise I'll try."

Sabina wrote to Cecilia at once and waited anxiously for a reply. It came several days later:

Dearest Sabina,

I'm replying to your letter immediately due to the urgency of its tone. Do not worry, sister. Anne's zeal is to be commended, not feared. The young are prone to strong emotions and rebelliousness (as you well know, for you yourself were quite the rebel). Since you are neither devout nor an avid churchgoer, your daughter is merely defying you. If this honest observation offends you, forgive me. Perhaps my niece should visit our convent more often. Our abbess disapproves of violent carnal punishments, claiming that such extreme devotion is an affront to our Lord's sacrifice. Take heart and be patient. This phase, like all youthful phases, will pass and Anne will mature into a fine Christian woman. You are always in my prayers.

Your loving sister, Cecilia

Cecilia's letter did little to assuage Sabina's concerns, but she applied her sister's advice to be patient. Anne was indeed young and had obviously inherited her mother's passionate and somewhat volatile nature. Hopefully, her daughter's eventual maturity would lead to spiritual balance.

Aside from the constant preoccupation with her daughter, Sabina was immersed in happiness now that Massimo was by her side. Since Anne approved of the match, nothing prevented the loving couple from legalizing their union. They were married in a quiet, private ceremony.

Intent on making up for lost time, Sabina and Massimo became so absorbed with each other they were almost oblivious to what was taking place around them. Florence was steadily going downhill after Lorenzo's death and Piero was making a complete mess.

The trouble first started when King Charles VIII and his army invaded the Italian continent with the intention of conquering the Kingdom of Naples. Piero failed to rally enough soldiers to defend the fortress of Sarzana, so it fell into the hands of the French. After that military disaster, Piero managed to dissuade the French monarch from continuing his progress via the Florentine route. The king agreed to not occupy Florence but would occupy other cities, including Pisa. Piero returned to

Florence expecting the Florentines to be happy he had saved them from the French. Instead, they labeled him a traitor for striking such an odious bargain.

The consequences of Piero's negotiations were catastrophic. The Medici were viewed as enemies of the fatherland and banished from the Signoria. Piero and his brothers, Giuliano and Giovanni, were forced to flee in the middle of the night. They carried as much money and precious items with them as they could, abandoning the Palazzo Medici, which was later sacked by an angry mob.

The Florentines were forced to face the problem of King Charles VIII, who was welcomed by Savonarola as a liberator. The king took residence in the former Palazzo Medici and Florence slipped into a state of internal conquest as Savonarola's power grew. Even after the departure of the French king, the situation within the city did not improve. Savonarola's control over Florence only worsened matters and his political ascent was now unstoppable.

The Florentines were caught up in a strange penitential fury, driven by Savonarola's obsession with sin. Wealthy merchants and nobles exchanged fine clothing for plain religious habits, rejecting lavish lifestyles in exchange for a simpler existence devoted to God.

Sabina and Massimo witnessed these events with great dismay. They often longed for the happy days when Il Magnifico ruled the city, but Lorenzo was dead and his Florence was gone forever. They seldom left their home during that dark time, preferring isolation to the insanity taking place in the streets. On the rare occasions when they did venture out, they were careful to wear conservative clothing and little or no adornment. Anne dressed like a nun most of the time.

The Carnival of 1496 inspired what would later be called the Bonfire of the Vanities—a great pyre created in the center of the Piazza della Signoria. The Florentines fed the greedy flames with their fine paintings, rare and expensive books, luxurious clothing, wigs, precious jewelry, cosmetics, and anything else considered to be sinful or worldly in nature. Sabina's heart ached at the sight of so many exquisite things being consumed by fire. Even Botticelli was seen throwing his own paintings into the flames.

Anne, who insisted on attending the event as a family, turned to her mother and Massimo with glassy eyes and sighed happily. "Florence is finally cleansed of sin."

Sabina clenched her jaw in anger but said nothing. Massimo shot his wife a look that conveyed his empathy. "Let's go home," he said.

Once inside the sanctuary of their home, Sabina sulked in her study.

Massimo stood in the doorway. "Don't be upset with Anne."

"The girl is obsessed!"

"Calm yourself, my love. I'm sure this is a phase, like Cecilia said."

"I usually fell asleep in church; it bored me to tears." She sighed, shaking her head pensively. "My father forced a marriage upon me because we were poor. Anne will never have to do that. She is my heir, and I want her to be educated and independent. I want to provide her with the things I never had. She'll marry only if she chooses to do so."

Massimo sat down beside his wife and took her hand in his own. "That is dangerous talk in these times. Savonarola admonishes women to be submissive toward God and men."

"Bah! I have challenged our patriarchal society since I was a girl. I never want Anne to feel the confines of male domination."

He raised an eyebrow. "Is that how you feel about me, too?"

"No, my love. You're an exception to the rule."

"I'm glad to hear it. It's a pleasant evening—far too pleasant for you to be moping about like a child who has just lost her favorite toy."

"I've lost something far more precious than a toy—I've lost Anne."

***

Sabina discovered through Massimo that there were many Florentines who, like them, did not support Savonarola and his

271

teachings. Some of the magistrates in the Signoria were grumbling. Tired of the constant criticisms and of being blamed for the city's decline, an anti-Savonarolan party was formed called the Arrabbiati.

Pope Alexander VI was also growing very weary of Savonarola's daily sermons and moralizing. When the friar went as far as questioning papal authority and openly criticizing Rome, the pope was forced to take drastic measures. At the end of 1497, the Signoria received a request to turn Savonarola over to the papal justice, but no action was taken until the following year. Having lost most of his support in Florence and abroad, Savonarola was arrested, imprisoned, and condemned to die. On May 23, 1498, he was burned at the stake in the Piazza della Signoria—the same place where the Bonfire of the Vanities took place.

Anne insisted on being present for the execution so she could pray for Savonarola's soul. Sabina could not bring herself to go, but she reluctantly allowed her daughter to attend in the company of Massimo and a pair of armed guards. Anne was teary-eyed for days afterward, cursing papal corruption, and the injustice of Savonarola's death.

"How could God allow the pope to do such a thing? Savonarola was a true servant," Anne cried.

"Be careful, daughter," Sabina advised. "Never say such things aloud in the presence of others."

Anne stared at her mother before locking herself inside her bedchamber.

Two days after Savonarola's execution, Sabina received news of Camelia's sudden death. She was deeply saddened by this, and mourned the loss of her dearest friend.

In December of the following year, Anne made an announcement to Sabina and Massimo. They were in the middle of eating the fine meal Sabina had arranged in celebration of her daughter's eighteenth birthday, when Anne abruptly stood from her chair.

"There's something I must tell you," Anne said. "I plan to take my vow as a novice in the Convento di Santa Lucia, where

I will devote my life to God."

There was nothing Sabina could say or do to dissuade her daughter from her godly calling. Anne left for Lucca the following month.

As Florence continued to suffer from internal strife, its former prestige dwindled. Once the center of European culture and trade, it lost much of its importance with the discovery of the New World. Spain and Portugal were becoming increasingly rich and powerful thanks to colonization, the spice trade, and other maritime exploits.

In the years following Savonarola's and Camelia's deaths, Piero de' Medici attempted to recapture Florence three times and failed miserably. He then tried to curry favor with King Charles VIII by joining forces with him to conquer Naples. In the end, Piero died an inglorious death. While transporting artillery in 1503, his ship encountered a storm and the vessel was shipwrecked. Piero simply vanished among the waves.

Massimo's mother passed away the same year. Caterina, who had been courting a successful spice merchant named Carlo Castagno, was married as soon as her period of mourning was over. She became pregnant almost immediately. Her husband's trade eventually led him to Tuscany, where there was an abundance of rich noble clients. They purchased a large villa in the Mugello, which was located in the province of Lucca, high in the hills and far from the city center. Massimo was happy that his sister would now be closer to Florence and he looked forward to becoming an uncle.

The years continued to pass quickly, and Sabina sighed in resignation every time she found a new gray hair or a wrinkle on her face. She aged gracefully and kept her slim figure. As for Massimo, he remained a good and loyal husband. They visited Lucca once a month to see Anne, who seemed happy and fulfilled in her role as nun. The thought of life without grandchildren was grim, and Sabina often wondered why God had blessed her with only one child.

In the year 1504 something very special happened in Florence. On a sunny June day, Sabina and Massimo watched the painstaking installation of a massive sculpture at the entrance of the Palazzo della Signoria. Carved from white Carrara marble, the stunning male figure stood over fourteen feet tall in a classic, contraposto stance. To the shock of everyone present, it was completely nude.

"It's supposed to be David, you say?" Sabina asked of Massimo, unable to tear her eyes away from the sublime male form. "He looks more like Adonis."

"See the weight of the stone within his right hand?" He waited for Sabina to nod then pointed to the figure's left hand and said, "David is holding a sling that falls down his back."

"I see."

Massimo studied the statue while rubbing his chin. "Botticelli thinks the statue should be closer to the cathedral. Do you agree?"

"I don't know."

Sabina caught sight of Michelangelo di Lodovico Buonarroti Simoni across the piazza. The well-known artist and sculptor was commonly known as "Michelangelo" among the Florentines. She remembered him as a clever and extremely talented boy—one of the many protégés in Lorenzo de' Medici's court. He was now a man in his late twenties, and Sabina suddenly felt old.

Massimo followed his wife's gaze. "He's being hailed as a genius for this piece, you know."

"I can see why. This statue will certainly restore a bit of glory to our city." Sabina noticed that David's right leg was attached to a tree stump and inquired, "Is it true that the marble was defective and another artist was commissioned to do the work but he abandoned the project?"

Massimo nodded. "The stone was full of striations and nobody knew what to do with it." He chuckled. "Leonardo da Vinci is envious of the praise being heaped upon Michelangelo, whom he refers to as nothing more than an 'arrogant, young upstart.' "

"Michelangelo was the only one who succeeded in freeing the figure from within the stone's depths; I believe that merits a bit of arrogance."

"Especially since he only started the project three years ago. Leonardo advised placing the statue beneath the roof of the Loggia dei Lanzi."

Sabina shook her head and laughed. "Oh, how absurd!" She paused. "I think I like David there, in front of the Palazzo della Signoria. He's heroic; a fine example of the weak conquering the mighty."

"I suppose you have a point," Massimo agreed. "He's a fine representation of our Republic against tyranny."

Massimo used the word "tyranny" but Sabina knew that many Florentines, especially the magistrates within the Signoria, would have used the word Medici.

***

In the year 1510, shortly after Anne's twenty-ninth birthday, Sabina received news from England. James was dead. The letter was written in female hand and signed by James's widow, who most likely felt a sense of duty toward Anne. James left almost everything to his eldest son but allotted his wife and other children a sizeable sum of money. Since Anne had not been in contact with her father for two decades, he bestowed only a small inheritance to his estranged daughter. Anne donated the money to the convent and accepted the news of her father's death with indifference.

***

The years continued to pass uneventfully and Sabina welcomed the lack of excitement. She had endured so many dramatic episodes and emotional upheavals in her lifetime that monotony was a blessing. She and Massimo had settled into a happy routine and were grateful for their domestic bliss.

All was well until August of 1519 when Sabina received a disturbing letter from Cecilia:

Dear Sister,

I hope this letter finds you and Massimo in good health. I'm writing with news that may surprise you. Our dear Anne is completely smitten with the new bishop, who possesses the same zeal of the late Savonarola. He has been assigned to the Chiesa

275

di San Michele where Anne attends mass daily. Remember when we attended mass there as young girls? Of course, her love and admiration for this man of God is chaste and strictly spiritual. His Excellency is none other than Marco Alfani! Can you believe it? God works in mysterious ways, indeed. On a much sadder note, Sister Olivia passed away last week after contracting a fever. I'm sure she is looking down on us from Heaven right now. You are always in my thoughts and prayers.

With much affection, Cecilia

Sabina reread the letter. Marco Alfani...Bishop of San Michele. According to Cecilia, Anne was "completely smitten" with him. The mere thought of it made her nauseous.

CHAPTER 22
LUCCA, TUSCANY
AUGUST 1519

The church bells rang loudly and the sun shone brightly as Anne approached the Chiesa di San Michele. Almost forty, she possessed a spritely step and appeared much younger than her age. She was slim and in good shape due to a sparse diet and hard work at the convent. When she walked through the streets, men still stared at her with lustful eyes.

It was unbearably hot outside and she wiped the perspiration from her brow. The surrounding Tuscan hills were scorched from lack of rain and she prayed daily for God to end the relentless drought.

Anne walked into the church and was grateful for the coolness of its marble and stone interior. She loved being a nun and her life had recently become more spiritually fulfilling thanks to Bishop Marco Alfani. The thought of him made her smile. Despite being old enough to be her father, he possessed youthful vigor and a handsome countenance—although she would never admit such a thing aloud. Of course, she appreciated his physical beauty the same way one would appreciate any of God's creations, like a flower or a tree. At least, this is what she told herself whenever she gazed upon his pleasing face.

She spotted Bishop Alfani praying in the nave. Mass was not for another two hours, but Anne usually arrived early to pray and hopefully engage in conversation with him. He was authoritative and spoke the word of God with fiery conviction. The mere sound of his deep voice was enough to make her feel giddy.

Oh, God, such wicked thoughts…

Bishop Alfani crossed himself and stood, and Anne could not help noticing the width of his broad back. She murmured an apology to God for being weak and sinful. When he turned his head, she lowered her eyes and her face grew hot.

He smiled. "Hello, Sister Anne."

"Your Excellency."

"You have come to pray."

"Yes, but I also have a question."

Anne's upper lip trembled slightly as he approached her. Marco was experienced enough to know when a woman desired him, and this pale flower had been coming to his church ever since he transferred from Rome.

Her hands shook as she extracted a small Bible from her pocket. "I'm hoping you can offer some clarification on this scripture," she said, indicating the passage with her fingertip. "What did the Apostle Paul mean by this?"

When Marco moved closer, gooseflesh broke out all over her neck. The woman was undoubtedly a virgin. As he began to explain the scripture, he noticed that her eyes glazed over.

Marco had left for Rome shortly after Savonarola's execution, and things had gone well for him in the Eternal City. He befriended a bishop who had instructed him to carry out certain tasks deemed questionable by the Church. In exchange for Marco's "services" (and more importantly, his silence), Marco had been given his own bishopric and a handsome monthly stipend. Everything was going smoothly until he met a duchess who took a fancy to him. The woman's lust was insatiable. Their amorous relationship ended when the duke discovered his wife's infidelity. The prideful noble insisted on Marco's expulsion from the church and from Rome. His friend, the bishop, arranged for Marco to be sent back to Tuscany with a papal letter of introduction to the Archbishop of Lucca. He was assigned the church of San Michele shortly afterward. Marco missed the excitement of Rome and needed to find other ways to entertain himself in Lucca.

Perhaps he would start with the pretty nun who came to hear his sermons every day…

Marco studied Anne's face discreetly as he spoke. There was something hauntingly familiar about her features, something about her eyes and the way she tilted her head.

***

In the winter of 1519, Marco was surprised to discover that Sister Anne Wynne was actually Sabina Rossi's daughter. He vowed to conquer the girl, who would no doubt prove to be more willing than her stubborn, arrogant mother. Sabina had spurned and rejected him, but her daughter desperately sought him out like a lost lamb after its shepherd. The irony was priceless.

Marco learned the art of patience and vendetta in Rome—being discreet and waiting for the right moment to strike were imperative to the success of countless church dignitaries. If people knew how much corruption existed within the Vatican's walls, they would be shocked. He continued to act as Anne's mentor and spiritual guide, as was his duty. Slowly and carefully, he drew the naïve woman into his trap. Whenever she showed him something from her Bible, he would "innocently" place his hand on the small of her back or gently take her elbow when walking down the nave together. He also made it a point to stand in close proximity and look deeply into her eyes whenever they engaged in conversation.

It was not long before Anne was completely enamored with him. Although she lacked experience when it came to men, she was old enough to know the symptoms of lust. Whenever Bishop Alfani was near, a thousand butterflies took flight in her stomach. Whenever they were apart, she yearned for him to the point of feeling ill. The very touch of his hand was enough to make her tremble and burn with longing, but the thrill was always followed by guilt.

Always the guilt…

***

Marco chose a bitterly cold, rainy day to carry out his plan of seduction. Few people attended mass midweek since most of the congregation was poor and forced to work during the day. The number of attendants was even lower when the weather was particularly nasty, but Anne always came, rain or shine. She was among the nine people who had braved the storm to take

279

Holy Communion.

When everyone had left the church, she remained behind. Her Bible was clutched to her chest. "Bishop Alfani, I have a question to ask you."

A smile lit up Marco's face as he stretched out his hand. "Come."

She was taken aback. "Where, Your Excellency?"

"I'm more than happy to answer your questions and discuss scripture, but I must do so in the warmth of my private quarters. I'm not well today."

Her face expressed genuine worry. "Oh…I hope it's nothing serious. Perhaps I should leave so that you may rest."

"No, no… I just need to warm myself by the fire before I catch cold."

Marco took Anne's elbow and urged her to keep pace with him. At first, she was reluctant to be alone with him, but since the chamber was attached to the church itself, she thought it harmless. After all, they were both in God's house. She followed him down a short corridor past the sacristy, then out of the church into a tiny courtyard leading into a side building that served as the bishop's residence.

Marco took out a key and unlocked the door. "Please," he said, motioning for her to enter. "We can speak in my study."

Anne walked into the center of a room containing a table and two ornate chairs. A thick fur rug was set before the hearth and on the table was a tray containing two silver chalices and a pitcher of wine. One wall was completely devoted to books and the opposite wall flaunted a tapestry and a doorway leading to the bishop's bedchamber. Anne heard a click as the bishop turned the key in the lock. A feeling of uneasiness swept over her as she glanced at him. He stoked the orange embers within the hearth then poured some wine.

"Here," he said, offering her one of the chalices. When she hesitated, he placed it in her hand. "Timothy said a little wine is good for the stomach. Go on and drink."

"But it's not diluted," she pointed out. The nuns avoided drinking wine unless it was mixed with plenty of water.

"Jesus transformed water into wine. Besides, it will warm you."

Anne did not taste the aromatic red wine until the bishop had poured some for himself and drank deeply. She took a small sip and found the wine sweet and very strong.

"Please sit," he said, indicating one of the chairs. As he leaned his crozier against the wall, he asked, "How long have you been at Santa Lucia?"

"I've been a bride of Christ for twenty-one years."

"A long time. You were born in Lucca?" he asked, removing the miter from his head and placing it beside the silver tray on the table.

Anne's eyes followed him as he moved around the room. "No. I'm originally from England."

He removed his jewel encrusted robe, revealing a simpler wool tunic underneath. "From England, you say? Yet you speak like a native Tuscan."

The wine was delicious and Anne took a deep sip. "My mother is Lucchese and my father is English. I came to Tuscany when I was a child."

Marco brought the wine over and refilled her chalice to the brim. "How very interesting. You felt the calling at a young age?"

"It was always my dream to serve God."

He sat across from her. "Most commendable. Tell me, who are your parents? Are they still alive?"

"My father died several years ago. My mother is alive and living in Florence. Her name is Sabina Rossi."

"Rossi…a noble name." He paused. "So, what was your question?"

The wine had gone to her head so quickly that she had completely forgotten her question! She blushed in embarrassment. "Ah…"

"Well?" Marco urged in a soft tone.

"Forgive me, Your Excellency. This wine is too strong for me. I have forgotten," she confessed, wide-eyed.

He burst into laughter and she followed suit. "Oh, Sister

Anne, you're like a breath of fresh air in this austere place."

She blinked several times at the compliment and her blush deepened. Not knowing how to respond, she took another deep sip of wine and regretted it instantly.

"Do you want to know a secret?" he whispered in a conspiratorial tone, forcing her to incline her head toward him. "I look forward to your daily visits." He stared intently, drinking in her innocence.

"Oh…I…" she began but did not finish.

"I must confess that you are by far one of the loveliest creatures I've ever laid eyes on. God is indeed an artist."

Anne placed her hand on her chest, flustered.

Marco's face grew serious. "Oh, dear. I hope my honest confession didn't offend you, my child. I'm a man of God but still a man, with all the imperfections of a man."

They were seated, facing each other. He looked down at her mouth and she bit her lip. It took most of his resolve not to attack her in that moment.

"May I ask you a delicate question?"

"Yes…"

"Have you ever known any man in your lifetime?" he whispered. "Answer me honestly, as if you were in the confessional."

"Known?"

"In a carnal sense?"

"No!" she exclaimed. "Never."

"Good girl," he said, gently touching her face.

Anne didn't move a single muscle when he leaned forward. Like a snake who hypnotizes its prey, Marco kept his eyes locked on hers as he moved closer and kissed her lips ever so gently. She had never been touched by a man, let alone kissed, and was thrilled by the act.

Removing the chalice from her hand, he slowly deepened the kiss and took her in his arms. When his tongue ran across her lips, she instinctively opened her mouth. Every inch of her skin tingled as his hands caressed her body. She gasped when he cupped and teased her breast.

You are just like your mother, he thought as his excitement grew. "Sweet child, let me purify my soul…let me bask in your innocence," he whispered. "I need you, Anne."

She came completely undone. Within seconds, they were sprawled on the fur rug. Marco undressed her, kissing every bit of exposed skin, but when he turned Anne on her side and saw her back, he froze.

"My God," he said. "What have you done to yourself?"

He was unprepared for the angry red scars crisscrossing the delicate white skin. Self-mutilation was both excessive and unnecessary in his opinion. He experienced a surge of pity for this obviously troubled woman.

Anne was too far-gone in the throes of passion to notice his reaction. She instinctively pulled him on top of her and moved rhythmically against him. Not expecting the sharp pain when he took her maidenhead, she cried out. Marco quickly covered her mouth and lay still until she was ready to proceed. She possessed surprising passion, meeting each of his thrusts until she came as wantonly as a slut. When he pulled away and looked down at her flushed face, she was crying.

"What is it?" he asked.

"We have sinned… we have sinned so terribly!" she sobbed. "Fornicators! We are fornicators!"

Marco covered her mouth and glanced at the locked door. "Hush! Do not say such things! We fell in a moment of weakness—nothing more. God is forgiving and He'll accept our prayers of repentance." When she continued to cry, he added, "Don't worry. I'll hear your confession."

She sniffed. "And who will hear yours?"

He didn't expect such a quick retort. "God," he replied. "You should get dressed and go."

Anne covered her nudity with her hands as she sat up. Marco turned his face away in courtesy as she donned her nun's habit and wimple.

"Bishop Alfani?"

"Yes?"

"Will I burn in Hell for this?"

Anne was obviously plagued by an unusual and exaggerated sense of guilt. She would, no doubt, punish herself for this deed and create more scars. "Not if you repent," he said sincerely.

"I do… I should have never come here with you alone. I'm so sorry."

"Anne, please stop."

When Marco unlocked the door, she ran out. The images of her scarred back would remain on his mind for the rest of the day.

***

Anne reached the convent and went straight to her cell. She threw herself on her cot and cried. What had she done? Dear God, she had committed fornication!

But it had felt so good.

She already knew she would commit the sin again (and again) if given the chance. Why did she allow herself to be alone with Bishop Alfani? How could she continue living at the convent after what she'd done? Would the other sisters find out?

Anne missed supper that evening and Cecilia went to her cell. "Are you ill, my dear?" she asked from the doorway. "You didn't come down to eat."

Anne was stretched out on the cot, staring at the ceiling. "My head hurts and I had no appetite. I'll be fine by morning."

"Well, rest up because tomorrow we're expected at the orphanage."

"I will. Goodnight."

Anne couldn't bring herself to attend mass the next morning with the other nuns, but helped at the orphanage as promised. The scent of Bishop Alfani's skin, the memory of his touch, and the taste of his mouth haunted her thoughts throughout the day.

After a week of avoiding mass at San Michele, Anne received a message at the convent from Bishop Alfani. He needed to speak to her as soon as possible and she could not ignore the summons of her superior. She went directly to the church and found the bishop waiting for her near the high altar. There was not a soul in the church. He led her into a dark chapel and within seconds they were kissing passionately. This time, their lovemaking took place in the sacristy!

Their secret affair continued throughout the winter with Anne fluctuating between spiritual agony and carnal ecstasy. By late spring, she realized something was terribly wrong. Her monthly flow had ceased, her stomach swelled, and she was sick every morning. When she informed the bishop of her symptoms, his face paled.

"There's an old woman living behind the Chiesa di San Romano who goes by the name of Ursula. Go to her now and she will cure you of your ailment," he instructed. "Tell her Bishop Alfani sent you."

In an attempt to appear anonymous, Anne pulled the hood of her long cloak low over her brow. She found the house easily and was taken aback by the old crone's ugliness when the door swung open. "Donna Ursula?" The woman nodded. "Bishop Alfani has sent me."

Ursula smiled in a strange, knowing way. "He sends many."

Anne failed to grasp her meaning. "He said you could cure me of my ailment."

"That depends. What's the problem?"

Anne described her symptoms, and Ursula calmly collected various herbs and powders. She placed the ingredients in a pouch, knotted the top, and tossed it on the table. "Mix that with wine or water and drink it tonight before you go to bed."

Anne took the pouch. "All of it?"

"Yes. You may feel some pain, but the baby will come out in the morning. Burn the remains in the fire so nobody finds out."

"Baby?"

"You're pregnant. His Excellency sent you here to rid yourself of the burden." When Anne continued to stare at Ursula in horror, she added, "You cannot bear the child of a bishop, can you now? Think of the consequences!"

"I'm going to have a baby?" Anne asked, shocked.

"You certainly will if you don't take these herbs and follow my instructions."

285

"They'll kick me out of the convent…"

"You're a nun?" Ursula chuckled, but it sounded like a witch's cackle to Anne's ears. "Oh, this is a first! Bishop Alfani usually toys with simple village maids or whores. He's taking risks these days."

"Village maids? Whores?" Anne repeated, her eyes wet with tears.

"What? Did you think you were his one and only true love?" Ursula demanded cruelly.

Anne dropped the pouch on the floor and ran back to the convent. Bishop Alfani wanted her to abort their child! She was not about to add murder to her long list of immoral sins. After procuring a quill and a piece of parchment, she wrote a letter to her mother stating that she was going home.

CHAPTER 23

The moment Sabina and Massimo came out into the courtyard to greet Anne, she burst into tears and confessed the sordid affair with Bishop Alfani. Sabina's face paled in shock, but she kept her wits and tongue in check.

"There's more to the story," Anne sobbed. "I'm pregnant…I'm bound straight for Hell."

Massimo met Sabina's eyes and discreetly left the courtyard to allow them some privacy. Sabina's mind raced frantically as she absorbed the disturbing news. Marco had fathered her future grandchild! The entire situation was immoral and disgusting. Anne would be devastated if she knew Marco had bedded her mother in the past.

Anne could never know the truth.

"God should strike me down," Anne muttered.

Sabina winced. "Don't say that. Everyone makes mistakes in life."

"I'm a nun!" Anne stepped back and covered her face with her hands.

"You have served the Lord faithfully since childhood and spent twenty-one years in a convent. There are worse sins in life than bearing a child out of wedlock—believe me."

"There were others," Anne said, sniffing and wiping her tears. "The old crone who gave me the herbs told me so."

Sabina's brow creased in confusion. "What are you talking about?"

"Bishop Alfani has sent other women to rid themselves of babies." This brought a fresh onslaught of tears. "I was not his only lover."

Damn you, Marco! "Oh, Anne…"

Sabina wanted to take her daughter's pain into her own heart, but all she could do was offer comfort. For the next several months, Sabina did everything to keep the outside world at bay so her daughter could feel at ease. Anne's pregnancy was difficult right from the very beginning. She was sick until her eighth month, then bedridden until the end of her ninth month. Massimo was always close and ever solicitous toward Anne, often inquiring if she needed anything from the market. Sabina loved him all the more for stepping into the role of a caring stepfather.

Shortly before Anne was due to give birth, Sabina wrote Cecilia a letter. Her sister had sent many letters inquiring after Anne and demanding to know why her niece had fled the convent so abruptly. Sabina finally penned the truth, begging Cecilia to keep the information confidential. Cecilia's response was swift, expressing regret for Anne's "unfortunate situation" while assuring the utmost secrecy.

After a long and painful labor, Anne delivered a healthy baby girl. Sabina saw traces of Marco in the child but refrained from commenting on them. "She is the spitting image of you. A perfect little girl."

"What should I name her?"

Sabina found it odd that Anne had not thought of any names. "Well, I've always been fond of the name Stefania."

"Stefania. So be it."

To Sabina and Massimo's immense relief, Anne was delighted with her new daughter, but the joys of motherhood were short-lived. The guilt of sin weighed too heavily on Anne's conscience, and she began to act strangely, remaining listless for hours or staring out the window.

A letter arrived a few weeks later addressed to Anne bearing the official seal of the Vatican. Rather than deliver the correspondence to its intended recipient, Sabina hid the letter in the folds of her gown and read it within the privacy of her bedchamber.

Dearest Anne,

I hope this letter finds you and the babe in good health. After not seeing you at mass and not receiving word from you, I paid your aunt a visit at the convent. Cecilia informed me that you had retired to your mother's home in Florence for your pregnancy. I must admit that I was shocked to discover this news. You should have sent word to me. I'm willing to provide for you and our child, and hope you will consider returning to Lucca where I will set you up in a comfortable household.

M.

Sabina threw the letter into the flames and instructed a servant to procure a horse for her at once. As she prepared to depart for Lucca, Massimo appeared in the doorway.

"You cannot ride alone," he protested. "It's too dangerous. I will accompany you."

"My men can accompany me."

"That is well and good, but as your husband, I'm also responsible for your safety."

"I have words for my sister and Bishop Alfani, and I wish to deliver them alone."

"Very well," he acquiesced. "We can spend the night at an inn. I shall wait there while you conduct your business."

Sabina told her daughter that she and Massimo were visiting Caterina in the Mugello for a couple of days. She hated lying, but she had no choice. They arrived in Lucca late at night and, after a restless night of sleep, Sabina awoke early and set out shortly after the sun had risen.

Exhausted and angry, she barely glanced at the beautiful façade of San Michele as she stormed through the door. The church was empty except for a few people who were praying inside a chapel. She strode down the nave and went into the sacristy.

"Marco!" she called out. "Where are you?"

When no one replied, she went down a corridor and crossed a small courtyard that led to an unlocked door. Marco was seated by the fire reading a book. Balling her hands into fists, she ran into the room and began hitting him with as much force as she could muster.

"You bastard!" she cried.

He gripped her wrists and stood. "Calm yourself, please!" Sabina was as lovely as he remembered, and a wave of desire washed over him.

One of her hands escaped from his grip and she slapped him hard across the face. "You knew she was my daughter! How dare you lay your filthy hands on her?!"

"I suppose I deserve that," he admitted.

She spit at him. "You deserve that and much more!"

He grabbed her shoulders and shook her hard. "Stop it!"

"Have you no shame? My God, Marco—you and I were lovers once and you take my daughter into your bed as well?"

"She sought me out."

"You are the older, more experienced one who should have known better. You are a bishop!"

"Anne is no child."

"She may as well be. She's an innocent soul who has never cared for the things of this world. Anne was meant for a cloistered life of quiet contemplation and devotion to God, and now she's lost and miserable."

She began to beat Marco once more with her fists. He grabbed her wrists again. "Please stop! I want to see my child, Sabina."

"The one you wanted Anne to kill?"

He looked away. "I didn't know what else to do."

"Apparently, there were others who were sent to this vile woman named Ursula."

"I'm not the first clergy member to father a child and I won't be the last," he pointed out in his own defense. "Even popes have bastards."

"That's no excuse."

"I'm truly sorry," he offered contritely.

"Your irresponsible behavior ruined my daughter's life."

"I never meant for this to happen." He paused, averting his gaze. "Did she have a boy or a girl?"

"A lovely girl whom you will never see."

"What's her name?" he inquired tentatively. When she remained silent, he added, "I want Anne to return to Lucca where I can provide for them."

"So you can set her up as your mistress? Your whore?"

"Sabina, that's not—"

290

"Leave Anne alone! Don't send anymore letters—they'll only be tossed in the fire, unread. Stay away from me and my family!"

"But—"

"I'm serious, Marco. I will kill you if you come near my daughter or my grandchild. You've done enough damage already."

"I'm not the monster you think I am."

"I haven't forgotten what you did to me in the chapel," she reminded him through clenched teeth before storming out of the church.

Sabina went straight to the convent and knocked on the door of her sister's cell.

Cecilia opened the door. "Sabina! What are you doing here?"

"Why did you tell Marco?"

Cecilia flushed to the roots of her hair. "What choice did I have? He came here demanding the whereabouts of Anne and asking questions. He's a bishop—I couldn't lie to him. Besides, he has a right to know."

Sabina's eyes flashed in anger. "He has NO right whatsoever! Do you hear me? He wanted Anne to rid herself of the child—she is under no obligation to him."

"If what you say is true, then you're right," Cecilia conceded. "Does Anne know that you and Marco…?"

"No, and neither does Massimo. No one knows about my past with Marco and it must remain that way."

"Of course. Forgive me, sister," Cecilia offered. "I meant no harm. Marco would have found out sooner or later."

Sabina ignored the apology. "I cannot dally. Massimo is waiting for me and we must return to Florence at once."

"How is Anne?" Cecilia asked.

"Miserable and overwrought with guilt. I'm worried about her."

"I'll visit Florence soon, I promise." Cecilia placed a hand on Sabina's arm. "I'm sorry."

Sabina covered her sister's hand with her own and sighed.

291

"Come spend Christmas with us. Anne would appreciate the visit and any words of encouragement you have to offer."

"I will. God be with you, Sabina."

***

"Mother!"

Sabina dropped the book she was reading and ran upstairs at the sound of her Anne's scream. She found Anne crying hysterically, cradling her blue-faced infant daughter.

"She's choking!"

Sabina took hold of her grandchild and stuck her finger in the baby's mouth before turning her on her stomach and gently patting her back. Stefania began to cough and took a deep, shaky breath. Color began flowing back into her plump cheeks as she let out a loud wail.

"There, there, my precious girl."

Visibly shaken, Anne went to stand by the window as Sabina rocked Stefania to sleep, then put her in the cradle.

"I'm a terrible mother," Anne lamented. "Had you not been here, Stefania would have died."

"Nonsense," Sabina said, sounding more convincing than she felt. "Your instinct would have guided you."

"It didn't...I have no maternal instinct."

Sabina often thought the same thing but would never dare say so aloud. Anne had already suffered too much in life. Both women turned to look at the sleeping baby.

"Sometimes I wonder how my gross sins could have produced something so beautiful," Anne commented softly.

"I wish you would stop talking like that. You've repented and prayed over and over again. You seem to forget that God possesses infinite capacity for forgiveness."

Sabina was truly worried about Anne's mental state, which was obviously fragile and seemed to be deteriorating on a daily basis.

"I want to go back to the convent," Anne admitted.

"Anne..."

"I can never go back, I know," Anne said, tossing an accusatory glance at Stefania.

292

"Don't resent the child," Sabina gently admonished. "Stefania did not ask to enter this world. It's not her fault."

"No, it's not," Anne agreed. "Why should I be punished for my sins while Marco remains unburdened? His life hasn't changed at all."

Sabina took note that Anne no longer referred to Marco as Bishop Alfani. Her daughter had learned a hard lesson in life: the world belonged to men, not women. There was a separate set of rules for them and a different price to pay for the exact same sins.

"It is indeed a man's world," Sabina said. "It has always been and perhaps will always be."

Anne looked at her mother with eyes filled with pain. "Sometimes I just want to die, Mother," she whispered.

"We love you so much and you have a wonderful daughter to raise. Massimo and I are here to help you in any way we can."

Anne lowered her head and cried. Sabina knew her daughter was suffering, but she had no idea what to do about it. The consoling words she and Massimo offered seemed to fall on deaf ears. Cecilia would surely have better success with Anne during her upcoming visit.

***

Anne ran into her aunt's arms the moment Cecilia arrived at the house. It was a few days before Christmas and the weather was dreary.

"You look well," Cecilia lied, smiling into her niece's face.

"I've missed you, Aunt. How are the sisters?"

"Everyone is fine and they send warm greetings."

Anne's smile vanished and her brow creased with worry. "They still believe that I'm…"

"Battling a strange illness," Cecilia assured, finishing her niece's sentence. "No one knows the truth, so do not fret." She paused before changing the subject, "I'm anxious to meet my grandniece."

Sabina came out with hands extended toward her sister. "Cecilia. You must be tired and hungry."

"I am, but first take me to Stefania."

The three women made their way to Anne's room where a wet nurse was feeding the child.

"She's perfect," Cecilia said, accepting the baby from the robust woman. "Look at those big, green eyes! Her mouth is a little rosebud."

"How are the sisters of Santa Lucia?" Anne asked.

Cecilia frowned slightly. "You've already asked me that, dear. They're fine and send their love."

Anne wrung her hands nervously. "Yes, I forgot." She bit her lip. "Are you sure no one suspects?"

Sabina sighed. "Anne…"

"No one knows the truth but me," Cecilia assured.

Anne burst into tears. "If they knew the truth, they would hate me."

Cecilia and Sabina exchanged a worried glance.

"Hate is a strong word," Cecilia pointed out. "The nuns would feel sorrow that you fell into temptation, but they could never hate you." She smiled. "Everyone loves you, Anne."

Anne stayed behind in the room to put Stefania to sleep while Sabina led her sister to the main hall. "I'm extremely concerned about her," she whispered. "She's always so melancholy; I'm at a loss. She wants to return to the convent."

Cecilia pursed her lips. "She cannot."

"I know that and she knows that, too. I think Anne secretly resents the baby. She believes her life is destroyed."

"Anne's life was destroyed because two adults committed a sin." Cecilia sighed sadly. "Anne must take responsibility for her actions and assume her duty as a mother."

Sabina frowned. "She is doing her best under duress, yet Marco's life continues undeterred. It's unfair."

"Very unfair, I agree, but life is unfair," Cecilia conceded. "That is the way of the world."

"Could we not report Marco to the Archbishop?"

Cecilia laughed without mirth. "We could, but the Archbishop has four bastards of his own."

"Cecilia! What a pleasure to see you again!"

Both women turned to see Massimo standing in the

doorway. He still looked dashing despite the gray hair he sported at the temples and the crow's feet around his eyes. He kissed his sister-in-law's cheek in greeting. The servants brought out wine, soft cheese, and dried figs.

"Is Stefania not the sweetest thing you've ever seen?" he asked proudly. "We've fallen in love with her."

"She is, indeed," Cecilia replied. "A lovely little angel."

The fact that Stefania was born out of wedlock from a sordid affair between a corrupt bishop and a naïve nun did not matter to Massimo. He loved the baby with all his heart and Sabina loved him for it.

"How long will you be staying with us?" he asked.

"A few weeks."

"Why not a few months?"

"Thank you, but I have to get back to my charity work."

"Stay as long as you can," he said before kissing his wife's forehead. "I'm going out and may not be back in time for dinner."

"He's a good man," Cecilia commented as Massimo walked away.

"Yes, he is."

Cecilia spent the majority of the following days with Anne, doing everything within her power to lighten her niece's mood. Sabina gave them privacy to speak and often heard the sound of her daughter's sobs.

Sabina was pensive one night as she sat at the dressing table getting ready for bed. Massimo came into the room and, seeing his wife's expression, took the ivory comb from her hand.

"Here, let me do that," he said. After a while of combing his wife's long hair, a tiny smile settled upon his lips. "I can't believe we're both past our sixtieth year."

Sabina grimaced. "My gray hair and wrinkles are daily reminders."

"You're as beautiful as the day I met you."

"And you are as charming as the day I met you," she said with a glance over her shoulder.

He put down the ivory comb and caressed her shoulders.

They did not make love as often as they used to when they were younger. The fiery passion had become a mellow but steady flame. Massimo was involved in Florentine politics and often came home tired. Sabina worried constantly about Anne while caring for an infant, which was both physically and emotionally draining.

Massimo bent his head to kiss her neck and Sabina smiled at him through the reflection in the looking glass. Slowly, his hands undid the laces of her dressing gown and slid down to caress her breasts.

"Mmm…are you trying to seduce me?"

"Does a husband need to seduce his wife? I would think you would comply willingly." Still facing the looking glass, she reached behind and slipped her hand between his legs. His breath caught in his throat. "You can still make me burn with desire for you, Sabina."

Their lovemaking was sensuous and satisfying. Afterward, they watched the fire in the hearth until there was nothing but glowing orange embers.

Sabina traced patterns on his chest with her fingertip. "Massimo?"

"Hmm?"

"Do you think Anne will be all right?"

"She should count her blessings. Many of the people I know would not be so lenient with their daughters."

"That's because many people are close-minded with no sense of compassion. By the way, have I ever mentioned how lucky I am to have you as a husband?"

He kissed the tip of her nose. "Not lately but feel free to do so now."

She propped herself up on her elbow and drowned in the gaze of his blue eyes. "I'm so lucky to have you. I love you, Massimo."

"I love you, too, Sabina. I always will."

***

Sabina woke up the following morning and was surprised to see Massimo still in bed. He was usually in the Signoria with the other men at that hour. The lovemaking from the night before had probably left him exhausted. Smiling, she debated whether or not to wake him. It was the day before Christmas and he may have important business to deal with before holy day celebrations began in the city. "Massimo," she said softly in his ear. "Wake up, my love. The sun is high."

He didn't move. She called his name again a little louder. Nothing.

Sabina placed a hand on his bare shoulder to nudge him and recoiled in horror. His skin was cold. "Oh my God," she gasped as her nervous fingers pressed into his icy neck to find a nonexistent pulse. Holding his stiff, lifeless body, she cried, "No! Massimo! You can't do this to me! You can't leave me! We have a beautiful granddaughter to raise!"

Teresa rushed into the room and crossed herself at the sight of Sabina embracing her husband's corpse. A moment later, Cecilia's concerned face hovered in the background while Anne cried over the loss of her stepfather.

The servants brewed calming draughts for Sabina and Anne while Teresa summoned the physician. During the examination of Massimo's body, a strange, dark bruise was found behind his ear. The physician offered a ruptured vein as the probable cause, and assured Sabina that her husband's death happened suddenly, perhaps while he was sleeping.

"At least he did not suffer," Sabina said, her eyes filling with tears.

Many people came to pay their respects at Massimo's funeral, including Caterina, Carlo, and their three sons: Giovanni, aged sixteen, Marcello, aged ten, and four-year-old Vittorio.

On that day, Sabina's heart was entombed along with her beloved Massimo. She would never love another man again.

***

Prior to their departure a few days later, Caterina and Carlo invited Sabina to stay with them in the Mugello. She thanked them for their generosity but politely declined. She had to remain in Florence in order to help Anne with the baby.

Sabina missed Massimo so badly that her heart physically ached for days, but nothing could prepare her for the tragedy that occurred shortly after her husband's funeral. On New Year's Day, 1521, poor Teresa found Anne swinging from a makeshift noose attached to the ceiling rafters. Stefania was peacefully asleep in her crib. A suicide letter had been placed on top of the coverlet.

Dear Mother,

I have been praying for the courage and the right moment to end my miserable existence. You are already grieving for Massimo, so you may as well mourn for me at the same time. Since I cannot rejoin the convent, my life is no longer worth living. I hope you can forgive my act of selfishness and cowardice. I have forfeited the prize of Heaven in taking my own life, but Hell cannot be worse than the guilt and pain I suffer every day. Besides, I cannot live with the shame of the truth. Please take care of Stefania and tell her I'm sorry. I do love her, but she is much better off without me. Thank you for everything, Mother. I love you. Tell Aunt Cecilia that I love her, too.

Your Daughter, Anne

Cecilia read the letter to Sabina, who merely stared at her daughter's swinging corpse and purple face. When Cecilia was done, Sabina walked to her bedchamber and stretched out on the bed.

"Sabina," Cecilia said, the tears streaming down her face. "Say something, for God's sake!"

Sabina was numb to the world, staring at the ceiling in silence. The next day, Cecilia arranged for Anne's body to be buried. Since her niece's death was a suicide, no priest could pray for her soul and her body would be interred in unconsecrated ground. Sabina did not cry during her daughter's meager funeral and merely stared at the wooden coffin being lowered into the grave. As the gravediggers began to shovel dirt, the sound jolted her from her stupor and she began to scream. Teresa and Cecilia tried to calm her, but she kept on screaming until she fainted and fell to the ground.

When Sabina opened her eyes, she saw worried faces hovering above her. It was raining and the cold water seeped through the fabric of her garments, but she didn't care. One line from Anne's suicide letter kept tormenting her: *Besides, I cannot live with the shame of the truth.*

The moment she was back at the house, Sabina raced to Anne's room and began going through her daughter's things. Cecilia and Teresa stood in the doorway while Stefania fussed inside her crib.

"What are you doing?" Cecilia finally asked gently.

Sabina continued to search frantically. "She knew…"

Teresa took a tentative step toward her mistress. "Let's get you out of those wet clothes, Signora Sabina. You should rest now."

Sabina's eyes were wild as she dug through piles of clothing, flipped through books, and peeked into the corners of a chest. Teresa wrung her hands nervously before picking up the baby and leaving the room. Cecilia watched as her sister slowly lifted a small piece of red wax from the floor. After examining it closely, she got down on her hands and knees and peered under the bed.

Reaching under the mattress, Sabina extracted a letter and handed it to her sister. "Read it."

Cecilia recognized half of the Vatican's red seal on the partially broken wax. With shaking hands, she unfolded the letter.

Dearest Anne,

I pray to God daily for your health and that of our child. I want you here in Lucca where I can provide for you both, but your mother strictly forbids it. She has even threatened me with physical harm if I go near you or the baby. Perhaps it's her jealousy that keeps us apart, for she and I were in love once, before she was forced to marry Tommaso Caravelli. I urge you to dismiss her poisonous counsel and return to me.

M.

Sabina laughed without mirth. The sound was chilling.

Cecilia regarded her sister with a mixture of fear and

concern. "You cannot blame Marco for this. Anne's mind was sick, fragile…"

Without a word, Sabina walked out of the room. She couldn't sleep that night or several nights afterward. She sat with the baby every afternoon, but there was no joy in her face, only sorrow. Cecilia did her best to lift her sister's spirits, but two great losses in such a short span of time was too much— even for Sabina Rossi. Cecilia woke up one morning to discover that her sister was gone. She went into Sabina's study and found a book of poisonous herbs on the desk.

"Oh, God," Cecilia cried before she got on her knees and prayed.

CHAPTER 24

Sabina patiently waited until the evening mass was over before sneaking into the church of San Michele. Sticking close to the shadows, she crept to the sacristy then to the bishop's private chambers. The door was slightly ajar to allow some fresh air into the room, and she watched Marco through the narrow crack like a silent cat. After several minutes, she knocked on the door.

"Who's there? Natalino, is that you?"

Marco's eyes grew wide when Sabina slowly pushed the door open. She took in the bishop's miter on the table and the golden crozier leaning against the wall before meeting his gaze. The torch flames flickered across her face and bathed her in golden light. He stood up in anticipation of another angry encounter.

"Forgive my intrusion, Your Excellency."

Marco's eyebrow shot up in surprise. "Why are you here?"

"I came to apologize for my behavior the last time we spoke." When he eyed her suspiciously, she added, "I overreacted. You're the father of my granddaughter and Stefania needs you in her life."

"Stefania," he repeated, happy to finally know his daughter's name. He suddenly frowned. "What tricks are you up to now, Sabina?"

"No tricks. I've been thinking about the situation for a long time. The enmity between us should end." She forced a smile. "I'm getting old and tired, Marco."

"So you came all the way here to tell me this? Why not pen a letter instead?"

"My sister is sick," she lied. "I have come to spend a few days with her at the convent." She licked her lips and tried to look demure. "I thought I would come and see you."

"I'm sorry to hear about Cecilia. I hope it's nothing serious."

She shook her head in response and sighed. "I want peace between us for the sake of little Stefania."

"I want peace, too." He visibly relaxed and his expression softened. "I swear I never meant for Anne to get pregnant and be forced out of the convent. She's a wonderful girl and I've always admired her zeal. I want her and Stefania here in Lucca. Rest assured, they'll be afforded every comfort they deserve."

Sabina fought back tears and smiled. "I believe you."

"What a relief. Let us put the unpleasantness of the past behind us for the sake of this child, shall we? We'll call a truce."

"You read my mind, Marco." Her eyes scanned the room and stopped when they found a wine flask on the sideboard.

He followed her gaze. "Shall we make a toast to seal our new pact?"

"A fine idea."

Marco poured two cups of wine and handed one to Sabina before holding his own high in a toast. "To new beginnings."

Sabina never broke eye contact with him as she raised her cup and repeated, "To new beginnings."

After they both drank deeply, he set down his cup on a nearby table.

"Sabina," he began and hesitated. "I want you to know…Well, what happened at the chapel…what I did to you—"

"I know you're sorry."

"Do you forgive me?"

Never. "Yes," she replied, her teeth clenching slightly.

"I only wanted to teach you a lesson."

"I know." She averted her eyes and added, "There's something I need to tell you."

"This sounds like a confession," he teased lightly.

"It is a confession. I've never stopped thinking about you. I admit, I was jealous when I found out about you and Anne."

Marco closed the gap between them. Taking hold of Sabina's chin, he forced her to look at him. "I always knew you loved me," he declared arrogantly. "You went off and married that old man who probably never satisfied you the way I could."

302

Sabina moved to stand beside the table where he had set down his cup. Turning her back to him, she said softly, "Many nights I would recall our passionate couplings in the woods near my father's house..."

A wicked twinkle appeared in his eyes as he remembered his lustful youth. "You were wild. I wonder if you still possess that fiery passion."

She peeked at him over her shoulder, her green eyes almost glowing in the dimness of the room as her hand moved discreetly over his cup. She quickly flipped open the top of her recently purchased poison ring to allow a small amount of white powder to fall into his wine. Fashioned from pure gold with a big oval jade from the East, it possessed a hollow compartment under the stone.

Sabina turned around as Marco approached to caress her face. When she did not flinch at his touch, his other hand cupped her neck and gently pushed her head back. "You're still lovely, even after all these years," he said before nuzzling her throat. Her body had aged, but her mind and spirit had mellowed like fine wine—and no aphrodisiac could have proved more powerful.

She placed a hand on his chest. "This seems rather inappropriate," she whispered in his ear. "Need I remind you that you are the father of my grandchild?"

Marco did not stop kissing her throat. Instead, he groped her breast. Afraid he would rape her again, she said, "I want you to make love to me, Marco. The way you did when we were young."

Ah, the words he had been waiting to hear for so long! "I want you, too. I never stopped loving you," he confessed as he began to press himself against her with urgency.

"Not here. Let us finish our wine and go to your bedchamber, where we can take our time and be more comfortable," she suggested, handing him his cup.

Sabina watched as he eagerly downed the remains of his wine and waited for her to do the same. As he pulled her toward his bedchamber, he doubled over in pain.

303

"What is it, Marco?" she asked innocently.

He straightened and smiled. "A little indigestion. I always get it after eating wild hare. I'll be—"

He doubled over again, only this time the spasm of pain was worse.

"You should rest a bit," she suggested, opening the door of his bedchamber.

She quickly took in the rich surroundings, ascertaining that Marco had done quite well for himself. The bed was hung with rich, red, patterned velvet and there were exquisite tapestries and fine paintings on the walls.

"I'll be fine," he said, reaching for her and untying the laces of her bodice with shaking fingers.

"I should fetch the physician," Sabina suggested with mock concern as she removed his hands from her bodice and led him to the bed.

Marco reclined on the velvet coverlet while clutching his stomach and retched. "What in God's name is happening to me?"

Another painful spasm took hold, draining him of color and causing him to perspire. When it was over, he said weakly, "I felt fine until…" Looking at her strangely, his eyes suddenly lit up. "You bitch!"

Sabina hopped onto the bed and straddled him. Since he was too weak and in too much pain to resist, she pinned his arms over his head.

"How could you?" he asked through clenched teeth as another spasm took hold of him. "I'm the father of your grandchild!"

Sabina put her lips to Marco's ear. "I have been searching through my books for days to pick just the right herbs and roots for you. I finally chose a poison that will take some time to kill you and cause you agony in the process." She paused, her chilling smile becoming a nightmarish grin. "How did I do? Are you in agony? Have I chosen well?"

Marco perspired profusely. Soon the pain would be too much to bear. "Bitch! Liar! Vixen!"

She cupped her ear mockingly. "What? Did you say something?"

His body began to convulse. She continued to straddle him in the same manner one would ride a horse. White foam escaped from the corner of his mouth and his eyes rolled upward.

Gripping his throat with both hands, she squeezed as much as she could. "Die, you filthy pig!"

Marco's last moments of consciousness consisted of Sabina's curses, damning him to eternal torment in Hell. When he lay perfectly still, she left the room without a backward glance.

There was a little boy in the corridor. "Where is Bishop Alfani?"

"Who are you?" Sabina demanded.

"Natalino, the altar boy. I'm looking for the bishop."

"Go home. Bishop Alfani is sleeping right now."

Cecilia sagged with relief when her sister finally arrived home. "Sabina, did you—"

Sabina lifted a hand in protest. "Do not say another word, Cecilia. The less you know, the better."

"But—"

"I've been riding for many hours and need to rest."

Cecilia crossed herself as she watched her sister ascend the stairs.

***

Sabina couldn't remain in Florence. Memories of Anne and Massimo lurked in every corner of the palazzina. In addition, news of Marco's sudden and mysterious death would eventually spread throughout Tuscany. How trustworthy was the goldsmith from whom she had purchased the poison ring?

Caterina wrote another letter to Sabina immediately after Anne's suicide, insisting that she come live with her family. The Mugello was quiet and charming—most of all, it was safe. She accepted Caterina's offer without hesitation.

"What will you do in the Mugello? There is nothing there," Cecilia inquired. "Would you not prefer to remain in Florence?"

"I want to raise Stefania in peaceful surroundings, far away from any trouble," Sabina replied. "Besides, there's too much political turmoil in Florence right now."

"I will keep you both in my prayers. I always do."

Sabina touched her sister's cheek affectionately. "I know you do. Thank you for everything."

Cecilia left for Lucca and Sabina moved to the countryside a few weeks later. Leo stayed behind to guard and maintain the house, while Teresa accompanied her mistress along with Donna Francesca, Stefania's wet nurse.

Caterina received Sabina and her entourage with open arms. "Let me see this little beauty," she said, reaching for Stefania. "I've always wanted a girl, but God has blessed me with three sons."

"How are the boys? Where is your husband?" Sabina inquired, looking around.

"The boys are well. Carlo had to deliver some merchandise to his clients in Rome, but he should be back in a few days."

"Thank you for offering your home to me, Caterina."

"We are family, Sabina. Having you both here is a good thing. Besides, it gets lonely with Carlo being gone so often."

"Florence is not the same without Massimo. And after Anne...."

Sensing her sister in law's potential tears, Caterina changed the subject by asking, "Do you plan on selling your home?"

"No. I'm going to keep it for Stefania." Sabina took one of the baby's fingers. "I must focus on this little one, and I'm more than happy to help you with the boys. I insist on funding their education from now on."

Caterina appeared stricken. "We invited you here because we foster great affection for you. We don't expect anything in return."

"No one knows that better than I do, but those are my terms. Allow me the opportunity to repay your kindness and generosity by providing your sons with the best tutors that money can buy. I'm old and have too much money, so let me spend it wisely."

Caterina smiled and nodded. Stefania began to fuss so

Donna Francesca came to take the baby for her feeding.

"Your nurse appears to be very capable," Caterina commented.

"Donna Francesca served as nurse to the Fanucci family and their children."

"Fanucci—he is a baron, is he not? Handsome too. I remember he had many children."

Sabina smirked. "Ten. Stefania has taken a liking to her and cries less now. She was crying all the time after…" She was going to say "after Anne's death," but stopped herself. Anne had wanted nothing to do with this life, with Stefania, with anything. Sabina believed that she had failed miserably as a mother, despite having done everything in her power to provide the best education and happiest childhood for her daughter. Where had she failed? How had she failed?

Oh, Massimo, how I wish you were here to help me through this…

Caterina's voice brought Sabina back to the present. "The boys are excited about having a baby in the house, especially a girl. They already feel protective of her."

"Stefania will love them. I'm sure."

Caterina put her arm around Sabina's shoulders. "I know you've been through so much. Let me do what I can to comfort you. I'll always be in your debt for making my brother happy."

"To be honest with you, I had no idea what to do or where to go after losing the two people I loved most in this world."

Caterina pulled her sister-in-law in for a brief embrace then led her to the garden located behind the villa. It was cold, dry, and lifeless, but, in a matter of months, spring would make everything green and full of life again. Hopefully, Sabina's spirit would be reborn as well.

The political situation in Florence was precarious. Fear of the Medici returning to reclaim power was prevalent among Florentine politicians, creating a tense atmosphere. Carlo kept abreast of current news and passed what he gleaned onto his wife and Sabina, who greedily absorbed any tidbit of gossip. The peaceful countryside proved to be a healing salve for Sabina and her granddaughter.

Stefania may have lost her mother, but she gained an adoring family who witnessed her first steps and her first tooth, and watched her grow into a healthy, happy child. Her surrogate brothers not only loved her, they were also extremely protective. Stefania became precocious and coy as a result; a deadly combination for a child who, at the tender age of five, was already exhibiting the physical traits of a future beauty. Her emerald green eyes were large and expressive, her mouth a red rosebud, and her dark spiral curls bounced prettily whenever she moved. When she flashed her captivating smile, it was difficult not to fall under the spell of her charm.

Lorenzo il Magnifico's granddaughter, Maria Salviati, moved to the Castello del Trebbio a while back, but Sabina was only introduced to her after Easter Mass. Maria's reputation preceded her; she was known to be a cultured and spiritual woman, totally dedicated to the raising of her son, Cosimo. Sensing the camaraderie between Sabina and Maria, Caterina graciously invited her to dinner the following week.

Maria and her seven-year-old son came to the house after mass the following Sunday. Caterina and her servants prepared a fine meal of stewed wild boar and roasted vegetables. Maria complimented the food and chatted easily with her hosts. Confident that she sat among Medici supporters, she finally disclosed her real reason for living in the Mugello.

"As you well know, Florence is a dangerous place for my son," Maria said. "He may be viewed as a threat to the Republic."

Carlo nodded in agreement. "You were wise to raise the lad here."

The adults sat together at the head of the table and their eyes slid to the little boy who sat at the opposite end with the children. Cosimo, being perceptive and intelligent, met their gazes with an expression of calm assuredness. His handsome brown eyes gave nothing away.

"I want him to grow up in a safe environment," Maria whispered while still looking at her son.

They understood the prudence of her actions. In such politically turbulent times, it was not uncommon for poison to find its way into someone's food or for a fatal accident to occur. A child would be an easy target.

"I remember when your grandfather, Lorenzo, ruled the city. It was the cultural center of Europe and an economic giant," Sabina reminisced. "Oh, how I miss those days."

Maria smiled. "The Golden Age of Florence…I wish I could remember those days, too."

"They ended when Giuliano died," Sabina said sadly.

"My mother told me the story of the Pazzi Conspiracy and how poor Giuliano was murdered during Easter Mass in the Duomo," Maria said.

Sabina's memory raced backward in time. In her mind's eye, she remembered the scene vividly. "Your grandfather was such a great man. The people loved him."

"Indeed he was," Maria agreed. "It's a pity his life was cut short by gout. That cursed condition has afflicted many in my family. I pray Cosimo will be spared."

The boy met Sabina's gaze. Like his great grandfather, Cosimo's eyes were piercing and steady. Anyone with a shred of perception could see that Maria was grooming him for a great future in politics. Cosimo was educated, strong in character, and already possessed the intelligence and cunning needed to be a powerful ruler in the future—should he survive into adulthood. One could never take such a luxury for granted.

Changing the subject, Maria asked of her hosts, "I hear that your oldest son is getting married in the spring."

Carlo replied, "Giovanni has made a fine match with the daughter of a Milanese banker. Perhaps you have heard of the Romario family?"

"Yes, I have. They are a good and reputable family."

Caterina and her husband beamed with pride before Carlo said, "Our son will be moving to Milan after the wedding."

"We will miss him," Caterina added. She sighed and glanced at the children. Giovanni, who normally sat with the adults, was away on family business. She remembered when all three sons sat together. Time passed too quickly.

Carlo was generous with his good wine, so the aromatic nectar flowed freely at the table. Even the children enjoyed a watered-down version mixed with honey. Cosimo and Stefania were seated side by side and kept smiling at each other. After cutting up several pieces of wild boar on his plate, Cosimo offered them to Stefania.

The act of male gallantry was not lost on Vittorio, who scowled and said, "I was going to cut the meat for Stefania."

Despite being two years older and considerably taller, Vittorio failed to intimidate Cosimo, who said, "Next time, you should seize the opportunity and act quicker."

This made Stefania laugh and Vittorio blush. Marcello, who was by nature extremely quiet and shy, merely smiled at Cosimo's quick retort. Nearly sixteen years old, he seemed unfazed by the fact that he was sitting with the children instead of the adults.

"How old are you?" Vittorio asked of Cosimo.

Cosimo continued to place tidbits of meat on Stefania's plate as he replied, "I'm seven years old, Stefania is five, and you are nine."

"How do you know?" Vittorio demanded.

"My mother's servants tell me everything."

Stefania looked at one boy then the other while she chewed

quietly.

"Did they tell you Stefania prefers my company to yours?" Vittorio countered saucily. "I'm her favorite, you know."

Cosimo's eyes slid to Stefania then back to Vittorio. "Are you sure about that?"

Vittorio frowned in outrage. "Of course, I am!"

"Do you not think it better to ask her?" Cosimo insisted.

Vittorio demanded, "Stefania, who do you like better—me or him?"

Not wanting to hurt either boy's feelings, Stefania pointed to Marcello, who playfully grabbed her finger and pretended to bite it off, making her squeal with laughter. The adults glanced at the children.

"She's such a pretty little thing," Maria commented.

Sabina beamed with pride. "She's a good girl, too."

"We love her as our very own," Carlo said and Caterina nodded in accord. "It seems like your son, Cosimo, has fallen under her spell just as our sons have."

For the first time in his young life, Vittorio experienced the sharp pang of jealousy. Stefania had always belonged to him; now this new boy was diverting her attention and making her smile. As Vittorio studied Cosimo, he decided to dislike the young usurper.

***

The years passed rapidly and peacefully. Sabina devoted herself entirely to Stefania's education. In time, the girl became knowledgeable, articulate, and well versed in Latin, history, and mathematics. In the year 1535, Stefania turned fourteen and Sabina turned seventy-six. Their birthdays were celebrated a few days apart during the month of October, when the autumn chill began to permeate the air.

Carlo continued to flourish as a merchant, only now he sold gemstones and precious metals instead of spices. He would sometimes travel as far north as Venice or as far south as Naples. Of his sons, the only one who displayed interest and talent for the family business was Vittorio. Not only did he accompany his father on these long journeys, he also dabbled in goldsmithing. Although Vittorio enjoyed working with his father, he hated being away from Stefania. At age eighteen, he pined for her attention and often fantasized about marrying her in the future.

Cosimo, who was now sixteen and very much a man beyond his years, was also not immune to Stefania's feminine wiles. His sexual appetite was healthy, which was not unusual for a young man of his age. Despite having bedded a few of the nubile servants in his household, he could not yet bring himself to seduce the young woman who had been his best friend since childhood. Stefania was his closest confidant, and he held a great amount of respect for her and her grandmother.

***

Stefania barged into Vittorio's room one day holding a stiff bodice against her bare chest. "Will you please lace me up? My maid is nowhere to be found," she lamented.

Vittorio, who had been seated at his desk writing a letter, put down his quill and merely stared at Stefania. She was wearing a cream linen underskirt and he could see through the flimsy fabric. To his chagrin, he felt himself harden.

She walked up to him and turned around, exposing her back. He stared at the silken skin, which was the color of fresh cream, and admired the way her slim waist curved into her hips. He wanted to run his hands on that skin, smell it, taste it.

"Well? What are you waiting for?" Stefania asked, peeking over her shoulder. "Go on. I need to get dressed for my lessons."

Vittorio could not stand up in his current state without humiliating himself. With trembling fingers, he carefully laced up the undergarment from where he sat. Each time his fingers brushed her skin, the desire increased. She also smelled of rose water, which only tormented him further.

"Almost done?" she asked.

"Yes," he replied.

"Thank you," she said, turning around and kissing his cheek. "Do you want to play chess after I'm done with my lessons?"

Vittorio nodded mutely, his mouth dry. She smiled and rushed out of the room. He exhaled and put his head into his hands.

Sabina did little to rein her granddaughter's passion and femininity. Instead, Stefania was afforded more freedom and education than most women her age. She loved the sport of falconry and hunting, which was not surprising since she was raised around males. She also loved to ride. Of the three brothers, Marcello was the most accomplished rider and hunter, but he was in love with a local young woman named Giulia and too busy courting. This left the second-best rider, Giovanni, who was more than happy to accompany Stefania whenever he and his wife, Anabella, came to visit. Unfortunately, his visits were infrequent. Finally, there was Vittorio, who traveled often. Whenever he was home, however, he preferred reading over riding but would indulge Stefania on occasion.

One cold winter afternoon, Stefania wanted to go riding. The bad weather had forced her to remain indoors for many days. To make matters worse, Marcello was not home. Since Sabina did not permit her granddaughter to go out into the woods alone, Stefania was doing her utmost to convince Vittorio.

"Please Vittorio," she pleaded as she paced around his chair.

Vittorio was reading a book by the warmth of the fire. "Stefania, it's so cold outside. Look!" he pointed out the window. "There's snow on the ground."

"Only a light dusting. You know I'm not permitted to go out alone. The falcons need exercise."

He sighed tiredly. "Father and I returned only yesterday. Let me rest a bit, will you?"

After a few minutes of whining, it became obvious that Vittorio was not going to budge, no matter how much she pouted.

"I'll go riding with you."

Both Vittorio and Stefania turned toward the sound of the voice in the doorway. It was Cosimo.

"Your grandmother let me in," he said to Stefania. Looking at Vittorio, he added, "Buongiorno."

"Buongiorno," Vittorio replied with forced pleasantness.

Cosimo turned his attention back to Stefania. "I would be

more than happy to accompany you riding or hunting or whatever else you wish to do. A lovely lady should never beg for the company of a gentleman."

Stefania smiled and blushed.

Irritated, Vittorio stood. "Of course I would not allow her to go alone. I'm only concerned with her health. I would hate for Stefania to catch cold in this weather."

Cosimo laughed. "One with hot blood cannot catch cold."

Vittorio witnessed the electricity in the look that Stefania and Cosimo shared. In that moment, he experienced a jealousy so fierce, he wanted to strangle his opponent.

"I'll fetch my cloak," Stefania said before rushing off.

There was a tense silence between the two young men before Cosimo asked, "What are you reading?" Vittorio held up the book for him to see. "Ah, Plato. Always a good choice."

"How is your mother?" Vittorio inquired courteously.

"She's well, thank you. She's looking forward to Christmas. Your parents have been kind enough to include us in their celebrations this year."

"How thoughtful of them. I'm sure it will be a merry time for us all," Vittorio stated flatly, feeling the exact opposite.

Another tense silence passed.

"Ah, Stefania is blossoming into an extraordinary woman, don't you agree?"

Vittorio heard a touch of mischief in Cosimo's voice. "Yes, she is."

"Like her grandmother."

Vittorio nodded in agreement. "She was quite a woman in her day, from what I hear. Beautiful, courageous, strong, and a talented writer."

"And exactly who fits that wondrous description?" Stefania asked as she waltzed back into the room with a fur cloak around her shoulders.

"Your grandmother," Cosimo replied. "She was incredible."

"She *is* incredible," Stefania corrected. "After all she's been through and what she's done for me, I owe her everything."

"She does it out of love, I'm sure," Cosimo said. "Are you

314

ready?"

She nodded and looked to Vittorio. "See you at supper."

"I'm going with you."

She raised her eyebrows in surprise and Cosimo's face broke into a sly, knowing grin that made Vittorio's face turn red.

"Are you sure?" she asked. "I thought you wanted to rest."

"I'm sure, unless my company is unwanted," Vittorio retorted defensively.

"Don't be silly, my friend. We would enjoy your company," Cosimo said smoothly.

"I'll change into something warm and meet you in the stables shortly," Vittorio said.

Once outside, Cosimo placed his hand in the small of Stefania's back as they entered the large wooden stable. His face was close to hers and the presence of his hand on her back felt pleasing.

Seeing her horse, she said, "Hello Nero."

"I like that you named your horse after a notorious Roman Emperor," he commented, his breath brushing her cheek like a feather.

The coldness in the air was turning their noses and lips red, and their breath came out in vaporous clouds. Stefania did not move when Cosimo took another step to close the gap between them. When the hand on the small of her back pulled her toward him, she did not resist.

He held her close. "I wonder if your lips are as sweet as they appear."

Her mouth curved into a smile. "Why not discover for yourself?"

Cosimo's eyes lit up with humor. "What a bold thing for well-bred girl to say. How many other boys have you kissed?"

"You are about to become the first."

"Are you so sure that I'll kiss you?"

She giggled softly. "I am."

"You're very pretty, you know."

She blushed. "Thank you. My grandmother tells me that, too."

"Your grandmother is right," he said softly before lowering his head and gently kissing her lips.

Stefania was timid at first and her lack of experience was evident, but she was a fast learner. She greedily accepted his tongue into her mouth and pulled him closer. They stopped kissing and stepped away from each other when they heard approaching footsteps.

Vittorio entered the stable a moment later and took in their guilty expressions. "Why have you not saddled Nero yet?"

When Stefania did not answer, Cosimo interjected, "We were trying to decide which horse I will ride."

Vittorio frowned. "Did you not ride here on your own horse?"

"Ha! Of course, I did. How silly of me!" Cosimo exclaimed, making Stefania laugh before tossing her a conspiratorial look.

Vittorio knew something had transpired between the two of them and, as usual, he felt left out. He suddenly wished that Cosimo and his mother would move to Florence where they belonged!

"Are we going for a ride or not?" Vittorio demanded impatiently.

Stefania summoned the groom to saddle Nero while Cosimo sought his horse.

Vittorio stood beside Stefania. "What were you two doing before I came in?"

"Nothing."

Her expression was innocent, yet he didn't believe her. "You like him."

It was not a question. Stefania shrugged. "We all like him."

"You know what I mean."

She smiled slyly. "Are you jealous, Vito?"

Stefania was the only person allowed to still call him by his childhood nickname. He crossed his arms and turned away from her gaze. "Jealous of a sixteen-year-old boy? Stop being silly."

The sly smile turned into a knowing grin. "You *are* jealous!"

"You're being ridiculous."

"We were kissing."

Vittorio swung his head toward her. "*What*?"

"That's what we were doing before you walked in."

"You allowed him to kiss you?"

"Yes," she admitted without the slightest hint of shame or regret.

"But…"

"But what?"

You're mine! Instead, he shook his head in disgust. "Nothing."

Cosimo was handsome, charming, and possessed an enviable level of sophistication. While Vittorio was also good looking and charming—when he wanted to be—he lacked the experience with women that Cosimo obviously possessed. He was furious with Stefania for engaging in a kiss behind his back.

"Are you angry with me?" she asked as if reading his mind.

He touched her cheek gently then quickly lowered his hand. "No, Stefania. I could never be angry with you."

Cosimo whistled to them from outside the stable entrance. The three of them mounted their horses and trotted in the snow.

"Should we take the falcons?" Stefania asked.

Vittorio peered up at the sky. "It may rain soon. I think a quick ride is all that this day will allow."

"I believe he's right," Cosimo agreed, looking at Stefania.

She pouted and spurred Nero forward in order to keep up with her two companions. She studied each one carefully. Cosimo was lighter in skin tone and fairer in hair color than Vittorio, who had inherited his mother's olive skin, black hair, and blue eyes. She loved his blue eyes. Cosimo's eyes were brown and he was more than a palm's width shorter than Vittorio.

In an act of spontaneity, she kicked her horse and took off at a gallop. She shouted over her shoulder, "A kiss for the one who catches me!"

Cosimo and Vittorio looked at one another then kicked their horses, urging them forward with shouts. Stefania crouched so low in the saddle that Nero's mane tickled her face. Her heart pounded in rhythm to the horse's fast pace, the sound filling her

317

ears.

As they emerged into an open field, she laughed from exhilaration. Peeking over her shoulder, she saw her companions approaching. She laughed again, reveling in her youth and the joy of being alive. Nero began to tire and slow down. The young men were on either side of her, both trying to overtake her horse. It was Vittorio who finally succeeded.

"Whoa," she cried, making Nero come to a halt.

Vittorio glowed with pleasure as he leaned in his saddle. "I want to claim my prize."

Stefania noticed Cosimo watching her expectantly, but, as usual, his expression gave nothing away. As she leaned toward Vittorio, she saw something in his eyes—something that made her feel strange but in a good way. Unsure of what to do, she kissed his cheek. She noticed the flicker of disappointment on his face. Vittorio glanced at his opponent; it seemed as if Cosimo was the true victor.

Later that night, after the family had supped, Stefania read aloud to her grandmother. Sabina's eyes were still good, but they grew tired quickly. Besides, she liked the sound of Stefania's voice. She noticed that Vittorio seemed agitated throughout evening and had said little during the meal. She was also well aware that he was completely enamored of Stefania.

"That will do, my dear. Thank you," Sabina said.

"Are you sure you don't want me to read until the end of the chapter, Grandmother?"

"I'm sure."

Stefania marked the page then set the book down. They were alone, facing the warm fire burning within the hearth.

Steeling a sidelong glance toward her granddaughter, Sabina asked, "Vittorio was unusually quiet this evening. Why is he upset?"

Stefania knew it was jealousy, yet said, "I have no idea."

The girl would undoubtedly break many hearts, including poor Vittorio's. "He is fond of you."

"I'm fond of him, too."

"You could do far worse for a husband."

"You would have me marry so soon, Grandmother?"

Sabina was suddenly reminded of a dry, hot day long ago in her father's courtyard. She had once thought of marriage as repugnant, too. "Most girls your age are eager to marry and start a family."

"Not I!" Sabina laughed and Stefania frowned. "What's so funny?"

"I was the same way at your age. I loved my books and cared little about marriage or babies. Don't worry, child. I won't force you to marry anyone."

Stefania's relief was evident. "I didn't say that I don't wish to marry ever…just not now."

Sabina nodded slowly, amused. "Understood, my dear."

After a brief pause, Stefania said, "Cosimo would also make a good husband."

"Oh, so it's Cosimo you fancy?" Sabina asked, knowing full well that it was. She had already noticed how her granddaughter's eyes followed the young Medici whenever he came to the house.

Stefania blushed. "I'm simply stating that both Vittorio and Cosimo are fine young men who will someday make good husbands for two fortunate ladies."

Sabina tried hard not to smile. "I see."

"Besides, at my age, I shouldn't even be thinking of such things."

Sabina coughed to cover up her laughter. "I think you're right. Concentrate on your studies, practice your Latin, perfect your mathematics, and leave the boys to their silly games."

"It's not as if I don't like boys…" the girl trailed off and shrugged.

"I know, sweetheart," Sabina assured. "No need to say another word. You're growing up so quickly. I'll wager there are many thoughts and feelings inside of you that seem strange." Stefania nodded, her eyes a bit sad. "I experienced the same thing at your age. Keep in mind that what you feel is normal and it will pass."

"Cosimo kissed me today," Stefania blurted out.

Sabina peered at her granddaughter. "Is that all he did?"

"Yes."

"You're aiming high, child."

Stefania was hurt. "Am I not good enough?"

"That's not what I meant, Stefania. You're good enough for a king as far as I'm concerned." Sabina lowered her voice. "The problem is that Cosimo is being groomed for a political future. He has a destiny to fulfill and his mother has dedicated her life to make sure he assumes that role."

"I thought we were never to talk of this."

"You're right, it's a secret. Never speak of this outside of our family circle. The point I'm trying to convey is that you should be careful. Don't allow your heart to love someone you cannot have." Sabina paused, her expression serious. "Cosimo will need to make difficult decisions soon."

"Such as?"

"Making political alliances that will enable him to take over Florence."

"Like marrying someone he doesn't love?"

"More often than not, those kinds of marriage arrangements occur with political leaders." Stefania looked down at her hands, compelling Sabina to add, "I'm only telling you this because I want to protect you. I've never lied to you and I never will. I love you and want nothing but your happiness. If you set your heart on Cosimo, you must be aware of the risks involved. Do you understand what I'm telling you?"

"Yes."

"Good. It's time you get to bed, young lady. Goodnight."

Stefania ascended the stairs while pondered her grandmother's wise counsel. Turning the corner, she ran into Vittorio.

"I heard you coming up the stairs," he said, grabbing her shoulders.

She smelled wine on his breath and tried to push past him. "I'm on my way to bed. Goodnight, Vito."

He refused to let her go. "I want my prize."

Before she could protest, his mouth came down on hers and

he pressed her roughly against him. Stefania struggled and finally managed to pull away. He staggered back and put a hand on the wall to steady himself.

Stefania's eyes flashed. "How dare you!"

"You promised a kiss to the winner…I won."

"You claimed your prize this afternoon."

"A mere kiss on the cheek? No, I want you to kiss me the way you kissed Cosimo in the stable."

"I kissed him because I wanted to, not because I had to."

Vittorio winced at the sting of her words. "Stefania…"

"Goodnight, Vittorio," she said coolly.

***

Sabina didn't know what transpired between Vittorio and Stefania, but their comportment toward each other had changed. Drastically. There was no more carefree laughter, tickling, or jokes. They were always polite and cool when they addressed each other, but their close friendship had evaporated. Cosimo frequented the house often and since both he and Maria were invited to stay for Christmas, he enjoyed most of the festivities at Stefania's side. Their admiration for one another was obvious to everyone.

Cosimo shared his secrets with Stefania. Since she knew about his political strategies, he trusted her with information that he normally wouldn't reveal to another soul. He also confessed personal things, which she guarded within the locked confines of her heart.

Stefania lost her virginity to Cosimo shortly after the New Year. He had come to the house while everyone was attending mass. Stefania and Cosimo had previously conspired to stay behind on pretenses of ailments while their families went to church. There, in Stefania's bed, Cosimo gently made love to her. She had disliked the pain of that first encounter. The second time, she experienced pleasure and her body responded naturally and without inhibition.

After he had come twice, Cosimo stretched out beside her, panting. "You are a wonderful lover, Stefania. Had I not taken your maidenhead myself, I would think you quite experienced."

321

She blushed. "I please you then?"

"More than you know."

"I know I'm not the only girl..."

"I won't lie to you. There are others, but I neither confide in them nor care for them. They are merely used for brief pleasure."

"I see," she said, her expression one of disappointment.

"I'm very fond of you, Stefania."

She would have preferred to hear the word "love" but remained silent.

"From this day forward, you have possession of my heart and some other parts as well." He rubbed against her playfully to emphasize his point and they both fell into peals of laughter. "I should go before your family arrives."

"Everyone knows you and I are dear to each other."

"I know, but…"

He sat up in bed and reached for his shirt.

"Just like that? Without so much as a goodbye kiss?" she said, her pout irresistible.

He slid over and pinned her under his weight as he kissed her. As her tongue found his, she moved her hips slowly and soon felt his manhood grow yet again.

After Cosimo had gone, Stefania busily prepared an emmenagogue to prevent pregnancy. Like her grandmother, she had a knack for flower lore.

CHAPTER 26

Throughout the years of Cosimo's childhood, Florence witnessed the Sack of Rome in 1527 and the siege that followed in 1529. At the time, Alessandro the Moor was vying for power in Florence. His parentage was obscure, however. Many believed he was the bastard son of the Medici pope, Clement VII, and a Negress, thus giving him the look of a mulatto and his nickname.

Alessandro was unpopular with the people and viewed as the puppet of the pope's delegate, Baccio Valori. In 1532, Alessandro took firm control of the city and began his tyrannous rule. He was detested for his lack of refinement and coarse behavior. In addition to prohibiting the Florentines to carry arms, he employed the service of foreign guards and imposed heavy taxes.

There was much talk in the Salviati household regarding the events taking place in Florence. Maria was always careful not to say anything in front of her servants that could later be repeated and used against her or her son. The same held true in Castagno household.

Meanwhile, news of a tremendous scandal in England reached the ears of everyone in Europe. King Henry VIII asked the pope to annul his marriage to Catherine of Aragon in order to place his mistress, Anne Boleyn, on the throne. When his request was refused, he went against the pope and married Anne, crowning her Queen of England in 1534.

"The world is changing," Carlo said one Sunday while they were seated together having their midday meal. "I have received news that the English whore was crowned queen. No one respects God's laws anymore."

"We are living in troubled times, indeed," Caterina agreed. "I fear for the future of our children. What kind of world will it be for them and for their children?"

"One without morals or God's law," he replied grimly.

Sabina quietly listened as she ate another spoonful of soup. She glanced at Stefania, who was looking down at her plate and wondered what the future held for her as well. It was now common knowledge in the Mugello that Stefania was Cosimo's lover, but no one commented on that fact. Sabina knew her granddaughter fostered secret hopes of becoming Cosimo's wife one day. Sooner or later, she would have to accept the harsh reality that he would never—could never—marry her.

Stefania finished her meal and excused herself from the table. Cosimo was expected soon to take her hunting. Sabina knew the young couple spent many of their afternoons in the hunting lodge belonging to the Castello del Trebbio rather than chasing game, but she never said anything. Her granddaughter, like herself at that age, was far too rebellious and sensuous to retain her virginity. Because of this, she offered practical advice rather than moral ideals. Stefania knew everything she needed to know about the act of love and how to protect herself from becoming pregnant.

When Cosimo arrived, Stefania wasted no time fetching her cloak and leaving the house. It was a clear, spring day and she and Cosimo laughed as they steered their horses through the trees. The lush greenery and fresh scent of vegetation was intoxicating. Stefania wanted to speak with him about a certain matter for quite some time and resolved to do so that afternoon when the moment was right.

They dismounted and entered the cozy hunting lodge. They undressed while kissing and teasing each other. Passion soon gave way and their young bodies became united as one. Their lovemaking was simultaneously intense and tender.

How can he not love me? Stefania thought as he rested against her bare breast, panting softly. After a long moment, she said, "Cosimo, there is something I wish to ask you."

"What is it, my love?" he asked without moving.

"Am I?"

"Are you what?"

"Your 'love?' "

He leaned on his elbow to look at her face. "You know I care deeply for you, Stefania. I bare my soul to you."

"Do you love me?"

"Yes, but…You know there can never be a marriage between us. We've discussed this before."

She looked away. "You would rather marry for a political alliance instead of love?"

"Love and marriage have nothing to do with each other. People in my position do not have that luxury."

"Exactly what is your position? Alessandro the Moor does not appear to be going anywhere anytime soon."

"That damned tyrant won't be in power forever. When the time comes, I'll claim my right to rule. I'm the next legitimate Medici in line of succession." He sighed. "Why are we discussing this again?"

"Because I love you, Cosimo!"

His expression softened and he caressed her cheek. "Dear sweet Stefania. Do not think my refusal to marry you has anything to do with how I feel. I adore you. You are my confidant, my lover; I want the best for you."

Tears streamed down her cheeks as he spoke. "But we'll never marry or have a family," she whimpered. It was the first time she exhibited her true feelings.

He gathered her into his arms and kissed the top of her head. "We cannot." They remained in a silent embrace for several minutes before he spoke again. "I promise that you'll always have a special place in my heart and you will always be well looked-after."

Stefania never spoke to Cosimo of marriage or love after that day. She played the part of lover without demands or complaints, and enjoyed every moment with him as though it was her last. Raw strength ran in her blood, just as it ran in Sabina's blood.

***

In the fall of 1536, Sabina received a letter from the Convento di Santa Lucia. Her sister was very ill. The last time Sabina paid her a visit, Cecilia had complained of frequent and intense headaches.

Sabina summoned Teresa. "Pack my belongings. I'm going to Lucca at once." She paused, her eyes watering. "I think my sister is dying."

"I'm so sorry," Teresa offered. "Shall I come with you?"

"No, and don't tell Stefania until I'm gone. She'll want to accompany me and I wish to go alone."

Sabina was taken directly to Cecilia's chilly cell upon arrival. A single candle sputtered atop the bedside table, and the sparsely furnished room smelled musty.

"Sabina?" Cecilia called out in a weak voice. "Is that you?"

"Yes, dear sister." Sabina approached the bed and the shock of Cecilia's appearance made her gasp.

Cecilia laughed weakly before having a coughing fit. She winced at the pain in her head. "I'm a frightening sight, I know."

"Not at all," Sabina lied.

"I see the expressions of the young novices who are assigned to my care." She held up her bone-thin hands. "I haven't left my bed in weeks, and my hands reveal that I've lost much weight."

Cecilia, always robust and healthy, had wasted away to the point of skin and bones. To make matters worse, the dark circles around her eyes accentuated her ghostly pallor.

Sabina knew her sister would not last much longer. She knelt beside the bed. "I cannot find the words for what I want to say."

Cecilia smiled wryly. "That's funny, sister. Of all people, I think you would be the last person to be at a loss for words. Sabina the poet…Sabina the writer." Sabina bent her head and wept. "Stop that nonsense. We all have to go sometime. I'm actually looking forward to these headaches finally ending."

Composing herself, Sabina inquired, "Have you been properly examined by a physician?"

"Yes…he said it's a tumor. I have bouts of blindness and moments where I see intense light. At first, I thought they were visions." Cecilia shook her head. "Imagine me having visions? Such arrogance on my part! As if God Almighty would send visions to a miserable sinner like me. Ah, human pride is

326

limitless."

"I cannot think of anyone more deserving of God's divine favor."

Cecilia closed her eyes as a spasm of pain took hold. "You're being kind to a dying woman."

"What else did the physician tell you?"

"I have less than a month to live."

Sabina swallowed the lump that rose in her throat. "I'm going to do everything in my power to make your last days as comfortable as possible. You will not die alone, Cecilia."

Tears filled Cecilia's eyes. "Thank you, dear sister."

After making a sizable contribution to the convent, Sabina arranged Cecilia's transfer to a large cell with two comfortable beds. She also procured warm blankets, rugs, books, plenty of candles, and the best pain-relieving herbs that money could buy.

The draughts eased Cecilia's pain to the point that she developed a small appetite. After a few days of sipping chicken broth and nibbling on fresh bread, some color crept back into her cheeks. Sabina didn't fool herself into thinking Cecilia would recover, however. The attacks of blindness and bright light became more frequent and eventually the painkillers began to lose their effect. When the dose was doubled, Cecilia became numb and incoherent.

"Sabina?" Cecilia said one day in a moment of lucidity.

Sabina, who was wiping the drool off her sister's chin, paused. "I'm right here, Cecilia."

"Tell me…Marco's death…Did you…"

"Shhh….Let's not discuss that now." *Or the rape, either*.

Cecilia nodded. "Thank you, sister…for everything. I love you."

"I love you, too." Sabina gave Cecilia's hand a squeeze.

"I need to apologize."

"For what?"

A spasm of pain caused her to wince. "For thinking badly of you."

Sabina adjusted the coverlet, tucking it neatly around her sister's shoulders. "This is nonsense, Cecilia."

"I have secretly envied you for years. You were talented, beautiful, clever…I was plain and dull-witted. The only thing you lacked was reverence for God. That's why I joined the convent." Her eyes shone with unshed tears. "I wanted to have at least one thing in my life that I could hold over your head."

"Oh, Cecilia…"

"I can't die without confessing my sins of envy and pride."

"There were many things you were better at than me—you simply failed to see them." Sabina paused and smiled. "I never got that sweet tart recipe right. You made them perfectly, whereas my tarts always ended up raw in the center. Oh, and let's not forget your skill with needle and thread. Remember when we were young girls and commissioned by the local parish to make a tapestry for the altar? The half you worked on was lovely, whereas mine…" she trailed off and shrugged.

Cecilia chuckled at the memory. "Your half was a mess!"

Sabina burst into laughter. "Well, you could be a bit kinder."

"It was terrible! With crooked stitches and knots."

"You were also a better mother than I ever was."

Cecilia waved her hand weakly. "Do not say such things."

"Had I been more like you, maybe Anne would still be here today."

"I was a good mother to my little Paolo because I loved him. You were the same way with Anne—nothing more, nothing less."

"Ah, Paolo…"

"I think of his smiling face every day." Cecilia sighed with delight. "I'm looking forward to seeing him again in Heaven."

"When you do, give him a kiss for me. I shall meet you both shortly."

It was the last conversation the two sisters shared.

CHAPTER 27

In January of 1537, Stefania suspected that she was with child but kept her condition a secret. Her paleness and frequent trips to the privy brought suspicious stares from Sabina. In that same month, Alessandro the Moor was stabbed to death in an assassination plot. Florence had rid itself of its tyrant, but news of his death was kept quiet for a time in order to prevent an uprising in the city. When the incident was finally made public, the Florentines hoped to restore the Republic. The new pope, Paul III, had no designs to rule, leaving the city free for a new government.

This was Cosimo's chance to claim his birthright and become the next Medici ruler. First, he had to convince the Senate, which would not be an easy task. Prior to his departure, Cosimo went to see Stefania to bid her farewell.

"The time has come at last, Cosimo," Stefania said, trying to keep the sadness out of her voice.

"My mother and I will ride to Florence tomorrow. My fate is in the hands of God now." He caressed her cheek affectionately. "Hopefully, we shall see each other again soon."

They embraced and he held her tightly.

Now is not the time to tell him that you are carrying his child. She whispered in his ear, "You're going to win them over, Cosimo. I have complete faith in you."

He inhaled the scent of her hair and kissed her cheek before pulling away. "Take care of yourself and your grandmother."

She nodded. "Now go. Promise me you'll write as soon as you can."

"I promise."

He left the room without looking back and Stefania wept. Sabina, who was outside the door, heard the familiar sound of a heart breaking and closed the door to afford her granddaughter some privacy.

329

***

Maria and her son arrived in Florence and immediately sent a message to the city leaders announcing their arrival and her son's wish to appear before them. The request was granted, and the next morning she and Cosimo made their way to the Piazza della Signoria in the company of heavily armed guards. Maria had waited too long for this moment and was not about to take any chances.

Cosimo assured the Senate that power would remain in the hands of elected magistrates whereas his presence would be symbolic; a mere figurehead. Convinced by his sincere and humble manner, he was named head of the government with the clause that the Council remained in full control.

Cosimo wasted no time exploiting the use of his newly bestowed title and the influence of his many supporters. By the time his electors realized the mistake they had made, it was too late. When several members of the Council rebelled and attempted to form an army to defeat him, Cosimo had them decapitated.

When the dust finally settled, Cosimo proved himself to be a skilled statesman, regaining much of the economic and political stature that had been lost in Florence. Some people even called him the next Magnifico because, like his great grandfather, he was educated, cultured, and politically shrewd.

***

Sabina took the news calmly. "When were you planning to tell me?"

"When I was certain, which I am," Stefania replied.

"I suspected as much. Does he know?" Stefania held back tears as she shook her head. "Come here, child."

Stefania ran into Sabina's arms. "I love him, Grandmother."

"I know you do," Sabina said, stroking her granddaughter's hair. They were sitting by a warm fire in her bedchamber. Outside, the wind howled against the closed shutters.

"When are you going to tell him?" Sabina inquired.

"I was going to write a letter."

"This kind of news is best delivered in person. Besides,

Cosimo may want you close now."

"I know."

"Which means that I would have to accompany you to Florence."

"Nothing would make me happier."

"I know, my dear. For you, Florence has so much to offer. For me, I have nothing but memories there."

"Good memories, Grandmother, not bad ones."

Sabina smiled and her eyes took on a faraway look. "Yes, very good memories. I shall sleep on this matter and make a decision in the morning. Does anyone else know of your pregnancy?"

"My maid suspects."

"They always know everything that transpires in our lives, but your maid is a good girl and knows how to keep secrets. I'm tired. We shall talk tomorrow."

"Goodnight, Grandmother."

The following morning, Stefania let out a sigh as she watched the sunrise from her window. The sun's golden rays were bathing the earth in a bright light and the frost-kissed trees and grass glistened like crystal. She and Cosimo had made love on the grass once, in the springtime.

Her maid opened the door and poked her head into the room. "Your grandmother wishes to see you. She is breaking her fast in her bedchamber and wants you to join her."

Stefania went directly to her grandmother's room.

"Sit down, my dear," Sabina said as she buttered a piece of bread before holding it out.

"You said you would have an answer for me this morning," Stefania said, accepting the bread.

Sabina began to smear butter on another piece of bread. "Before your aunt's death, I thought I wanted to die here." She paused to take a bite. "But after much thought, that's no longer the case. I want to die in Florence, in the bed where Massimo and I made love, in the house where we laughed and talked of so many things—in the house where Anne lived. I want to die in Lorenzo's city with my memories around me."

Stefania leaned forward and embraced her grandmother. "My heart is lighter knowing that I will soon see Cosimo. Thank you."

Sabina eyed her granddaughter steadily. "You do know that he already has a child from another woman, don't you?"

"What?"

"He never mentioned Bianca, his daughter?"

Stefania paled. "I knew he was no saint, but…"

"She's almost three years old."

"Have you known for a long time?"

"Maria told Caterina and me in confidence, but I never had the heart to tell you." She sighed tiredly. "You need to prepare yourself for certain situations in life, especially those that take you by surprise."

"I had no idea…Cosimo never told me."

"Obviously, he doesn't want you to know."

"I'll demand an explanation when I see him!"

"Only if you wish to lose him." When Stefania stared at her askance, Sabina continued, "Cosimo is not a man you can control, my dear. The game of love must be played by his rules, not yours."

"What should I do?"

"Absolutely nothing. According to Maria, he has a great sentiment for Bianca, which means that he will love your child, too. Take comfort in that knowledge."

Stefania nodded, albeit reluctantly. "I will follow your advice."

Sabina announced their upcoming departure to Florence during supper that evening. Caterina and Carlo were saddened by the news. Vittorio was away on business and due to return the next day.

Caterina said, "We hate for you to go, but we understand your reasons. Stefania will thrive in Florence."

"My home is your home whenever you are in Florence," Sabina said.

"We promise to visit as soon and as often as we can," Carlo assured her. "Who will run your household?"

"I have sent a letter instructing Leo to hire servants and prepare the palazzina. I want the rooms aired and the kitchen and wine cellar fully stocked prior to our arrival."

Carlo looked to Stefania. "You must be overjoyed."

Stefania nodded. "I'm sad to leave you all, but I'm happy to embark on this new adventure. I'll also be closer to Cosimo."

Sabina and Caterina exchanged knowing glances. Later, when the two women were alone in the kitchen afterward, Caterina said, "Stefania is going to get her heart broken."

Sabina nodded sadly. "I've already warned her, but she's too in love to think rationally."

They both leaned forward at the same time to warm their hands near the hearth's fire. Caterina ladled some hot, mulled wine into a cup.

"Only half a cupful for me," Sabina said, inhaling the strong spices. "It's good to get your heart broken when you're young. You learn to protect it in the future. Stefania is a smart girl."

"Don't you wish you could prevent her pain?" Caterina asked once she had filled her cup and taken a sip.

"Absolutely not." When Caterina gave her a puzzled look, Sabina explained, "I don't have much time left on this earth. I want Stefania to be strong enough to stand on her own. Once we're in Florence, I'll introduce her to the right people and fill her head with wisdom and good advice, but the rest is up to her."

"She'll always be welcomed here—this is her home, too. You know we love her as our own daughter."

"I know and she knows, but it's my blood that runs in her veins. She's as headstrong and tenacious as I was at her age. After Cosimo breaks her heart, which will be soon, she'll toughen up and learn to survive in a man's world."

"Sometimes I envy you."

"Why? You've had everything a woman could want in life: a loving husband, three healthy sons, and a beautiful home. What could you possibly envy?"

"Your strength and independence."

"You have the same qualities, Caterina. From where I stand,

333

your life is perfect."

Caterina sighed wistfully. "It would be perfect if my son was happy."

She referred to Vittorio, who was handsome and successful but plagued by sadness. He was desperately in love with Stefania but she barely acknowledged his existence. Throughout the years, his parents had contrived various introductions to available young women, but their efforts were in vain.

"He'll be heartbroken when he discovers that you're leaving for Florence," Caterina lamented.

"I know and I'm sorry for it."

"My poor boy." Caterina shook her head and smiled. "I do not blame Stefania. One cannot control Cupid's arrow."

"I wish my granddaughter would forget Cosimo and give Vittorio a chance," Sabina admitted. "Stefania could do no better than your son as far as I'm concerned. I would die with peace of mind knowing she was in his loving care."

"Amen to that," Caterina agreed.

As expected, Vittorio was devastated when he learned that his beloved Stefania was making a permanent move to Florence. He remained stoic when Sabina and Stefania hugged and kissed everyone goodbye. When their carriage finally rolled out of the courtyard, Vittorio retreated to the privacy of his bedchamber. Caterina went up a few moments later and placed her ear against the locked door. It was the first time she had ever heard her adult son weep.

***

Leo greeted Sabina and Stefania in grand style when they arrived in Florence. The house was immaculately clean. Flowers graced tabletops and the delicious aromas of roasting meat and fresh bread filled the air.

A special bouquet of flowers and a bottle of wine had arrived earlier that day. The attached note welcomed them on their return to Florence and bore Cosimo's signature and the Medici seal.

"What a nice gesture," Sabina commented. "We shall have

to invite him to dinner."

"I shall send the messenger at once," Stefania offered.

"What do you think of tomorrow?"

"I would invite him today, but perhaps you're right."

Sabina raised an amused eyebrow. "A woman should never appear overly eager. Always keep a man guessing because as soon as he thinks he has you, he'll become bored and begin to notice other women."

Stefania always listened to these tidbits of advice with only one ear, half believing everything her grandmother said.

As though reading her granddaughter's mind, Sabina said, "I know you must think me a silly old woman, spewing old proverbs and telling you what to do, but it's only because I care about your well-being. You may not take my advice seriously, but it doesn't make it any less valuable. When the time comes, you'll remember my words. Hopefully, they'll benefit you."

"I appreciate everything you do for me, Grandmother. I will always remember your words."

"Good. Now go send a message to Cosimo inviting him to come dine with us tomorrow."

Cosimo declined the invitation due to a series of meetings demanding his attendance, and invited them to dine at his residence on Saturday. Stefania immediately began worrying about what to wear. By the time Saturday arrived, her maid had pulled every gown out of the wardrobe and even Teresa was called upon to help. When Stefania finally wept in frustration, Sabina ushered the maids away.

"I cannot believe you're actually crying because you don't know what to wear. This is not the Stefania that I know and raised," Sabina said in a slightly hard tone.

"I haven't seen Cosimo in so long and I want to be perfect."

"You are perfect."

"You don't understand…"

"You have several charming gowns and any one of them will surely please him."

"It's not about the gown, Grandmother. I heard our servants talking yesterday and…" Stefania trailed off and began sobbing again.

"Get a hold of yourself, child. Why are you so upset?"

"There are rumors that Cosimo has been wife hunting, and that he's already found a potential bride."

Sabina quirked a brow. "Yes, I know. You've already been warned of this, Stefania."

"Why didn't you tell me?"

"I thought it better if you heard it from Cosimo himself."

"What about the child? I was planning to tell him tonight."

"You can still tell him. You knew his marriage would not be one of choice but rather one of politics."

"I know, but my heart can't accept that."

When Cosimo saw Stefania later that night, his eyes lit up with joy. She had chosen to wear an emerald satin gown that complimented her figure and green eyes. Rather than kiss Stefania's hand as he had Sabina's, he took her into his arms and embraced her before kissing her tenderly on the cheek.

The conversation during dinner was pleasant. While Sabina and Maria chatted away, Cosimo and Stefania spoke in hushed tones with each other, like they had when they lived in the Mugello. When Cosimo suggested they take a walk alone in the garden after dinner, Stefania shot her grandmother a look. Sabina smiled knowingly and turned to continue her conversation with Maria.

"It's chilly outside," Cosimo said as he led her toward the doorway. "Let me get your cloak."

"Thank you."

They walked out into the garden. The moon was full and Stefania could see the first buds on the trees.

"Spring will be upon us soon," she stated in an attempt to hide her anxiousness.

"The weather has been mild," he agreed. "I expect the flowers to bloom early this year."

"Yes." *Why were they talking about the weather?*

They walked to the far end where the fruit trees and shrubs offered privacy. Without saying a word, Cosimo took her into his arms and they shared a passionate kiss.

336

"I've missed you so much," he said softly against her lips.

"And I you," she replied before being kissed again.

His hands began to explore the familiar territory of her body, taking in the supple curves beneath the fabric of her gown. When he slid his hands around her waist, he hesitated. "You've put on weight," he teased.

"I have, and with good reason." She paused and he pulled away, staring intently. "I'm carrying your child, my love."

His face was a mixture of joy and pain. Joy at the thought of another child, only this time with someone he truly cared for, and pain because he could not give this woman what she wanted of him.

Worry creased her brow. "Are you displeased?"

Cosimo embraced her tightly and when he spoke, his lips caressed the skin of her neck. "Of course I'm not displeased. On the contrary, I'm very happy because I know this child was conceived with great affection. I will love the baby dearly."

"I'm much relieved," she sighed.

His eyes narrowed. "Did you doubt for one moment that I would reject you or the child?"

She chose her words carefully, "I knew you would not reject us, but I also know that you are procuring a political alliance."

"You mean a wife." Stefania nodded, unable to meet his eyes. He took hold of her chin, forcing her to meet his gaze. "I've asked for the hand of Marguerite of Austria, widow of Alessandro de Medici."

"Is she beautiful?"

Cosimo laughed aloud. "Not in the least!"

"You would marry an ugly woman, then?"

He placed his hands on her shoulders and smiled. "Darling, I've already explained that my choice of wife must be for political gain. I need to make a strong alliance in order to secure my position."

Encouraged by his words, she slid her arms around his neck and pressed her body against his in a very suggestive manner. "Since your marriage will be only for a political alliance, does that mean that your heart can belong to someone else?"

337

"My heart *and* my body…"

From that night onward, Stefania became his official mistress in Florence. The weeks passed and, as Cosimo had predicted, the flowers bloomed early. Stefania's belly grew, yet she did not get fat the way many women did. Her skin glowed and her hair was lustrous; she looked as radiant as a gilded Madonna.

Sabina knew the blissful period Stefania was enjoying with Cosimo would end soon enough. She refrained from stating the obvious, however. Why spoil a good thing when all good things sooner or later came to an end? Better to live and love fully and pay the price afterward. Stefania would learn to survive any storm, as she herself had learned to survive them.

Although Sabina knew that her granddaughter's joy would be cut short, she did not expect it to happen only one month after their arrival in Florence. Sabina awoke to the sound of screams and running feet. Teresa burst into her mistress's bedchamber with a troubled expression.

"The physician is on his way," she cried, wringing her hands.

"Physician?" Sabina asked, sitting up in bed.

"Stefania—"

Teresa did not finish her sentence. Sabina got out of bed, pushed her maid out of the way and ran to her granddaughter's room. She found the door open and two female servants hovering over the bed. Stefania was curled into a fetal position, clutching her abdomen. The bed sheets were soaked with blood.

Sabina knelt by the bed so she could see her granddaughter's face and stroked her cheek. "Oh, my sweet girl…I'm so sorry."

Stefania's eyes were half closed. She turned them slowly toward her grandmother. "He was so happy."

"I know, but right now, we have to worry about you."

"I wanted this child very badly," she whispered as the tears streamed down her face. "We both did."

"You'll have other children—strong, healthy ones."

"Please summon Cosimo. I want to see him."

Cosimo arrived shortly after the physician had examined

Stefania. He found her resting peacefully. Her eyes were red and puffy from crying. Taking her hand in his, he said, "My heart aches."

"Oh, Cosimo..."

His eyes grew teary and he said nothing more as he laid his head on her bosom and allowed her to stroke his hair. Sabina, who had been standing by the door, stepped back and out of the room.

CHAPTER 28

Cosimo's power continued to grow, and so did his popularity with the Florentines. A little over a year had passed, and Sabina was convinced she had made the right decision by coming to Florence. In addition to watching Stefania flourish, she was content to spend her last days surrounded by the beautiful memories she had shared with the love of her life, Massimo.

Lately, he haunted her dreams. Sometimes she would wake up smiling and expecting to see him beside her, smiling back. When the cobwebs of sleep dissolved, she was faced with the harsh reality of his absence. The terrible sadness that gripped her soul on those mornings was more than she could bear. Why had God been so cruel? Why could they not have ended their days together?

Why ask why? She was old. *Too old.* She knew it was time for her to die. In fact, she was ready for it, but she refused to do so until she was certain that Stefania was in good hands.

Cosimo finally found himself a suitable bride: Eleonora di Toledo. She was the second-born daughter of Don Pedro, viceroy of Naples and lieutenant governor to Charles V. Eleonora's father was also head of one of the richest and noblest families of Spain. Cosimo had chosen very well. His future wife's aristocratic ties and immense wealth would do much to advance his political career.

Nobody expected that the marriage would be a love-match. Not only did Cosimo fall in love with Eleonora, he forsook all other women in her favor. He was very careful in his choice of words and timing—and demonstrated extreme kindness and tenderness—when breaking it off with Stefania. Naturally, she was devastated. He spoke to Sabina privately afterward, promising to find a suitable husband for her granddaughter. Sabina thanked Cosimo for his concern and kindness and wished him and Eleonora much happiness in their union.

Stefania suffered for many days. She slept little, ate little, and cried much. Sabina knew the pain would eventually pass. After all, she had gone through the same pain herself once…

Was it really so long ago?

When Stefania finally emerged from her self-imposed confinement, she was thin with dark circles under her eyes. Sabina was outside in the courtyard, reading under the shade of a Juniper tree when she noticed her granddaughter's presence.

Stefania looked down at Sabina and said, "Basta. I'm ready to live again. I cannot grieve anymore."

Sabina smiled from ear to ear. "I'm glad to hear it, my dear. We're so much alike, you and I."

"I hope so."

"It just so happens we were invited to a private birthday celebration this evening at Signora Nadia's home."

"Good. I like her daughter. I'm going to bathe and change now."

"I think that's a good idea," Sabina said, closing the book.

"Also, I'm going to eat. I'm starving."

"I'll have one of the servants bring a tray to your room."

"Thank you." Stefania took a few steps toward the house, stopped, and turned around again. "Grandmother?"

"Yes?"

"Does the pain of lost love ever go away?"

Sabina thought for a moment. "It never goes away fully, but it does become less painful with time. The greater the love, the longer it takes the wound to heal. You're young and you'll be fine. Trust me."

***

Cosimo and Eleonora were married by proxy on the twenty-ninth of March 1539, but it was not until the twenty-ninth of June that she made her official entrance into Florence. She was welcomed warmly to the Palazzo Medici by her new husband and his mother.

The lavish wedding celebration that took place spanned several days. There was much feasting, dancing, music, acrobats, and performances to be enjoyed by guests and citizens alike.

Sabina and Stefania enjoyed the festivities and, when they were properly introduced to Eleonora, their congratulatory wishes were heartfelt. Eleonora was well-bred and lovely; no wonder Cosimo fell in love with her. He caught Stefania's eye and smiled gratefully. She returned the smile with sincerity. She loved him still, but the fiery passion and her desperate heart had cooled considerably. He was no longer the last thought in her head before she fell asleep or the first one when she awoke. She had finally managed to put Cosimo behind her and move on with her own life.

The summer of 1539 drew to a close with Cosimo and Eleonora as the new rulers of Florence. The people were happy and enjoyed peace and prosperity, just as they had when Lorenzo was alive. Like his predecessor, Cosimo was a generous patron of the arts and possessed an open mind. It was not long before he made the daring move of making the Palazzo della Signoria his home. By doing this, he let everyone know that he was power incarnate. The artist, Bronzino, was commissioned by Cosimo to paint Eleonora's name on the walls of her private chambers. It was further evidence of the tender feelings he had for his wife.

***

It was the first day of September when a letter from the Mugello arrived at the palazzina. It announced Vittorio's upcoming visit to Florence and his desire to visit both Stefania and her grandmother.

After reading the letter, Stefania announced the news to Sabina. "Grandmother, Vittorio is coming."

"Our Vito?"

Stefania grinned and nodded. "Yes, our Vito."

"When?"

"According to the date this letter was written, he should be here any day now."

"Well, tell the servants to prepare a room for him."

Stefania nodded and walked away.

Teresa, who sat beside Sabina mending a hem, commented, "I think she looked rather pleased."

"Hmm, I got that impression as well."

"Ah!" Teresa said as the thread escaped from the needle. "It will take me forever to thread this needle again. I can barely see with these useless eyes."

Sabina chuckled. "We are too old, my friend."

Teresa put down the needle and laughed, too. "Much too old."

"All I want before I die is to see her settled and happy."

"I wish for the same."

Sabina looked intently at the woman who had stood beside her for a lifetime and asked, "Why did you not leave me and get married? Have a family of your own?"

"Surely, you jest! After I saw how much you suffered with Massimo and James, I wanted nothing to do with men."

Sabina sighed tiredly. "Perhaps you were the wiser for it."

"I have no regrets. I've seen and done so much, thanks to you. It has been a great privilege and pleasure to serve you."

Sabina reached out and squeezed Teresa's hand. "You've been a true friend to me." Changing the subject, she asked, "Will you help me make a match?"

Teresa giggled. "You were reading my mind. I think Stefania and Vittorio would make a fine pair."

"Splendid!" Sabina cried. "This will be my last and most important project before I die."

"Please don't talk like that."

"I'll be eighty-two this coming October. I've outlasted most of my family and friends…I'm tired, Teresa."

***

Vittorio arrived a few days later, fashionably dressed and as handsome as ever. Sabina noticed that his shoulders were wider, his voice deeper. He had a fine physique and displayed his male prowess with confidence. Whatever experiences he had gone through in the last few years had transformed the boy she remembered into a formidable man.

Stefania came out to greet him and paused in her steps.

343

Sabina and Teresa exchanged knowing looks and hid their smiles. Vittorio took Stefania's hands in his and bent to kiss her cheeks.

"You are prettier than I remember, Stefania," he said in a smooth, deep voice. "It's good to see you."

Stefania blushed. "Thank you. You look very well, Vito."

The corner of his mouth shot upward in a crooked smile and he quirked his eyebrow. "No one has called me that for a long time."

"Forgive me."

"No, I like it."

The young couple stared at one another as if for the first time. If Sabina had not cleared her throat, they would have continued to do so. "Come give me a hug, my dear boy!"

Vittorio embraced Sabina and Teresa in turn.

Sabina pulled back and eyed him from head to foot. "Your mother and father are well? The last letter your mother sent described a hard winter, and fever taking the lives of several villagers."

He nodded, his expression grim. "My parents were ill for most of the season. They managed to recuperate but their health hasn't been the same ever since."

"I'm sorry to hear it," Sabina said. "We can talk during supper. Right now, you need to rest. Stefania will show you to your room."

Stefania led him upstairs. Once they were alone, she confessed, "You may not believe it, but I've thought of you many times."

"Why wouldn't I believe it?" he asked softly.

"We were not on the best of terms when I left the Mugello."

"That was long ago. We're both different people now."

She smiled up at him. "Yes, we are."

In the weeks that followed, Sabina and Teresa did little to match-make the young couple because they were doing fine on their own. It was good to hear music and laughter in the house again. Sabina soon saw the telltale signs of love blossoming.

It was no surprise when Vittorio came to speak to her

344

privately in order to ask for Stefania's hand in marriage. Sabina was overjoyed. During dinner, she gave both of them her blessing and wished them many years of marital bliss. She had never seen Stefania so happy and felt a huge weight lifted from her shoulders. Her granddaughter would be well cared for by Vittorio.

Sabina sat at her dressing table that night, staring at her crisp reflection in the fine Venetian mirror Leo had procured on her behalf. At her advanced age, she preferred the slight distortion of an old-fashioned looking glass. These new ones from Venice were too honest. Sabina sighed as she recalled the beauty of her youth. Now her looks were as faded as her memories. Glancing down at her papery, veined hands with their brittle nails, she tried to envision what they had once looked like. She tried to remember the feel of Massimo under those worn fingertips…

Massimo visited Sabina in her dreams that night. They were both young again, standing outside in the sunshine, laughing. Sabina opened her eyes and was overwhelmed with joy; she was no longer alone.

Massimo smiled at her from the opposite pillow. "I've been waiting for you, my love."

Eyes as blue as the sea…

"I've missed you so much, Massimo."

Stefania entered her grandmother's bedchamber the following morning and found her dead, yet she did not cry. Teresa and the servants were crying beside her, but she smiled inwardly. Sabina had deliberately chosen the right moment to depart from this world. Her grandmother had always done everything with forethought and purpose—even her death.

Stefania walked to the window and threw back the wooden shutters. The sun shone brightly on the Arno River and upon the red tiled roofs of Florence. It was a new day and the beginning of a new life for her and Vittorio. She looked over her shoulder once more to the peaceful resting form of her grandmother and, this time, smiled outwardly.

Did you enjoy this novel? The author would appreciate your review on Amazon. Thank you.

The intrigue of Renaissance Florence and the Medici family continues with the exciting sequel, ALLEGRA. Turn the page to read a sample.

ALLEGRA

A Novel Set in the Italian Renaissance

C. DE MELO

ISBN-13:978-0999787816 (C. De Melo)
ISBN-10: 0999787810

CHAPTER 1
FLORENCE, TUSCANY
OCTOBER 1547

"Never was anything great achieved without danger."

—Niccolò Machiavelli

The Tuscan landscape remained shrouded in gloom as a tempest unleashed its fury upon the city of Florence. Rain hammered against the windows of the spacious workshop where Vittorio Castagno sat repairing a gold necklace by the light of flickering candles. A servant entered the room to stoke the fire in the hearth.

"Fetch me some undiluted wine when you're done," he said, hoping to drive the chill from his bones.

"Yes, Signore."

He disliked fixing jewelry, but the exigent clients he'd inherited from his father were accustomed to the extra service. His father had transported exotic spices for a living for many years until Portugal undercut the Venetian spice trade by sailing around the Cape. With the need for middlemen eliminated, the resourceful businessman began moving precious metals and gemstones for the nobility who needed vast sums of money to fund wars. Jewelry served as portable wealth; a precious commodity always in high demand. Within a short period of time, his father had acquired a client base that spanned from the pope in Rome to the doge in Venice.

The door opened and, without looking up, he pointed to a vacant spot on the cluttered workbench. "Set the chalice there, girl."

"Vittorio."

He didn't expect to see his wife standing in the doorway.

"Stefania."

"I am with child," she said flatly, her face expressionless.

He hesitated. "That's wonderful news."

"Is it?"

An awkward silence followed the question.

Averting her gaze, she said, "The hour is late. I'm tired."

"Sleep well, my love."

He watched her go before resuming his work with a heavy heart.

Gianna crept into the room shortly afterward. The faithful servant exchanged a meaningful look with her master. "The midwife is hopeful."

Vittorio pinched the bridge of his nose. "And the physician?"

"The dottore believes that perhaps *this time…*"

"Isn't that what he said last time?" He'd only caught a glimpse of the premature infant before the servants wrapped the tiny body in linens. The sight of his son's blue lips would haunt him forever.

The servant girl appeared, handed Vittorio a chalice of red wine, then swiftly departed. He took a long sip of the ruby elixir, grateful for its numbing warmth.

Gianna wrung her hands. "Signore—"

"Go now," he interjected. "Tend to your mistress. She could surely use one of your potent draughts tonight."

Without another word, Gianna slipped out the door, leaving her master alone with his troubled thoughts.

Meanwhile, Stefania surrendered to despair in the privacy of her bedchamber. She'd been poked and prodded all afternoon until she was sore. Both the midwife and the physician seemed positive, each promising to pray for the health of the unborn babe. By now, she could see through the veneer of false hope and empty words.

Sitting before a Venetian mirror on the dressing table, she studied her reflection in the mottled glass. A pale, weary face stared back at her. Where was the vibrant young woman who had accompanied her grandmother, Sabina Rossi, to Florence

349

eight years ago? Oh, how happy and naïve she had been back then, pregnant with Cosimo de' Medici's lovechild. Her grandmother had tried to warn her of life's unexpected pitfalls, but she'd paid little mind to the old woman's unsolicited advice—until a bloody miscarriage, followed by Cosimo's betrothal to Eleonora di Toledo, shattered her idyllic world.

Gianna entered the room and handed her mistress a ceramic cup. "Best to drink it hot, Signora."

Stefania took a cautious sip. "What am I going to do?"

"What you always do. Pray."

"I don't believe it will be different this time. Do you?"

"Yes, I do," Gianna replied with forced conviction.

"I wish I had your spirit, Gianna."

"You possess more spirit than everyone in this household put together. I'll be praying for you—all of us will."

Stefania attempted a smile. "Thank you."

"The dottore said you need plenty of rest, so I bid you goodnight."

Stefania stared blindly into the distance as she slowly drank the herbaceous brew. Despite her anxiety and racing thoughts, she went to bed and eventually fell into a deep slumber.

Gianna went out of her way to glean as much helpful information as she could from the city's apothecaries and various midwives. She oversaw her mistress's diet with special care, stocking the kitchen with the finest quality wheat, non-acidic fruits, and dry red wine—all of which, supposedly, produced healthy boys.

After years of bitter disappointment and heartbreak, Stefania remained stoic in regard to her condition. She quietly submitted to her maid's dietary administrations and bitter green concoctions without complaint, and didn't raise any objection when Gianna began applying foul-smelling plasters to her abdomen once a week.

***

Invitations for the Medici Christmas banquet were distributed in early December. The most prominent members of Florentine society were expected to attend, including the

Castagno family. Plagued by persistent nausea, Stefania had no desire to leave her home.

"Go and enjoy yourself, Vittorio," she urged. "Given my condition, you can easily make an excuse for my absence."

"Gianna will prepare a tonic to settle your stomach."

"None of them work."

"Then I will personally consult with every apothecary in the city until I find one that does."

"I am not well," she persisted. "I feel weak."

"Your cheeks are radiant and you've grown robust! The way Gianna frets over you, I'd wager you're the healthiest woman in Florence."

"I don't want to take any chances…"

"Stefania, I honestly believe it will be different this time."

"Dear God, I hope so."

Pulling her into his arms, he kissed the top of her head. "Why not take a respite from the constant worrying and celebrate the birth of our lord in high style? The Medici are generous hosts who always provide excellent food and entertainment."

"Eleonora is pregnant again."

Vittorio knew that Stefania's reluctance to accompany him to the banquet had more to do with the duchess's condition than her own. "We cannot refuse every invitation we receive during your pregnancy, my love. Especially from the Medici."

Stefania acknowledged his prudent words with a nod. Social occasions served as opportunities to keep a close eye on rival families while forging new alliances. "Very well. I will accompany you."

He smiled encouragingly. "That's better."

On Christmas morning, Stefania consumed the bitter elixir her husband had procured from the Santa Maria Novella monks. Thankfully, the expensive medicine diminished her nausea, allowing her to confront the day in relative comfort. Arrayed in a velvet gown matching the green of her eyes, she accompanied Vittorio to Santa Maria del Fiore cathedral for Holy Mass, then followed the Medici retinue to the Palazzo Ducale, formerly the

Palazzo della Signoria. Transforming the government headquarters into his private domicile had proved a cunning strategy on Cosimo's part since it further solidified his power in Florence.

Stefania stood beside Vittorio and did her best to maintain a cheerful disposition. At one point, she discreetly studied Cosimo while he addressed a cluster of elderly magistrates. What was it like to embody such power? His marriage to Eleonora had secured an alliance with the formidable Kingdom of Spain, and his distant cousin, Caterina, had become Queen of France last March. The cards seemed to be in his favor.

Her eyes slid to Eleonora, who hovered near her husband in a costly gown of burgundy brocade. The growing mound beneath the luxuriant fabric drew many stares. Cosimo's broodmare was pregnant. *Again*. She had to admit, the woman's fecundity was impressive. By sheer coincidence—or God's cruel humor—she and Eleonora had been pregnant roughly around the same times throughout the years. One woman was blessed, the other, cursed.

Two ambitious courtiers drew Vittorio into conversation, compelling Stefania to wander off in order to afford them a measure of privacy. She walked toward an adjoining room where a few guests were congregated beneath the much-acclaimed portrait of Eleonora. Bronzino created the fine painting shortly after she had given birth to her fifth child. Dripping with gemstones and pearls to accentuate her royal status, the duchess was depicted in an exquisite black and white gown flaunting the pomegranate motif—a symbol of fertility.

Eleonora, the perfect wife.

At the sound of rustling fabric and footsteps, Stefania tore her eyes from the propagandistic portrait to see the duchess standing beside her. Surprised, she immediately inclined her head in greeting. "Your Grace."

"Bronzino's talent is impressive, is it not?"

"Most definitely, but it was aided by your natural beauty."

The corners of the duchess's lips lifted a fraction of an inch. It wasn't the first silver-tongued compliment she'd received that day, and it certainly wouldn't be the last. "I wish to have a word with you, Signora Stefania."

Many sets of eyes followed the women as they retreated to a quiet corner.

"I know how difficult it has been for you and your husband these last few years." Eleonora's eyes dropped to Stefania's belly. "Be assured that His Grace and I are praying for you and your unborn child."

"You are most kind, my lady."

Taking hold of Stefania's hand in an unprecedented gesture of friendliness, she said, "God will bless you." Although she didn't say the word 'eventually,' her tone implied it. "You must never give up hope."

"We never do."

She offered Stefania a genuine smile, then retreated to the main hall.

A moment later, Vittorio appeared carrying two chalices of mulled wine. Offering one of them to his wife, he inquired, "What did she say to you?"

"Everyone is staring at me," Stefania observed, ignoring his question.

"The most important woman in Tuscany has gone out of her way to speak with you privately," he pointed out. "Naturally, people are curious."

"She is praying for me and the baby."

***

Vittorio departed for Rome in mid-February. The night after his departure, Gianna was startled from sleep by the sound of Stefania's cries. Scrambling out of bed, she uttered a quick prayer before grabbing a handful of linen cloths from the cupboard. Running to her mistress's bedchamber, she mentally prepared herself for the gruesome task ahead.

She pulled back the coverlet and froze. *No bloodied sheets?* "Wake up, Signora!"

Stefania sat up in bed. "Santa Madonna!"

"There, there, it was only a nightmare. Shall I fix you a draught?"

"I had a dream," Stefania said, her voice trembling with emotion. "I saw a baby girl seated upon on a bed of jewels, completely covered in gold dust. She even smiled at me!"

"God be praised."

"My baby is alive, I know it."

Gianna crossed herself before kissing the silver crucifix around her neck. "Thank the Blessed Virgin. This is an omen."

Stefania's hands flew to her belly and her eyes welled with tears of joy. "The baby moved inside of me! Another sign!"

"We should attend Holy Mass first thing in the morning to thank God for this miracle."

"I want you to summon the city's best astrologer as soon as possible."

Gianna almost recoiled. "Signore Vittorio would not approve of an astrologer coming here. Would it not be better to go to church, instead?"

Stefania's brow shot upward. "My husband will be none the wiser as long as the matter remains between us."

Nodding reluctantly, Gianna murmured, "As you wish, Signora."

Snuggling under the warm covers, Stefania went back to sleep with the mental image of her healthy, golden baby.

A few days later, a dark eyed man in a fur-lined cloak and orange doublet arrived at the Palazzo Castagno.

"Messer Mancini is waiting downstairs," Gianna said from the doorway of her mistress's bedchamber.

Stefania closed the lid of her jewelry chest. "Mancini?" she repeated with a furrowed brow. She'd heard the rumors about him and wondered if there could there be any truth in them. "Are you certain he's the best?"

"Everyone seems to think so. The Strozzi and the Pucci employed his services not long ago."

Pandolfo Pucci was one of Cosimo's close companions, a man of considerable influence within the Medici court. Stefania's curiosity was piqued. "Help me don this necklace, hurry."

The maid wrung her hands nervously before obeying the

command. "It's not too late for me to send him away. We can still go to church."

"I shall meet with him in my sitting room."

A moment later, Messer Mancini's presence dominated the small, feminine room. Doffing his plumed hat with flourish, he said, "Signora Stefania, I am at your service."

"Please, sit." She waited for the extravagantly dressed man to take a seat before inquiring, "Are your readings accurate?"

"*Certo*," he assured. "Perhaps you've heard that my father was a famous astrologer, as was my grandfather before him. I am proud to say that even the Medici children have benefitted from my expertise."

Surprised by this revelation, she said, "My maid mentioned the Strozzi and Pucci, but she said nothing about the Medici."

"I don't share that information with just *anyone*." The enormous topaz adorning his pinky finger flashed in the sunlight as he stroked his black goatee. "May I speak frankly?"

"You may."

"The duchess herself summoned me more than once," he bragged in a conspiratorial tone.

If this astrologer was good enough for Eleonora's children...

Stefania cleared her throat. "Can you perform readings on the unborn?"

"No one in Florence can do that." Sensing her disappointment, he added, "My mother's midwifery skills were legendary, and she taught me how to discern the sex of a child inside the womb."

"Can you see if my baby will survive the birth, too?"

"I can determine its progress," he replied cautiously.

Stefania hesitated, embarrassed. "My husband doesn't approve of such things. He's unaware of your visit here today."

"I assure you, madam, that I'm the very incarnation of discretion." Messer Mancini slowly reached out his hands and paused two inches short of Stefania' midsection. "May I proceed?"

She nodded and the man pressed both of his palms against

the bulge beneath her satin gown. After several seconds, she prompted, "Well?"

"You're carrying a healthy girl."

"Thank God and all the saints!"

The astrologer's eyes focused blindly on Stefania's gold necklace as a crystal-clear vision unfurled in his head. "She'll be gifted; a blessing and a curse," he whispered unwittingly.

"A curse?" she repeated, alarmed.

"Forgive me, I misspoke," he lied, regretting his lapse of judgement.

"What did you see?"

Witchcraft was a serious offense in Florence. Performing a public Act of Faith or hanging from the gallows at Fort Belvedere held little appeal for him, so he replied blandly, "I saw nothing, Signora Stefania. Rest assured that she'll be a healthy child, fortunate to have such loving parents."

Stefania regarded him dubiously before placing some coins in his upturned palm. The moment her fingers brushed against his skin, his eyes grew wide. "Is something wrong?"

"Not at all," he lied again, hastily pocketing the coins. "Be sure to record the exact date and hour of your daughter's birth so that I can create an accurate astrological chart."

Stefania watched from the window as the astrologer exited the courtyard. He took a few steps down the street, stopped, then turned around to meet her gaze before disappearing around the corner.

CHAPTER 2

On the seventh day of April in the year 1548, as the church bells rang under the midday sun, Stefania Rossi, wife of Vittorio Castagno, gave birth to a living infant. The delivery wasn't without serious complications, and the physician quietly informed the parents that this child would be their last.

Vittorio took a seat beside his wife and gazed in wonder at the baby in her arms. In that instant, Stefania was more beautiful than all of the Madonna and Child paintings in Florence.

"Look at our daughter, Vittorio. She's perfect, is she not?"

"Yes," he replied, gently stroking the downy hair on the infant's head. "Her hair is the color of burnished gold."

"I was told my mother had light hair." She paused, her expression serious. "I know you would have preferred a son."

"Hush," he chided, already smitten with the child. "I'm overjoyed to have a fine, healthy daughter."

Stefania and Vittorio reveled in their new roles as first-time parents—it didn't matter that she was twenty-eight years old or that he was thirty-two. As the days passed, the love they bore for their child grew, but so did their anxiety. What if something happened to them? Who would care for their precious little girl in their absence?

Stefania arranged a private audience with Cosimo soon after recuperating from the birth. A liveried page led her into one of the public rooms of the Palazzo Ducale where the Duke of Florence sat behind a desk.

"Thank you for meeting with me, Your Grace," she said once the servant had departed. "Regrettably, Vittorio could not accompany me today, but he sends his warmest greetings."

"I've told you before, Stefania, there's no need for such formalities when we're alone." He smiled broadly. "You look exceedingly well. I hear congratulations are in order."

"We're so happy, Cosimo. She's a healthy baby, thank

God."

Cosimo crossed himself. "Thank Him, indeed. My wife and I prayed frequently and fervently for the safe delivery of your child. She would have liked to congratulate you personally, but she and her ladies are at Santa Maria Novella with the Spanish ambassador." He paused. "Have you chosen a name?"

"She'll be christened Allegra."

"How fitting. I look forward to meeting her."

"Allegra is the very reason why I've asked to see you. As you know, I have no family and Vittorio is estranged from his brothers. If something were to happen to us, our daughter would be completely alone in the world."

"Are you asking me to be her godfather?"

"You're the only person I trust."

"Rest assured, Stefania. Should anything happen to you or Vittorio, I'll take Allegra into my household and protect her as my own daughter."

"My husband and I are forever in your debt."

An impish grin stretched across his face, instantly transporting her back in time to their youth. He stood. "Come."

"Where are we going?"

"It's a surprise."

She followed Cosimo into an antechamber where he summoned his valet and whispered something into the man's ear. After casting a glance at Stefania, the valet nodded and left the room.

Feeling giddy, she inquired, "What mischief is afoot?"

"You'll see."

They talked of idle things as they waited, but Stefania's curiosity was making it hard to concentrate. At length, the valet returned carrying a tray containing two painted ceramic cups.

"This was gifted to my wife by the Spanish ambassador," Cosimo explained. "I want to share some with you in celebration of your daughter's birth."

She accepted a cup from the valet with a grateful nod. The mysterious brown beverage gave off a strange but pleasant odor.

Cosimo held up his cup. "To Allegra's health."

Stefania took a small sip. The cold, bitter beverage was flavored with vanilla and spices. "What is this?"

"The best-kept secret in the Spanish kingdom. The Dominican monks who accompanied the Spanish ambassador to Tuscany call it *xocolatl*, and they claim it's good for your health, particularly the stomach."

"What is it made from?"

"Cocoa beans from the Viceroyalty of New Spain."

"From the New World," she whispered, intrigued.

"The beans are finely ground into a powder and serve as a base for this drink. You and I are the first Tuscans to taste it. What do you think?"

"It's very good," she said before indulging in another sip. "Adding a bit of honey or sugar may improve the flavor."

"You always did have a penchant for sweets."

***

Vittorio, who could barely tear himself away from his daughter's side, was obliged to visit clients in Venice during the last week of May. Stefania instructed Gianna to summon the astrologer the moment her husband left Florence.

Messer Mancini arrived at the Palazzo Castagno arrayed in red brocade and sporting a massive garnet on his forefinger. A black satchel with strange markings hung from his shoulder. "Felicitations, Signora Stefania."

"A healthy girl, exactly as you predicted," Stefania said, indicating the wooden cradle in the corner.

The astrologer gazed down at the pink-faced infant, then at Stefania. *Her first and last child.* He hastily lowered his eyes before she caught his impertinent stare. A servant entered with a tray containing two glass vessels and a bowl of dried apple slices.

Accepting a goblet from his hostess's hand, he said, "A toast to your daughter's continued good health." He took a sip. "When was she born?"

"On the seventh of April."

"And the time of day?"

"Noon. I heard the church bells ringing."

Messer Mancini sat down and opened his satchel. Inside were scrolls depicting the horoscope and astronomy charts, a journal, a few pieces of graphite for jotting notes, and a deck of tarot cards. At the very bottom was a heavy book bound in black leather.

Opening one of the journals, he wrote: *Allegra Castagno, 7 April 1548, noon.* "I need to consult with the almanac to make a few calculations."

Stefania watched in fascination as he flipped through the book and wrote down several numbers. "I know a bit about astrology..."

He continued writing without looking up. "Oh?"

"Allegra is in the House of Aries—the ram."

"Mmm-hmm."

"From what I hear, it's a good sign. A strong sign."

He turned a page and ran his finger down a column of numbers. "Stubborn would be a better description." He stopped writing and met Stefania's insistent stare. "Are you aware of the direct relationships between the signs of the zodiac, the planets, the stars, and the parts of the human body?"

"No."

"Your daughter is ruled by the planet Mars and her element is fire, which is powerful."

"Detrimentally so?"

"Fire can destroy, but it can also melt something hard in order to make it soft and pliable. With fire, things can be reshaped, *reborn*. It can be positive if used correctly." Leaning over his notes, he added, "I will draw up a chart indicating the most auspicious days for certain decisions or events."

"What about the unlucky days?"

"I will include those, too."

Pointing to the stack of tarot cards, she inquired, "Is it possible to see her future?"

"She's rather young for a reading."

"Do you know any other methods of divination?"

The desperation and fear in the woman's eyes startled him.

He had seen that look before. Miscarriages, stillborn infants, until—*finally*—a living, breathing baby…

Glancing at the closed door, he said, "Fetch the infant."

Stefania gathered Allegra from the cradle and placed her in the astrologer's arms. "Please, tell me anything you can."

Awakened from sleep, the baby stared at the strange man with a frown.

"Hello, little one," he said, caressing her plump cheek with his forefinger. "Aries rules the head and your daughter's eyes are as lively as I expected them to be." His gaze was drawn to the baby's perfectly formed hands, her greatest asset, capable of creating incredible things; pity she wasn't born male. "This child is strong and will live a long life."

A grateful smile tugged at Stefania's lips as she retrieved the baby.

He started collecting his items and placing them back in the satchel. "I'll have my servant deliver the completed chart to your home—"

"No!"

"If you prefer, you may dispatch one of your servants to collect it."

"That would be better," she said before placing Allegra in the cradle.

"Very well. It will be finished by the end of next week. As always, you can count on my discretion."

When he picked up the deck of tarot cards, Stefania asked, "Would you do a reading for me?"

He hesitated. "Perhaps another time."

"Please, I insist."

Although he already knew the woman's future, he reluctantly spread the cards face-down on the table. "Pick one."

Stefania selected a card, which he took from her hand without revealing its face, then placed it at the bottom of the deck. It was the Major Arcana, a skeleton upon a pale horse with sickle in its hand. *Death.*

"Please select another card," he instructed.

"What's wrong with the one I chose?"

"Nothing," he lied. "I have my own method." At least that was true.

The second card she selected depicted a cloaked woman and child seated inside of a boat with six silver swords standing upright.

Stefania's brow creased in worry. "What does it mean?"

"The Six of Swords represents a difficult past, which is now behind you," he replied. "The problem you've been grappling with for a long time has finally been resolved with the birth of your child."

Stefania breathed a sigh of relief before asking two predictable questions. The astrologer replied with two blatant lies.

Unhappy clients were not good for business.

CHAPTER 3

Stefania insisted on feeding Allegra herself rather than follow her husband's suggestion of hiring a wet nurse. When the baby became colicky and her breasts failed to produce enough milk to satisfy the child's growing hunger, she begrudgingly accepted defeat.

Fortunately, procuring high-quality breast milk for babies was an easy task in Florence. Lactating women often advertised their services, and parents were cautioned to be extremely selective since it was widely believed that diseases and humoral qualities could be passed onto infants via breast milk. Some families sent their children to the Casentino Valley because the women from that region were supposedly healthier, and the pestilence-free air of the countryside enabled babies to thrive. Wealthier families maintained a wet nurse in their household.

Before long, little Allegra had her very own live-in wet nurse; a bonny young woman with a cheerful disposition and excellent, abundant breast milk. In a matter of weeks, the baby's weight doubled, much to the delight of her parents. In addition to this, Messer Mancini's astrological chart delineated Allegra's favorable alignment with the moon, which governed over the female sex.

The year 1548 may have brought good fortune to the Castagno household, but it left the opposite on the Medici doorstep. Eleonora gave birth to an unhealthy son in July. Little Antonio was hastily baptized and died shortly afterward. A year later, she gave birth to a healthy son and they christened him Ferdinando.

Eleonora birthed nine children so far, seven survivors. Many Florentines assumed she would stop bearing children, especially when her belly remained flat for the next three years. The duchess took advantage of this childbearing respite to improve their living conditions. After convincing Cosimo that their expanding family was too cramped in the Palazzo Ducale, she used her own funds to purchase the Palazzo Pitti in 1549.

Longtime rivals of the Medici, the Pitti family attempted to build the biggest palazzo in Florence with its very own piazza—a luxury normally reserved for civic or religious edifices. Their plan backfired when the grandiose project forced them into bankruptcy, thus allowing Eleonora to strike a bargain by negotiating a much lower price than the property's actual worth. The Boboli Gardens, specifically created for the duchess's pleasure, were conveniently located directly behind the palazzo, making it the ideal residence for the Medici family.

Plans were drawn up to enlarge the existing structure. The furnishings and artwork procured by Eleonora reflected her refined taste. The Medici continued residing in the Palazzo Ducale and their many country villas during the ongoing construction phase. When they began spending more time at the Palazzo Pitti, entertaining guests and impressing dignitaries, people nicknamed the Palazzo Ducale the "Palazzo Vecchio."

Members of the nobility followed the ruling family's example by purchasing property in the Oltrarno, making it fashionable to own a home in the greener part of town, away from the foul-smelling streets of the city center.

While Eleonora fussed over her new home across the river, Vittorio and Stefania fussed over their daughter. Allegra grew too quickly for Stefania's taste, and the initial joy she had experienced as a mother gradually faded as she became less needed by the child.

"She's getting so big," Vittorio said to his wife one day as they both watched Allegra play with Gianna in the sunny courtyard below.

Stefania sighed sadly and stepped away from the window. "I know. In a way it's such a shame."

Taken aback, he frowned at his wife. "You should be happy."

"I am, but Allegra grows too fast. She rarely sits on my lap anymore, and she doesn't allow me to coddle her."

"She prefers to run and play, which is normal for a child her age. Our daughter is blessed with robust health," he pointed out impatiently. "This is something to celebrate, not weep over."

"I'm not weeping…I want another baby."

"Not again," he said, pinching the bridge of his nose in annoyance.

"Vittorio, please."

"Are you mad, woman?"

"Don't be angry, husband. It's natural for women to want children."

"After years of disappointment, we finally have a perfect daughter. Why can you not be grateful for the gift God has bestowed upon us?"

"I *am* grateful, but Allegra isn't a baby anymore. She doesn't need me."

"Of course, she needs you!" Lowering his voice, he added, "Have you forgotten the difficulty of the birth?"

"I haven't forgotten, but I've prayed to God on the matter many times. He can help me deliver another healthy baby if I put my faith in Him." She paused, her eyes wild. "I need this, Vittorio. My heart is heavy and my mind is restless. Only a baby can cure me."

The bouts of melancholia his wife often suffered throughout their marriage had temporarily subsided after Allegra's birth, but they were gradually returning. As a result, their daughter spent many hours playing alone, usually under Gianna's watchful eye.

He paced the room. "You've inherited your mother's illness—"

"Stop!"

"It's happening again with more frequency."

She covered her ears. "Vittorio, I beg you."

Grabbing hold of her hands, he gently pried them away from her head. "She, too, suffered from this malady and took her own life because of it."

"Please, let's not talk of her..."

"I don't want the same thing to happen to you." In a gentler tone, he suggested, "Maybe you should go to church daily instead of only twice a week. God's Holy Spirit will ease the restlessness within your soul and guide you toward peace."

"All the masses in Florence cannot help me."

Vittorio stormed across the room to close the door. "It's bad enough that I defy Holy Mother Church by wasting my seed in order to not impregnate you. Now you want me to commit the sin of murder?"

She recoiled. "Murder?"

"Lower your voice," he snapped. "Yes, *murder*. If you carry another child to full term, there's a good chance you'll die during the delivery. That's precisely what the physician told me."

"My body is still strong," she insisted. "We need to have faith."

"You should heed your own counsel, wife, and have faith in God's wisdom. If He wanted you to have more children, then He would have provided them."

"I know for a fact that I'm destined to be a mother many times over."

"How could you possibly know such a thing?"

She hesitated, debating whether or not to reveal her secret. Finally, she confessed, "Messer Mancini informed me that I would bear more children and enjoy a long life."

His eyes narrowed. "You consulted with him behind my back?"

"I invited him here shortly after our daughter's birth." Seeing her husband's expression, she quickly added, "You were away on business."

"You allowed that warlock into my home?"

"He is a respected astrologer."

"The practice of divination is clearly forbidden in the Holy Scriptures."

"I had him draw up Allegra's astrological chart, nothing more. Besides, he's been employed by various noble families, including the Medici." Vittorio's icy stare compelled her to add, "I refrained from telling you because I knew you wouldn't approve."

"You try my patience, Stefania."

"He read my cards," she pressed. "I asked him if I was destined for a long life and if I would bear more children."

"Whatever that unholy man told you—"

"He answered 'yes' to both of my questions."

"I will not hear any more on this matter."

"But, Vittorio…"

Vittorio left the room without a backward glance.

Meanwhile, Allegra had managed to escape Gianna's watchful eye and wandered into her father's workshop. Scattered upon the long workbench were several colorful gemstones sparkling in the sunlight. She climbed onto the chair, teetering precariously on its seat. The yellow gleam of a broken bracelet caught her eye.

"Gold," she whispered, her blue gray eyes wide with wonder.

Taking hold of the shiny bracelet in her chubby hand, she examined it with a studious expression before reaching for a set of small pliers. She aligned the links accurately and tightened them, exactly as she had seen her father do on many occasions.

Vittorio entered the workshop. "Allegra, no!"

"I fix it," the little girl cried triumphantly.

Surprised to see the bracelet properly repaired, he embraced his daughter and kissed her forehead. "Yes, you did."

Gianna appeared in the doorway, breathless with flushed cheeks. "There you are! This clever girl is getting too fast for me."

Vittorio attempted to hand Allegra over to Gianna, but she clung to her father. "Papa, no!"

Gianna put her hands on her ample hips. "Come along, child, your father has work to do."

Allegra's lower lip quivered and tears gathered in her eyes. Seeing this, Vittorio sighed and waved Gianna away.

"You'll spoil her, Signore Vittorio," the wise servant muttered.

"Perhaps," he conceded, setting his daughter down on a stool beside him.

In 1553, shortly after her fifth birthday, Allegra suffered a serious bout of fever. Stefania feared she would perish, but the fever broke by the end of the second day. After that harrowing experience, the child was immune to almost every ailment that befell the city, yet that did not stop Stefania from becoming an overprotective mother.

Eleonora gave birth to a girl around the same time, but little Anna did not survive long. Some people whispered that the duchess's birth canal was ruined; worn away from too much usage. After all, she already walked with a slight limp from damaged hips. Maybe it was time for her body to take a much-needed rest. Eleonora stopped the wagging tongues when she delivered her eleventh child, Pietro, in June 1554. He was a healthy boy who thrived, and the last child she would ever bear in her lifetime.

CHAPTER 4

The last remaining rival left in Tuscany for Cosimo to conquer was the Republic of Siena. Their refusal to acknowledge Medici power in the region instigated a series of drawn-out battles that came to be known as the Italian wars. The Battle of Marciano in August 1554 marked the end of the fighting. Despite a valiant effort, Siena lost its independence to the Duchy of Florence. It was a humiliating defeat for the proud Sienese. Cosimo added insult to injury by affixing enormous Medici coats of arms throughout the city for all to see.

With all of Tuscany submissively under their rule, Cosimo and Eleonora could concentrate on forging and strengthening political alliances outside of the region. They hosted a party at the Palazzo Pitti in the spring of 1557 to celebrate the betrothal of their firstborn, Maria, to Alfonso II d'Este. The marriage was an attempt to seal a peace treaty between the Este family and Cosimo's ally, King Phillip of Spain.

Banquet tables groaned beneath the weight of delectable treats as minstrels performed enchanting ballads.

"Do you think Allegra is all right?" Stefania asked for the third time.

Vittorio sighed. "Can't we enjoy ourselves for one evening without your incessant worrying?"

"Forgive me, husband."

"Gianna will put her to bed soon, and she'll have sweet dreams." He brought her knuckles to his lips. "Now, let's eat. I'm famished."

They supped on roasted venison and wild boar stew accompanied by fresh vegetables and cheeses, followed by an array of sugary cakes and pies.

After the lavish meal, Cosimo approached Stefania. At age thirty-seven she was still a striking woman and, despite his devotion to Eleonora, he could not help but admire his former lover's beauty. "I'm happy to see you and Vittorio here tonight. I hope you're both enjoying yourselves."

"The party is wonderful." Looking at Maria, she added, "Your daughter seems pleased. She's such a lovely young woman."

Following her gaze, he said, "How quickly they grow up. I can hardly believe she's to be married." He paused. "Tell me, how is my godchild?"

"Allegra is doing well. She's a clever girl."

"I can't remember when I saw her last—or you, for that matter."

"Vittorio is away on business so often…I rarely go out."

"You must instruct him to remain in Florence." She laughed without humor, prompting him to add, "There's no reason why you can't attend our gatherings without him. We grew up together, Stefania, you're practically family. No one would dare speak ill of you for being present in my home without your husband."

"Thank you, but my daughter takes up most of my time. As you probably know, I'm completely devoted to her."

"She must get lonely."

Stefania lowered her eyes. "I wish I could have provided her with many brothers and sisters."

"God has his reasons, my dear. Be grateful that you have Allegra."

"We are, Cosimo. She's a source of constant joy to Vittorio and I."

"I don't doubt it." He paused. "There are several boys and girls from noble households who come to play in the gardens," he said with a sweeping gesture toward a nearby window.

In the Pitti family's attempt to outdo the Medici, the windows were designed to be as big as the front door of the Palazzo Medici on Via Larga. Well, at least that was the rumor. Regardless of whether or not this was true, they offered a pleasant view of the Boboli Gardens. Stefania's gaze fell upon pathways and fountains amid the expanse of greenery.

He continued, "I believe Eleonora is organizing something

for the children this week. Why not bring Allegra?"

She hesitated, unsure. "I don't know…"

"It will be good for her to play with other children."

Finally, she relented. "That would be lovely, thank you."

***

The young Medici hosts were charmingly dressed in red and gold, the colors of their family crest. Sections of the Boboli Gardens were decorated with festoons of yellow and white flowers, and the servants had set up a Maypole with multicolored ribbons. An assortment of tiny cakes and sugared fruits were prettily displayed on a nearby table.

Eleonora and a spattering of noblewomen fanned themselves beneath the shade of trees while servants kept a close eye on the children. Allegra dutifully kissed her godmother before two Medici girls, Isabella and Lucrezia, took her by the hand and led her to the Maypole. Stefania politely greeted her impeccably dressed hostess, smiled at the other noble ladies present, then took a seat among them.

Maria de' Medici, considered an adult after her betrothal, sat with the women. She appeared abnormally pale, coughing frequently into a lace handkerchief. Stefania couldn't help but wonder if she was contagious. The women indulged in harmless gossip until a liveried boy arrived with a tray of chalices containing diluted white wine.

"It's delightfully cold," one of the ladies commented after taking a sip.

"We store the bottles in our grotto," Eleonora explained as she waved her bejeweled hand toward the garden. Her gaze fell upon Stefania. "Signora Stefania, I'm glad you accepted our invitation. We have not seen our godchild in a long time."

"My apologies, Your Grace. Thank you for the invitation. Allegra was overjoyed at the prospect of playing with your children."

Eleonora glanced at the laughing children. "My husband should be here shortly. I'm sure he'll be pleased to see you and your daughter."

The eyes of the other ladies slid in Stefania's direction as

371

she replied, "It's always an honor to see His Grace."

"Signora Stefania and her husband, Signore Vittorio Castagno, grew up in the Mugello alongside the duke," Eleonora explained for the benefit of the curious women, although the majority of them were already aware of this fact.

Maria leaned forward in her chair. "Was my father a precocious boy, Signora Stefania?"

"Oh yes."

"Was he a troublesome lad?"

Eleonora frowned. "Maria."

Stefania smiled. "No more troublesome than any other child, my lady. Your father was exceptionally clever and well-read. It was clear to everyone that he was destined for greatness."

"You also knew my grandmother."

Stefania nodded. "We all held Signora Maria Salviati in the highest esteem. She was considered a moral pillar in the Mugello."

"Your grandmother was her good friend, isn't that so?"

"Yes, the two were rather close," Stefania replied as the memories of her joyful youth flooded her mind.

Eleonora rose, ending the conversation. "I think the children must be thirsty by now. Shall we, ladies?"

The ladies followed the duchess toward servants bearing trays of watered wine mixed with honey. Standing off to the side watching the children was the Medici heir, Francesco, accompanied by his faithful friend and mentor, Bernardo Buontalenti.

Francesco was quiet, awkward, and somewhat reclusive. His interests were as odd as his manner—alchemy, chemistry, astrology, and the occult. Bernardo, who was ten years older than Francesco, was admired for his many talents, which included painting, sculpture, and architecture. Taken under Cosimo's wing at the age of sixteen after losing his family in a terrible accident, Bernardo quickly became a favorite of the Medici court. He had received instruction from the very best Florentine masters—Bronzino, Michelangelo, and Vasari—and he loved to cook. Due to his passion for fine cuisine, one of

Bernardo's responsibilities at court was to plan sumptuous feasts, which were always highly praised events.

Maria, who had not accompanied the ladies to the banquet tables, sat alone beneath the trees. Seeing this, Francesco and Bernardo went to keep her company. They had the young woman laughing in no time at all.

Cosimo quietly exited the palazzo and surprised his three-year-old son, Pietro, by swooping him up into the air. The little boy squealed in delight.

Allegra greeted her godfather before running off with the other children. The blonde highlights in her hair shone brightly in the sun, creating a golden halo around her head.

"She's growing up to be a fine young lady. Pretty, too," Cosimo said, his eyes following the graceful movements of his willowy godchild.

Stefania smiled proudly. "Thank you."

"Does she ride?"

"No."

Cosimo met her gaze. "An accomplished lady should know how to properly handle a horse. I employ highly-trained grooms to teach my children. Every morning they ride to San Miniato al Monte and the countryside beyond. Why not have Allegra join them? I have plenty of horses in my stables."

Allegra could fall off of the horse, break her neck, and die. "I appreciate your generous offer, but..."

The fear that crept into Stefania's eyes did not go unnoticed by Cosimo. "I know you worry about Allegra—as you should— but your daughter isn't made of glass. Children are incredibly resilient. I should know, I have many. They fall and scrape their knees, but they get back up and run off as if nothing happened. You can't hide your daughter from the world forever."

"You're right, of course. I only worry about her getting hurt."

"Have you forgotten how much *we* enjoyed riding our horses? Why deprive Allegra of something that once brought you such pleasure?"

Stefania recalled the exhilaration of galloping through the

lush green hills of the Mugello with Cosimo at her side. They were young and carefree back then, oblivious to danger. The invigorating feel of the wind in her hair as the horse beneath her pounded his hooves against the earth was forever engraved into her memory.

"I miss those days," she admitted quietly.

They shared a brief, intimate look before he cleared his throat and turned away. "Speak with Vittorio and, if he agrees, Allegra can begin her riding lessons immediately."

Later that day, Stefania and Allegra described the party to Vittorio in vivid detail.

"Lucrezia called me her god sister," Allegra announced proudly.

Vittorio chuckled. "I hate to disappoint you, dearest, but there's no such thing as a god sister."

"Cosimo offered our daughter riding lessons," Stefania said. "He told me to speak with you and, if you're in agreement, she can begin at once."

Allegra added, "Lucrezia has already picked out a pony for me. She's gray and white, and her name is Dolcezza because she has a sweet temperament."

"Isabella and Lucrezia went out of their way to make our daughter feel welcome today," Stefania explained. "Since Lucrezia and Allegra are close in age, the two of them were inseparable this afternoon."

"Please say yes, Papa."

Vittorio nodded. "I think it's a fine idea." *One is never too young to form valuable alliances.*

The lessons commenced the following week. To her parents' surprise, Allegra's newfound interest in horses didn't diminish her passion for goldsmithing. Every afternoon, she sat beside her father and fashioned discarded scraps of precious metals into whimsical shapes.

On a hot August morning, Lucrezia said to Allegra, "I want to tell you something, but you must swear not to repeat my words."

"I swear."

374

"I'm worried about my sister."

Lucrezia wasn't prone to hysteria; she faced life with practicality and levelheadedness. For her to be worried, the situation must be serious, indeed. "Maria isn't getting better, is she?"

"I overheard my parents whispering last night. They said she may have contracted a serious illness. I fear she's going to die."

Allegra crossed herself. "Don't say such a thing."

Lucrezia crossed herself, too. "Forgive me, but her upcoming marriage is so important…Mother keeps telling us to pray to God for Maria's swift recovery." She paused, her eyes glistening with unshed tears. "If she dies, I'll be offered to Alfonso in order to salvage the peace treaty."

"Hopefully, it won't come to that."

"There's a good possibility that it will, and there's nothing to be done. Isabella was betrothed to the Duke of Bracciano against her wishes, but what can she do? What can any noblewoman do? My sisters and I have been groomed since birth to be the wives of men chosen by my father. In truth, I don't want to get married to anyone."

It was common knowledge that noble daughters were little more than political pawns to be used by ambitious fathers for the gain of money, lands, and military support. The stakes were even higher for the Medici.

Allegra thought for a moment. "You could claim sanctuary in a convent."

Lucrezia laughed bitterly. "One prison in exchange for another?"

"I'll continue to pray for your sister's recovery. Don't worry, God will answer our prayers."

"I hope you're right, dear friend."

By mid-September, Maria was bedridden. The best physicians were summoned, several cures were prescribed, but her condition worsened daily. The poor young woman was bled, forced to drink crushed pearls, and bathed in hot milk. Despite these measures, she died at the tender age of seventeen on the nineteenth of November.

Maria's funeral took place in the Basilica of San Lorenzo, where she was laid to rest in a gown the color of lilacs. Cosimo walked down the nave after the service and knelt on the circle of porphyry marble located directly before the high altar. Buried beneath the royal stone was his great ancestor, *Cosimo Pater Patriae*, whom the Florentines began referring to as *Cosimo il Vecchio* in order to distinguish between the man who currently ruled the city and his long-dead ancestor.

Crossing himself after uttering a brief prayer, he stood and walked toward his daughter's coffin. Eleonora and her black-clad ladies followed him at a slight distance like an undulating murder of crows. Heavily armed guards quietly accompanied the Medici retinue.

The church overflowed with mourners who had come to pay their respects, including the Castagno family. Allegra noticed that Lucrezia seemed particularly distraught, and she did her best to comfort her friend. Their attention was diverted by Bernardo, who came to stand beside Lucrezia. She looked up to him as one would an older brother.

"Do you see that man over there?" he asked.

Both young women followed his gaze. A richly-dressed nobleman stood on the far side of the church staring at them.

Lucrezia inquired, "Who is he?"

"Alfonso's uncle," Bernardo replied. "He's here to represent the Este family, as a gesture of respect for Maria."

"He's also studying me closely in order to offer an accurate report."

Allegra commented, "I'm sure your beauty and good manners will be highly praised." Bernardo snorted derisively and Lucrezia made a face, prompting her to add, "I'm sorry, did I say something wrong?"

"You lack deception," Bernardo observed. "Your naiveté is endearing, Signorina Allegra. You are living proof that there is hope in this world."

"Forgive me, Signore Bernardo. I don't understand…"

Lucrezia intervened, "The Este family isn't concerned with my beauty or my charms."

376

Allegra's brow creased in confusion. "I thought he's here to make a report on you."

Lucrezia narrowed her eyes at the man across the room, then said, "He's been sent here to make certain that I'm not sickly and frail like my sister, Maria. The only report Alfonso wants to hear from his uncle is that I look healthy enough to bear him sons. That man over there is the farmer, you see, and I, the broodmare."

Do you want to keep reading? ALLEGRA is available on Amazon.

20982012R00224

Made in the USA
Middletown, DE
11 December 2018